Tintin Meets the Dragon Queen
in The Return of the Maya
to Manhattan

TINTIN
MEETS THE DRAGON
QUEEN

in

The Return of the Maya

to Manhattan

a novel by
Alain Arias-Misson

Black Scat Books
2013

Tintin Meets the Dragon Queen
in
The Return of the Maya to Manhattan

a novel by Alain Arias-Misson

Cover art & design by Norman Conquest

ISBN-13: 978-0615865386

First Edition

Black Scat Books
E-mail: **blackscat@outlook.com**
Web: **BlackScatBooks.com**

The narrator and a select team of real-life friends, eminent Spanish philosopher, Ignacio Gomez de Liano, German shamanic artist/poet, Carlfriedrich Claus, Dada erudite, Parisian Marc Dachy and the sophisticated American novelist, Walter Abish, along with assorted cartoon figures, Tintin and Captain Haddock, investigate bizarre sightings of historic Maya personages and the apparition of ghostly Maya pyramids in the streets of Manhattan. They discover that the bloodcurdling Dragon Queen and her marauding, illegitimate, campy son and S&M mate, Smoking Rabbit, who introduced bloody "axe" warfare in the Petén Peninsula in the seventh century, are pushing through the time-boundaries of ancient Tikal. The legends and exploits of the latter are bizarrely paralleled in the marital mayhem of the dysfunctional New York couple, Augustus and his (maternal) spouse. Their risky voyage into the past climaxes with the deadly Maya ball-game, pok-a-tok, in which the captain of the losing team—loses his head! And the narrator's romance with a Maya princess is doomed.

PART I

FIRST APPEARANCES

I'x 5
(Day Eleven)
The jaguar

It would begin with a slight optical tug at the corner of an eye, a glint on top of a Manhattan office tower—remote, uncertain, then on further observation a pyramid quite discernibly would flash out, sloping upwards into its converging peak, perched on this summit, much like the "Gothic" or "Renaissance" palaces which adorn the skyscrapers of New York. On a desultory promenade up Seventh Avenue as he passed by the corner of West Fourth on Sheridan Square, he came distractedly upon the vast elephantine foot of another such construction in the street and stared unbelieving at its huge expanse jutting upwards, leaning back on a sixty degree angle and towering to a vanishing point a score of hypothetical floors above the regulation three or four stories of the surrounding Greenwich Village buildings: a full-scale pyramid! Its walls were translucent and evidently permeable to city-life—he could recognize people and traffic "in transition" within—things, that is, did not progress without a break, smoothly and tightly as would have been the case if the pyramid had been a mere visionary device wrapped about this section of the street. His impression was all the more pronounced, as the pyramidal walls were not quite transparent but translucent, thus allowing his disbelieving stare to make out, but not clearly define, the figures within. The monolith appeared to have crashed down from an invisible apex to the ground below where it now straddled the "Village Tobacconist" where he always bought a particularly noxious Brazilian cigarillo, as well as the whole of Sheridan Square: a gleaming crystalline cataract falling inside out in pyramidal form toward him.. He leaned forward to touch it—and still could not accept the evidence of the balls of his fingers as these slid across the surface of the artifice.. It was no dream experience, he had never conceded any weight to even those philosophical arguments which address the ambiguity of dream and reality, reality was straight up and down, he had a very firm grip on it, but then what was this, a holistic projection? Augustus Sykey skittered mentally on the glossy surface—tremens. Obviously he shouldn't be able to scale this glass mountain which offered no grip, no toe-hold, but his feet oddly appeared to adhere as he stepped cautiously onto the inclined wall, and despite his non-assenting, logical mind he found himself walking not strenuously bent at an acute angle close to the slope of the Pyramid as anyone would normally expect, but at a right angle to it, perpendicular, which defied gravity. What at first had seemed an unbalanced and risky posture quickly became quite mechanical as he tentatively walked up the side of the tower, delirious with the contradictory character of it all, glorying in these physically impossible actions as if he had suddenly arrived at the preternatural condition he had longed for all his life. And he peered at the busy scene below his feet within the pyramid, stunned by their obliviousness of him. Those crowds down there swirled murkily within the enclosed space of the pyramid, the effect like the smoked glass of limos in New York. Perhaps they couldn't see out of the enclosed space? He must have been fifty feet up the side of the Pyramid by then. In order to get a better look, he crouched down on all fours and pressed his nose against the surface. It was not glass, but to him it appeared to possess the properties of transparency and impenetrability of glass, like a solidified layer of air, a kind of interface with the real surroundings, which made the pyramid itself barely visible. When people in the open area of the street and in Sheridan Square came up to the inclined wall, they simply slipped through unnoticing (unlike himself). Perception was staggered, like an old, jagged film: he would see someone for a second in one spot, and a second later that   person had skipped several steps away, as if there were some mechanical defect in a film take. Between the Once and the Once as his spirit-brother, the artist of writing, Carl[1]

1   Carlfriedrich Claus, from the East German town of Annabeg-Buchholz, poet and shamanic artist, in his book, Zwischen dem Einst und

would have called it. He was high enough above the crowd to get a good overview to the other sides of the Pyramid, but not so high as not to be able to see the faces below. His knees and hands had the same adherence as his feet, yet he could shift them without any sticky resistance. One face, because of the sharp contrast its high color offered to the surrounding tide of gray complexions, caught his attention. To his astonishment it looked exactly like Tintin, the famous Belgian comic book character he had adored in his boyhood. Tintin also merited having a footnote beside his name, which would send the uninformed reader to the bottom of the page.[2] It will not surprise the reader to learn that both Tintin and Augustus were from Brussels—even now, for a moment, he could perceive in the place of the grit of the city street, the broad oak-lined avenue in front of his childhood home as he had hurried off in the still dark morning at the clanging approach of the tram, a Tintin comic book clasped tightly under his arm, the scent of the grass and of the fallen debris of twigs and dead branches mixed with the glutting electrical smell of the tracks so rich he almost sobbed with emotion. No doubt sorrow for the lost innocence of his childhood before he had understood about his father and mother.. The Tintin albums, in which the cartoon episodes were collected at the end of a particular series such as *Tintin and the Return of the Mother of the Maya*, actually did more to preserve the streets and shops and trams and traffic of his native town than any other book. Tintin would have to have been older than Augustus, since he was conceived (and that full-blown in his late teens) more than ten years before the latter. He was originally drawn with a crude, more naive stroke than the mature work, which appears here. Hergé had not yet endowed him with the Zenlike reduction of feature he was to become famous for. However, cartoon characters are blessed with eternal youth, so that even now below Augustus' hands and knees, he walked with his old bounce. Augustus pivoted on his knees and scuttled back down the Pyramid in order to intercept this childhood hero lookalike, and even so, with his head lower than his posterior as he hurried on the downward slope, he experienced no pull from gravity, the inclined plane of the Pyramid's surface maintaining all the characteristics of a horizontal. And as he caught up with the

dem Einst, deceased in 1996.

2   Tintin, world-famous character created by Belgian cartoonist Herge in the late 20's. Tintin was a boy-journalist of uncertain age, somewhere between 16 and 21 at the most. The Tintin comic-book came out once a week in Belgium on Thursdays, his new adventures awaited with excitement by Augustus and his comrades when he was a boy going to school in Brussels..

odd-looking personage below, the latter glanced up with that perfect 0 of a face, empty except for the pin-pricks of eyes and stubby
turned-up nose and taut line of a mouth, his expression not one of
pleased recognition but of utter disbelief. Eye contact was brief, a
shock of recognition, and he realized the young man before him
actually was the real Tintin—or better, the unreal Tintin. However
real Tintin had always appeared to him, his appearance here was
out of the question—some fraud, some masquerade. And the
same dismissal of his presence was evident in Tintin's eyes.
However this hallucination instantly passed, because there floated
overhead the vast voluptuous figure of a Woman with Butterfly
wings, naked, wave after wave of her, the whale-like glossy flanks,
the ivory hush of thighs, the great swelling pubic mound, the tidal
up-surging breasts: he could feel the heat of her body, its "breath".
He and the comic-book hero, open-mouthed and round-eyed,
looked up as she swept by, float or blimp or whatever publicity
marvel she was, and as he searched her seductive forms, intoxicated with the intimate curves and delicate skin tones, he quickly lost
touch with Tintin in the press and shove of the crowd. Then she
was gone and his entire body was left shuddering as if from the vibrations of some ineffable bar of music. He looked about at the
people in the street, revelers—Friday evening in the Village, faces,
gestures, exploding with desperate animation. Not one of them
had noticed the inexplicable sight. Something poked him in the
calf of a leg, and he glanced down in time to see Milou, Tintin's
white cartoon doggie with the curly tail, scamper away. He did not
have any desire to talk things over with the Hergé character that
would probably only confuse planes of reference in his mind. But
still he followed the darting hindquarters of the animated dog as it
raced through the festive street. Who else in this anonymous
crowd—he jostled his way through the crowded sidewalks, dark
closed faces, greedy faces, empty raucous faces, ancient savage
faces—who else could possibly provide any guidance? All this
was, of course, still under the protective cover of the pyramid
which he hardly was aware of, so transparent from within were
the soaring walls, that if it had not been for the occasional gleam
of the evening sun rays on the corner angles of the construction
one would not know it was there. Again he caught sight of Tintin
as the latter stood on the far edge of the scene, his features working like punctuation marks in the cipher-like face. Milou of course
was joyfully jumping about his legs. Augustus strode over with a
show of self-assurance. He would ignore the internal contradic-
tions of this affair and play it by ear, he decided.

Ah Monsieur Tintin, he began, holding his hand out in front of him in a pose he had seen a dozen times in the comic strip of a variety of people approaching Tintin: Maharajahs, scoundrels, oil magnates, thieves etc., Monsieur Tintin, I am so pleased to have found you after all these years! The eternal youth's voice came back not quite a falsetto, but cracked and adolescent. To his amazement he saw rather than simply heard, written in bold characters in a speech-balloon above his head-

Monsieur Sykey, I am just as surprised! After seeing you so unexpectedly crouching on top of that illusory pyramid I hardly expected to find you so soon again! Milou glanced back at him with a reproachful squint.

What? Exclaimed the latter. What do you know about the Pyramids? No one else seems to.. Tintin tossed the famous forelock back, and answered, with the same speech-balloon effect—

No, of course you're not the only one who knows. A number of us have been observing this phenomenon, and I have been trying to get to the bottom of it for my newspaper. How did you get in here, may I ask?

Augustus was not a little amused but also a little put out at having to justify himself to a cartoon character, and said shortly, I just came upon the Pyramid near Christopher Street and was "translated" inside.

I believe, said Tintin with an intense look, an index finger pointing outward under his nose in a gesture Augustus could remember exactly from an ancient cartoon frame that something quite mystifying and entirely illogical is going on here. Some illicit "mix".

And, um, Augustus wasn't sure how to broach this delicate subject, how is it that you yourself, coming from a different—he searched for the appropriate term—a different frame of reference—Tintin turned an indignant face on him, an expression in which his eyebrows peaked in circumflex accents ^ ^, so.

Do you think you have an exclusive *droit de cité, Monsieur Sykey?* he inquired. Let me tell you one thing. I do not yet understand the origin of these pyramids, but one thing I do know. Anybody, from anywhere, may be here! He turned away, snapping his fingers at Milou, and the two of them trotted off into the crowd. He watched them go, stunned and bemused. I suppose "cartoonism" might be considered a form of discrimination, he thought. There was something in what he said—what would have been altogether unacceptable in Christopher Street in the ordinary course of things was somehow more credible in the "shadow of the Pyramid". This was the phrase that came to him, a rather Hergé-like phrase come to think of it. He had wanted to share impressions with Tintin about the female vision. Whatever she was, she seemed inextricably linked to the meaning of the pyramids. Of course it's true that Tintin, while courtly, was quite asexual, and probably would have little to say. He shrugged and set off. The crowds had dispersed; the buildings about him were shadowy owing to the fact that he was plunged in such a muddy brown study. He hastened his pace and tucked his chin in with an air of determination and a New Yorker's don't-mess-with-me look. He had turned off Christopher going East and had no idea what side street he was in. Even though he had (also) grown up in this city (indeed Augustus' dual childhood in Brussels and New York was no doubt the root of his ambivalent character), he invariably got lost in the Village. The street was deserted and dark; he had heard of a horrendous mugging in the seemingly innocuous neighborhood--a couple found with throats slit with box cutters—and quickened his pace. A scrabbling noise, like a footstep slipping in street grime, struck terror to his heart, and he walked as fast as he could without breaking into a trot, which would have betrayed him. He heard the scrape again, more regularly, as if someone was dragging something behind in the street like a clubfoot. The hair prickled along the nape of his neck and a chill crawled up his back. He could no longer help himself, and turned around. He could not remember having ever screamed in public, at least not since childhood, but when he saw it his full-throated scream was independent of his will. Only a few short yards behind him was a squat, powerfully built, almost cubic being, swarthy and hook-nosed, rubbery-lipped, but what—what he could not credit to his senses—was the enormous under slung mandible, a simian jaw which hung open exposing razor-sharp, shark-size teeth. In its right hand this humanoid avatar held up a primitive-looking, black obsidian axe, and in its left he tendered toward Augustus the bleeding, severed head of some savage beast which still bared its own large fangs in rigor mortis. It was as if he had taken a wrong turn into a nightmare—nonetheless the fetid emanations of this demonic figure so suffocated him with dread that he took to his heels and rushed breathlessly for the nearest corner of the street. This instinctive flight may have saved him, because the creature appeared to have been taken unawares, which allowed him a head start. Moments after he had raced down the next dark, shuttered side street, he heard the clatter of footsteps behind him. Why "clatter"? The noise was more of an animal than a man, a large goat, something with hooves or claws instead of feet. The thought urged him on in a cold sweat, and he abruptly burst with a whoosh into a little square. He looked behind him and saw no one—like light off a knife blade, beyond the dark mouth of the street he had issued from he glimpsed the angular edge of the Pyramid that he had just transited through. Still shaking, he hurried across to the opposite corner to a cunning art-objects shop on the second floor above LUV Drugs where the owner was a friend, and stampeded up the stairs. The latter appeared, a lion's mane of white hair haloing his face and arms spread, and roared a welcome. Then he stared at Augustus.

Man, you're as white as a sheet! You look as if you're seen a ghost!

Well in a manner of speaking I did, said Augustus, I've had a difficult evening. I ran into what looked like a pre-Columbian demon in there—it—

Oh, said the other, deadpan, Pre-Classic, Classic, or Post-Classic?

Don't joke, he said, pained, it was horrible, with a mandible more insect than human.

Ah said the other, trying to sound serious, what was he doing, panhandling? Those kind look dangerous, but they're harmless really. Just your everyday Village folk. Augustus ignored the levity.

He wielded what I think was a ritual obsidian axe. And he stretched out the severed head of a bloody slavering dog or hyena.

The other looked interested. My god, Augustus, he was offering you his trophy!

His trophy? he inquired.

Yes, said the shop-owner, it's all a part of Mayan Ritual Bloodletting. Jaguar Kitzle.

Mayan Ritual Bloodletting? asked Augustus, sounding obfuscated. Kitzle?

Tz'ikin 5

(Day Ten)

The bird, the vision

He gazed out the window down the broad Avenue lined by great compounds. He no longer felt quite so disconcerted by these incidents. After all, he had read about the Maya for years, fascinated by the intertwined strands of a highly sophisticated, esthetic culture and a repugnant cult of personal cruelty. Perhaps he had been more troubled emotionally than he had realized. The peculiar toys of the shop accompanied these thoughts: the doll whose head would fall off when you activated the little guillotine, the forks and spoons twisted and transpierced in amorous positions, the nutcracker in the shape of female thighs.

Why do they call it Avenue of the Dead? he asked dreamily. He was remembering how he and his ex-spouse, Milena, had moved there before getting the apartment uptown. The shop-owner glanced sharply at him.

They usually call it Avenue of the Americas, he said, glancing out the window. But instead of Sixth Avenue, they now took in a broad clear view of the four-mile long Avenue of the Dead with the Pyramid of the Moon at its end and the great Pyramid of the Sun somewhat to the right. Both did a double take and stared again. Augustus' one thought crowding out any reflection was "delirium". The shop-owner's face turned white. He stumbled back a couple of feet, putting out his hands for moral support. He glanced about his shop as if to reassure himself the familiar surroundings were still there. He peered out the window again, cautiously, with Augustus, and together they contemplated the stage-set of the Pyramids against the backdrop: the mountains ringing the valley; the vast Avenue and the terraced palaces with their grand ramp staircases, the intersecting geometry of the streets, the monumental bas-reliefs in the walls, worthy of the

neobaroque vision of a German-expressionist film decor or of an
Albert Speer, all dotted with colorful and variegated people. They
looked away and considered each other gravely, as if they shared
some insanity—then burst out laughing and went on laughing for
a minute at least, until Augustus, spluttering, rested a hand on the
other's shoulder, and said

Let's go see what the hell is going on out there, Phil.

You never know, said Phil, I should mind the store, but—he
followed his friend down the stairs and into the street. The dusty
heat of the street was like walking into a brick wall. The men and
the few women who passed by were for the most part half naked,
the former wearing a sort of girdle and loincloth, the latter a skirt.
Most of the people they came across had a compactness of facial
traits, brows pressed down above the eyes, nose hooking out at the
brow and down to the mouth, mouth bulbous and lips rubbery
and large, and they were so squat of body and limb that they appeared cubic. He and Phil mixed in with the crowds and nobody
paid much attention to them, aside from an occasional curious
glance. They floated down the main avenue, sustained by the
dense human medium. Now and then an elegant and slender individual strolled by, taller than the others, sometimes with a jaguar's head-skin perched jauntily on top of the head, or a bobbing
array of brilliant blue and green plumage. These men (for in fact
they had not yet seen one such woman), while of the same ruddy
complexion and angular noses as the majority, nevertheless appeared to be another race—with their slanted, cruel eyes, their
sneering mouths, their height and bearing. The bare dusty street
and the plastered walls of the monuments and compounds glided
by in a blur before their incredulous gaze. Transported in the rush
he could not deny his senses. He determined to take it as it came,
sure that eventually it would resolve itself in some return to reason. The more magnificent Sun Pyramid lay farther down, but
they noticed that the colorful crowd drifting down the Avenue of
the Americas beside them was winding off to the left, an excitement lighting up the otherwise incurious, black eyes, and now
they all milled about in the huge plaza beneath the white-plas-
tered Moon pyramid, as if awaiting some sign, and a shout went
up from their throats, a collective roar, some word or name, *ahaw*,
repeated over and over, and they looked up in the same direction
as everybody else and saw, walking somewhat unsteadily, drunk-
enly perhaps, out onto the platform at the top of the pyramid
from the rear and left from what appeared to be a temple, but was
barely visible because of the height and the angle of the platform,

a small figure in a brilliant splash of blue-green feathers streaming about head and shoulders, a simple white tunic about his midriff, and a gleaming green jewel on his bare chest that sent brilliant sparks reflecting in the bright sunlight.. By his side appeared a portly woman, bulky breasts barely veiled in a filmy blouse, a long bright-green embroidered skirt, and hands cupping her face. Flanking the couple at a respectful distance, were half a dozen priestly figures in bright scarlet robes. Now a half-swallowed, collective sob gulped upwards from the otherwise silent crowd, as if they had one throat and one breath, and peering up he realized why: a dazzling red stain was spreading on the white tunic just below the male figure's groin. At the same time the lady now took her hand away from her face, and a similar but smaller red glitter was apparent on a whitish strip beneath her mouth. These revelations were so sharp, so pointed, that it seemed to Augustus and Phil that they might have witnessed the solitary hierophantic act which doubtless had been performed minutes earlier inside the temple.

For when Lady *Wac-Chanil-Ahau* had arrived in the holy city, she performed the sacrificial act of bloodletting at the top of the holy pyramid, a sacrament consecrated in the glyphs of stela 24. She approached the prince consort (who in this close-up appeared young enough to be her son—indeed he may have been her son), her tongue pulled out as far as it would go, swaying on her feet like a dancer, unseeing, and he searching in the darkness of her eyes.. The rent which he sliced open in her tongue by means of a razor-sharp, obsidian lancet gushed with blood, but that first bright shattering stab was nothing compared to the rasping intimate invasion of the rope she pulled through the hole in order to bring on and guide the healing spring of her blood down the paper bandages and toward the near-hysterical praying masses below. Her eyes clouded as the unutterably harsh body of pain swelled throughout her tongue—the pungent tormenting scrape of the rough hemp across the papillae of this most tender organ of sensory perception, as if it were drawing some soul-killing horror up from inside her womb and belly and out her throat—and suddenly the rushing sweetness of her own blood filled her mouth and eyes and nostrils, and then her mind was seized with ecstasy as a huge shuddering presence filled her, voluptuous-scaly, penile-slippery, delicious coil of a gigantic vision serpent which writhed throughout her entire body, exquisite in its erotic heaving and rippling flanks, her breasts swelling in its embrace, her nipples protruding as if to suckle this otherworld progeny, her thighs split apart to receive it.. How else to conceive of their union? Then the prince squatting above a pot, pushed aside the loin cloth, pulled out his thick dark penis with one hand, drew out the loose foreskin, with the cruel stingray spine in his other hand, deliberately, carefully, pierced through the skin three times, and as the blood leapt out, pulled the strips of white paper through the cuts and allowed them to soak the blood. How could Augustus have realized at this exotic and repulsive spectacle that his own domestic relations were prefigured here? What could seem more removed from a Manhattan couple's domestic agony, sexual anomie etc.? He could never have suspected..

Now however, though the eerily familiar couple were on the top of the pyramid, visible to thousands and ringed by the shamans, and at a greater remove by warrior nobles in full regalia, with nodding plumes of a blue bird on their helmets, they appeared to be alone together in a saffron-illumined room, the play of the sun light on the glossy tile surface, and they started to dance. It is true that Phil and Augustus were several hundred feet below with the huge and now silent but perceptibly vibrant, or more exactly, shivering crowd, but it was evident to them all, was it because the member was hugely tumescent, or painted in a ceremonial white? A low, stricken, awed murmur rose out of the crowd, while she, a queen beside this obviously kingly figure, had now opened her mouth, just a dark O, and pulled out—her tongue! They could distinctly see the blood sparkle now at her mouth and then drip down the pyramid's glossy skin. A low groan of excitement went up from the surrounding crowd. The were becoming increasingly agitated as the twin rivulets of blood dripped along the enormous decorated wall and slithered over the relief figures of skipping and dancing demons, of regal figures with eagle's heads and claws, of bowed, shackled and tortured victims. Then much to Augustus' and Phil's alarm, next to themselves a short thick dense man wrapped in what looked like a towel, face pentagonal, brow hirsute and bullock shoulder, flicked a wicked snakelike leather-thong whip with shards attached out of his tunic and slashed down on his own sloping back, blood played hopscotch and drops flip-flopped through the air even catching Augustus' jacketed arm. The Indian's eyes were fixed glassily, dreamily, on the little figure on the pyramid. They noticed that others were similarly engaged, some slashing or nicking or slicing at their flesh with razor-thin obsidian knives, others flailing and snapping and whipping at themselves with thong-whips and switches, others pricking or perforating noses and ears and tongues and nipples and the externalia of sexual organs with the same sort of peculiar serrated fish-spine instrument the "queen" had delicately wielded above. And throughout the throng the sprinkles of bright blood created a fine connecting reticulation. Many occasionally took a swig from gourds at their belts; all were caught up in the same agitated ecstasy. The squat brown and red bodies which were covered by a mere loin cloth in the case of males, short skirts for women, glistened with blood and sweat and sperm, necklaces and earrings and nose plugs of jade and shell and amber jiggling as they danced. The collective odor—which began to have a distinctly sexual aura—became oppressive. They decided to get away from the pressing jostling crowd and headed off quickly toward a temple out of the traffic flow: the Quetzal-Butterfly Palace.

The large entrance room of the Temple was cool and ovoloid in form, as if a giant egg had once been laid in its midst. They entered quickly to leave the sun at the door. There were large frescos on the curving walls and the sense they had was of *contemplation*, yes, much like the Louise Nevelson chapel at Fifty-first and Third if memory served him right. A sort of rhythmic shuffling noise drew their attention, and they saw a small group of six highly ornamental if near-naked warriors (so they seemed, for they carried weapons) skirting the far wall in a rhythmic march. Actually only the four in front wearing great nodding blue feathers carried the axes, short spears and spear-slingers—behind them trod with gravity two massive and lordly figures, one with particularly menacing brow and narrow predatory gaze. This *Ahau* whom he contemplated with some apprehension (he appeared to be of high rank and only later would Augustus learn that this was the fashionable "look") carried a cylindrical pot in both hands with a lid on it, as did his companion. A brilliant little set of tableaux like a comic strip marched in a frieze around the pot, showing identical figures, i.e. the two pot carriers with their tasseled headdress, the four warriors who preceded them, weapons in their hands, and he thought he could make out a figure similar to himself leaning against a wall in the brown ink pot drawing (as he was doing now), watching the Visit of Glory (as the Ambassadorial mission was called). All in all, the ceramic scene had a threatening atmosphere about it, and the sky was a preternatural dark blue. He took his courage in both hands and walked up quickly behind the squat and powerful lord, whose left rear eye-corner widened at his approach, but who continued forward behind his companions at a military pace. Now that he was close to the *ahau* he noticed a pungent odor, sweat mingled with dense musk, and was startled to realize just how short the Teotihuacanoo was below his massive headdress, since his face reached barely to Augustus' shoulder, but what he lacked in height he more than made up for in breadth and brawn, sinewy muscle slid fluidly on chest and arm and thigh like a great cat's. The man's face seemed twice as dense as an ordinary man's: the sneering thick lips, the heavy arched brows, the eagle-beak nose coalesced in the heavy mask of a flat clay-red face. Make-up—if not special effects—obviously accentuated these traits, he observed. He was at loose ends as to how to address this personage, "Johnny" was out of the question, but "*Ahau*" seemed too anthropological, self-conscious, stagy, so he settled for—

Excuse me, Sir! May I accompany your party? The mask glared, then grunted—

The name is Jhonny, he said, to Augustus's astonishment. And why should you accompany our 'party'? The word was lined with mockery. Augustus was startled by the smartness of the warrior's reply.

Because, He answered unhesitatingly, I would not wish to lose the opportunity to visit the Maya people. Now while it was true that he was devoted to the study of the Maya, it was also true that something else had moved him to this trip—something far more intimate which he could not quite put his finger on. *Cherchez la femme..* It was always that way with him.

Yes but why really, coaxed the other, as if guessing at these self-doubts, somehow I can't see you in the role of archaeologist or of a scholar of any sort, you're too—*je ne sais quoi*—dispersed. And in any case what scholar..? The *Ahau* looked at him skeptically, then grunted again and turned forward to resume his march. Augustus followed at a discrete distance, and the other made no sign to dissuade him. It was evident that the group was preparing to leave the Temple of the Butterfly, and indeed the city itself soon, on its way through the jungles and deserts of the Meso-American heartland south to Maya country and this was a fatiguing prospect. If only one could dispose of it in a couple of sentences—after the act! —translating the difficult conditions of the trek across mountain and valley. There was no question of following in the steps of his dear and admired friend, Walter Aleph, multiple prize-winning novelist, who had absorbed a deliberately fictitious experience of Palenque and the virgin forest from travel books and history books: as a surrogate experience.[3] No, for Augustus, embedded in the Mayan milieu, the trip had to be on foot, not even the

---

3   Eclipse Fever by Walter Abish

local buses would be available at this time. The only conveyance apart from one's feet was the long canoes that they would take to travel the Usumacinta River and its tributaries. And what of the physical inertia of the vegetation, the hostility of nature, need anything more be said? The poisonous, maddening insects? The intolerable sun! It has been told before, the situation is well known. A hiatus in the text, an indrawn gasp, will do as well as a score of paragraphs! The shadow he sought might be that of a woman; or the delight that woman had always been for him might be the shadow of something else. Whatever it was, he knew that this shadow led him to the Yucatan and beyond. The trip was instantaneous—between an instant and an instant[4], that is—because their departure was at the same time their arrival as all such departures are[5]. The Usumacinta stretched on for ever it seemed, its banks golden with rushes and swamp grass, the sky a canopy of theatrical blue, silence so perfect that the dipping of the oars in the immaculate water was delicately percussive, heartbreaking. A prickly red flower caught his eye, its large fuzzy petals passion-red, and he knew the end of their long march was at hand even if it had barely begun. He could remember hardly anything of the journey, the muscular torque of a back, the aggressively penetrating scent of a flower, and the "journey" was over. Already the welcoming Maya figure loomed in the foreground, the strident blue-green of the Macaw's long feathers bowing in his hand as the Teotihuacanoos advanced, the warriors with their campy Quetzalcoatl feathered tails bouncing at their rears, and the two emissaries with their precious cargoes in the brilliantly ornamented lidded jars, and the tassels of their headdress jiggling as they shuffled forward in a ritual offering. Augustus felt positively clumsy in the wake of such staccato rhythms, but having been absorbed by some osmosis into this ambassadorial group, probably by virtue of his own "godlike" otherness, he did his best to follow in the dusty footsteps of his new friend, "Jhonny": it was a grunting, consolidated group shuffle forward a few steps, then one or two back a little with incurving torso and belly (concave, a sort of bow), not graceful but with a vigorous irregularity that pumped up out of the viscera and was situated between the grotesque and the ecstatic. The Mayan host appeared to be delighted as he tapped his feet in rhythm (which dangled from the stone throne he occupied on the two bottom steps of the temple). Augustus was at a disadvantage in this ritual footwork, as he really couldn't keep up—it was

4   from Zwischen dem Einst und dem Einst, by Carlfriedrich Claus
5   This is graphically clear in the above-mentioned Maya ceramic pot which determined this episode.

both primitive and highly sophisticated in its counterpoint rhythms. Now, as they bumped and ground to some syncopated backward shuffle, which included a lateral outward thrust of the posterior, he followed the step of the envoys in front of him. With the tap-tap of the Mayan's toe and the visceral shove and rub of the group body, in the hazy drift of the mind as he thudded with the others, he became aware of a different quality of space in the incantation of the dance.

Ajmaq 7

(Day Nine)

Sin and forgiveness

The glaucous lagoon-emerald reflections which had dominated his sense of this habitat of the deep Yucatan did not so much disappear as recede into the slanted hyperreal gloss coming off the translucent walls of the original pyramid with which this whole episode had started. Only the Pyramid no longer plunged into the middle of the West Village but somehow enveloped, like a second glowing skin, the pyramidal structure that sits on top of Met Life at 24th street and Madison. He determined this location the moment he teetered in his precarious position just within its sloping translucent wall above the abysmal narrowing canyon, an existential motif in keeping with slapstick films of the era of the building itself, he wearing the vertiginous awe-struck gape common to the Harold Lloyds who inhabit the latter. The iridescent glint was fading quickly and with it the Pyramid seemed to melt from within its seemingly intractable mass. Since he had been standing just within the soaring glassy wall, in the wake of its dissolution he was left shivering and unbelieving at the vanishing of the Petén rain forest, for he now stood on a thirty-inch wide ledge, which ran around the base of the building's concrete "pyramid", amateurish in the extreme. His one concern, at this height, was a hurried exit away from the vertiginous abyss into the building. Without looking behind his shoulder into the honking, traffic-ridden street below, crablike, he sidestepped his way along the ledge around the building searching for an entrance, cursing his stupidity at finding himself there in the first place. The ephemeral, entranced, coruscated Pyramid had been fully eclipsed now, and here I am, he realized with a thud of sober panic, on top of a building with a miniature stone parapet about the edges of a roof-pyramid! After he had pried himself around a slanting corner of this "pyramid", he leaned over supporting himself against the inclined, grainy wall, over-compensating for the vertiginous pull of the *de profundis* of the street below. The grainy surface was milky soft under the balls of his fingers. Two to three stories of peculiarly arched windows punctuated the walls above of this pseudo-pyramid (which might more aptly be compared to a Walt Disney *Chateau de la Loire* with its mediaeval buttressed balcony-parapet stuck on the top and hanging over the void, and above that a peculiar octagonal temple, in turn capped by a golden Byzantine dome, the latter crowned with a turret with a final spire spun out from its center like a feather on a cap). He came upon the small black metal door he had been hoping for and popped in. It was not a sarcophagus. No axe-in-head god guarded it. Instead it was uniformly lit, the windows blocked out from the inside, and white walls slanted towards a single pointed apex along triangular slopes. The spacious room had no aura of mystery, bareness was its most compelling attribute. He had noticed a line or crack in the wall opposite and hurried over, heels resonating dully with a "clack clack" on the oak floor. It was the elevator door, discreetly concealed in a wall of similar texture; he rang and rode it, immense and noiseless, 49 floors down. At each stop smoothly plump-jowelled, briefcase-clutching, featureless look-alikes got in and faced the door or looked up at the ceiling with fleeting evasive eyes. An occasional female, dressed in a caricature of male, white-collar severity, joined the herd without eliciting a glance of recognition of her female otherness. Only at the last stop, the seventh floor, did someone with definition get on: swarthy, short, chunky, in 3-d and tru-color, the gentleman had pronounced Guatemalan features, and his eyes appeared to leer at them all. As they elbowed and squeezed out in a dull cattle shuffle at the ground floor, Augustus found himself in the vicinity of this loutish "other". Glancing briefly toward him he found himself enveloped in the violet shadow of the other's closest eye and heard him hiss with a distinctly Cholan accent—he had learned some elements of the tongue to prepare for his trip one day into the Mayan lowlands—

I s-see, s-sir, you have s-s-spied on the white room. He glanced at the Indian with astonishment.

What, what, why, what on earth would I want to spy on an empty room? He sputtered, not thinking to ask how the man could have known of his visit there. As the Indian slipped out of the crowd and away into the crowded lobby the words drifted back towards him in a ghostly cartoon balloon, it is not ours to mind, is it? He had disappeared, leaving a perfectly senseless phrase floating in midair.

Augustus dismissed the absurd—if intriguing—encounter and hurried back to his apartment. He had urgent business. His urgent business was Woman. The other day he had mentioned to his friend, Phil, in passing, that his passion for the *ewige weiblichkeit* had been the fatal distraction of his life—literally drawing him away from what his life was, or should have been, about. And why "business"? Shouldn't he have been about his father's business in the Yucatan, for example? With these thoughts and others crowding his mind he fought his way through the thickening evening rush-hour crowds down past the Municipal Building with its Disney-demonic Bald Mountain, an open-winged embrace which would transport him across Herald Square past City Hall to the subway station. Before the Metro entrance swallowed him up, he gazed up at the Woolworth Building just opposite, staring at its crown of pseudo-Gothic spires with a premonitory fascination—or trance? After all, the five-and-dime store napoleon had built the Woolworth in emulation and envy of the MetLife building some fifty years ago, bettering it by several floors.. Forty-five minutes later he popped up out of the subway entrance uptown on Broadway like a delivery out of a pneumatic tube. Minutes after that he was at the door of the Apartment fifty-five floors above the street floating beyond the racket of the real city below, and when the door opened the first thing he saw was the frond of an exotic plant poking across the entrance. Behind its emerald undulation Milena's red-lipped smile (she was into rich ripe reds) and behind her head the riotous profusion of a sub-tropical plant world, great fronds and tendrils and splayed veined leaves wandered across ceiling and walls and crowded out the light of the wall of windows which peeked out at the sky and clouds and the spacious margin above the lower buildings in front.

Milena.. He was no longer tormented, for only the facades, the décor, were left standing. She greeted him with a sanitized, sisterly kiss and led him in by the hand, and he had to duck and weave in order to penetrate a veritable jungle and its undergrowth of fleshy, near-animated plants. He had to push aside the painted drapes that constituted the vestibule of her being but was still unable to get at a core. Her resistance to his inquiries was as tenacious as any jungle cover. Was there a monster within? Perhaps, he thought with a shudder, finally we are only this decor (de-core) we draw about us. He bumped against a coffee table because the shrubbery was so dense that it hid the low-lying furniture. At one point he actually had to grab hold of her hand as she flowed ahead of him in her floor-length, plant-green, satin gown because he was not able to discern his way through a flourishing stand of bamboo. They had been married more than a score of years before their separation, a little more than the difference between her age and his. A fine line of pain underlay this divide. He and Milena had blithely ignored it at first, but through the years this mutual, unspoken but acute consciousness ate its way into their shared flesh. Mouthing it over, a sticky filament was left in the wake of his lips as they slobbered over this crest of an old wound, some antique rite.. A waste of words, he thought gazing at her lips, wasted breath! Décor! What about the script then? His college friends had urged him not to drop the all-American sweater-model sweetheart he had been dating for a middle-aged Latin adventuress, but his mind was colonized by an alien horde of emotions and images he was helpless to resist. Even Harvard, where for the first time he had felt at home after all the bullying, jock-culture, boarding-school years in Massachusetts away from his family in Europe, and where he had found himself effortlessly at the top of his class, he now neglected and almost abandoned for his trysts, within a couple of months of the start of his infatuation with her. His friends tried to recall him to common-sense but he rebuffed them indignantly, caught up in a cloud of mystical sensuality, and they gradually resigned themselves to the loss of their companion: he had started on his voyage outward, god knew where. He would declaim Rainer Maria Rilke's Elegies to her and talk of the mediaeval Christian mystics—and her sexual touching of his privates when they went to a church together created a confusion of the senses and religious sentiment which he had never imagined in the context of his father's northern "Calvinist" Catholicism, and which thrilled him and left him entirely helpless. After one of their passionate rendezvous over the weekend, he would lie awake in his bed at college, his body vibrating like a tuning fork to the memory of her fingers, her tongue, her sex. This interleaving of uninhibited eroticism and numinous sensibility determined their relationship. How could he guess that it was in the intoxication of this moment that the rest of his life was being coiled and shaped? His father had put a detective on her tail when he first got wind of the affair while he was still in college. Augustus was outraged but she—she never forgave his parents their suspicions. His mother was desperately jealous of this rival, proxy mother only a few years younger than herself, and his father saw his dreams of an aristocratic marriage and a diplomatic career for his brightest son quickly fading—but Milena worked at cutting them off from him far more successfully than they had managed with her. She would read their letters to him and his letters to them, excising any expression of affection that he might use, alleging disloyalty to her. His father tried to bribe Augustus with a Porsche, and in desperation even suggested that he take the older woman for a mistress. His sallow, rough-shaven, somewhat jowly cheeks shook with the intensity of his argument.

Just look around you, my boy, he pleaded, you have your pick of any of these delicious young girls in our society, and he could swear that his father's trembling lower lip betrayed more than concern for him. In vain—he spurned his father with superb disdain for such amorality and with youthful certainty of his perfect love. Only holy matrimony would do! Who was she really? A question he could not have asked himself at the time with his mind rushing in the wake of his body, when his thoughts and emotions were only an immediate response to the thrilled touch. Even though he could see that this glamorous older woman was touched by the child-man she had awakened, he in turn was wounded deliciously and debilitated by her mothering lust. When she turned her lush exotic features to him in coitus, he saw reflected there not only a lover's desire but also a curious maternal greed. For that matter, she was the mother of a girl not much younger than himself, and was caught up in a difficult post-marital situation, divorced four times, supported by the penultimate husband, a prominent New York lawyer who had handled her divorces from the previous husband (an OSS, operative persona non grata in the United States), as well as from the parenthetic parasite-hippy (thirty-day marriage) who followed his own marriage to her, in exchange for maintaining the family home—and appearances. His luxurious ex-wife and her loyal black servant (who, she regularly informed others, owed her everything) referred to her financial mainstay as "Tribilin", a choice Cuban mockery for a cuckold, and when the obese lawyer with his pursed plump lips approached her, what had become a permanent expression of petulance on her sensual face only deepened. While the lawyer was sadistic and impotent (he once threatened to cut off her legs, a telling fantasy of amputation), the company of his beautiful and elegant ex-wife was without doubt a highly prized asset when taking important clients out to dinner after drinks at the little jewel of an apartment he had bought for her near the Cloisters. And the couple was on show at all the latest Broadway hits and drank at Lindy's, the Twenty-One Club and the Rainbow Room in an extravagant and conventional life that was anathema to Augustus' style and preferences—later when he saw a photo of

them in the Rainbow Room he was saddened by the bored hard-
ness which so aged her beautiful features.

Yet her situation was oddly comparable to his parents' life
when they had lived in New York, before returning to Brussels.
His mother had become the social secretary of a famous director
of the Museum of Modern Art, a position that she owed to a major trustee of the museum who had been close to her father—as
well as to her considerable social charms. She was a good-looking
if not beautiful woman, with an enticing Spanish darkness of
complexion and eyes surprising for a thoroughly English woman
from Devon, but then her father was of unknown (English, and
perhaps Jewish?) origin, a self-made man who came out of nowhere and made a fortune, before marrying into the landed gen-
try of his spouse's family. Being the daughter of one of London's
shipping magnates, she had traveled with her father about the
chancelleries and embassies of Europe, met Oscar Wilde and
Cocteau in le beau monde, and as a young woman gossip column
for a London paper. She had the accent and all the requisite tal-
ents for just such a Museum position. She entertained for the
trustee in her husband's penthouse apartment just off Central
Park, and Augustus remembered as if it were yesterday the perfumed and superbly groomed company for whom he played doggie at the age of eight or nine: they would toss him canapés, and
he, on his knees and yapping, would catch them in his mouth in
mid-air, to their distracted and amused applause. After the party
he would do a tour of the living room and finish off the cocktails
left in the glasses. He was particularly fond of his mother's favorite, which was a whiskey sour. It was in the course of one of these
investigations that he found tucked into a corner of a sofa chair a
pair of his mummy's minuscule *cache-sexe* which he promptly put
on with tremulous excitement, trying his best to understand how
Mummy must feel in them, imagining the ins and outs vividly and
exotically, and quickly wetted them. He hid them away and kept
them for further solitary occasions, always parading in the living
room with its great glass wall and its invisible audience across the
street. His father caught him with them on one day, and after
cross-examining him as to the provenance of the garment, gave
Augustus what appeared to him to be an unfairly savage beating
with his belt. This association of events no doubt contributed to
the obsessive proclivities (lingerie, whips, and bondage) that he
developed later on in life. In any case that was the extent of his
mother's professional responsibilities—although there was good
reason to believe that she was also the trustee's mistress. In fact

rumor—and an uncanny resemblance with the trustee—had it that Augustus' much younger brother was the love child of this union. Such a liaison would explain the somewhat unhealthy emotional symbiosis between his mother and that late-born son, as well as the bitter alienation of son and father. The latter took to sleeping on the opposite side of the large dark house in Brussels from his spouse and infant son, after she gave birth to him there. Augustus remembered still the dramatic shrieks of his parents and the slamming of doors and his mother locking herself in the bathroom not long after the *cache-sexe* episode. However his much younger, presumably bastard brother, whom their mother had practically venerated in his persona as guru, had long since departed for some clime where one surmised he practiced mystical rituals. Augustus felt obscurely responsible, but had lost all touch long ago.

In any case the apartment on the Upper East side of Manhattan exhibited several fine Edward Hoppers on the walls as well as a Mirò (none of which the family could possibly afford), which the trustee with his immense collection would not even miss, and which were later to make the younger brother's fortune. His father's presence at the parties was always appreciated in any case, with his thick French accent and his baronial forbears whose portraits frowned up and down the stairs and on the walls of the duplex. He put up with the situation until he was invited to the regal Long Island estate of the trustee to participate in what were quite precocious wife-swappings in the late forties, and then he put his foot down. Augustus doubted his mother shared his father's reluctance.

A couple of years before Augustus' encounter with Milena, she had begun to dabble in art at the Art Students' League, and went out painting with a group of idle-rich women guided by a seductive Greek sculptor of no mean reputation who tried his luck first with Milena and then with her teen-age daughter, much to the mother's rage. Especially since she suspected that her fifteen-year old had indulged in her usual exhibitionistic streak. Then in one of the art-club outings, she discovered Abstract Expressionism and was swept off her feet by the great glowing lozenges and rectangles of Mark Rothko. Henceforth she would dedicate herself to the spiritual art of abstraction and would either sink or swim as a true artist! she declared to all and sundry. Which explained her presence at the tip of Cape Cod (Provincetown) where several of the abstract artists worked during the summer, in particular Hans Hofmann who taught classes which she attended with something

akin to religious fervor. Her "conversion" to abstraction had an in-
dubitable flavor of old-time religion; she also abandoned all her
old acquaintances and friends (in particular the now-despised art-
club) in order to sit at the feet of this guru, booze up on weekends,
take lovers (of whom Augustus was the latest and final one) and
set up a thoroughly professional studio, thanks to her ex-hus-
band's bounty. On a vacation trip from college to the Cape,
Augustus had caught sight first of her tall, blond daughter leading
a white horse by their frame house on a hill on the morning before he met Milena (so he learned much later), and had lusted after this leggy American classic, and indeed had returned to the
spot that very evening with high hopes—and clearly the entire
course of his life might have changed if he had followed this
prompting. On the other hand maybe it wouldn't have, since the
bitterly jealous daughter confided in him that her mother would
always come on to and if possible seduce her boy friends! He never dared tell daughter or mother however how closely he had
missed the one or the other. The mother was resentful of her
daughter's youth and her generous display of large breasts when in
company with herself and anybody in pants, and the daughter
hated her mother with a passion for her beauty, her fascination
and her succession of lovers. In any case the daughter was undeni-
ably a standard and boring young American woman, whereas her
mother was the mythical seductress. Milena didn't conceive of
herself in that way. If asked she would have said she felt herself to
be the seventeen-year-old virgin she had once been in her native
Cuba; a role Augustus could not quite grasp. For he was the real
demi-vierge. This disparity of roles was to determine the paradoxi-
cal and ultimately fateful nature of their union. And the question
of who she actually was remained unanswered.

Now, more than thirty years later, a touch more of the wreathy
interior in their apartment and he would have sworn he heard the
cry of the macaw and the hoarse cough of the jaguar: the meto-
nymic rendering of the lower Yucatan was undeniable. Was that,
he wondered, why he had gone into that mosquito-ridden swamp-
land alone? Was it somehow linked to her perfumed elusive essence? Later, as he sat with her in a clearing and they drank a bottle of Chateau St-Emilion (definitely doc), her tragic, reproachful,
glances reminded him it wasn't. This episode had originated with
his rumination on women, or the "essence woman", and he wondered now, as she passed from looks to the habitual and explicit
"stream of consciousness" recounting of bitter memories, whether
humorous detachment really would not be a preferable alternative

to romantic despair? It had occurred to him earlier in the street that the red meat of impassioned discourse lay not in its major parts of speech, the semantically defined subjects and verbs and predicate phrases, i.e. in the overt meanings, but rather in the minor adverbial parts such as the "whatevers" and "in any cases" or "actuallys" where people put all the emphasis. Whatever the case might be, he winked at her one moment over their increasingly giddy wine glasses and in the middle of her recital of a particularly heinous and hoary crime (against Love) of his, and she almost broke into a self-betraying grin, but caught herself and carried on. Even though he had come to this encounter persuaded that such passionate relations (or crimes of passion) were the stuff that any authentic life-story should consist of. Is that, after all the misery they passed through together, what this Maya adventure amounted to?

Augustus, she said, with a phrase she had used often before in their years of marriage, you know very well I practically brought you up. Everything you've learned—I could have been your mother! The superb unconsciousness of this declaration always left him stunned—as well as oddly embarrassed and touched.

Milena, he said, trying hard not to use one of the phrases he had used often in their years of marriage, isn't it time we moved away from these cardboard figures which have impersonated us for so long, and tried to get at something lighter? He resisted using the word "fundamental" because, or such was his conviction, the emphasis on the "serious" was exactly what had wrecked their marriage. As soon as he had said this, however, he realized by her frown that he had put his foot in it, because his "levity" and lack of deep "principle" were exactly what she had always reproached him for, so they were back in the cardboard box. She glanced at him with an expression that could only signify loathing.

You were always such a superficial fool, she said. I should have suspected from the very beginning when you—

—when I went back to that party, he finished the sentence. This reproach had been repeated a hundred times over the years.

But how could you do such a thing! You claimed to love me, I was the great romance of your life! She rolled her eyes with revulsion and disbelief. He felt that nervous prickling in his chest, the nerve-rending machinery had started up again. Was there no way its course could be altered? The party had been a big social event at Harvard, and after an —emotionally and sexually—intoxicating but equally exhausting weekend, he really had wanted to get back to it as a form of psychic relief. He did not realize for many years that he had, in effect, been sexually kidnapped!

But Milena," he said again with ingratiating gentleness, we are not just one thing, I was not only passionately involved with you, I also had the light-heartedness of any student, frivolity even—. The usual insidious note of pleading had crept into his voice; he couldn't bear this weakness in himself. From her flashing glance he realized that he had gone too far again, any reference to his lesser age was a deliberate provocation.

The frivolity of a student, she echoed in a nasal falsetto, mimicking maliciously the tone of pleading, you weren't a child, you knew exactly what you were doing. You disgust me, Augustus, why did you pretend to be something you weren't? He really couldn't agree more with her, why had he thrown himself into that passionate embrace when all he had wanted after all, then (and now) was a good fuck! But of course he did not dare to tell her so. And this was where he could pinpoint the exact moment when the torture-recall machine would roar into full throttle. Why had he never been able to demystify the process just once? —once and for all! Because of his mother? Because he wanted to be what she had expected of him, he couldn't disappoint her? But she wasn't his mother, was she!

But I did love you, Milena, I really did! Even to himself his words sounded empty and cracked. And he felt uneasy about the past tense. He tried to soften it: I have always loved you! This latter phrase was so weak it was barely audible.

You liar! she exclaimed with a sneer, you've always been a liar. You don't know what love is! Her voice had a firm fullness, not a tremor to it. He had always noticed this tendency as their "conversations" veered toward emotional turbulence, her voice became increasingly secure and sure of its ground, whereas his grew increasingly inchoate and uncertain. The more he tried to correct or fortify his tone, the more he would begin to stutter. You have no idea what it means to love, my whole life has been devoted to love. She reclined in the sofa with these words, luxuriating visibly in the glow of her own love. At this very moment he was overcome by the extreme tedium of this conversation and her emotions, every phrase had been said and repeated ad nauseam in hundreds of such "conversations", yes, and his responses were unchanging as well, it was a well-oiled piece of machinery. It was the "deep" form of their communication.

Milena, he began with a fresh attempt at common sense and finality, we've been through this so often, can't we just drop it? It won't make any difference.

Oohh, the poor little darling, he's had enough! Well come on, sweet darling, let's see what it's all about, and she reached out an arm from her semi-prone position and hooked her fingers into the waist-band of his pants and began pulling them down. A wave of revulsion swept over him.

Stop it! he said weakly, leave me alone. And to his humiliation, he felt like a girl whose virtue was threatened. She leaned forward with sudden fury and thrust her face within inches of his.

You bastard! she growled, tell me, what is it like with that little South American tart, is it much better, have you been enjoying yourself with this little girl, my darling? She pronounced the latter sentence with an exaggerated tone of solicitude, as if inquiring of her son. Her shifts of register baffled him, and at the same time he admired them with a certain detachment as if a Sarah Bernhardt were performing in a tinny unworthy theatre.

Milena, was his tone actually one of begging now? I don't have any 'little South American tart'.

You deceiving hypocrite! she spat out, and the last word was punctuated with a painfully stinging slap delivered with full force.

Oh fuck it! he exclaimed allowing himself this first impropriety, and made as if to get up. He would have liked to escape at this moment; she was of course quite right, but how could she know about his girl? Fortunately, at that moment the doorbell rang, and she got up instead with assurances of "to be cont'd" and rustled off into the brush with self-conscious sway of hips and grace of movement. Milena had always given him the impression of being perpetually on display. He heard voices through the gloaming at the front door, and now she was back again with in her tow a short, blocky, swarthy, Mesoamerican Indian type—in fact quite clearly the same lower-Yucatan or Guatemalan Indian who had hissed at him in the elevator yesterday. He jumped up from the table a little defensively with the wine glass in his hand and in the other the bottle, which he proffered now to the visitor.

Augustus, his ex-spouse said with a society smile, without a trace of the emotions of the interrupted "discussion" and a warning glint in her eye that he show no distress, and a hint of spiritual loftiness, I want to introduce you to a friend from Church—Juanito. These instant switches from emotional confrontation to composure and normalcy when company, especially of the churchly variety, turned up was an injunction he had never wavered from, although his face was still smarting and, he hoped spitefully, still reddened.

The Indian's eyes glinted, and the grin of complicity on his face showed he was not dupe, although the emotion conveyed was not sympathy. Rather it suggested some ulterior motivation regarding Augustus' Ex. Following their bitter separation, she had fallen into the clutches of a fundamentalist sect on Times Square, and danced about and mumbled in tongues with the best of them. With her childhood in Cuba and the magical culture of *vaudou* that lay in the shadow behind every Catholic church in the land, it was an easy transition. She quarreled with anyone who did not respond with equal spiritual enthusiasm to her advances. Besides, she was not that partial to blacks, or only so long as they knew their place, even if it was only in the Church. Actually her romance with the Church did not last long; her susceptibilities were as easily provoked by the churchgoers, by the "prophets" and pastors whose authority she disputed, as by her past lovers. Juanito was an Indian however—he clearly had designs on her, whether of a churchly or solely mercenary nature was uncertain. They sat at the table and she went off to the kitchen to get another glass for her guest, but they hardly spoke although she carried on in a religious chatter about the sublime nature of the sermon of the last guest pastor at the church, which neither he nor the Indian probably heard a word of. Instead they pursued some other agenda which seemed to have begun a long time ago, before the church and before the "white room". The next time Milena got up and went to the kitchen to fix something or other, he and the Indian arose on common impulse, and he followed the sure-footed swinging pace of the other into the deep brush of the living room until they could no longer hear her tones of surprise but only the occasional grunt of a peccary and the mock-anguished scream of the macaw. Juanito, or Jhon, because evidently it was he even though he had not recognized him at first—slipped ahead on invisible paths along which the other's practiced step carried him effortlessly.

No'j 8
(Day Eight)

Cosmovision

And with this classic «script» it was evident that they were already in the virgin forest. He could tell, because when he looked up, the forest ceiling or panoply was at an altitude that no New York apartment could afford. He huffed and puffed in the effort to keep up with the Indian who glided ahead of him, business suit and squat figure notwithstanding. In fact the latter's toad-like lumpishness and closeness to the ground appeared to favor him now, unlike his first appearance in the midst of the elongated (human and architectural) figures of the vertical city of Manhattan where he was definitely at a disadvantage, endowed with a stature not unsettled by the low-hanging branches and trailers, and a specific gravity enabling him to plough irresistibly through the dense underbrush. Augustus was largely assisted by the ground-clearing action of the former. He could not pause in this headlong flight (why? where?) to reflect on the bizarre transition from a sophisticated and difficult city life to a quite different habitat, although the jaded would doubtless dismiss it. He, however, was trained in the classics to be both skeptical and logical (in syllogism and inference) and this turn of events was distressing to him.. At one turn about a *ceibal*—the immense pot-bellied trunk, the vast spreading crown of foliage of the sacred tree, they almost collided with a small group of three Indians going in the same direction but coming from the right-hand side (in light of the greeny saturation of this interior atmosphere there was no way you could tell where the sun was and thus determine the cardinal points): all three men, short and swarthy, were dressed in ordinary American businessmen's attire and were running with the same elegance, the same suave motion as Jhon. He could make out even in that gloaming that they were very similar to the group of envoys he had originally accompanied to the Maya temple. Was it possible, he wondered, they were the same? The group of five thudded along the jungle floor almost in unison (he couldn't get the step quite right; the different stature, the weight, gave the Teotihuacanos' feet a drum-like percussiveness), and when they came about another bend in what looked increasingly like a trail, he was not surprised to see a couple more Indians, also short etc. and dressed similarly come around the bend. Now the original group was reconstituted, in fact it drew itself together so as to run in formation, and Augustus with it, odd man out. As he ran, in spite of the fatigue and the raw gulps of humid air, his mind could wander, and he reflected on the difficult relation he had with his spouse.

It all appears quite inevitable to me now, quite inevitable, he murmured. I should have known from the beginning. Unless on this journey.. What was it he was seeking in the damp heart of the Mesoamerican forests? What massive female penetration? What monstrous vulva and organ was he being absorbed by? Some intuition had fluttered over the runes of his mind—the monstrous female with the butterfly wings had impelled him to this journey! He was overcome by a sudden certainty that he had been only half-conscious of his acts most of his life. And would learn to open his eyes on this journey! He was caught up out of this disquieting reverie by the grunting of his companions and their physical proximity, the smell of sweat and some exotic musk, and it was as if it awoke him to the actuality of his situation. The transition had been so bizarre and unexpected that he had observed subsequent events (the trek through the tropical forest, the converging paths of the indigenous businessmen) as so many artifices or constructs, but it was obvious to him that something besides pattern and ploy was going on. Some tracing of life's meaning? When he glanced at his companions, he noticed how their brows were fiercely bent as denoting total concentration (not one of them glanced at him) and how distinct and defined in features each of them was, not to be summed up in thumb-nail one-liners, such as the bushy eyebrows of his neighbor to the right, or the pig-eyes and swollen chops of his neighbor to the left. Well in the meantime that would have to do. The group uttered a collective "Huh!" every few steps, and finally he caught on—it was not a grunt, any more than the other grunts, instead it was a military pacesetter. It abruptly ended and the formation of six men stopped so suddenly—in their tracks—that he stumbled into the warrior ahead of him who did not budge. He looked where they were looking and distinguished in the thick undergrowth (which had earlier covered Milena's coffee-table) a pile of white stone and what appeared to be broken bits of faded pink stucco, possibly a crumbled stela from the look of the weather-beaten carvings on some of the stone surfaces. No trace of the coffee table. The two priests and the four military escorts commenced a jumbled natter, from the tone of which he understood that they were startled and apprehensive. No longer in formation, but moving ahead in cautious reconnoitering mode, each man peered into the impenetrable brush and advanced slowly, as did he, although he had no idea what to look for. After about twenty minutes of this discreet rustle through the undergrowth, during which time the Teotihuacanos, in spite of their dark business suits which by now were salty-pale with sweat in great rings about their necks and powerful shoulder-blades, looked more and more like the warriors they were and less and less like New York hustlers. One of them let out a shout of discovery and alarm, and they all hurried over to where he stood and pointed with trembling hand toward massive stone ruins. It was immediately evident that before them lay the ruins of the temple where they had met the *Ahau,* and which was the northernmost building of the North Acropolis of the sacred city of Tikal. Now Jhon pointed with another guttural cry at a white slab which had evidently collapsed from the overhead pediment: it showed part of a great plaster mask with the blood-scroll unraveling from the maw of the monster-god which once was mounted on the temple facade. They appeared baffled by the sight, speaking in low urgent tones. They approached the ruins in an anxious mood, and then sat among the rubble, careful not to desecrate any fallen stelae or fragments of statuary. They looked like a bunch of despondent business commuters who had missed their train. He approached Jhon who was the only one he had talked with yet.

Jhon, he said, what's happened, what is the matter? Jhon looked at him from under beetling brows and over aquiline nose, forlorn:We've arrived too late, Augustus. Or rather, we have not returned to when our *pochteca* were carrying out the Ambassadorial Visitation to Tikal, but have remained in the same nowness as when I slipped out of the apartment with you.. So there is no more Holy City of Tikal. Nothing but the remains of that calamitous event that ended it all. Jhon's face, so weather-beaten it appeared rubbery, worked briefly. Then he went on—but you, Augustus, this is what you have not understood about your ex.. I realized that during your acid chat with her. You cannot force your way back to a time before, with her. Before the ruins of your grand love affair, that is.

No, answered the other, but neither can I sift for the rest of my life through the archaeology of its ruins! I must find some other manner of relating to woman. If one axiom was fundamental in his life, it was the wan hope that the energy of love could not be wholly dispersed, that it was transmuted. His life had not borne out this faith. One or two of the other Teotihuacano ambassadors or warriors glanced curiously at the conversational duo, the others glumly fixed on the ground and the rubble. It occurred to him that this belief might have only been his way of preserving some ultimate residue of the romance.

You see, continued Jhon, it's like our arrival here. Translation is not easy. You must achieve it somehow. We are here accidentally if "magically", so we have not really come back in any meaningful way. Why we are here at all is due more to an edge that we crossed in your mother's bedroom. The Maya world is full of such edges. They are profoundly ambiguous—and so, potentially dangerous, if often fruitful. But of course we thrive on danger! Augustus could-n't tell if the gleam in his new friend's eye was mocking or warn-ing.. But why mother's bedroom?

What edge, insisted the latter, fascinated by his companion's ar-ticulate exposition.

No, no, insisted the Teotihuacáno, the problem is not one of logic or good reasoning—it is the shaping of the world, of the am-bient reality! And anyway, the edge is around unconsciousness, which is power. Do you realize when that occurred this evening? Augustus shrugged. When you recognized me. Or more exactly, when your mother introduced me. Or perhaps when I crossed the threshold of the apartment, the act of allowing me—me! —to cross it. Augustus was nonplussed by this—revelation?—and stared at the wide-dark-eyed Indian. What edges of conscious-ness?

She's not my mother, he said. He gazed thoughtfully at the hir-sute fellow—his hair was dressed up the forehead in the terraced fashion, in the Maya manner. The other's eyes had gone blank, dark pools, as if he felt he had already said too much. And as his friend's (?) dull gaze now pooled with the others, his thoughts re-turned to his mention of Milena.. What was done could not be undone or the past revisited. As the saying goes. This creates only the gnawing of time disembodied. An excited cry broke into his reverie—he glanced up with the others, and saw Jhon a few feet away, staring down into the grass. He bent down and lifted up into the air some small object that flashed dully in the sun—the others crowded around him and Augustus rushed up as well—in Jhon's hand, held triumphantly aloft, was a small, very thin, very fine edged, one might say razor-edged, black piece of glass; no, he thought, looking more closely, black obsidian. Jhon's companions jumping about him to get a better look thudded blankly, monstrous squat schoolboys in Sunday's best, those Katzenjammer rascals, grunting under their breath—with the effort? Expletives? Sacred mumbo? He did not know, but they couldn't manage really, being a good six inches shorter than Jhon's five foot two inch giant (for a Teotihuacáno of those times) stature. They jostled him as they leapt with their dense bodies; they seemed to look through Augustus, a somewhat aggressive rugby team. He had only to bend over their heads to peer more closely, and he could make out now the fine lines scattered over its surface, but the waving hand of Jhon prevented him from making out any more.

Oooh shit, Jhon, stop waving it about and let us take a look at it! he blurted, and right away they did all pipe down, and Jhon lowered his hand with great precaution and placed the ritual object on top of a crumbled stone stela the height of a stool, and they all crowded around to see.

One of them, with extra-flaring eyebrows and a huge crow-beak nose said,

It's a Vision-Serpent ritual accoutrement, obviously, and the others nodded in agreement, murmuring with interest and approval. Now the lines were sorting themselves out for Augustus' eye as well, and suddenly they resolved into the dancing, stick-limbed, fat-headed, Negroid, pot-bellied little god of *Xibalba*, the Maya Kingdom of the Dead, who did this hum of incantation: mmmmmmmmmm. He snapped his gaze away, as if he had been half under hypnosis. A heavy blanket of silence draped over them all. He reached out a hand to take, to take—but the verb could not follow through to its object, and now their eyes drilled into his including those of the one he called "Jhon", whom he thought was his friend. Jhon's own brown block-hand shot out and easily grasped the obsidian knife again and pushing up the black cuff and sleeve of his jacket three quarters of the way up his muscle-rippling arm with his fist, sliced smoothly in it just below the shoulder as if into a *guanavano* causing the blood to spurt out in a scintillating spray anointing Augustus' brow.

Why! why? blurted the latter, haggard.

Because, answered Jhon, now wrapping his torn shirt about the gaping grin of the wound, the god wanted blood and I couldn't give him yours, my guest. And my companions here knew the

god's thirst. Augustus understood without further talk. The chaps
began a heavy-rhythm dance following Jhon's lead, and the loose
ends of the torn shirtsleeve flapped up and down showering the
ground—and them—with his blood. No doubt it was his imagination, but it seemed as if from the depths of the jungle he heard the
piercing moan of the great wooden trumpets and the cavernous
beat of the *Tunkul* drums as they danced. And somehow the sight
of half a dozen, squat, brown body-builders in dark business suits
treading the ritual step and chanting no longer seemed anachronistic. After the ritual was performed, their spirits appeared to
have revived, and they took seats on the various fragments of the
temple and chatted about the day's events.

But then what did really happen, asked Augustus, appealing
with his hands out, palms turned upwards, what happened to the
original temple?

The other ambassador—whom he recognized now, he had
more refined features than the others, a thin nose, thinner brows
and delicate fine-beaten gold ear flares, said:

We've just left the present time in your mother's living room,
we're barely forty minutes out of it, what, September 19th, 2001 at
6:40 pm. But when we were at the original temple it was
8.17.1.4.12.11 *Muluc*- that was the *Tzolkin* sign (or day), Jhon,
wasn't it? —At a nod from the other he continued and 15 Mac or
about 376 AD on your calendar—and we're nineteen hundred and
twenty-two years out of that time. So the temple has disintegrated.
It was a matter of time. The fine features relaxed into a satisfied,
sensitive state of repose, and the others murmured their approval
or admiration, it was evident that this date-counting feat was no
mean one, and it was also evident to Augustus that he had in front
of him an *its'at*, a class-A1 mind, an artist or scribe, one used to
reflecting on enormous time spans and concrete events as he chis-
eled them out of the stone stelae..

Well, he murmured respectfully, since we're not going to get
much farther in here this time, wouldn't it be better to go back to
the apartment. But it's not really my mother's..

Jhon put his ham-heavy hand gently on his knee. Augustus, he
said, it's not so simple. We have to do some searching here, turn
up some sign. Perhaps you should go back, though, you could detect something there. Augustus looked at his new friend quizzically. He weighed the pros and cons. Perhaps this was the wrong
time—here.

All right, he said. Thanks, Jhon. Thanks for everything. And he
shook hands pensively with him, and with all the others. Then

with Jhon pointing him the way, he headed back, threading his way through the undergrowth and the overhead trailing vines and low luxuriant branches, the whole atmosphere redolent with exotic perfumes and the occasional heady shocking animal odor, until he bumped into a solid but soft obstacle, and pulling the wild grass apart, saw the edge of Milena's sofa footstool. And he called out her name with sudden urgency, and her voice sounded back, preternaturally close at hand.

I'm here, in the kitchen! He went in to see her. The fixed familiar patterns. The immutable coffee cups and dishes, the Ivory liquid hand soap on the sink. For a moment his heart stopped. Would nineteen hundred and twenty-two years change that? Does the heart change?

Milena? he said, I am willing to talk about anything, you know. So much had passed between them. So much love, so much fury, so much sorrow and disappointment. But she said nothing. She asked him if he would like another glass of wine. And he said yes, and they talked about concerts, and that was all. He touched her hand. Words were painful or had lost any substance they once had or given rise to that irresistible mechanics of further interlocking and unfree words. She looked at him from the other side of a chasm of thirty years. He gave her a hug and she hugged him back in this mute communication of the bodies. Perhaps bodies have a better and simpler mode.

Milena, he said, I have to go now. I have to see a friend.

Oh, your friends, she said, from depths of insuperable bitterness and incurable envy. You always loved your friends best. He suppressed his customary disavowal. He let himself out amid the whisper of the leaves of the Yucca tree as the door shut. As he walked down the long corridor to the elevator she opened the door again and watched him go, the long elastic bond of love and possession still tied to him. Once he was in the street again, the enormous vigor of the city revived and purified him.

Tijaax 5

(Day Seven)

The sacrificial knife

What was his error, then—Woman in general? And for a brief instant, mind drifting, he was able to perceive his mother as his father must have first seen her, lovely, darkly romantic, opaque, at a party at the Spanish ambassador's where he mistook her for the ambassador's daughter. She was able to coincide very briefly, strenuously with this image, to satisfy his pater's longing for that unreal and never-to-be-realized mirage of womanhood, which in reality she in no wise resembled—sardonic, lucid, anti-romantic, thoroughly sensible Anglo-Saxon that she was. Why on earth she had chosen his father, Augustus could never fathom. Perhaps some last romantic spasm from her girlhood? What she missed in her very sentimental husband was a little whipping. How was it that Augustus was so convinced of this? Perhaps because he resembled her? She had told him, when he was thirteen or fourteen, that in all couples one always loves more than the other; he did not have a moment's doubt that she was the other. Was there more pain in loving or being loved, he had asked her, and she didn't answer. He would have to discover for himself that the guilt of loving less was far more painful. Love always finds a certain comfort or consolation in its gift of self: one's own irrefutable generosity.

Thus musing, he found his way to the aperture of the Lincoln Center subway and down into its ornate entrance: the *Witz* monster's maw, which adorns the facade and doorway of the temples in Tikal. Descending into the depths with the warm animal mass of the evening rush hour, anonymous hands, knees, feet, hips and breasts in impersonal intimacy, it had always been a source of excitement for him, well before any differences between himself and Milena had appeared, a sort of deception that was impersonal and involuntary, and which compensated for the rigid fidelity which she claimed as an absolute right. He wondered at the length of the descent and admired the deco art on the walls, the *repoussé* stucco masks, clever idea he thought, this Maya motif in a subway station. And for several hundred meters the procession of warriors carrying spears and axes (no doubt an allusion to the ax-wars of *Tlaloc* warfare introduced in Tikal by visiting emissaries and traders from Teotihuacan in the fourth century) wound along the walls accompanying them. Brilliant as the mural was—the reds, ochres, browns, were delicious—the descent appeared excessive to him. He was a habitué of these subterranean depths but he didn't remember the 1 and 9 trains running so deep. The human herd about him seemed to be afflicted by the same doubts, and for the first time their grunting and heavy breathing drew his attention, and it was only when he glanced about and saw the near-naked bodies clothed mostly in mere tunics and sometimes a great feathery head-piece that he realized what it was. Only in a Manhattan subway, he thought wryly, could this sort of ambiguity be countenanced. It was obvious that the city was suffering from instability, its boundaries in some condition of oscillatory double identity. In any case, in view of its notorious racial multiplicity the exotic crowd could easily be explained by other factors (an ethnic block party, a Greenwich Village gay Mexican convention, *que sais-je*), so he decided to ignore this particular group, although he was surprised by the brown, highly visible, not unpleasantly shaped if a bit too Botero for his taste, damsel in a *huipil*, the classic, transparent, lacy gown that was obviously *la delicia* of the *Ahauob*, since maidens in their presence were invariably so dressed, except in the case of warlike spouses or mothers. He glanced more closely at the damsel thus attired right behind him, who in her swinging barefoot pace thrust into his purview at every step her chunky nipples protruding under the filmy material. On closer view, her face even had a certain wedge-like delicacy, as if it were cunningly cut out of a block of jade. However he would not let that distract him, he was becoming quite anxious about the 1 and the 9 trains, and the murmurs and muttering which rippled through the crowd expressed similar concern. Then the entire procession came abruptly to a halt, and piled up on itself (and he along with it) accordion-like. He was acutely conscious in the meaty crush of what must be the girl's breasts crushed up into the small of his back (yes, she was that small), but resisted the impulse to look behind, and in any case he was so tightly held in place and squeezed on every side that it would have been difficult, so instead he leaned forward straining to see beyond and above the backs of the crowd to what was holding them all up. He could not see beyond the end of the tunnel, or rather it was not evident in the poorly lit conditions whether there was an abrupt turn in the tunnel and for some reason the front of the crowd didn't want to go around the corner, or whether the tunnel had itself come to a stop and up front the people were all up against the wall. He was too far at a hundred feet to tell, but all those brown squat bodies appeared to be pressing against a wall with nowhere to go, hands and arms stretched out flatly and no movement to left or right. Behind him murmurs, cries, curses of frustration, and in his back a shifting of pressures as the breasts slid upwards to his shoulder blades and the warmth of the groin into the small of his back as the girl strained no doubt to see over his shoulder to what was happening. He could not help, no, guiltless, he did not need to help the tingling physiological reaction at his crotch. Apart from this sensual provocation, he felt distinctly uncomfortable about how things were going—the simple act of taking the subway tunnel had been so bizarrely distorted, it was injurious to a fundamental sense of what one could expect in such an everyday situation. Add a sense of mental saturation of such fantastic developments, a *trop-plein* of unconscious events, and his confusion was complete. Things were coming to a head about him now, people were pressing up hard from behind, those in front were shouting in protest and gesturing to get back, and the girl in his back with her lacy *huipil* was practically glued to him, and this became acutely embarrassing because she started to make spasmodic jerking movements, her groin thumping against him, and he thought she was performing some sexual act and felt close to coming, but when he twisted his head backwards to see her face and could only see the top of her electric black hair below his shoulders, above it he saw the hirsute, ferociously grimacing face of the dark-red man behind her (certainly no educated *Ahau*) who was taking advantage of the over-crowded circumstances to copulate with her from the rear. He wrestled himself out of the almost inextricable embrace of the group about him with a gut-bursting effort, and hurtled a couple of yards forward through pivoting bodies like revolving doors. It was not the touch of the woman's body that caused this revulsion, his susceptibility to female magnetism was unexceeded by anyone he knew, but the disgust inspired by receiving the impact on his body surface of a male rhythm. Squeals and raucous cries from the now turbid zone he had just quitted convinced him of the timeliness of his self-extraction. And now he found himself with just a few dozen rows of bobbing heads in front, and it was perfectly clear that the tunnel had come to an end, no exit, narrow or otherwise, one way or the other: just an absurd wall curving in from the two side-walls and up to the top of the tunnel thus executing a closure. This was inconceivable in a subway tunnel, he had never seen anything like it before, and absurdly he felt indignant! He noticed a different tint or cement stain of the in-curving walls, which clearly demarcated them from the normal tunnel walls. They were of a paler tone, thus suggesting that they were a quite recent fabrication. He was excited by this realization, and wanted to put it to someone in this hysterical mob. The front rows of the small reddish block-like men in tunics right up by the end-wall were engaged in fending off the others pushing up against them, some had even drawn the axes they wore in their belts and the short obsidian-tipped spears they carried on their backs to ward off their fellows.

No, no, he cried, finally getting it out, the wall, the wall! Cut into the wall! Because of the advantage of height he had over them (most of them were just over five feet high) many in the crowd turned back to look at him. Mustering the best of his threadbare *Quiche* (the Maya tongue, not a trendy Manhattan snack) interspersed with *Nahuatl* with which he was more familiar and which he knew some of them had to understand even if it was a Mexican dialect and not proper Maya, but with the frequent trading missions from Teotihuacan many had become familiar with it—he cried again, Hit the wall, attack the wall! They looked at each other doubtfully a moment, then with a hoarse warrior cry turned and started stabbing and cutting and digging at the wall. And indeed, the relatively fresh mortar gave way little by little under their blows, and with a roar the others pressing behind them ran at the wall as well, and there were scores of axes gouging the crumbling surface now, and suddenly with shrill hoots and yowps it gave way, and they broke through a narrow opening and now were streaming through the wall, he carried along with the rest of them as the opening collapsed about them at the edges and spread wider. On the other side he halted for a moment in the midst of the crowd that had smashed their way through, and stared with amazement at the sight: it was a cavernous room, lit only by the electric light which was shed through the hole in the wall, so that it receded into gloom, but from it emanated a sense of pure architectural proportion cut from great stone blocks, and yet it was not so much an esthetic perception as a feeling of symbolic solemnity, awe. And the people who kept on pouring in through the break in the wall immediately fell silent as they entered, and soon a couple of hundred were standing about the walls of the room facing toward the center, the note of hysteria which animated them earlier now completely vanished. He did not even question the experience, it was so wholly surprising: in the center of the room lay a single four by eight foot slab of stone, on which was engraved the figure of an elaborately armored *K'ul Ahau*, a lord of lords, with a human skull at his belt and in his hand a stick with the puppet like, long-nosed figure of the Jester God at its end. Augustus could only stab out wildly in conjecture at some archaeological discovery. But the Maya here, in a New York subway! Perhaps they had broken by accident into some underground storeroom of one of the city Museums?

As his eyes became accustomed to the dim atmosphere, he could make out on the walls the gathering of the Maya warriors and priests who had accompanied them along the frescos on their trip down the subway tunnel, and who strangely resembled the contemporary crowd standing in front of them around the room in something like funereal silence. People were still trickling through the breached wall noiselessly. Then the dead silence was shattered theatrically by a scream, coming as it did from the other side, off-stage, and then more screams as several people jostled their way through the opening jerking and heaving, and it became obvious that several men were dragging another man inside who struggled and screamed as he was literally carried in, the echoes of his screams deafening and reverberating in the otherwise mute and motionless room. Behind this small group limped a practically naked woman, since even the lacy *huipil* she had been wearing was torn apart, so that she had to clutch it about herself for decency. She was weeping noiselessly and was supported by another woman, a servant apparently in a simple coarse gown, and an old man wearing a tasseled headdress and a long gown. The several men dragged their prisoner through the crowd which fanned open to allow them through to the center of the burial chamber (for it had become clear to him that that's what it was), and the muscularly compact, wild-haired, dark-red-faced man (like most of them) in their grip suddenly stopped screaming and looked at the stone slab and about at the watching crowd with breathless and fixed attention. By now the entire procession was inside the chamber, perhaps three hundred people, standing several rows deep against the walls, so that little space was left about the stone slab. The man was laid down on the slab unresisting, he gazed about at his fellow-Maya with an interested, inquiring gaze. Another gowned man pushed his way through the crowd carrying a small container of some kind, and kneeling beside the prisoner began to daub on his body a blue ointment or paint. The prone

man shivered slightly, doubtless because of the wetness in that
dank atmosphere, but continued to watch what was being done to
him with the same detached and interested expression, as did the
rapt audience. Then each of the four men kneeling beside him laid
hold of his ankles and wrists, these were the *chac*, the assistant
priests responsible for this holding action (Augustus was informed of the various *termini tecnici* of the shamanic rite after the
event by his informant, Jhon). A fifth man in a scarlet gown and
many macaw plumes nodding about his shoulders and in his
headdress (where had all these props come from? he wondered)
approached. The latter, the *nacom* or executant priest, squatted
beside the quietly waiting, spread-eagled man, and passed a hand
gently over the hairless chest and dwelt for a moment at the left
nipple, which caused the man to shiver slightly, perhaps an involuntary erotic response? A hum was audible, and Augustus realized that several men had come up closer about the absorbed little
group, and were murmuring or chanting in low tones. The *nacom*
was now passing his hands up the chest and then down the sides
or ribs of the supine man who began to twitch faintly at the seeming caress. The chanting of the *ahmen* (who specialized in shamanic prayer) grew louder, it had a soothing, even hypnotic effect on
Augustus and the rest of the audience, to judge from their slight
swaying motion, and the latter began to think of it all as a rite
similar to the Catholic confession and absolution he had experienced as a boy, the seduction it had exercised upon his boyish
soul and the troubling erotic atmosphere it evoked (what other
sins does an adolescent agonize over?). Here however the rite was
done with a kinesio-therapeutic laying on of hands, cathartic in its
rhythmic collective pathos, perhaps charismatic-Catholic. The object of these ritual gestures was jerking more spasmodically, and
now and then the *nacom* would draw a hand down across his
brow and eyes to calm him. One of the chanting priests came forward now with a small white bundle in his outstretched palms,
and held it out to the *nacom*. The latter stood up and Augustus
saw that he was a dignified five-foot three or four, inches taller
than the audience as a whole, and with professionally graceful
movements of the fingers, like a Catholic priest unfolding the
communion napkin posed on the chalice, spread the white cloth
open as the chanting reached a higher, more emotive pitch, hovering at a cusp between exquisite delight and anguish—and drew
out a dully scintillating, curved and pointed black flint instrument
like an eagle's beak. Kneeling down quickly, leaning suddenly with
his left hand on the shaking victim's left breast, whose limbs were

tensed now by the four *chac*, his right hand swept down in the midst of a billowing of the plumes on his shoulders and headdress and in a final upward convulsive leap (*saccade*) of the victim's entire body in spite of the restraining hands of the *chac*, a single scarlet arc snaked up into the air and maculated the feathers of the priest in absolute silence. The *ahmen* had fallen silent for the victims of the Maya heart sacrifice, known as the "Gentle Death", never utter a sound. Augustus felt some moisture on his wrist and wiped off his sleeve compulsively. He had a sense of post-ejaculatory satiety and relief together with a gut feeling of utter disgust and vomit and incredulity. In this moment he hated (and feared) the Maya. He recognized what might be called the orgasm of cruelty. He realized he had been at the "heart" of a shamanic experience. He wished he had not been but it was too late now. Was there not at the core of his revulsion some recognition of a deserved and delectable punishment? Does not his horror and delight reflect his own identification with the victim? The priest's sensual and murderous gestures obscurely desired? The people about him whose rite it was were not quiet. They were in fact dancing, at first a stirring in the crowd like leaves rustling, then more pronounced and excited. Later he learned it was called the *Xibalba ocot*, the dance of the demons, the dance of the dead. They danced with an orgiastic excitement, a pulsating rhythm, some hollow drumbeat in the background, but mostly it was the spasmodic, difficult beat of their feet that generated the obsessive rhythm. He was not inclined to follow the step, indeed he could not accept the entire event as even happening in his familiar New York subway—but he felt the visceral tug. He looked down (from his six foot height, minor in a New York subway but considerable in present company) at the crowd with revulsion. The *nacom* was standing in their midst holding up his prize, the slippery raw organ (was it pulsating still or was he hallucinating?), the blood sliding down his outstretched arm. The dancers were gathering steam, locked into a mechanical coherency as if they were all driven by a single dynamo, and as they throbbed and jittered little spurts of red appeared like blossoms about them, and he saw that many were nicking or pricking at their own arms or thighs or breasts with little obsidian or flint knives as he had witnessed earlier at the pyramid, and behind he heard muffled groans, and he half-turned and saw the very girl who had been the crux of this incident drawing her *huipil* aside and a half-naked man fumbling between her thighs, blood dripping down his back, and across the room was a confused jumble of bodies, another woman interlocked with two or three men in spasmodic movements, the smell of blood and sweat and sex viscerally shocking, and he himself began to dance now, unable to help himself, unconscious, a puppet joining the other puppets, first one leg rising up to one side and next the foot slapping down, then the other leg, while he rocked from side to side. He who had always laid claim to being aware! It reminded him of a bizarre and painful store window-dressing he had once seen of a ragged puppet monkey jerked rapidly and spasmodically on strings for hours on end. The grimace on the puppet's face seemed set in rigor mortis and the strings appeared to be Kafkaen instruments of torture rather than of play. In any case their gods must have been pleased, *Itzamna* or *Kitzle* the Head-Eating Jaguar, because the cloying smoke arising from the cooking organ assumed an elaborately wreathed shape about the ceiling which might well be interpreted as the Vision-Serpent. The dancers fell to an awed hush as the figure deployed about the ceiling. A vast, satiated "ahh" rose from their collective throat. He did not feel justified in joining in this sort of festivity, and he stroked his chin and looked about at the others absurdly embarrassed. There was no reason to be because no one was looking at him; but he was looking at himself, wasn't he? At the opposite end of the room from the breach in the wall where he was still standing there appeared to be an eddying and backing in the crowd, it was difficult to see in the gloom, there was still some dancing but obviously the heart had gone out of it, and after a moment he realized the crowd was thinning at the other side and was evacuating the room from a still invisible exit. He noticed they were leaving from the same direction as that followed by a small pipe or tube which protruded from under the great marble lid upon which the figure of the *K'ul Ahau* was engraved—no doubt a source of air! The still packed crowd on his side began to dwindle and to stream out in that direction as well, and sucked along in their wake he came upon a little rectangular doorway in the shadows through which he was engulfed along with everybody else. The narrow tube also ran along up the side of the doorway and along one corner of the ceiling of the tunnel. It was a very different atmosphere than the route, which had led into the funerary chamber. This tunnel was obviously ancient, it was no subway tunnel, and he had to stoop to walk up the inclined and dark passageway that was lit only by the flickering light of torches carried by some of the Maya crowd. No wall decorations this time, just a rugged, steep tunnel hewn in rock or packed rubble. Sometimes when the gradient was especially pronounced, steps were cut in the ground, and the group was now proceeding in single file, there was no extra room next to him, so that he could only see a pair of powerful red haunches in front of him and hear the scrabble of bare feet behind. There was grunting and plaintive moans, and the on-winding procession seemed very long to him, it spiraled on and up for at least an hour. Occasional grunts and complaints-"*ai hermano, basta, no!*" he heard in plaintive insular Spanish, the tunnel lent itself to a loss of awareness of anything except the immediate sensations. Its physical conditions evoked the sense of relative time, which he cherished: the conviction that time was a present spiral and that at $x + 1$ time he would hold and contain what was so viscerally present to him at this moment. Shouts ahead, excited clamor, suggested to his numbed mind that that moment had arrived, and irresistibly like a cork popping out of rushing water, he spilled out of the dank tunnel with the crowd into fresh, sparkling, black air. Vastness, a staggering, vertiginous opening onto the star-dotted sky struck his solar plexus first. He thought for an instant he had come out onto one of those great pyramidal platforms of Tikal, the Temple on top jutting out behind him and the little spirit-tube (for air) poking from the ceiling of the tunnel above him like a snake's head into this atmosphere, and it made a small hiss as it also sucked in the air. Then the perspective of enormous height when he gazed down into the canyon below with its fluttering scintillation of tiny lights, and mind and eyes had to adjust to comprehend that they were the tiny headlights of traffic and blinking store-lights a couple of score of floors below. He and the crowd of Maya swayed as if drunk with the dizzying reversal of perspective as they found themselves on the top of one of the great skyscrapers of New York. He did not recognize immediately which one it was, but he realized from the look of the snarled street patterns below that it had to be Midtown Manhattan, and closer perusal revealed the avenue to be Madison, so he guessed that this could be the Supreme Court building with its pyramidal hat on its summit. Meanwhile the indigenous Guatemalan, Yucateca, Belizean crowd about him was now chattering excitedly in Spanish instead of Quiche or some other Maya dialect so he understood without difficulty, about how late it was, what had happened to the party, what about dinner, as well as a couple of references to the "Yanqui" and querying glances in his direction, and then something about the police, and the tone changed, now suspicious glances shot toward him, and the volume of the excited conversations dropped to a mutter as the people bunched together in small groups their backs turned to him, and he decided prudently to take advantage of the momentary distraction to withdraw, and so nonchalantly he extended one leg out to the side and just around a corner of the wrap-around terrace, which the rest of his body followed instantly like a cartoon character, and breathlessly he hurried along the walkway until he came to an iron door which he pulled open with a heart-stopping rusty creak, and he vanished within pulling the door to and slamming home the rusted bolt. Perhaps he was taking this whole thing too dramatically, he thought, but his pounding heart told him otherwise, and he clattered down the iron staircase to the next floor where he found a carpeted hallway and an elevator which he promptly rode down to the ground floor, promising himself he would not mention the Maya crowd's situation to the guards. He had no wish to embarrass them, but neither had he any desire to be ejected bodily from the rooftop which he feared might be their conclusion as to how to rid themselves of a potentially dangerous witness, since it was in their mores to roll people down very high steep stairs. With that he sped into the street, ignoring the guards' questioning cries. He dropped into the first coffee shop he came to, to mull things over.

Kawok 10

(Day Six)

The great community of the Universe

Momentarily unbalanced by the gravity of the dark column of the crowd he had left behind, he gazed up into the atmosphere gathered into the summits of the skyscrapers. This was another, celestial Manhattan with the letters of its name written in a filigree of golden light: a delicious theatre detached from the vulgar city or just barely tethered to it like a buoy straining on the bouncing waves. He knew he had to get back to the Maya peninsula one thousand year three hundred years ago but he didn't know how to get there. He couldn't go back via his mother's, it was a decoy, and it would never get him there in time anyway, that was already proved. He could still see the troubled expressions on the faces of his Maya companions as they stared at the millennial ruins of their former habitat. Plunge deeper, he murmured, as he trotted down the street with the familiar mental blinkers on either side of his temples. This was an old technique, neither hearing nor seeing anything (or very little) of the outside world, he would drive himself on. When he crossed the Bowery, around the corner of a "blank" he glimpsed a couple of blocks north a round-backed, black-patch-eyed fellow who tilted his head so as to enable his good eye to shoot a rapaciously inquisitive glance in Augustus' direction, why did he look so familiar, he wondered. And it was thus he traversed the East Village and came unto the text-world of Alphabet City, across Avenue A, past Tompkins Square into little cross-streets which were vaguely threatening, with that thread of anxiety which underpins the fabric of the entire city but is more perceptible in these neural nodes, and on into denser undergrowth, in the shape of stray animals and stray humans, famished addicts and moonstruck purple-and-orange headed punks with gimlet eyes, indeed everything in the neighborhood appeared razor-sharp if gazes could cut. What first swam into his ken was a trim, utterly different sort of human being whose most striking feature from behind was a curlicue or extravagantly twisted coil of bright yellow hair, which stood up on top of his head. He was dressed in old-fashioned knickerbockers, like bicycle-pants which tuck in and are suspended by elastics above the calves, which he might have worn himself once when he was a small boy bicycling in the *Foret de Soignes* (Swine Forest) on the outskirts of Brussels, a town also frequented by—yes! Tintin! For clearly, unmistakably, it was he. The last character he had expected to see here. However the inescapable fact was that Tintin was there, in flesh and blood, before him. Beyond Tintin's briskly striding outline the landscape was oddly flat and graphic. It was still New York, and yet it was not the New York he had perceived while on the front side. The landmarks had not changed, he could now see a couple of hundred yards down the street which had been blocked previously by the wall, and at the end of the street was the East River where it should be, and he could even make out the Pepsi Cola plant farther north on the Brooklyn side of the river, so it's not as if this were a fictitious *Tintin en Amérique* place, a figment of Augustus' (or more accurately Hergé's) fevered brain, which would not have been surprising in light of the weird Shamanic events of the last 24 hours. No, he was where he should be, in his hometown. An optical displacement had taken place; a psychic Kepler effect. While he was studying these matters, Tintin's brisk pace had taken him down the street toward the river.

Tintin, he cried out, the cry reverberating just above his head. Tintin did not stop but disappeared about a corner at the end of the street. Augustus took off in a spurt and raced to the corner, but Tintin had disappeared. He found himself not far from the foot of the Williamsburg Bridge, with FDR Drive vibrating in front of him with its lethal swish of vehicles. As if with the disappearance of the Belgian character the gritty reality of Noo Yok had reasserted itself with no margin left for charm. The fine-tuned lines of the city decor of moments ago had given way to the corroded wear and tear of stone and steel. Disappointed, he walked down Columbia Street (near the Williamsburg Bridge), thinking he had lost track of perhaps the only person who could assist him in this chaotic train of events. He was also concerned about Tintin who probably had no idea how dangerous this drug-infested neighborhood could be. He appreciated that Tintin, unlike many other characters used to a—well, more schematic world, understood the risks associated with a certain urban setting, and had been in tight spots. Still this was not the New York Tintin had known: crack and racial violence were not a part of what after all had been a simpler world. At that moment through the generalized blare of traffic, he heard a high-pitched voice cry out, and immediately recognized Tintin's still-adolescent tones. He raced once again down the street along the elevated riverside throughway to the next corner, and swinging about the corner breathlessly, heart pounding, came upon a scene not startling to anyone familiar with many such episodes in Tintin's career: two swarthy men, possibly Latinos, were circling Tintin with sticks in their hands, the latter, with his fists up in classic Marquess of Queensbury boxing stance. Augustus, who was no hero but no coward either, ran at them screaming hysterically something about the police. This distracted the thugs sufficiently, who turned toward him in alarm, so that Tintin shot out his famous left hook and knocked down one of his assailants. Augustus was almost upon them now himself still screaming, and the man who had been knocked down scrambled to his feet with the help of the other and they both took to their heels. Tintin watched them go with satisfaction, dusting off his immaculate tweed jacket with patches on the elbows, and gave Augustus a warm grin and a manly handshake and, pointy eyes twinkling, asked how he happened to be in the vicinity. The latter explained what had transpired above, while Tintin listened in silence, and then he suggested they go and get some refreshment at a bar down the street because he would like to get Tintin's view on a matter. Tintin nodded enthusiastically, and they walked quickly, and it was not easy to keep up with Tintin's animated gait, to an establishment with a pseudo-antique sign hanging above the door, *La Licorne*[6]. Comfortably ensconced at a table by the door in the cozy boozy bar, the first thing he asked Tintin was why he had seemed so surprised and even—he endeavored to phrase it non-contentiously—a little put off to see him when they had first met "in the shadow of the Pyramid" on Christopher street.

Augustus, said Tintin, leaning forward earnestly and lowering his voice, I have been on the *piste*, the track of some very peculiar developments. The waitress, a buxom redhead in her late forties, who looked as if she had seen more glamorous days in a more seductive profession to judge by her cleavage and her baited gaze, leaned on the table and asked what was their pleasure, gennelmen, seeming to promise much more than beverages. Augustus said a beer and Tintin asked if he could have a glass of milk. She gave him a withering look and said the best she could fix him up with was a glass of water, did he think he could manage that? Without flinching he said yes, if she had a Badoit or a Perrier, because he would not drink the river water.

A bad wow, a pear yay, she asked, pouring on more withering scorn.

Oh all right, he said, I will have a Coca. Heavy-lidded she turned to Augustus, and said,

We don't push that shit here, and he said,

My friend would like a Coke.

After she left, he began again: yes, *mon ami*, I have been following these transmigrations between the Maya world where I myself have been occupied[7], and your Great Apple. When I saw you, my friend, I was suspicious that you might be involved if unwittingly, and that you might tip them off without meaning to as to my identity. I first became aware of the nature of these events when you arrived in the Petén rain forest where I was winding up the Picaro business. I did not witness your arrival personally but was told about it as I and the *Capitaine* were preparing to leave for Belgium. He came to a stop as the buxom waitress who, Augustus

6 This name is found in one of Hergé's best albums, *Le Secret de la Licorne*

7 *Tintin et les Picaros* ; Tintin actually preceded Augustus in this adventure in Maya country in the thirties. So Augustus was able to benefit therefrom.

noticed, ever attentive to such details, had buttoned up one or two buttons of her plummeting neckline after Tintin's disapproving glance, plopped down their glasses with a flounce of her red wig and left. He listened with half an ear to Tintin's background sketch. He had difficulty in paying close attention because Tintin's gestures, even his facial movements, appeared at times to swim in and out of focus with the surroundings. It was as if they were taking place in a parallel space. And that in spite of Tintin's well-known attention to detail and realism. It was precisely those qualities, he reflected as he half-listened to Tintin's sprightly account that would make him an ideal mediator.

By the way, he interjected, how come Milou isn't with you? Something seemed wrong with the picture even though he could not put his finger on it. For one practically never saw Tintin without his dog whether in the most formal circumstances or the most arduous of adventures. If Milou were not in one frame he would be in the next. This was one of Tintin's saving graces, who otherwise was so perfectly behaved that he could verge on the priggish. And Milou had the further virtue of being a thinking dog. His thoughts and emotions were simple, childlike, but explicit.

Oh, he's right here, said Tintin, here boy, he whistled and the curly-cued, sprightly terrier appeared at his feet.

Tintin, he said tentatively, why were you even here? Tintin looked at him out of those piercing pinpoint eyes. His eyebrows were raised in circumflexes above the pinpoints. Alert.

There was information regarding a tramp steamer, the "Maya Princess", which has just docked down here. Tintin waited for a moment as if to let the import of his words sink in. My informant also said that a group of Maya had disembarked at Pier 43. Augustus glanced at him, in turn with piercing gaze or at least doubtfully. "Doubtfully" would be more accurate.

And who, may I ask, was your informant?

Dupont and Dupond, of course.

Oh dear, he said. What had aroused his suspicions was the style of the account. He could practically see the squat brown Maya with their *harape* or colorful indigenous shawls wrapped about their shoulders in pleasing contrast with the gray tones of the wharf. It was too much like a classic Tintin scene. Not quite real. Too pleasing graphically to be real. And did you see them, he asked, to see how far he would go.

Yes, said Tintin, just minutes before those two swarthy fellows approached me.

And what did they look like?

Oh you know, that squat type with those colorful indigenous shawls.

Tintin, he said, rising, I think we should leave.

All right, just a moment, I'll finish with the Coca, said the other and he raised his glass to his lips and swallowed it down. Not even a drop on his lips, Augustus noticed. Obviously there had to be some points of synapses with the empirical world, i.e. New York, and the, say, animated one which his friend came from, which gave rise to incoherencies.

In my world, he said deliberately as they went out the door, the Maya in New York wear business suits. For the sake of argument, he forgot about the procession in the subway tunnel.

Well, said Tintin glancing sharply at him, they probably had their business suits in their luggage. He nodded, that seemed quite reasonable. And just then, as if to prove the point, trooping across Abraham Kazan Street from Delancey, came a goodly group of, yes, Maya Indians in colorful dress, carrying suitcases and assorted bundles and packages carefully balanced on their heads or protectively wrapped in their arms, as if these were sacred artifacts. As they came closer Augustus and Tintin saw that a couple of them even wore brilliantly plumaged blue and purple headdress, which nodded as they walked. They appeared to enjoy some special regard among the others, judging from the space afforded them in the midst of the group. From the records Augustus remembered of Father Diego de Landa (the notorious Jesuit who burned most of the Maya books but preserved their writing and the famous Dresden Codex—which after all contained the essence!), it seemed to him these must be the priests, and in fact it was now evident that the group escorted or protected them in the formation of the procession. They had almost reached Augustus and Tintin and while none of the Indians returned their curious looks, Augustus recognized a couple of the dark faces, one with more finely delineated features, and the other with bushy brows brushed upwards, flaring. The group continued on past them, and they watched them go, gaping, Tintin's mouth a little round o, the Indians' colorful drapes in pleasing contrast with the prosaic, gray three- and four-storey buildings characteristic of the old Jewish quarter. As the group dwindled down the street, it was evident that a psychic energy held them in its magnetic embrace, and even the buildings and the street seemed to vibrate about them, a bounce in the air which had more of an aura of graphic electricity than of an indifferent urban environment. And he realized that it was not simply the group, but the street, the waterfront, the skyline which shimmied so energetically, and when he turned his eyes back to Tintin who walked beside him, and noticed how his face turned and bobbed, how his hands flapped in the air with spasmodic speed, how in a word it was difficult to hold in his sight the quicksilver movements of his friend, it dawned on him that he was participating as much in Tintin's provenance as vice versa.

Tintin, he said seriously, as they turned from the vanishing dot of the group and looked back across the river, I have been a fan of yours for many years, but I never expected, well..

It's nothing to be ashamed of, said the other gently, we all have different backgrounds, different life experiences. The soap opera tone was not what he would have expected of Tintin, but of course he must have a deeper dimension than was generally apparent in his various *Aventures*.

Tintin, he continued, feeling that the moment might have come for a more intense and to-the-point conversation, I realize it's funny to want to get at some underground level with you, because—

Because you see me as a two-dimensional comic-book character? put in Tintin without any ironic inflection.

No, no, I didn't mean that at all, he objected hastily, but because you are a man—well, a boy-of-action, always living a life of adventure, saving your friends from certain death [8] or discovering treasure [9], without question other-directed, generous and altruistic.

Oh come, come, my friend, objected Tintin with a wave of the head and the hint of a blush in his cheeks, you are exaggerating. But in any case we all have our *pecadillos*.

Well I know you don't have a girl friend or pick up prostitutes. This time the blush reddened Tintin's cheeks like a young girl's, and not a girl of 2000 plus.

There are other ways to express affection, he demurred.

You live alone at the Chateau de Moulinsart with your closest friend, le *Capitaine* Haddock and his faithful retainer, Nestor, and the Professor Tournesol. When one is a role-model for young boys.. I do not intend to pry into your private parts, said Augustus hurriedly, I had in mind rather self-reflection, introspection.

You think me incapable of interiority, said Tintin softly, and brushed the back of his hand across his cheek, although those gimlet eyes seemed scarcely capable of squeezing out a tear. I have emotion when I stand across from a magnificent snow-capped mountain[10] in Tibet, for example. A surprising play of emotions ran across the reduced, indeed basic traits of Tintin's face.

8   The Temple of the Sun or The Blue Lotus
9   The Secret of La Licorne
10   True, see Tintin in Tibet

Yes, of course I know you have a sensitive appreciation of atural beauty.

And of the arts, interjected the other with a touch of pique, Bianca Castafiore has been a guest in our home more than once[11].

No, no, of course I realize that, said Augustus emphatically, wishing to soothe his friend's feelings, please understand me. I refer rather to a sense of one's own nature, of our place in the scheme of things. Because in fact, Tintin, and he stopped here and put both hands on the shoulders of the other, as if to speak from the heart, but really in order to steady the other's rapid fluctuation in and out of the purely physical context, what I'm getting at is whether you—from the position you occupy—

Leverage, interjected Tintin, leverage is what you want from me.

Yes, he said, to mediate for me with the others, who are from a different and more alien environment, one that might be called shamanic, which, even though I realize of course that you do not share in, nevertheless when you consider the avenues we have borrowed to gain access to their world, perhaps you have some means to comprehend, some alternative approach. He knew he was being excessively vague, but he felt he could not afford to take a more direct tack.

But Augustus, said Tintin, you yourself have remarked how realistic and attentive to detail I am, in fact how I have always played a demystifying role[12].. How could I possibly intervene in the sort of fantastic or mythomanic scenarios you indulge in..

It's not a question of outlook, he said as delicately and as firmly as he knew how, it's a matter of intersecting planes of the non-real.

Ah, said the other in the tone of one hardly surprised but nevertheless disappointed by human frailties, so it's come to this. You are not the first human being to—

Tintin, I don't mean to offend you, it's just that there are discontinuities I cannot resolve and perhaps you—

Oh yes, I know, people like you think they have a monopoly on the real. Do you have any idea in how many languages and how many millions of copies the Albums of my *aventures*—mentioned surreptitiously in your footnotes—have been sold, and what their impact on the "real world" has been? The extent to which young minds have been molded, including your own, may I add?

Of course, said Augustus, but of course! And your very presence here, and your on-going investigation! That's what I mean!

11   Cf Herge's The Jewels of Bianca Castafiore: the Italian Diva, forever chasing the Captain Haddock.

12   Cf The Black Island

Ah, said Tintin, mollified, well of course that's a different matter. Augustus breathed a sigh of relief.

Well then, he said. Now it is clear that the Maya we just saw are a clandestine group with their own agenda.. Do you know anything more of them?

No but I've heard things, said Tintin.

From your informant?

Yes, yes, the Dupont(d)'s are very reliable.

Oh dear, said Augustus. [13]I know what you are thinking, said Tintin, but in their own way they are thorough. They collect facts. What they are incapable of is ideas. My difficulty with your proposal, he added after a moment of thought, is that fantasy is foreign to me. I am incapable of operating in a world of shadows and illusions without attempting to shed light upon it.

In that moment Augustus felt he had captured exactly Tintin's essence, and that was what he had been after.

I see, he said, I see. Whereas in my case it is probably the need to be accurate and quite literal. It's not so different. Perhaps we can manage some collaboration. Everything appeared to be still around them. He could no longer hear the throb of the huge city as if it were in abeyance.

Hem, coughed Tintin, finger pointing across the lot at a pyramidal shaped building, if the step-level construction rising hundreds of feet into the air above them could be accounted a pyramid. At the first step or landing a number of figures were milling about, a couple of hundred feet higher at the next, smaller landing, a few figures could still be spotted, but at the last landing which constituted the top of the building, none. About Tintin and Augustus, at ground level, no traffic was present. The gradualism of their perception was uncomfortably evident to both of them, a difficult construction, as if slivers or sections of the surroundings seeped out of their field of vision. Augustus rubbed his eyes and Tintin followed suite rubbing the dots, which passed for eyes, as if to broaden the perception. Now the lay-out of the vast ground-level square swam into that field of vision, and of course Augustus, let alone Tintin, had adopted the psycho-mnemonic device of "blinkering" his field of awareness, so that it should hardly be surprising that now as he (and Tintin, since the latter was an active participant in this process) built up the setting,

---

13   Notorious detective duo who often turned up in the Adventures of Tintin at difficult moments such as the above. It is true they were better known for comic relief than for their detecting skills, and it was perhaps that Tintin had in mind.

things should fall into place thusly: yes, avenues radiated out
from this square, the geometrical loveliness or coolness of the
plan was uplifting with the other temple-like buildings spaced at
right angles and set back symmetrically from the corners of the
"pyramid" building.

However it looks like nowhere in the East Village, that's for
sure, he said to Tintin.

Tintin who stood eyes popping (if such pin-points could be
said to be popping) and small straight nose aquiver at the grand
layout, nodded,

Nowhere that I know on the East Side.

No, no, don't think so, said Augustus shaking his head in disbelief, maybe somewhere down toward Bowling Green, they're always building something new down there. But both of them knew
this could not be, and besides how could they be at the tip of
Manhattan having just crossed a street in the East Village?

I assure you, said Tintin, with a pout, that there is an explanation for this.

He said yes, but it may not be the one you want. Tintin's figure,
it should be noted, had taken on an increased luster in this context, an added vivacity. It was as if he were more at ease, more
used to it. Without question the atmosphere had changed in the
last few minutes, the air was shot through with a glassy brilliance,
the hues of the buildings about them had taken on depth, richness, the lines of the above-mentioned "layout" were spectacularly
clear-cut and graphic, design-intensive, whereas before the streets
had been quite indifferent. Even the little figures strutted about on
the platforms above with the same sort of mercurial vivacity that
characterized Tintin's own flux of movement. In a word, this was a
world in which Tintin could feel more at home than the more
sluggish Augustus Sykey. And that, of course, was exactly what he
had suspected. With his bicycle pump pants and tweed jacket he
even looked more at home than Augustus, in fact did he not resemble, say, Alfred P. Maudslay in the course of his exploration of
the Maya monuments in the late 19th century? Of course it is true
that Tintin who spanned several decades was a figure from the
mid-twenties, but as a pre-War figure he kept a moral flavor of the
nineteenth century. In any case, Tintin now pointed an unwavering index finger toward a feature neither of them had taken cognizance of earlier: what had appeared to be a vertical ornamental
strip running up the middle of the Pyramidal structure now was
seen to be very steep steps running straight up the slightly inclined face of the Pyramid, leading through from one platform to

the next without interruption.

My goodness, he said, like walking up the face of a skyscraper. I wonder what the *Capitaine* would say?

The *Capitano* would say, gadzooks, me hearties! It's like climbin' to the fore royal sailin' close to the wind! The hearty voice marked with a strong French accent boomed behind them, and he and Tintin swung around, dumbfounded. There, big as life, in flesh and blood, was the old sea wolf himself, black beard bristling and blue eyes piercing, weather-beaten creased face, the very stereotype of a sea captain, with that air of bonhomie that characterized him, every inch a man's man. Le *Capitaine* Haddock was striding towards them, and close behind was Phil, the shopkeeper-poet, shaggy white mane and equally blue eyes and a broad smile.

Captain Haddock, said Augustus, delighted to see you again! Can't remember when I last had the pleasure, but—but this could be—

Tintin et les Picaros [14]! joined in Tintin and the captain, laughing.

Yes, I suppose it could remind one, said Augustus, a little self-consciously, but this is the real thing. An aura: the terraced buildings, a lunar stone garden in a subtle play of planar surfaces, of pyramidal structures, massive, looming, set off from one another at delicately staggered symmetries, yielded an aura of power from above and supreme esthetic intelligence.

Look, Augustus, said Tintin, here comes that group again, and they watched the assembly of Maya immigrants from pier 48 approach from the far end of the plaza, the same two plumed heads nodding now in a staccato dance-rhythm, the people about them doing a sort of simple two-step forward, one-step back rhythm, and other similar groups streamed in from all corners of the plaza. Many were now dressed in the Wall Street style, pin-stripe business suits somewhat peevishly recommended by Augustus, while others went half-naked in native costume, see-through lace *huipils* and tunics, macaw feathers and jaguar and peccary and serpent skins, although many of these incongruously wore bowler hats and fedoras and borsalinos; then there were the pilgrims in white capes with red spondylus shell clasps, and right next to them the joggers, male and female, in crotch- and thigh hugging black spandex or dainty neon-bright loose racing shorts, the Huaxtec women, their hair braided with feathers of red and blue and green and wearing provocative nose-plugs, the Yucatan and

---

14   *Tintin et les Picaros*, album by Hergé.

Campeche Maya with red and yellow cotton shirts and skirts embroidered with variegated colors of feathers, the *Muchuppip* and *Cochuah* provincials in feather vests woven into the shape of a jacket, and many with the large ear-flares, all with their faces painted in the indispensable iron oxide red; and then the more elegant tourists in the velvet-glove fit of strapless Armani suits, the trendy locals of the Soho neighborhood in overalls and hairless chests, the intellectual visitors from the West Village in corduroy pants and tweedy jackets, but most impressive were the warriors in cloth armor and skulls hung at their broad belts, sporting leather head-bands flashing with jade emblems, wearing helmets of stuffed deer and jaguar and peccary heads perched on top of their own, and some with the great blue and green tail feathers of the Macaw nodding behind them, every manner of clothing in fact that appeared to its wearer holiday-like and celebratory, and the vast plaza was fast filling up with this festive crowd. Augustus wondered aloud to his companions that perhaps it was a block party or a parade. Tintin attempted to calm the frantically yapping Milou, and the Captain sucked on a pipe redolent of his favorite and intoxicating Dutch tobacco, and listened with a distracted ear to Augustus's talk of a putative pirate ancestor, since the Captain had a sea-faring ancestor of his own, Chevalier François de Hadoque (to whose buried treasure the Captain owed his magnificent home, the Château de Moulinsart[15]), who may have crossed swords with him in that very adventure.[16]

I would like to go there myself, Augustus remarked to the captain, to seek out any traces of the ephemeral pirate republic, when a brouhaha swept the crowd, mingled in little groups, excited murmurs, scattered chatter across the entire square, fingers pointing up and Tintin and friends witnessed a sea of up-turned brown faces, like some gigantic bronze chalice cupped to receive the sun's rays. They looked up as well and saw that the small clusters of ornately blue and green robed and jade- and obsidian-jeweled characters on the step-levels of the Pyramid were gazing up

---

15   *Le Secret de la Licorne.*

16   Augustus's ancestor was a Breton bearing his family name, from the second half of the seventeenth century, who after plundering Portuguese slave-ships off the coasts of Bahia and Dahomey had finally settled in Madagascar where thanks to his looted treasure and inspired by the Encyclopedists he founded the first free republic of Liberatoria. Cf. Daniel Defoe, *The Grand Dream—Buccaneer,* Chapter 20, *The Story of Captain Misson and his crew.*

toward the summit of the building where there stood a small block-like temple with a roof-comb on top. The facade of the temple was covered with a great stucco mask which measured at least forty feet wide by fifteen high and figured a *Witz* mountain monster festooned with coiled serpents and a row of severed jaguar heads. Its maw enclosed three entrance-ways between its fangs. But it was the extraordinary figure that had issued out of the left or east doorway of the temple and now advanced toward the front of the platform, which had arrested everyone's attention. At that height of course it was almost impossible to make out any details, some flurry of movement is evident, scarlet-robed priests seemed to be dragging a naked figure across the platform toward the first figure, who evidently was a woman despite the powerful build because protuberant bare breasts were prominent.

Lady Wac-Chanil Ahau, hissed Tintin, and the Captain slipped a small cylindrical pouch from his vest pocket and extracting a fine collapsible telescope, handed it to Augustus through an aromatic puff. Coughing he thanked the Captain, and put it to his eye: *Lady Wac-Chanil Ahau* stands, as if enshrined in a stone image, on the naked prostrate body of an enemy. She is dressed in gorgeous symbolic finery, the plumes of a quetzal swept in azure feathers behind her head, her long-nosed, heavy-lipped, double-chinned profile turned approvingly to the side, ears pierced with bone adornments, heavy neck sunk in a couple of voluptuous folds, broad sensuous shoulders, her arms clasped under massive breasts bulging behind a brassy pectoral holding what he supposed to be various sacrificial implements, a shield made from a flayed face, her lower waist trussed in an elaborate belt, with a huge jaguar-buckle hanging on it, its lower jaw gaping open on a knee-length battle-skirt just in front of her groin, her feet clad in elaborate, high-backed shoes, and these firmly and securely anchored as, impassively, she bears down with her full willed weight on the back of the collapsed, naked, near-fetal form of her captive as he awaits execution. He carefully conceals the shame of his bared testicles, a humiliating exposure in Mayan custom. With everything else crowded out of his mind by this spectacle, Augustus had lost track of goings-on around him. Now he realized that a dead silence had overtaken the crowd. Even the captain had stopped sucking on his pipe, held just inches from his open mouth. Tintin, usually the guide in these events, was speechless. Milou pressed apprehensively against his master's leg. And Augustus, his back wet with sweat, felt a cold shiver run up his spine and quiver in his throat. He had recognized her.

No, he hissed back at Tintin.

Pinned under her heels now, Augustus stared up at his mother's indifferent face. The inscription on the medallion that dangled between her powerful buttocks just above his head: "celestial is his penis"—was clearly legible. Beyond the medallion in the dark recesses of her thighs he could just perceive the foul brush.

He adjusted the focus of the telescope and blinked through the sweat dripping from his forehead into his eye. One of the attendants of the Queen Mother, a prince of the blood probably, with jade pectorals and a quetzal plume through the black hair of his ponytail, presented her with a short spear. Taking it with her free right hand, she raised it high, a thick, purple-nippled breast sprouting with hairs slung out from behind the pectoral, and without even glancing down she buried the blade beneath her victim's left nipple, the splash of bright red that stained her battle-skirt greeted by a roar of approval.

Tintin and Augustus exchanged horrified looks. Only the Captain, that (authentic) descendant of the Barbary Coast, did not flinch.

Eh oui, he said. Such are the norms of symbolic mastery and the ritual of blood. The others nodded gravely. The act was obviously a crowd-pleaser. Grunts of approval, eye-rolling, feral yaps, and rumps began to swing, the women were particularly pleased with this female exhibition of power, the bare breasts of many women present began to shake with the drum-beat in the background, amber lip plugs and nose-pendants a-jangle. At one side of the arena a foursome of loincloth clad youth drummed on knee-high drums clasped between their knees. The tossing of rumps and the rolling of breasts spread, the excitement was palpable, intimately so. Men were quaffing the *balche* honey-mead liquor and women were munching on the little red fruit of the *uqa* tree, known for its inebriating properties; other men in small groups were exchanging the aphrodisiac *xulu queh çaqul* herbs with knowing winks, and more than one woman tilted her elegantly narrowed forehead archly glancing at Augustus and his friends, with a flirtatious shake of the breasts under transparent *huipils*.

Try to walk naturally, without hurrying, said the prudent Tintin. The noise of rattles and the plaintive cry of flutes burst upon the ear, and they sensed that the atmosphere was really heating up. Above, on the terraces, where the nobility had gathered along with those merchants and professionals with enough clout to join them, some individuals whirled in long rapturous loops.

There was a great deal more of this local color, what with instruments such as the *tunkul* war-drums and the long mournful wooden trumpets and the singing gourds, but when the crowd began to draw little round obsidian blades and razor-sharp spearheads and leather thongs out of their leather bags, and started to whirl about with the cutting instruments in outstretched hands, they decided it was time to leave. One becomes satiated with the bloodletting. They pushed and elbowed their way through the crowd with the Captain in the lead, the dancers and whirlers and flagellators oblivious of them, threading a path around the groups which bunched and swung hypnotically, until they came out of the dense mass to the edge of the crowd next to the pyramid, in fact practically at the foot of the enormous flight of steps which soared to the top of the building. They were relatively free of the bumping and bouncing of the crowd there because people were giving wide berth to the area at the bottom of the steps, so they stopped and gathered their breath and took stock of things for a moment. It was not dancing for the joy of rhythm and music as in the case of a Caribbean festival, it was dance of such intensity that the people appeared driven, the glassy look of their eyes and difficult staccato of the steps was impersonal, otherworldly, inexplicably frightening.

Tintin: I would not have believed it if I had not seen it. There must be thousands of people here. It's not credible that this is happening in New York on the lower East Side. Certainly nothing like this has ever happened in my *aventures* as they are popularly known.

No, said Augustus, it's a zonal divide. The border is blurred, that is what gives rise to confusion.

It is, said the Captain finally, turning his eyes away from the frantic crowd, the numinous that estranges; it is something that goes beyond language, and he stroked his porcupine beard and his brow furrowed as in deep thought.

Oh! Look, said Tintin, ever alert and observant. His index finger pointed up the towering stairs, and they all stared as a tiny white bundle teetered at the top, two minuscule reddish figures on either side of it, then the bundle appeared to tip over the edge very slowly, and an enormous vacuum seemed to form behind them in the plaza, and they realized the huge crowd had stopped moving and had fallen dead silent, but none of them turned to look at the crowd but instead watched the bundle as it toppled over the top, and then bounced again like a ball onto the next step some ten or fifteen flights below, and picked up force and sped

bounding down the steps with approaching force like an ava
lanche, so that it seemed that it was upon them almost as soon as
it had gone over the top edge. When the white ball leapt off the
last step and landed flatly almost at their feet, collapsing in on itself, it was revealed to be about the size of a good load of laundry
for a large machine, the white linens flecked unmistakably with
gore. What appeared to be part of a blue foot poked out of the top
of the bundle. Two men stepped out of the crowd, dressed in scarlet robes and each with a blue quetzal plume nodding at the back
of their heads. One of them carried a long flint knife, the other a
deep ceramic dish painted with figures. The man with the knife
reached down to the bloody laundry pile—. It had the wholly ordinary and routine character of nightmarish horror for Augustus.
He could not lift a finger. Who was it? he wondered.

O Mon Dieu! Non, non! cried Tintin and leapt forward and
with that notorious left hook laid low the sacrificial priest with his
flaying knife, and the latter now lay awkwardly on the ground, his
robe awry, an air of utter astonishment arching his bushy eyebrows. The other priest stared at Tintin, ear-flares a-tremble, and
bending low stretched out a cautious arm to help his comrade up.
Augustus realized that they were fascinated or appalled by his
friend's minimal features. Others, however, *Ahauob* who were
gathered on the various terraces of the Pyramid, were staring
down at the small group at the foot of the steps, and excited cries
and howls of rage could be heard drifting from those heights, and
some started down the steps in a flurry of robes and carrying
spears or knives which flashed in the sun. The four companions
cast hurried looks at one another, the Captain said,

Mille sabords! We'd best scram lads, and they took to their heels
in the dry hot dust of the plaza, curiously no one in the glassy-
eyed crowd lifting a hand to prevent them, on the contrary as the
four companions charged around the front of the Pyramid, people
gave way. Their attention was elsewhere, the entire plaza was in a
state of frantic celebration, acrobats performed, hunchbacks and
dwarfs slipped in and out of the throngs with ribald jokes to judge
from the hooting of the women, women were being fondled intimately by men wearing loin-cloths only as was embarrassingly
obvious, and necromancers performed their illusionist arts.. The
little group with Tintin in the lead disappeared around the corner
from the distracted gaze of the celebrants. They found themselves
once again in a wide plaza with another three- or four-tiered pyramidal construction on the other side, but this plaza was quite
empty with the exception of a single odd-looking individual, who

approached them now from the middle of the plaza, unusual for his height, well over five-foot six and any one over five feet was tall by Maya standards, smoking a long zoomorphic pipe and treading a slight fantastic gait—picking up his feet in large but dainty steps and weaving as if dazed. Augustus who had been shaken by the roll-the-victim-down-the-steps ritual sat on the ground with his back against the inclined *talud-tablero* base of the building, his head resting against the scaly back of a stone-hewn feathered serpent in deep relief in the wall, and scratched in the dusty plaza floor (for the entire plaza was actually paved in hard plaster). Captain Haddock stood with hands thrust in his pockets, a broad and ingratiating smile frozen on his lips, while Tintin stood a little to the fore as was his wont, both hands out, palms upward, in the universal attitude of peaceful greeting.

Yes, said the other as he weaved nearer, his immaculate white hip-cloth folded around his hips and up and between his legs and knotted together in a broad flourish of the cotton cloth at the hip, a jade necklace his only adornment with a little blue Quetzal feather at the bottom, yes, yes, and he took another puff on his pipe with a duck's head as the bowl, delighted to have you here at all, and he looked around amiably at all of us.

Tintin glanced back in astonishment, On behalf of my companions, he said, I thank you, Sir, for your gracious words.

Oh no, no, said the eccentric gentleman waving the long stem of his pipe at the little group, it is you who grace us with your presence here. The Captain in the meantime, emboldened by their visitor's ways, drew out his own pipe and snuffing deeply at it as he snapped a match over the bowl, blew out a great white cloud as in greeting to the other's curling tobacco smoke. Ah ha, ah ha! cried the visitor, obviously delighted and walked up to the Captain and grasped both his hands and shook them up and down vigorously. This is how you do it, is it not? I am Smoking-Rabbit. You are from the other side, are you not? Welcome, welcome.

Augustus had risen to his feet, and he walked forward, And you, Sir, are you—he was going to make some reference to the royal family, because the rank of their distinguished visitor seemed evident from his height, his delicate hands, his demeanor (even though his gentleness was decidedly un-Maya, the *Ahauob* without exception preferring to present themselves to the world with scowling brow and sneering lip) of absolute unselfconsciousness.

The *Ahau* said, I am merely *its'at*, a writer-artist, I do this, and he gestured with a flourish in the direction of the Pyramid.

Augustus understood it as an artistic gesture. He introduced himself and his companions.

I am Augustus Sykey from New York, these gentlemen are Tintin and *Capitaine* Haddock from Belgium, if you are familiar with the Hergé comic strip.. Out of the corner of his eye he could see Tintin wince. The Captain on the other hand puffed away imperturbably, a violet cloud lacing into the still hot air. What do you mean, the other side, said Augustus as casually as possible.

Um, said the other, on the other side of there, pointing.

Augustus pursued the thread of thought: When you intimate you have been expecting us—

The "visionary serpent" said the other, rendering the quotation marks himself, it is emblematic of our way of perceiving things or designing events. We might also say, on the other side of the "World Tree", the upside down side. He smiled self-deprecatingly. I mean that we have been observing you, ever since your accidental entry. We have problems with the exhaustion of our events. No time left, no words, almost. You "other-siders" take it all so literally.

Well, said Tintin, who had been taking it all most literally as was his wont, rolling a man trussed up in a ball down a thousand steps is not exactly "tripping the light fantastic"! Moral indignation was Tintin's forte. You will recognize, Smoking-Rabbit, that you Maya have an exquisitely developed sense of personal cruelty! Tintin was practically breathing fire.

Tintin, said the *its'at*, you are the Tintin, are you not? You see, I delineate this, it is what I do! An exquisite sense of pain—and ecstasy! That is at the heart—and I use the word advisedly—of our way, and it also exists on that other side in which you, moralist, participate—but on the margins of your society. When you exclude the divinity of cruelty, divination and vision, from the core of your relations, it flees to the margins—and so you have madness, cruelty, useless blood seeping from the extremities of your social body. We practice extreme cruelty on ourselves, our *Ahauob* shed their blood and the blood of their noblest captives in sacrifice—and we save the social body!

Ah *Monsieur*, said Tintin, I cannot concede nobility to a human ball!

Monsieur Tintin, echoed the *its'at*, perhaps that is because you are lacking a dimension in your world, interiority.

Augustus shook his head vigorously, Smoking-Rabbit, he said, when you said that what you do is to delineate this, I think—and I have tried to persuade Mr. Tintin of the same—that you and he inhabit worlds of similar high tension. This was a sudden intuition on Augustus' part. Captain Haddock looked at him aghast.

Moussaillon, he exclaimed, are you trying to suggest that..! In fact Augustus was quite convinced that he was also being changed in this regard. As if squeezed inward at the waist, his own personage was being flattened, so to speak, rendered filiform.

I think, said the latter, if we just hang on to this figure of the line, it will all become clear. I.e., forget about local color, descriptive filling in of detail, drawing in the round, it won't get you any farther. The entire little group was seized with creative adrenalin. And at the same time with lassitude. It was as if they were caught up in a cloud of cognition, an intense flutter of mental ions in swift exchange and filling the air. A little more, and they would produce an intellectual precipitation of consciousness regarding this delicate situation.

Instead the *its'at* broke the bond of "charm" which held them (like the bond of elementary particles), and said: Haven't you asked yourselves how you were able to escape to this tranquil space?

I don't know, said Augustus wryly, but I seem to have been attempting to escape for most of my life.

Why yes, the Captain suddenly erupted from a reverie, now that you mention it I have been asking myself just that question— where has that horde of *va-nu-pieds, chenapans, bachibouzouks* all gone to!? They were at our heels.

I would suggest to you, sir, said the *its'at* softly, that they are all where you left them—piled up at the corner you came around minutes ago—suspended in the midst of that "hot pursuit". For this is a place of reflective "suspension". Augustus craned his head backwards toward the corner of the Pyramid. In fact the corner was not vertical it may be remembered, and anyone who had advanced as far as the base of the corner would be partially visible above it. He tried to sketch a line in his mind's eye which would be the cut-off point, but wasn't sure. Tintin had been watching him with curiosity. Now he joined him.

Augustus, he said softly, let's go take a look. The latter assented with a nod of the head, and they walked a score of feet back to the corner. He almost shouted from the shock and Tintin's hand clamped onto his upper arm convulsively: at his shoulder level was a grimacing warrior's face, predatory hawk-nose set in the broad red face, brow receding sharply into the angle of the contracted narrow forehead, naked except for a heavy loin-cloth wrapped around his hips and groin and a skull bound to it, a necklace of black beads and shell-pendants, a turkey-tail spread of feathers sprouting at his posterior and a spear-thrower in his hand with a short spear set in it, but more shocking yet, piled up at behind him was a panoply of similarly war-painted faces, of gesticulating limbs, of shields of flayed face-skin, of bristling flinty spears, violet-robed shamans as well, all with raging open-mouthed faces—but not a movement perceptible, not the blink of an eye, not a whisper could be heard, as if they were all immobilized inside a monstrous aquarium squashed up against the glass wall. The two friends tiptoed backwards from the spectacle fearful of setting them into motion. They found Smoking-Rabbit and the Captain discussing a Northern Italian recipe for polenta and stewed duck and comparing it with a Maya recipe. After all, the *its'at* was saying, polenta came from us.

Excuse me for interrupting a no doubt lubricious exchange, said Augustus dryly, but is that—and he nodded over his shoulder toward the corner—what you meant by "suspension"?

You might call it, added Tintin, suspended animation.

The *its'at* looked at them, a humorous crook of an eyebrow—but that's exactly what it is, he murmured. I told you that's what I do. And this was a time for reflection.

Why reflection, asked Augustus, already guessing the answer.

Because you have entered the picture, said Smoking-Rabbit softly.

You mean, you mean, stuttered the Captain, looking thunderstruck, his eyes dwindling into the dots of the pupils and appearing to spread wider apart in his face, a vacant look in the slightly raised line of the brow, and the usually gruff voice reduced to a childish plaint, you mean, that means, that we are mere—Tintin was listening to the Captain and nodded grimly.

No, no, said the *its'at*, with a self-effacing wave of his hand with its long, delicate tapering fingers, it is certainly not my pen that—

Tintin spoke up forcefully now: Smoking-Rabbit, he said, the *Capitaine* Hadoque is a simple but honest mariner, and he has probably seen more of this world than you or I can ever hope to, however he is not given to metaphysics, and I would prefer not to discuss these matters in front of him.

I merely wished to clarify that whatever you—and for that matter anybody in the audience who might be listening in, the *its'at* rejoined, raising his voice—might conclude from the "cruel practice" of "step-ball", I must assume my own responsibilities. And as my profession as *its'at* implies, there is no distinction between the thread that extends from the eye to the hand and the thread that ties the hand to the brain, and so the responsibility is entire. For that matter I believe your case is no different, he addressed himself to Tintin as conscious reflection of one's own Penmanship, and Tintin acknowledged the courtesy with crooked brow.

Yes, yes, of course, he replied, but I am more concerned with investigating certain stories than with speculation.

But let me ask you a question, said Smoking-Rabbit, taking a long puff on his zoomorphic pipe, why are you here?

Why? said Tintin. Because we have noticed unusual movements as well, he said, and we wanted to give a hand to our friend. Besides, this sort of contamination risks seeping into our domain, and Moulinsart is already sufficiently polluted, what with the garbage dump near our forest[17]? But enough, he said, turning to the Captain, and patting Milou, who was sitting mournfully at his feet, having obtained precious little attention from anyone today, let us go. The Captain got up, hurrumphing apologetically to the *its'at*.

Tintin, appealed Augustus, must you go? You know that I hoped you might be able to play a transactional role.

Sorry, smiled Tintin, who appeared to be in a hurry, uncomfortable. It's the only way out just now and the threesome walked off, Milou trotting happily at their heels. Augustus was shocked at their abrupt departure, but tried not to show his disappointment. They walked off in a tight little group across the white-paved arena, in the opposite direction from the corner they had so recently arrived at. Soon they were a compact horizontal rectangle on the other size of the arena, tiny puffs of dust rose about them, and they began to dwindle still further to a black dot.

The *its'at* now snapped his fingers in the air. Enough, he said, enough! The time for reflection is done, and he waved toward the Pyramid with the same gesture as when he had first described to him what he did as *its'at*. And as if at a secret signal, with a savage roar as from a single throat, the horde of Maya which had been pursuing them before their encounter with Smoking-Rabbit poured from the corner in a torrent, shell-trumpets braying, tassels and feathers "making the air to dance" as the saying has it, shaking their flexible shields with the dried head masks affixed and flexing their spear-throwing arms with the spear-thrower. They ignored Augustus as he was with the scribe and dashed across the Great Plaza in hot pursuit of the little group of friends who had almost disappeared on the opposite side of the plaza down the beginning of another avenue and toward the distant

---

17   See *Les Bijoux de la Castafiore*, page 1.

corner of another step-pyramid in the direction of yet another step-pyramid which was partly outlined in the distance beyond in the characteristic honey-tones. He was unable to see beyond that one but was convinced that pyramids and plazas and avenues radiated outward beyond it wheeling one about the other as far as the eye could see. The horde raced on in any case, the hollow beat of *tunkul* drums urging them on and other realistic warlike noise-makers, and soon they also were nothing but a cloud of dust disappearing down the distant avenue.

Augustus, said Smoking-Rabbit, now that things are peaceful again, would you like to accompany me to the palace chambers? I have to see the crown prince about a jadeite image. And indeed while there were a few stragglers from the crowd lolling about the corner, a juggler tossing clubs in the air without an audience, any hint of a threat had disappeared.

I would be delighted, said the other, and the *its'at* arose, gathering his hip-cloth about him and patting down his loose black hair which floated about his shoulders, and with an elegant pull on his long duckbilled pipe blew smoke up into the air, and Augustus walked off with him shoulder to shoulder if not arm in arm. Half an hour later, hardly conscious of the path they had taken so entranced was he by his new friend's discourse on Tikal urban design, the deliberate dreamlike *mise en scène* of the city through which the people's minds were molded, the obsessive verticality of the steps going nowhere which brought Escher to mind, the wide dove-tailing of the planes of plazas and ball-courts and terraces below terraces below other terraces which alternated with a lush and implacable rhythm, he realized they had come to the foot of the wide shallow steps of the Great Palace. The horizontal blocks of the four-storied, colonnaded, rose-colored building with broad simple cutouts of windows and doorways recalled late Italian Renaissance or Mannerist buildings, their careless powerful sweep spoke of elegance and supreme assurance. And now close up, what at a distance had appeared to be a rippling texture of brick, revealed an astonishing play of inset and extruded blocks of stylized jaguar jaws and overhanging serpent tails and monster masks as of an immense and magical game both hugely diverting and inexpressibly menacing.

Yes, here we are, my dear chap, Smoking-Rabbit's voice broke into his reverie, just follow me up to his chambers, and they started up the broad flight of steps as wide as the building itself, the sky tilted over the roof in a radiant, furnace-fired, ceramic blue and the sweat poured down his back as they climbed to the top floor. The central entrance was flanked by squat muscular guards in feathered skirts and with animal headdresses as immobile as any of the statuary in the courtyard below. As soon as they passed through the doorway and into the dark chamber within the sweat turned cold on his skin, a cool condensation precipitated by the great stonewalls and ceilings. As his eyes became accustomed to this interior gloaming, he could make out wall-relief sculptures of the *Ahauob* inflicting unspeakable cruelties upon themselves and each other with impassive dignity.

By the way, Smoking-Rabbit, said Augustus, taking his companion, who had been waiting patiently by his side as he looked about the large room, by the elbow, I've been meaning to ask you—how did my mother come to be involved in these sacrificial rituals? Ever since that agonizing moment on the Moon Pyramid I've been asking myself this question.

I don't know, said the *its'at*, you're at the right place, though, why don't you ask the crown prince, since she's his mother too? He looked at the *its'at* aghast, his thoughts momentarily in an uproar, his familiar models upside down. His mother—the crown prince's!! In this Maya palace! *Lady Wac-Chanil-Ahau*, continued the Scribe, has her chambers in this complex, she likes to be quite close to the young crown prince, and some conjecture too close, his voice dropping discreetly. So saying, he steered Augustus out of this room, which he now recognized to be an entrance-chamber or lobby, and toward the next room. A low throb of voices was audible as they approached, and then a jagged but melodious music of sorts, what sounded like wind-instruments, and they came into a smaller room well-lit by a large sunny balcony window and full of people and noise. His attention was immediately caught by the corpulent and gaudy chocolate-brown figure on a raised dais in the center of the room. The gentleman—and it was clear that he was an *Ahau* by his bearing—large bare belly slung outward, slouched back against a huge white pillow, clothed only in a white hip-cloth embroidered with gold thread, and on both wrists wide bracelets of pearls sewn together in a fine yellow cotton, and on his head a globular headdress with goggle-eyes and behind it several braided colorful tassels flowing down his back, and finally a large pearl necklace about his neck. In his left hand he held a fan of white feathers, and his right hand was raised in an exquisite and difficult gesture, its remarkably long and tapered fingers with inch-long sharp nails pointing outwards. His mouth was curved up in a smile in the jowly chinless face almost to the white ear-flares, but his eyes were cruel and cold and the heavy hooked nose a raptor's. As soon as Augustus was able to detach his fascinated gaze from this portentous figure, he realized that the man was admiring himself in a green jadeite mirror being held up at his feet by a monkey; no, what he had for an instant taken for a monkey evidently was a very small, two-foot high simian dwarf in a red hat and red hip-cloth. The *Ahau* seemed to be saying something as was apparent from the row of glyphs proceeding from his mouth, but the music blaring from off-stage (two wooden horns and one conch-shell trumpet behind the palace wall, although the musicians could not be seen) drowned it out at least for Augustus and his companion. At that moment the warrior guarding the pillow-throne from behind caught sight of the latter two with a sharp fierce glare and down-turned sneering lips (which seemed to be the fashionable Maya look—almost everybody wore it), as if to challenge their entry or to harpoon them on the spot. But another plump gentleman sitting on the floor below the dais of the great Lord, more reddish than brown and wearing a saffron hip-cloth and wielding a large white-plumed fan also and a great white cap tipped back and large white ear-flares also saw them, and with an unusually pleasant expression bade them enter.

Ah Lord Smoking-Rabbit, he said, welcome, welcome!

The portentous brown Lord turned his massive head part way, the fat neck not allowing all the way, toward them. Yes, good my lord *its'at*, come on in, spoke the Lord with bonhomie, what, still scribble scribble, is that what "it's at"? The other *Ahauob* tittered dutifully, a lord holding a small bouquet of white flowers in front of the dais simpered, a servile and hunch-backed lord seated beside him, and a fat dwarf who was quaffing from a wide translucent bowl of some reddish liquid (probably the intoxicating *Uqa* fruit liqueur), the entire scene redolent of Aubrey Beardsley decadence.

Ah yes, said Smoking-Rabbit cheerfully, taking care of you chaps, I am!

The Great Lord did not laugh, and asked instead with a sudden unpleasant interest, And who is that charming young foreigner you have on your arm, you old rake? Augustus who was not all that young did not appreciate the qualifier, understanding it for the derisory put-down it was meant to be. Smoking-Rabbit took a puff from his pipe.

He is an ambassador from the other side, he said urbanely. I am taking him to the crown prince.

Ah yes, said the *Ahau*, caught out, well please, do not let me detain you Sirs, and, harrumph, he cleared his throat and shot an arch of spittle accurately into the bowl from which the plump dwarf was serving himself, causing a general outbreak of hilarity, which restored the *Ahau's* good humor, please good Sirs, do not allow me to detain you in the least, we would not want to keep the crown prince awaiting his pleasures, would we? Breathless laughter. With this the *its'at* and Augustus passed on through the door.

I thought at first he was the crown prince, said the latter softly to his companion and guide.

Oh no, answered the other, he is not even from here, a guest of the crown-prince's, a lord of Motul de San Jose.

What are those, asked Augustus nodding toward three goose-necked flagons, which stood in the doorway just outside the room where the Lord of San Jose de Motul held forth.

Oh those are enema bottles, said Smoking-Rabbit, they are quite popular among our upper classes, in fact the smaller enema bags make an acceptable gift to the ladies. I am sure the Lord de Motul makes good use of them. Augustus was left musing on the possible uses the Lord of Motul might make of his enema pots. They walked through dank, gloomy corridors lit only by an occasional lateral flare of light from a room, which gave onto one of those large cutout "Mannerist" windows.

He was rather rude to you, said Augustus, isn't the artist well considered on this side?

Oh yes, replied the other with a faint smile, Jose de Motul affects the fashionable Maya nastiness, it has afflicted our social relations ever since the Teotihuacanos exported it here, with their warring ways, it's all the rage. But the artist is venerated, in fact it's overdone, he added, after all where else would they get their material from (and Augustus understood "material" in the theatrical sense of "subject matter" or even "dialogue")? I mean this is what we do—and again that odd, encompassing flourish, pipe-in-hand, that Augustus conceived of as the artist's proprietary gesture. He had the impression they had gone through a labyrinth of corridors and empty rooms (or nearly—sometimes a small dark figure in a loin-cloth scurried by) with occasional reddish wall paintings, generally of some warlike scene. Well, here we are, said the *its'at*, finally stopping before a bead-curtained doorway, this is the crown prince's private chamber and a lower, respectful register in his voice was noticeable, a kind of + in his tone. In a loud ringing voice he called out some greeting, and a remote low response came back. The *its'at* turned to his charge with a pleased smile,

The crown prince has invited us to join him, he said. Augustus brushed through the curtain of green beads behind his guide, and found himself in a warm, luxuriously appointed room, a scatter of rugs and cushions, a polychrome painting of a sort of wyvern on the lintel under which they were passing, and at the opposite side of the room in the flickering light of a torch, a small not altogether distinct group of figures, which as they came into the room became entirely distinct: he was taken aback by an uncanny sense of familiarity with the quite beautiful young man who stood in sparse if elaborate dress (he later learned he was wearing the costume of *Hun Nal Ye* the maize god) between two entirely naked and high-breasted young women. One squatted behind him holding up his skirt (the crown-prince stood in profile opposite the entrance) and fondled his rear, while the other was rising in a half-kneeling position in front of the crown prince with her hands on his hips, having obviously completed an act of obeisance. It was the first time Augustus had seen Maya women without any clothes at all, and the sight humanized them—that is to say, brought them into the realm of instant familiar humanity—in a way no communication could have. The crown prince seemed oblivious of the women and politely solicitous of his two visitors.

Delighted to see you, Smoking-Rabbit *Ahau*, he said in a chime-clear voice. And is this our visitor from the other side, in the tone of an interested observation rather than a question.

Yes, Smoking-Squirrel *Kul Ahau* (Holy Lord). And with that the scribe and the crown prince both burst into giggles. Between giggles, the *its'at* gasped out in an aside, it's just the *drôlerie* of two little smoking animals greeting each other with such protocol, and they both burst into another fit of giggles. The crown prince removed his tall golden headdress and Augustus saw that he had to be much younger than he first appeared, an adolescent, tall and well built for his age, but one of the girls was a head taller than him; he couldn't be more fourteen[18]. With a startling burst of emotion he realized the prince was indeed familiar to him; his long-estranged and hostile younger brother! Instinctively he concealed his emotions, however.

So then, Smoking-Rabbit, said the latter, waving away the two girls and brushing his skirt back in place, what have you conjured up now? How did you come to bring this alien fellow here? He obviously had not recognized Augustus.

The *its'at* glanced at Augustus with some circumspection. He just came around the corner into my place of reflection, we conversed, his friends left and he stayed, and I realized that he was in

---

18   In fact Smoking-Squirrel Kul Ahau would have been almost fourteen at the time his mother stood on the hapless Kinichil-Cab at the dedication ritual on the top of the Pyramid.

it as well, and thought you ought to meet him.

Ah, said the crown prince looking at Augustus with curious intensity, I see. I don't know if you realize, my friend, that Smoking-Rabbit here is the author of our days. Scribe and descendant of the god Pauahtun, mage related to the kingdom of the dead, which determines our borders and is the condition of our kingdom of the living, he has been my teacher in the arts of divination, of manifesting the invisible world—he went on with histrionic brio.

Pshaw! interjected the *its'at*, not much of a teacher. Smoking-Squirrel here is a natural shaman like all his ascendancy, all he needs is a nod in the right direction. It is only a matter of weeks and his initiation will take him to *Kalomte*, accession. He was a natural from the age of eleven or twelve, all shamans have this precocious intuition as you know, Augustus, or perhaps premonition would be a better term. Augustus knew. He remembered.

Yes, said Augustus, seeking refuge in riddles, the ecstasy of a shared destiny high on a dark wooded lane.

Are you sure you didn't say anything to him up there? asked the Scribe.

No, no, said Augustus cannily, to whom?

That's all right, said Smoking-Rabbit, there is no one. Was there a hint of warning in his voice?

Augustus eyed the prince warily. No I suppose not.

Listen Augustus, said the boy-king, that is your real name isn't it?

Yes, it really is, he said, why? But he knew why. The other had also glimpsed some shadow of resemblance. But surely he didn't yet suspect?

Because a lot of people come here with pseudonyms, said the Scribe, it's part of the stock-in-trade isn't it?

I suppose so, said Augustus, realizing that any link between himself and the Prince would be inadmissible, threatening the dynastic heritage the latter lay claim to.

That is why we are shamans, said the Scribe, in order to see things that are not there. At least apparently not. What was he seeing, wondered Augustus.

Ecstasy, said Augustus again, is very ordinary living with a perception of things..

Yes, said the boy-king, I know where you mean there. We Maya cultivate the heart.

And the blood! said Augustus, thinking very private thoughts.

But don't you see, said the *Its'at*, very *Its'at* at that moment, don't you see that we preclude the secondary, the profits, the calculations, the small-mindedness, the guarantees, the hedging of your race?!

Exactly, said the crown prince, which is why we accept torture for ourselves—and for our enemies—who do the same for us: the blood. There is always a price, you know, Augustus.

Yes, I know, answered the latter. Since I was a boy I have repudiated such security. He no doubt was caught up in the visionary impetus of his friends, but why did he have such doubts regarding the prince's high-mindedness?

And, excuse me, added Smoking-Rabbit, what are you and your friends here for if not infiltration?

Psychic permeability, perhaps, suggested Augustus. I take your point though, he added. I hadn't thought of my own excursions in that way.

We never do, said the *it'sat* gently, just as we live in the shadow of our own death and we do not see it. Unless we practice its presence.

The boy-prince, who had sat down cross-legged on a sort of bench, shivered involuntarily. It is not easy to be Maya, he said. That is why, as Smoking-Rabbit and I have observed your comings and goings, we have suspected that there are disaggregate forces at work in our city—as in yours, no doubt. Fissures appear here and there. There is always reciprocity in these things. And do you think there are less sacrifices in Manhattan this year-end than in Naranjo, Palenque or Tikal? I assure you there are many many more. Only they are committed aimlessly, uselessly. You think these are entirely distinct acts, but they are both the fruit of our cities, do you see that? And while blood is illumined with consciousness here, much more is spilled on your side unconsciously.

Smoking-Rabbit looked approvingly at his initiate-king. When his day comes, he'll wow the crowds, he sighed. Parenthetically, it might be mentioned, it was difficult for Augustus to listen to the Kul Ahau without being distracted by the boy's unusual feminine beauty. And by this faintly menacing sense that their relationship was dangerous!

So why is this a threat, he asked, why are these infiltrations so troubling?

We feel, said Smoking Rabbit pulling on his duck-billed pipe, that it is your religious obtuseness, your lack of ritual sensibility that threatens our world. Augustus looked about the room with curiosity. It was sunken in like the marrow of the spine of the building, its faintly rounded cornerless walls contracting and swelling as if they were the walls of an organ, he could see them now, with huge pale glyphs which appeared to ruminate on those walls. As if the chamber were a hearing membrane worn thin between the two worlds, then the glyphs were simply the imprints on those fragile partitions of something spoken on the other side. The young crown prince's higher register of tone impinged on his hearing at that moment of his reflection,

And where did his companions, especially Tintin, who was rather acerbic and critical, go to, and why had he come? Both Smoking-Rabbit and Smoking-Squirrel were looking at him expectantly now, he realized, and he coughed in embarrassment.

Yes, added the Scribe, Tintin really has been quite aggressive, and one might wonder at his manner in light of the relative platitude of his life.

Why do you say platitude, objected Augustus for his friend.

Well yes, said the Scribe, the adventures, the pursuit of skullduggery, these boyish virtues, you know.

While what you say is true, said Augustus, and I can hardly cavil, I would say that his two-dimensionality is largely compensated by his absolute purity of intent. That is what his enemies, the predatory and the conspiratorial, most fear: his ruthless purity. You know that is the quality of the hero.

I would rather say, said the Scribe, that it is the quality of the shallow, of those who lack in complexity, depth and, yes, ambiguity.

Ah, said Augustus, the Pontius Pilate syndrome. Was he being overly defensive, he wondered? Both the others looked blank.

These are post-Columbian references, said the Scribe pointedly, and so should not be used. The boyish crown prince seemed to have lost the thread of the last few exchanges.

Well, what do you say to a game of *pok-a-tok* then, he inquired with boyish pep, your team against our team? You can get Tintin and the *Capitaine* Hadoque, and anyone else you fancy.

Yes, why not, said Augustus albeit with a slight frisson, knowing the Maya tastes.

Yes, said the Scribe with a faint smile, showing that he fully appreciated his guest's apprehension, well that could be down the road. Right now, though, King, *Kul Ahau*, I have a small present for you. Please accept this pectoral—and he extracted from somewhere in his hip cloth, a small six inch wide by three inch high blue-green jade plaque with a demon-mask cut in relief in the center and holes in the flanges through which passed a jade-beaded string. On the back, which would lie against the boy's chest, was a fluidly etched, full-length portrait of the boy-king himself

sitting on a bench in full headdress and pectoral and ear-flare regalia, with a couple of rows of glyphs opposite his profiled face
spoken by him.

Oh uncle, he cried in a fit of non-protocol feeling, I love it. He
jumped up and embraced the flushed and pleased Smoking-
Rabbit, and placed the loop of beads about his neck and adjusted
the pectoral against his hairless chest, then putting his golden
headdress back on and clipping on a discarded ear-flare, he sat on
the bench again in the same position as his portrait, i.e. profile
head and twisted upper frontal trunk and profile waist and folded
legs; a posture few apart from a shamanic crown prince or *its'at*
could manage. The young crown prince appeared limned in a
glaucous light, stiff and hieratic in his pose but simultaneously
with the sensuous nose and lips of a youth just out of puberty. He
had always had this tendency to adopt poses, mused Augustus,
and then caught himself up short. He hadn't, after all, seen his
younger brother since the age of four or five. He could hear a hum
from the other side which impinged upon the fragile ear-drum
walls of the room, and the jade-scene of the pectoral appeared to
be suspended in the gloaming: minute, perfect, wonderfully conscious and alive, yet petrified in this hardest of stone materials.
And striking against his own tympanic membrane with a tiny silvery ping was an insistent, minute voice, that had some relation to
the boy-king's high register, only this tone was higher still, almost
painfully musical, birdlike, the voice quite present and clear and
loud and voluble.

The Scribe said in a louder than normal voice, as if waking
them both from a deep dream, Lord! Lord Smoking-Squirrel! I
think it is your sister at the door!

The boy-king snapped out of his rigid near-cataleptic posture
into a more human all-frontal one, and called out, Oh yes, Lady
Butterfly, come in, we have a guest! Augustus looked toward the
entrance with curiosity, the beaded curtain shivered and through
it stepped a small slender figure, a girl—no, a young woman, in
fact tall for a Maya woman, just under five feet, uncannily like her
brother and yet the contrary. She was wearing braids which had
given him the impression of a girl at first, but full perfect breasts
visible under the *huipil* even to the delicate pink nipples made it
clear that she was definitely a young woman. Unlike most Maya
she had a small turn-up nose, but like the Maya black, one might
say blue-black hair, and her eyes were fathomless black *cenotes*[19].

19   Deep, natural, underground wells, greatly prized by the Maya
as entry ways into the Other World, and into which they cast much of their
treasure by way of offerings, as well as sacrificed virgins.

Her childlike appearance was quickly belied by her sharp and birdlike retort to her brother, obviously prefaced by some choice curse words (to judge by the shocked look on the Scribe's face), as to why he had kept her waiting at the door like a servant. Her brother had hopped off his throne with a grin and taking her by the arm steered her to Augustus. Shaking off her brother's grip with an impatient shrug, she gazed up into the former's eyes with a point-blank, nothing-can-deflect-me gaze, which took him in with one bite, digested him and spat him out again. Long in the jaw, with a doubtless involuntary, if very female, wolfish salacity. She turned away petulantly, but not before tossing out,

Don't let my brother convince you to play a football match with him. Don't lose your head—over such a lofty distinction! The young crown prince chuckled and Augustus stole a glance at her apple-firm buttocks as she walked back to the door, and ducked his eyes when he noticed the Scribe's frown. He recognized, astonished and fascinated, the intimate curves of the nude Butterfly Woman "float" that he had perceived above the pyramid in Manhattan.

Lord Smoking-Squirrel, said the Scribe to the crown prince, our guest would like to ask you about the Queen Mother.

Yes, said the crown prince pleasantly, what do you want to know? If she experiences pain when she pulls that thorny rope through her tongue? I've been asked that before. Oh yes!

Oh no, your lordship, blurted Augustus, of course not. No, I wanted to ask you—I wanted to ask you—and suddenly he realized it was very difficult to ask the crown prince about his mother when she purportedly was also his mother.[20] Your—your parents, the King and Queen, he said—

Actually she may be my mother but he's not my father, said Smoking-Squirrel, referring to the minor noble consort referred to in footnote 20—the Scribe coughed artificially, and the young

---

20   Actually there is no explicit statement in the records that Lady Wac Chanil Ahau, the great queen who inaugurated the glyphic steps in the gruesome manner we have seen above, *was* the mother of Smoking-Squirrel, one of the greatest kings in the long history of the Maya. This was *inferred* by Tatania Proskouriakoff, the great Maya scholar, upon observing the invariable appearance of the Lady Wac-Chanil Ahau on a stela paired with each stela that Smoking Squirrel erected of himself throughout his long career. On the other hand there is never any sign of his father, who had evidently been quietly disposed of. This suggested that his supposed father was of inferior rank—unless indeed Lord Smoking Squirrel

was the love-fruit of some alien union, so that in view of Lady-Wac Chanil's great distinction, the depiction of his mother alone served as the legitimization of his throne.

crown-prince waved impatiently at him, Oh come on, Rabbit, he said, it's just between us and these four walls. The Scribe nodded reluctantly. Proskouriakoff got it wrong, said the crown prince, *Lady Wac-Chanil Ahau* is a Grand Old Dragon Lady—and that makes her a minor god. Only *Itzamna* himself knows what her powers are capable of. I, on the other hand, am of a distinguished line of shamans and the son of—Smoking-Rabbit raised a warning finger—well never mind who, a powerful man, but in order to trace my lineage, to legitimize my accession to the throne after the Lady's hopefully not-too-distant demise, it will be necessary to derive descendancy exclusively from her. I'm sure she wouldn't mind, the old dear really dotes on me, she probably would be quite delighted. Nobody really knows much about her, she appeared out of the blue, a princess carried across the Petén marshes by warriors and priests from the Las Pilas Kingdom and who reconsecrated the glyphic steps and the kingdom—marrying an obscure member of the royal family, my alleged father, and after his untimely death becoming Queen-Mother. There was talk about a first son, the effete off-spring of that ineffectual gentleman, long since gone however, nothing that I need to worry about though, I was her favorite, and the long knives will be out as soon as she's gone as well of course

The candidate-king was altogether charming in his rapscallion account, and Augustus took none of it personally. While the Prince spoke, he had followed the little princess's exit and the swiveling of her thighs generously revealed by the so-short tunic, and the prehensile clenching and unclenching of his hands had continued in spite of himself. How would he ever be able to find her again? He wondered anxiously. But now he turned his mind to the business at hand.

Kul Ahau, he said in his best protocolese, I was deeply moved by *Lady Wac-Chanil Ahau's* performance this morning. I would be most grateful if it were possible to be received by her. I hope to speak to her about the tie between the voluntary self-infliction of pain and the visionary experience.

The boy-king answered with his characteristic spontaneity and lightheartedness. Why of course you may, my dear fellow, I'm sure she will be delighted to meet you. As he spoke the Scribe leaned over and whispered urgently into the crown prince's ear, and his face darkened. Don't forget about our ballgame, Augustus, he tossed out, go and get your team together on the other side. And may I suggest tomorrow afternoon. There was finality to his tone that smacked little of a sporting invitation. Augustus murmured mushily in apparent assent. What had the Princess Butterfly meant, he wondered, by "not losing his head over the distinction"? Was she trying to warn him? Had the prince recognized him after all, and was his ballgame "invitation" a way to resolve the difficulty?

Well off with you then, her chambers are just down the hall. The crown prince already seemed oblivious of them: he strapped on a jaguar mask and lay down on the short bench, his knees drawn up tightly. Augustus guessed why, because on their way out, one of the two girls, still stark naked, slipped past them, cup c breasts nodding, carrying an enema bladder in one hand.

Charming chap, murmured Augustus to his companion as they emerged in the gloomy corridor, not at all what I expected. I feel as if I'd known him all my life. A hint in time..he thought to himself.

Don't delude yourself, my dear colleague, answered the *its'at* wryly, if he feels his "dynasty" threatened, he can be quite ruthless.[21] If I were you, I would proceed with the utmost caution. So saying the Scribe touched long graceful fingers ever-so-lightly to his crotch, and Augustus understood instantly and without the shadow of a doubt that he had been castrated. He also understood that the *its'at* understood. He said nothing, dismayed, curious and embarrassed at once, but the *its'at* appeared entirely unperturbed. Down the long corridor, the scratch of dust and stone particles under his skin-sensitive Italian shoes, his fingers brushing the grain of the occasional stone warrior in relief. Finally the *its'at* broke the palpable silence, which had thickened about them following their visit to the crown prince's room,

We have arrived, he said. A double-headed serpent's floridly bearded skeletal jaws were painted on either side of the broad entrance so that upon entering one would have the impression of penetrating the maw of the dragon. Ma'am called out the *its'at* with a strong voice, it is I—and a visitor sent by the crown prince for your amusement. A sibilant whisper, or a hiss rather, came back in return, barely audible, and the *its'at* swept in with Augustus in his train. The room was unlike any other he had seen in the palace complex: vast, spilling over with the color the Maya

---

21   Smoking-Squirrel was said to be an "enthusiastic practitioner" along with his mother of the art of torture and blood sacrifice of his prisoners. He was known to have kept two of his high-ranking prisoners, Shield-Jaguar and Kinichil-Cab of Ucanal alive for many years so that he could exhibit them in public, draw their blood and inflict pain in various inventive ways. These and other prisoners were the result and reward of his military rampages through the Petén lowlands.

named *yax*, the lush, fleshy, profound green of tropical vegetation, palms and small all-spice trees, thick shrubbery, a *chicozapote* tree loaded with its oblong delicious fruit, creepers and vines clinging from trees and ceiling, thick ferns and grasses. Two of the large Mannerist windows Augustus had spied from outside the building shed a reddening late-afternoon light throughout the room; creamy white plaster walls enhanced the depth of color and the rubbery texture of the plants. Jaguar pelts were hung on the walls along with masks of jaguar and orange heron feathers, and more pelts and costly deep-purple and scarlet cloths were cast with casual grace about the various sofas, while small jade masks and obsidian figures lay on top of a low-lying furniture, which he and his guide were hard put to detect through the shrubbery—Milena's coffee table! And then the thin hard female voice came again,

Over here, Rabbit-Scribe, in the bedroom, and the Scribe who clearly knew his way around these quarters intimately, led Augustus to the dark entrance of the bedroom, and they both stood there a moment, letting their pupils adjust to the dusk. A tremulous outline of vertical and horizontal bars on the far side of the room gradually assumed the steadier state of a four poster bed, and now he could see a slight figure enveloped in bedclothes.

Come closer my darling, and the voice was an almost normal woman's voice.

Mummy! blurted Augustus in a pitch higher than his usual voice, shaking off the restraining hand of the Scribe, and taking two strides forward, he fell on his knees by the bed. The bed linen flew up in his face like a great white wing. He could see the shadowy figure had propped itself up on an elbow.

Now, *mon petit Auguste* (Augustus' mother sometimes expressed herself in French with a touch of snobbishness), what are you doing here? I was expecting your—the prince-heir that is!

Your what? he asked. Mother, said he, I lay under your feet this morning, one of your heels in my groin, I stared up into your noisome thighs, your incontrovertible sprouting bush. I want to know why I was in this position.

Why dearest, she answered coyly, you know you were always a prurient little chap! And the voice held an indulgent, mother's tone that he could not resist. He reached out a hand and saw her arm unfold toward him—

Ah, no! cried the Scribe, and the shock of the cry arrested Augustus' hand in mid-flight. A chill ran down the back of his scalp and down his spine to the back of his heels. Then he straightened said spine. He was not going to be frightened of a woman, he told himself!

Please, Mother. I just want to know why I was pictured in that position.

Because, came the hissed response, you insist on assuming your late father's long-suffering posture; your brother was never such a fool! He is a prince! Augustus saw that as a distinct possibility, he had often reproached himself for his supine manner. Why did he never oppose her? What did she mean about his brother? A flurry of emotions crossed between them. Listen, *mon petit Auguste*, just once, please tell me the truth. Like a *poignarde* this question slipped into a vital organ, a drop of blood scintillated on its point. Why did he never answer as she was begging him to, with the full charge of guilt, of sin, of betrayal that she believed of him? After all, she wasn't really his mother, was she? Wasn't the reason in this confusion of roles? Was he terrorized by the motherhood of her? Why didn't he answer: my dear (that was sufficient; no longer hiding behind the endearments that concealed the shallowness of their relationship)—I got bored with you. You harassed me incessantly, and I took my revenge, satisfying myself into the bargain. I cannot tell you how many other women I have caressed, how many women's mouths have fixed onto my penis, the numbers of women's thighs that I have luxuriated between! I am simply not interested in your sexual parts anymore. Instead:

But Milena, I do love you. I don't want other women (perhaps 'I don't want to want other women' would be true? But even that was no longer the case. He wouldn't trade his fleshly delights for her true love again. Ever.). I want only you. He heard that old fifties teen-age melody sung by The Platters mocking him, On-ly You-uuu! The ultimate lie.

You bastard, she said. I wish I had never set eyes on you. He broke into a cold sweat. It occurred to him that perhaps she heard everything he didn't say! I thought you were a poet. I thought once you were different from other men. That's where the shoe pinches, he thought. That she lose her illusions regarding himself. To disappoint the mother!

You cannot undo our whole life together, he pleaded, more to preserve her illusions, he told himself, than for his own sake. He passed over the word "unravel", too literary. He was beginning to stumble on words. Losing his composure, that always happened sooner or later. Becoming more stilted by the minute. He despised himself for it. She only became more unshakably sure of herself. And the more emotionally violent and outrageous these "conversations", the more eloquent she became. And anyway, he added, why here! What are you doing here?

Oh poor darling, she exclaimed petulantly, that you of all my children should ask me this! You, the alleged poet of the family! I am sure you understand metamorphosis.

Milena, darling, he mouthed, it was difficult for him to use that endearment, alright, let's be completely open and truthful then, and he bent over her, rediscovering a lost tenderness (was he being over-theatrical), resolved to—a predatory talon slashed across his face with homicidal savagery and he could feel the warm freshness of his own blood, a chill of the purest terror ran down the back of his scalp and into his spine.

You have murdered me, she rasped with an unnaturally hoarse voice, and with these words she reared up before him. He could not make out her features in the darkness, but her head appeared twice as big as he expected, too big for a human head. He jumped up in panic, stumbling backwards.

Th-thank you, he mumbled, I think I'd better leave now. He turned about and hurried for the lighted rectangle of the bedroom door, and her laughter rattled behind him. Then he felt the rush of feet, and ran as fast as he could for the door slamming it behind him. He heard her hands tear at the door, and raced down the corridor stumbling through the fronds and creepers and now she was after him again, naked, her large breasts shaking, laughing hysterically. His heart pounding uncontrollably, he fumbled with the front door and slammed it shut, and made for the elevator and pressed the button as hard as he could. Here, standing in the civilized, carpeted hallway he tried to reason with himself regarding the absurdity of the situation and his ridiculous fear, but he could feel his own face blanched and tight, and when the elevator door finally opened he dashed in, watching through the slowly closing doors as the apartment door opened, and saw Milena at the open door with the knife in her hand. He could not just hear but see her body slam against the just-closed doors as the elevator began its descent and he out of sight, eclipsed in her pure rage. There was a fleshliness, sexuality, in this manner of behavior as well, was his last thought.

Ajpu 11
(Day Four)

The lord of the sarbacan

And his first thought as he stepped out of the front doors of the apartment building into the street, nodding at the doorman while attempting to conceal the bleeding of his face was, Well that's settled--what a relief that things are out in the open now! And he actually felt quite happy about it all. And his second thought was, how on earth was he going to put together a *Pok-a-Tok* team? He decided to go and see his friend, Phil, at the store.

Obviously it's about language, said Phil after hearing Augustus' explanation.

Well, yes, said Augustus, metaphor and so on, but the ballgame, I would be lying to you if I said the ballgame could resolve itself in metapoesis. I strongly suspect the ballgame is dangerous, hence bears vital implications for all its players. I would only ask the friends I most highly esteem to play a part. Your tactic of feinting the obvious reference of, say, "football", and passing it on for a different play, should come in very handy in this psychic game. What do you say?

I'm game, said Phil jovially, and Augustus Sykey knew he could count on him.

Tomorrow, then. Listen, he added, there's another person in New York I know who has the wit for this game, and that's Walter Aleph, the novelist; do you know him?

I know him by reputation, said Phil, duplicity, psychological entrapment, he should be good. But will he agree? He's much in demand in high society. Yes, that's what bothered Augustus too, and he mulled over it on his way farther East to the Bowery where his distinguished friend lived. Walter Aleph was indeed the much-in-demand novelist of an influential social set, and he was not at all sure he would be able to lure him away, however briefly, from the seductive and delicately murderous society games, which afforded him such quiet amusement. The bait in which he put his hopes was Walter Aleph's well-known weakness for Mesoamerican artifacts, often of shadowy provenance. And indeed his friend took the bait. He understood the risks, but after all he reveled in dangerous games, or the personal relations which he converted into games. After his usual exquisite hospitality, the glass or two of wine, the inquiry into Augustus' troubled personal liaisons—indeed his sympathetic interest was at times so probing that it betrayed a mildly cannibalistic voracity for Augustus' persona, which the latter always felt duty-bound to deliver up—especially the incestuous relations which his friend particularly appreciated. Walter Aleph said, bending his large head like a kindly saurian, the good eye turned toward him, the blind, black-patched eye turned away—ah, yes, thought Augustus, it must have been him I saw on the way through Alphabetland—There are one or two loose threads from my last venture into the Mesoamerican lowlands which I wouldn't mind to pick up,[22]if only I could retrace that damned Codex! And my connections may be useful to you, after all one might as well be a survivor in the game. But I would keep a watchful eye, if I were you, on this "Butterfly Princess"; charming no doubt, but she exudes, from what you tell me, my dear Augustus, a seductive ambiguity which conceals some design, some—I don't know, threat. This was said with feather-light irony and with a wink that seemed to come from behind the piratical patch. Augustus looked up at his friend, startled, but aware of his friend's ambivalence regarding alluring women. However the friendly hand on his shoulder and the faint smile playing about the lips assured him that Walter Aleph was having a little joke at his expense.

I am drawn to her, Walter, I believe there is some psychic convergence between us, indeed, between many of the family. I can't quite understand it. It's as if it were all in the family! Quite incestuous when you think about it!

Ahh Augustus, Augustus, sighed Walter, quiet despair regarding his friend's tenacious illusions of love, resignation regarding his friend's incurable impulsiveness in the affairs of woman, I'll be happy to do whatever I can for you. Augustus embraced his esteemed (and quite famous) friend, and exited from this most cultivated apartment on the lower East Side.

Well, he thought, that makes three, with me. How many do you

22   *Eclipse Fever*, by Walter Abish. At the heart of the plot is an illegally smuggled Codex.

need for a *Pok-a-Tok* team anyway? Seven? And whom else could he count on? Tintin, I suppose, even though he is.. And then of course there was d'Hachis, Parisian luminary, exquisite friend, capable of the most delicate generosity with a friend and of the bloodiest mockery with a pretentious fool. Huge of girth and light-footed as a funambulist, he floated along the sidewalks and about the toniest cafes of Paris larger than life, a comic book character with his quirky pranks on anonymous passers-by and a savant with his warehouse memory and his ledger-like precision of phrase. These qualities would be of precious assistance in the shamanic head game. Augustus and d'Hachis had become the closest of friends years ago. For the former, d'Hachis had replaced the younger brother from whom his mother had separated him painfully many years ago, suspicious that he might have a bad influence on him (i.e. Augustus' wild pursuit of women). Their friendship was so intense, their communication so intimate, that Milena became hysterically jealous, accusing him of some homosexual attraction. She could never bear any of his close male friendships, as if she was afraid they might supplant her dominance of every aspect of his life.

Fortunately d'Hachis was on a traveling grant in the States from the French Ministry of Culture, and he should be in New York at this moment, no doubt staying at the apartment of his friend, the Ambassador of the Order of the Knights of Malta, on 12th street and Sixth[23]. Always generously available to Augustus in spite of the latter's sometimes obsessive insistence on staying in touch, nonetheless d'Hachis was difficult to pin down because with his esprit and his erudition, he was in great demand among the intelligentsia and cultural institutions: the man who knew everybody who was anybody, and many other intriguing bodies whom nobody at all knew. As a consequence he would frequently slip into what Augustus pictured as "blanks", unreachable by telephone, fax and email, doubtless absorbed by activities unimaginable to the latter, whether drugged bouts of erotic mania or State Dinners for the Cultural Elite in full regalia he could not tell. Finally one morning at 11:30 am he caught sight of d'Hachis sipping *une noisette and* munching a croissant at the French Coffee Shop opposite his apartment building, his powerful rhinoceros-like profile strangely married with a quasi-feminine beauty, bowed pensively over documents. After describing the recent events in

---

23   Unlikely, nevertheless quite true. Journalist and distinguished photographer, as well as Ambassaor, this Mr. Bekaert lived normally in Cambodia and so could let his friend use his apartment on his occasional research trips to Manhattan.

Manhattan, he invited his friend to participate:

d'Hachi, he said, I need the pellucid purity of your pen with which creative history and its actors are inscribed with such animation—if you take my meaning.

You are a friend after my own heart! I would be happy to contribute a text, said d' Hachis in his ineffably French accent which stood like a ghostly Notre Dame Church in the midst of the New York chatter, but you must be precise about the date and the hour because my engagements are such that I can only absent myself from Manhattan for a circumscribed period of time. Augustus said,

My dear chap! I know I can always count on you! There is an esoteric place where no tourists are allowed which I must show you —in the Municipal Building. Meet me there, and he continued in a whisper to explain just how and when they should meet, and they embraced and bid each other *aurevoir*. Augustus swung up onto the next bus while his friend waved good-by, his bulk easily distinguishable in the group of suspicious strangers that had suddenly gathered about him—for he noticed as the bus whisked him downtown their uniformly squat size and swarthy features. That was when he realized they were indeed engaged in the game of life and death. Manhattan is a city of great drifts of emotion, whether of the crowd along its streets, driven by a dollar-frenzy matched only by its panic of mortality, *vita* far too *brevis*, death and the dollar on the scales... or of the unceasing torrent of its imagery, digital and televisual, which is the specter of the crowd. He scoured the streets as the bus swept down to lower Manhattan but he didn't know where to begin next. He got out of the bus somewhere in the financial district, near Worth Street or Wall Street, and knew immediately he was in the heart of the financial district because of the shirts. All the young brokers and bankers wear the whitest, ritually immaculate shirts, the acolyte's vestment, of all New York. Not one wears a shirt, which is not *blendend mit licht* to cite Rilke's angelic description. What sacred event..? And at this moment a large group of these shirts was gazing up openmouthed towards a building on the other side of Broadway. Curious, he followed the direction of their gaze and saw, way up the forty-storey building, an ant-sized figure creeping across its vertical face, at this very moment edging its way around a corner with amazing chutzpa, and he could see why, because at a window some fifty feet behind the antlike figure a gross figure not at all antlike was furiously waving what even at that distance was clearly a revolver, unable to draw a bead on the fleeing ant which had vanished from its line of sight. Something about the ant's brown bicycle-pump trousers.. And then he realized who it must be— Tintin on his first visit to America[24] had become embroiled with the Al Capone gang and (no doubt modeling himself on some silent slap-stick film period-piece) at one point, in order to escape being "rubbed out" (the direst threat to a comic strip figure!) climbed out a window of a sky scraper (one of those Lower Manhattan buildings wearing a French Château as its crown) and edged around it in just such a manner. So Augustus had caught the original event and was terribly glad, because Tintin, it had occurred to him, would be just the ticket in his "football" game. Surely his metalinguistic peculiarity could provide them with a surprise element against their adversaries! In a few strides he reached the portals of the building in question. Glancing back for an instant before rushing in, he noticed the still rapt group of financial consultants with the red faces, burned by the first summer heat or by too many beers, hulking shoulders, thighs and calves bulging in their pants—as if the appetite for money was a high-protein, red-meat diet. He glanced about frantically but saw no sign of the gangsters; however putative and schematic they might be, they were always lethal! He made a beeline for the bank of elevators, but no sooner had he reached them than three of Capone's toughs slunk out and fanned across the lobby. He ducked behind an ornate plaster column, fully aware of the outdated style of the entire scene, but acutely preoccupied by the transcendent events concealed behind the *paravent* of this Saturday night b-movie cliché. It was not easy to disentangle a ready-made pop event from the intimate, spiritual occurrences at its edges. He watched for his friend's arrival, not sure what he could do. He heard a squeak-squeak, and glancing up saw the service door leading to the stairs was open a crack, and through it Tintin's beady eye with its look of resolute purpose. He cringed at the thought of what might be required of him—was there not something christic about the comic book character? In any case he did not hesitate an instant when his friend unexpectedly beckoned, crooking a finger. He backed up casually to the door, glanced about lazily to ascertain--and pressed against the crack which sucked him oops into the white stairwell, and Tintin's hand still clutching him by the collar of his jacket, one finger pressed against his linear lips and his button-nose, shh! he said, and, we'll be safe down the stairs, he added, they're not expecting us to go to the garage! Augustus felt slightly embarrassed at the predictability of the

24   Tintin en Amerique; actually this scene takes place in Chicago but poetic licence allows its transposition here to Manhattan.

situation although he could not be held accountable—could he? So of course he knew the sequence of the present action: clattering down the stairwell, the loud excited voices at the top of the stairs at the discovery of their giving-the-slip, the clangor of the metal door into the garage, then the getaway car—

Stop! Nothing of all this! Such was the Gallic exclamation (literally translated) shouted into his ears by an indignant Tintin who stood shaking him mentally. What's the matter with you, because you think I am a cartoon character, you can do anything with me! That I am gratuitous?

I certainly do not think you are anything of the sort, he said at last, apologetically, I understand the radical difference between the literary background you come from and the hopelessly labile milieu of the celluloid. And particularly, Tintin, I know how literate you yourself are, that is what distinguishes you from the rest. With that his friend appeared to be mollified, the wrinkled circumflexes above his pinpoint blue eyes smoothing out.

Ah, he said. Well. What you need to understand, Augustus is that a vast Maya substitution is taking place out there.

What do you mean, out there? Something about Manhattan? Tintin's eyes switched across his sharply, affirmatively. And the latter shivered inwardly. He had sensed some sacrificial aura, but not a subversion of the city. It had something to do with the left-over (or left-above) crowns of the buildings, like the tips of icebergs riding the flood. This is where the inversion of their world was taking place, the lacy palaces, the fretwork glyphic temples, the Châteaux de la Loire with Maya roof-combs towering among aspiring spires. It was the last place where New Yorkers would have expected subversion, always suspicious of their own underground, the subways, the *untermensch*, but here above it might be presided by *Itzamna*, supreme deity of the Maya and inventor of writing! He looked at Tintin dubiously. What could he really understand of writing—as such? And what did the writing have to do with the floating Palladian palaces, French châteaux and Gothic extravaganza of this upper city? Frankly he did not know, but he did remember the glyphic satiety of the Maya buildings, and this suggested a link. He knew who would have some inkling of this—the *Schriftmeister* (or "Master of Writing"), Carl—but would he be at their rendezvous? Tintin in turn gazed quizzically at his companion.

Have you ever thought, Augustus, he said, that you yourself might have stepped out of a comic strip? The latter burst into a brief laugh, but saw that his friend was quite serious and assumed a straight face.

Well, he said, you're certainly in a position to know. Why?

You're so insubstantial, said the other. And Augustus remembered the reproaches of Milena in her Sleeping Chamber.

Wasn't that really a matter of sex? he asked. You know, substantial contact? He shuddered as he remembered the "seduction" scene, but his shudder was directed less at the sexual than at its morbid overtones. For one thing, the Queen Mother is rather vulnerable, not at all the caricature she appeared in the Maya palace. Following that encounter, she had told friends and relatives, I thought he was going to try to rape me! It was terrifying! Actually the word she had used was "attack" but in view of the bedroom setting, of his posture actually sitting on her bed, and then the muffled quality of the dark curtained room, the dramatic inflation with which such darkness can affect the most anodyne of gestures—all of this converted the already hyperbolic "attack" into an attempted "rape". After all the atavistic relationship was there, was it not? And it did seem to him that while such instincts are buried most of the time beneath our humdrum intercourse, the sacred and the monstrous can surface at an unexpected moment. Nonetheless he was profoundly shocked by his "Mother's" insane distortion of the incident. Didn't it imply that beyond her bitterness and insistence on "the truth" was raw sexual need? What about her unhealthy symbiotic relationship with his younger brother? Wasn't there some suggestion of perverse excitement? Fathers and daughters have long been a common object of such suspicions—but between mother and son the relationship has always been deeply buried, subtle, inadmissible—for it is sacred. The son looks upon his mother's accidentally exposed flesh with a guilty mélange of disgust and identification. But the mother? For her it is so much easier, natural, simple! A revived, remodeled and ideal romance! Far removed from the coarse and brutal sexuality of the father. When Augustus finally resolved to secretly marry Milena, following two years of hysterical and bitter fights with his mother and father over the misalliance and leaving the family home, slamming the door behind him, he then wrote to his mother to announce the joyful event, and she answered by sending him a picture postcard of herself sitting on a rock in her bathing suit!

Such was the explanation he gave Tintin later on, as they sat in a bar that looked out on the twinkling lights of West New York on the other side of the Hudson and of the occasional bobbing vessel. Why this explanation? Because it was an attempt, however inadequate, to give his friend a sense of the atmosphere on his side. And of the risks. The *Pok-a-Tok* was not going to be a pic-a-nic!

As for the derring-do clambering about the building, said Tintin, and the Al Capone pursuit, well where else were you going to find me in New York City? And Tintin burst into hee hees over this heuristic stratagem. After all, sputtered Tintin in between hee hees, I don't exactly move in the same circles as Monsieur d'Hachis and I don't think he would welcome me as a compatriote if I did happen to move in one, and he was carried away in a gale of hee hee's and Augustus with him. On reflection, however, he could readily see d'Hachis, fine fleur of Parisian literati and eminent cultural historian, and Tintin, in consonance, the former because of the twinkling mischief behind his most erudite disquisitions, and the latter because of the Maigret-like thoroughness of his outlandish investigations. I.e. they were not so far apart as all that. Meanwhile Milou was giving those little impatient yips and nips at Tintin who cuffed him away a couple of times affectionately, and finally he got up dusting his pants and said,

Well thanks for the *chope* (Belgian for a beer), I'd best be off.

Wait a min, said Augustus pulling him by the edge of his unfashionably long (1940's!) tweedy jacket (Tintin affected this rustic garb, accustomed as he had become to the rural domain of the Chateau de Moulinsart of the Capitaine Haddock), I haven't told you about Lower Manhattan yet!

Quoi (what)? said Tintin, really *mon cher Auguste*, I don't have time just now for that sort of thing, but since they both knew that he really didn't have anything pressing to do in New York (other than the next gratuitous comic strip episode), he did sit down again and stare somewhat disconsolately at his empty glass (he had never known Tintin to drink; he had always been a clean-living, healthy young man with no known vices—*Le Capitaine* Haddock evidently had exercised a bad influence on him, in spite of his daily yoga!), upon which the buxom waitress quickly gave him a refill, then waddled off. Resisting the inclination to follow the jiggling retreat of her buttocks, he leaned forward confidentially and noticed that his long profile bisected the long wiggly blurred moon-reflections on the Hudson's waters that evening to his friend's intrigued gaze—at least he hoped so—and said:

Because this is where it all started in Manhattan historically—with our people! Tintin's shocked surprise was palpable, his cerulean blue eyes popped.

Don't you mean with the Indians? he inquired circumspectly, and Augustus just knew his incorrigible BD (comic strip) friend was thinking, in his naiveté, of the continuance of his own episode in Manhattan with the further trip to the Far West in which he would strap on a pair of wooly chaps and champion the down-trodden Indian.[25]He had no inkling you'd only find that sort of thing in the Village leather bars nowadays

No, no, Augustus shook his head vigorously, against the Indians and with our forbears.

Don't you mean the forbears of our Netherlander neighbors and the Dutch West Indies Trading Company?

On no, my dear friend, and with this Augustus quickly took a puff on his demitasse Dutch cigar, it wasn't the Dutch who came over, it was a group of 120 French-speaking Protestant Walloons who had sought refuge in tolerant Holland from their papist Belgian brethren. Then the Company sent them off to the Americas, and a group of them settled on Governor's Island, just south of this southern tip of Manahatta out of fear of the Indians, but a few months later when another two score of their fellow-Walloons joined them with assorted cattle they moved to the southern tip of Manhattan (or Manahatta as the Indians called it then) the better to feed and water the kine. That is why I have taken an apartment here in the southernmost residential building of the island, in order to amplify my receptivity on the same spot. Do you understand now why spiritual warfare, the Venus war as the Maya termed it, has been engaged with us? The bone they have to pick following their demise at the hands of the Conquis-tadores is with us here on *Manahatta*, the Pyramidopolis of the Empire of the Americas. You and I Walloons both, born and bred, comical figures retracing the steps of our forbears four centuries ago and accidentally stumbling on the deeper traces of a mysteri-ous race vanished eight centuries earlier.

Tintin tilted his soccer ball head skeptically at Augustus, the stiff cow-lick hardly wagging, and said, Come on now, we have known each other almost since the beginning, since my friend-ship with *le Capitaine*—isn't there some other interest for you on the other side, besides this threat to our entire civilization?

Soccer or not I think your head is secure enough, Augustus said jocularly, and replied that he had become very friendly with the *Ah dzib*, Smoking Rabbit, and expected their relationship to be fruitful.

No, no, said Tintin, wagging an admonishing finger, I mean someone else. Augustus blushed.

Yes, he answered after a moment's hesitation, the Butterfly Princess. I think I have found my life's companion. Tintin, who it seems had never had a girl friend, stared at his real-life and rather meaty companion with perplexity and not a little envy. I've only just met her, it's true, but some thrill, I don't quite understand. Listen, Tintin, please be discreet, he added. I have not mentioned this to anyone else. Now let me ask you a question—this question has been weighing on my mind since the beginning of our meeting. Can we interact, that is, with the harmonic constant of the Maya? I think you have a great advantage, you know, and that is your homology with their glyphs. Tintin looked long and slow at Augustus, not at all in sync with the usual rather staccato rhythm of Comic Books.

I can tell you this much, my dear Sykey—when we first met, do you remember? near Christopher Street with that meshing of pyramidal moving parts—that was the *Tzolkin*! The permutation of the thirteen numbers and the twenty symbols of the Maya calendar. When you had that hallucinatory vision of the Butterfly Princess. Yes: we function in a related universe. Comics, BD, cartoons—they have a compressed, hysterical, zoomorphic energy like the Maya and their glyphs. You can discern the wild glee in their blood.

Aaah, said Augustus. You mean the blood that courses through creation. The heart-sacrifice intended as a celebration. But that's odd, because the "related universe" you speak of always seemed to me peculiarly bloodless.

Well I assure you, Tintin said huffily, if you prick me I bleed the same red blood as any other man. Or woman, he added quickly. Tintin was politically correct. He had made mistakes in the past—ethnocentrist, racist, sexist—but he was definitely a reconstructed comic strip boy-hero, and trying hard. In any case he was so pure, so irreproachable with his good will and kindness that his lapses in the past could be explained more as a lack of taste rather than any ingrained malice. And if women are almost absent from his undertakings (with the notable exception of Mme. Castafiore[26], and her name is a clue), one cannot imagine Tintin going to a brothel!

Which reminds me, said Augustus, who had been looking for a pretext, I really must be going. I have a rendezvous. He was not referring to a brothel either, although unlike Tintin, with his runaway libido and weak moral character it was not unthinkable. But the truth is, he could not wait any longer to see the Butterfly Princess again. An entire imaginary bordello had been displaced by her lithe thighs! For the first time in his life, he really did not

26   "La Castafiore" or "The Chaste Flower" is a renowned opera singer from Milan. A close friend of Tintin's with a weakness for Captain Haddock, her voice has been known to shatter windows.

wish to go a'whoring! He bade his comic book friend farewell and they pledged to meet again soon for the *pok-a-tok* match, and he sauntered out of the tavern and into the evening heat in which the entire city appeared to be suspended in a state of semi-tropical stasis. He leaned out on the railing of the Battery Park promenade and stared down into the tremulous dark waters of the Hudson. The animal heat of the early summer evening rubbed up against his legs like a large feline familiar. He tried to imagine what it would be like to have her here one day, in his apartment over-looking the Hudson, her long black hair entwining him like the sinewy folds of the river. He had always been half in love with this river, remembering the long drives up its banks in his childhood when the family would drive up-state for the summer holidays: the delightful squabbling with his little brother and sister, the lazy hot air rushing through the open windows, his father's obses-sive machinal thrust forward and frequent, deliciously provoked shouts of temper at them, his mother's bored detachment from it all. The hot air blew through his fingers as he snatched at the leaves whipping by, then allowed his hand to glide and bounce on the billowing air like a plane wing. It was as if the River had spiraled around now from those years as he leaned over its flutter-ing waters and that small boy so close, almost within arm's reach. He decided to make off for the one site, which had suggested itself to his mind as a possible venue for the desired encounters: after all, if you couldn't find it at City Hall, where would you find it? Glancing back at the brightly lit windows of the Marina Clubhouse, he saw Tintin's sur-prisingly morose and wrinkled face (yes, the soft, hairless, almost girl-ish face of the boy journalist was wrinkled in the glare of the overhead lighting), an old and sad Tintin defeated by life, bowed over another glass of beer, and he feared the once abstemious paragon was bent on alcoholizing himself that very evening. Was he depressed by the absence of his fishy friend? The absence of Milou did not augur well either. Well, there was nothing he could do about this minute tragedy.

Imox –12
(Day Three)

Initiatic death

He turned resolutely back toward Broadway and headed north. Federal Plaza resurgent! Temples and palaces soaring upon the summits of the grim administrative buildings! He saw that he was at the heart, or better still at the belly, of Manhattan. At the north end of the great plaza hovered the spread-winged Municipal Building with a golden Walkyrie flaunting her Marilyn Monroe charms upon its summit: she held aloft a golden chalice in her right hand and in her left a round shield, her dress all billowing about the knees in neobaroque Hollywood 1950's kitsch. Hundreds of feet beneath her swirling robe arose no less than three colonnaded late Renaissance temples in Bramante's manner (a cupola with a dozen columns in full circle around the exterior), to whom however it would never have occurred to place three temples one above the other at stepped levels.. And as his eyes floated upward, these signs of an existence beyond the administrative ennui of Federal Plaza were further confirmed: four effete pre-Raphaelite caryatids spread their graceful limbs voluptuously upon the facade of the building opposite him at 15 Park Row on the South-East corner of the grand Plaza, and above them, remote, poked tumescent bulbous towers with copper-green monstrous phallic crowns. And just behind him, on Broadway that is, the fairytale-Gothic Woolworth Building soared upwards while it leaned rearward on tier upon tier of ornamental parapets and flying buttresses, and all around the Plaza at roof level fake gargoyles and triple-story Renaissance arches and tubular turrets and steeples were a-quiver and expectantly erectile in a state of a fibrillating excitation. But all this too is sacred! The Great Plaza of Tikal had popped into his mind with this observation, with its Temple I and its Temple II and the magnetic strip of its royal stelae. He distinctly felt the maternal eye watching him from some one of these unsuspected heights: withering, all comprehending, mocking. Little man, twist and turn in your labyrinth below, all paths lead back to Momma! His own head, of that he was quite convinced, was invaded by her consciousness. In any case he was disgusted with his redoubled, female-dominated subjectivity, he wished he could extirpate it like some tubercle. This humanoid insect below in the Grand Plaza with its poor web-like dreams, its glossy confabulations, did it really conceive that its mind reflected her universal Mind above? Now its spasmodic movements betray the illusion of thought as it heads across Broadway and then traverses the little park straight for the Municipal Building where it no doubt hopes to find some answer to its questions. Just as he crossed the threshold, he recovered his "illusion of self", and his first thought was that the critical lobotomy of consciousness does justify the gap between moment and moment. He glanced about anxiously and, yes, d'Hachis was arriving from the subway entrance as promised and saw Augustus with this look of anxiety, and thought to himself:

It is curious, the air absorbed of my friend, like Tintin, these accents circumflex over the eyes, they are the dead give-away! Augustus overheard his friend's excogitations, and guessed that this exchange of consciousness was an effect of the weak magnetic field set up about the Municipal Building by the Mayor.

d'Hachis, he called and waved to his friend, this way! d'Hachis pivoted like a bear in his tracks and with the extraordinary buoyancy of which he was capable, bounded in his friend's direction. There was a dividing barrier of rope channeling visitors toward the left side of the entrance, and he grabbed d'Hachis' elbow, we have an appointment upstairs with mumble mumble, he flummoxed the guard, and jubilant they popped through the right side into the busy hallway with administrative staff in a hurried hither and thither, and took the elevator that stopped six floors from the top. The dark brass ornamentation of the elevator doors, a fence of massive wrought brass with an open gate in the middle, a ponderous high-ceilinged construction; this was the "City Hall" of the twenties or thirties. Fraught with silence. Down a narrow hallway stacked high with dust-laden boxes of files, and after exploring long narrow corridors they found a corkscrew iron staircase. The staircase was exceedingly narrow and poorly lit and Augustus darted ahead of his friend whose bulk put him at a distinct disadvantage, and as he hurried on up he heard d'Hachis' labored breathing amidst the clangor of their feet, and an occasional window-slot spying onto a pediment suspended over the void, and it was as if the spiral were being pulled out and up as a child draws out a rolled ribbon of paper, the spirals tightening and the lighting dimmer floor after floor. Finally, out of breath, he arrived at the top floor: an unlit room, dark, the sensation of dust and obstacles scattered throughout—and an obscure sense of having been here years before. The womb, he thought. Is one never quit of the mother? The W, an inwardness, lips opening, a portal; then the hollowness of the OM, the resonance of the OM, its visceral vibrnation; and finally the soft closure of the B, its elastic tissue, its tenderness. It explained what he had intuited at first, the moist spongy walls, the organic non-geometric architecture: birth; also death, implicit in birth. When he had first visited Carl, his Brother in Life-and-Death had spoken to him of his mother's recent death:

Ah, *achi,* my brother, the first days of my return to this room after my Mother's death were painful. My eyes turned again and again to her coat in the closet, to her hat. A silver hair shone there, in the light. It seemed to me to be signaling from the other side. Your thoughts on time and identity move me. I often think of these central questions—they surround us, they bring us nearer to the puzzle within the puzzle from which enormous light streams: Death. *ki 'asah kamaweth ahabah;* for as powerful as death is love. That means the *Jodh* presses into the center, the heart. Does it not pulsate, does it not constantly produce new mutations, between, in, out, with, *ani* and *ajain*? Carl, who held the threads of death and existence and love in his hands as if they were fine threads of writing, had surely comprehended his own death in that moment. He had spoken to him then—from this moment. For this was without doubt Carl's room! The shadowy obstacles were coming clear—books: piles and stacks of books, little passage ways and barriers of books, sometimes waist-high from the floor up, sometimes perched in equilibrium on a table or on chairs and sofas, a labyrinth of books, but one in which the itinerary was perfectly sensible leading through this main room around to a threadbare sofa-chair with lamp and to a kitchen sink and range littered with coffee cups and more books, to the little bathroom (books balancing on the tub edge), and upon this architecture of books lay other books, open like windows and doors, foci of meaning, with their own intellectual itinerary. And altogether this house of books exuded through the shadow a luminosity, as if Carl had built, unfolded, opened up corridors of mental light, illuminating vistas in the small, pokey, closed-in room that an unseeing eye could not discern! Only moments had elapsed since Augustus had crossed the threshold, and he became aware of labored breathing and the magnetic warmth of a large presence at his back:

Books, hissed d'Hachis, what are books doing up here! His friend was a lover of books, not just of reading but of the body of a book, its beauty, its sex, its fine skin, its shape: for d'Hachis, bibliophile and lover of the written word, a book was a woman. In any case there was as much surprised delight as dismay in his tone.

d'Hachis, he hissed back, this is Carl's place, the architecture of his mind. It is the womb, which has nourished him, and he has returned to it.

Ecstasy! boomed a voice humorously from the shadowy recesses of the room, it was a voice that Augustus would recognize anywhere, for Carl's voice seemed to come directly from the belly and not out the mouth, even in this one word "ecstasy" the first syllable dropped to a guttural which vibrated like a Tibetan chant and his voice communicated directly with the fiber of one's own being, awakening emotion and a tonic to the brain. Yes, it is ecstasy, the voice continued growing louder, which is engendered by the vibrating fields of vowels, new emotional areas are stimulated by these layers of speech. Cries, emotions, are hugely amplified, and the psychic-physical economy is changed, healing forces are activated, subliminal contacts are established and phenomena and processes are produced which lead into the enormous realm of the Not-Yet-Conscious.[27] With these words which were chewed and growled in their conceptual working-out, and then abruptly pressed through explosively in a resonant "boom" of pellucid clarity, the small, wire-thin frame of Carl emerged somewhat lamely, lopsidedly. For his spiritual brother was, he knew, extremely ill, even to death, and yet he moved as if emanating from the freshest spring of energy. My brother, Augustus, and the words flooded forward in a warm current, and even before his eyes and wispy hair were fully visible the huge smile that gathered up and wrinkled his whole face radiated out through the darkness. d'Hachis' large hand clasped Augustus's shoulder from behind, his delicate nature able to perceive the passage of wordless communication beyond life. Now Carl was standing before them, skinny frame draped in the oversized sweater he always wore, and it was no longer his smile but the dark water of his eyes, a watery depth of warmth and understanding, fluid line of unreserved communication, the radiance of his eyes so intense and inquiring that they

27   The "not-yet-conscious" is a category from the work of Ernst Bloch, the great Marxist philosopher and correspondent of Carlfriedrich Claus.

appeared to float in the air. His actual physical appearance was that of a small, thin, large-eared, Negroid-lipped man, and the flashes of emotional intelligence that crackled in his eyes were of such intensity that they enveloped his objective appearance with an aura. He reached out and enveloped his dearest friend with both arms, who hugged him and patted him on the back as if to reassure him, and he felt the scratchy over-night growth of Carl's beard against his cheek and the large fragile forehead by his temple. Carl's almost simian features and large ears were eclipsed by the great dark eyes which overflowed with the warm intelligence in which his whole being was absorbed and then projected out to the other before him, and then his voice which vibrated with a resonance and volume which seemed impossible for the small wiry frame. This, he thought, gives meaning to the soft concept of an astral body, and he hugged his friend

Carl, my friend, he sighed, how long it has been.

Carl's gaze hugged Augustus' psyche, my dear brother! You know we are always in a bodiless communication; our minds and our hearts have kept an ethereal contact!

Augustus could not explain to himself why a sob broke from the core of his body. Yes, Carl, he answered, concentrating on the other's gaze and voice, even if you were not here in body I know this current could not be broken. He thought "gaze and voice", because these appeared to subsist in time independently of the body, a vibration of pure intellectual energy. They continue to vibrate to this day.

Carl took Augustus' hands in his, and their energy pulsated through him and swept away any anxiety. Soo, my friend, said Carl with the "s" like a z and the drawn-out Black Forest "zoo" a hum vibrating in the chest, what is it that has troubled you?

Carl, he said, the passing of the body in time, the vanishing of friends, of lovers.

Ah, my dear Augustus, we possess nothing. And love and friendship, if we lose the illusion of those bodies we dream we possess, whether others', or ours are energies, which never vanish, they are transmuted and continue to move through our lives and others. Then Augustus described to his friend the vision or the passionate intuition he had had of the Butterfly Princess, and his search for her, which took him now into the dense and surprisingly proximate jungles of the Petén.

Be careful, his friend warned, these are forces that you do not understand. And as he described his obsession with woman, this particular woman that is, Carl asked him whether eros for him was not the attempt to hold onto the body, to stop its slippage in time, and he said yes, that the savor of the body-spirit, the deep touch and odor of the other's body appeared to him the rarest embodiment of time; the roundedness and curves of the female form appeared unsurpassable to him. And Carl said to him, you cannot hold onto anything. Be aware, little brother! Beware! And as he gazed now on his old and beloved friend, he saw something he had never recognized before in his actual physical appearance: in the almost simian (Socratic?) features he discerned the identity of *Pauahtun*, the howler monkey, Maya god of the artist-scribe, *ah-dzib*. Carl, he exclaimed, are you related to Pauahtun! Because if so you alone can enable us to confront Smoking-Rabbit in our ballgame!

Carl chuckled in a bass rumble, do howler-monkeys have such oversized ears? Augustus burst into laughter as well, and d'Hachis, who had been as if spell-bound, spoke out:

Ah, *cher Monsieur*, my dear friend Auguste (he used the French version) has spoken so often of you that I feel I know you intimately! But how on earth did you come to have your underground place here in this altitude with your so numerous and wonderful books, and as he spoke, he had picked up one of the books from a mound at hand, and hmm'd with pursed lips, examining the book with the concentration of a connoisseur, brushed off a fluff of imaginary dust with the back of his hand, and replaced the book in the same position, adjusting it by a centimeter with a little tap of the pinky one way, then tapping it back less than half a centimeter the other way. For I use the term 'underground' not only for the nature of your drawings (and d'Hachis of course was a world authority on the "underground of art/writing"), but above all because I have known through Auguste of this legendary room where you lived with your mother for thirty years in the basement of an ancient movie theatre in Annaberg-Bucholz! Where I understand the shamanic rapport with the underground!

Come with me, said Carl, clapping one hand on the shoulder of the much taller and greater of girth d'Hachis and the other on Augustus', I will show you something. And he led them quickly to a door on the other side of the room, which Augustus had attributed to a closet, and opened it wide, and a large puff of wind entered the room. Be careful, he said, as they stepped out and found themselves just within the Bramante-like colonnade of the uppermost *tempio*. Lower Manhattan dropped away forty floors from under their feet, beneath the narrow ledge that circled the temple and allowed one to squeeze behind the columns. The side they had come out by looked over the East River and Brooklyn Bridge. Remembering her tossing skirts, d'Hachis and Augustus glanced up and only a few feet from their heads was the Golden Girl of the Municipal Building, flaunting her knees at the City. There is a portal here, said Carl in a soft tone, a quadrifoil portal of the Maya. That is why you find my room at this altitude, Monsieur d'Hachis. Their portals provide four possible doors out or in. You have to decide which. It is not that my old apartment under the cinema in Annaberg has changed or can change, Mr. d'Hachis. It is *irdisch*, earthly. It is just that the Maya have chosen it as an entrance from the Otherworld, or for me for that matter: it is known as the "Black Transformer". The intense consciousness of our death gives us a different sense of our life: between existence and non-existence. And to live in this certainty of our own death gives pause. More intense consciousness. Distance from oneself. *Distanz*, he said reverting to his native German, to dance away from the self. Augustus and d'Hachis looked at Carl wondering. They became aware of an abyss—not the one at their feet but between themselves and him. And speaking of their feet now, Augustus recognized in Carl's feet the *ak'ot* glyph, that is, the raised heel of Carl's left foot, the sign for the dance of death. Then his eyes rose to his friend's face in a slow arc of motion, accompanied incongruously by a windy flapping noise like swoosh, and he saw his friend's face then, it had a look of such intensity that it appeared to radiate outwards, the furry brows, the wispy electrical strands of hair, the hollow-cheeked, beard-shadowed, oblong jaws, which appeared to be rounded now, bursting outward in some divine animal-savage mask.

It must be his *way*, hissed Augustus (pronouncing it "why") to d'Hachis who was staring with lifted eyebrows at Carl, then at Augustus, then back at Carl.

Why a way? Said the art historian, recalling the Marx brothers' famous exchange, "Why a duck?"

The Mayan spirit-animal or double of the shaman who goes into trance! answered Augustus, and d'Hachis broke into a delighted smile—

Ah oui! mais oui! Now the left heel of his monster-friend arched higher and his foot floated into the air, and for a moment Carl was poised in this position, a huge raptor bird, stark carved nose and jaw inclined downward toward the streets and beyond, to the river, below. His lips were moving and he, always so attentive and welcoming to friends, seemed to be oblivious of them. Without placing the left foot on the floor of the narrow terrace again, he raised the right foot up several inches above the floor. Augustus made these observations very coolly and accurately, and afterwards he compared notes with d'Hachis who had also been observing, because the sight of Carl stepping up into the air was at once the most baffling and the most incontrovertible event he had ever witnessed. And now from Carl's articulating lips issued a glyph, obviously of Maya provenance but unrecognizable to Augustus. What alarmed him profoundly, what blew hot and cold now, was Carl's move toward the abyss, which lay at their feet. For he was at the very edge of the narrow walkway that ran around the *tempio*, and as he had somehow stepped up into the air, and Augustus, while he framed this thought, did not know what it meant because any normal physical explanation—for example that Carl might have leapt goat-like to the top of the balustrade—could not apply. Carl was there at the height of the balustrade but not on it, just hovering at this side of it, the toe of his right foot angled down delicately in the air and heel touching the ankle of the left foot and this foot with the heel slightly raised and one arm stretched out, left hand tilted up finely at the wrist, the ring finger and index finger bent inwards, the little finger and the thumb straight out. And as they stared in fascination hearts pounding it became clear that this was a stately slow-motion dance, and now in the next moment Carl stepped over the stone balcony with a high delicate dancing step and out into the empty air over hundreds of feet of sheer drop and their hearts jumped up into their throats, and Augustus, gagging, reached out weakly but his spirit-brother was gone, out of reach, not down the way natural bodies go but outward across the abyss. He knew this was impossible and looked around at d'Hachis for confirmation, but the latter was no help with the same look of utter bafflement. And now Carl, obscured in the night air, half-turned back to them and extended a beckoning hand and vanished into the darkness. Augustus started as if to jump forward to the balustrade, not of course over it like his friend, but by a sort of synesthesia was propelled forward, but d'Hachis caught him by the left shoulder and arrested him in mid-motion, and he pivoted on the hand-shoulder axis slowly into the large and shocked face of his friend.

Non, said d'Hachis, you can not go out there. But Augustus had no intention of going over the edge—he was terrified of heights! He was not at all sure of what Carl had done--he just knew he hadn't fallen to the street below. Not that one could really distinguish a fallen body down there from the others! But there had been no commotion in the air, no flailing about of hands, no fall in a word, a very characteristic event, an archetypal event one might say.

But d'Hachis, he said at last, where did he go? *Mon cher* Augustus, said the other, this is not possible. Your friend Carl must have disappeared behind a column. But there was no column within five feet of where Carl had gone over. He leaned over the parapet, both hands wrapped about the inside edge, and leaned out still farther to see if anyone might be holding on to the back of one of the columns. Pro forma. Of course not. Nothing out of the ordinary down there in the street, no break in the automobile rhythm of shifting headlights, no crowd, no ambulance siren. They turned as one man and walked back into the book-laden interior, the library landscape. Dreamlike he watched his friend pick up a book from a dusty pile and stare at it closely, then turn it around, and open it. D'Hachis, *fin bec* and *literatus exquisitus*, always appeared to taste when he read, and now his plump, sensuous lips moved as though he were savoring each word like an oyster, and then he set the book down slowly still open (which was unlike him) staring into space, and said:

But of course—why not! And he walked straight back to the exit onto the exterior circular walkway with a deliberate step, not looking at Augustus. A quick glance at the open page was enough for the latter to recognize a verse from *Le Bateau Ivre*, of course, he thought, and he hurried out after d'Hachis. The latter was already on top of the balustrade and a tough little wind was blowing and it was not all that stable on the terrace-walk. The rumble of the city echoed below and d'Hachis rocked crazily on the balcony, still anchored by his great bulk. Augustus' heart was stopped up inside his throat again, he felt a blank panic for his friend, and he stepped up without thinking, his right foot not quite able to reach up to the balustrade, and he pulled himself up next to his friend in the rushing air. Remaining very cautiously in a broadly braced position, feet spread and flat down, he did not feel too insecure. Then glancing forward he saw the near vertical drop forty floors down to the street just beyond the left foot, and his heart leapt into his throat. He glanced back to verify the support of his right foot, and saw that it was not resting on the balustrade but just in advance of it—in fact it rested on nothing at all! In a state of some anxiety, he dragged this foot forward toward the top of the balustrade, because he could not lift his forward left foot, which was solidly planted without losing his balance. This rear foot slid along quite agreeably until the toe of his shoe met the stone surface of the balustrade, at which point it grated over the rough surface with such resistance that he had to draw it along with little jerks of his leg. Finally it rested on the firm stone ledge and he grunted with relief. Now with his two feet solidly ensconced, he glanced forward with satisfaction—and saw to his consternation that his forward left foot also rested upon a void forty floors deep, and quite comfortably so. He dared not budge it lest he go crashing down. Throughout all this minute foot-maneuvering he had not looked once upon his companion, but now in his mental disarray he did, and was not merely astonished but dumbfounded upon noticing that his friend's very large forward foot, a foot of clownish enormity, rested well beyond the edge of the balustrade and thus also upon the abyss. d'Hachis looked down on him with that comical-malicious gleam in his eye, locks buffeted by the dark night air, but clearly not at all disturbed by their vital predicament:

Eh oui, he said, *mon cher* Auguste! We are at last upon the abyss. Augustus felt his rear leg shaking in little spasms, but replied in a steady voice to his friend:

Yes. It appears as if this is the way Carl went. And raising one arm with, not quite nonchalance, wrist crooked and fingers bent in that difficult gesture of the Maya, he raised his rear right foot high, and forward of his left foot, toe pointing downward into the abysm, and silence appeared to fall upon the night air. d'Hachis also raised an arm and drew his rear foot up and around, head cocked with an air of exhilaration, planting it also upon—the ghastly transparent air some four hundred feet above the midnight street, and looking back they saw the Quadrifoil doorway waver behind them, and close, like a reflection in the water which reconstitutes itself after a stone drops through: the Black Transformer as the doorway was known by the Maya, had allowed them through and on their way.

Iq' 13
(Day Two)

The breath of life

It was as if a new level of consciousness had been attained. Not just by Augustus and d'Hachis, although that was certainly the case, but for the enterprise as a whole: a transparency of these arcane figures and events. Once they had stepped off the edge of the Municipal Building, the sheer terror was over. Crossing the bridge over the abyss was intoxicating and exactly the opposite of walking a tight-rope—rather than having to seek out, blindly and dangerously, the lay of the land, wherever they set each dance-step they found support. And each succeeding step imposed itself as ritual. How could one walk with a casual and relaxed step? But neither with a fearful, testing step, feeling out a mortally danger-ous path! These could only result in death, since this walk was not simply dangerous, it was folly, swift and crushing death. It was dif-ficult because the foot is not accustomed to being used as a senso-ry organ—like the hand. It was like walking on water except that the eddies and currents had set and rigidified. After all, wasn't the abyss across which the Maya *ahauob* danced also the watery sur-face of the Underworld? He glanced at d'Hachis who danced in the same slow motion at his elbow with an *insouciance* and exhila-ration that made his great bulk expressive of pure buoyancy. The underside of death renders such ebullience possible. They had been walking for ten minutes or more, it was extremely dark, the moon having been swallowed by thick clouds, and the implau-sibility of it all had dulled their power or will for observation. His feet scraped a different sort of surface, granular, unpatterned. He stopped abruptly and looked down, and d'Hachis almost bumped into him from behind. They were standing on the same ledge—the balustrade—they had departed from, but they faced inward now. His first wild thought was, had they ever really left it?

His friend was maneuvering behind him to get a foothold.

You're thinking it has been a joint hallucination, murmured the latter now beside him.

Perhaps, said Augustus, from the shock of Carl's stepping off—or seeming to.

Yes, said the historian of the avant-garde, the room itself, the books, all a sort of dream. I don't see anything here though that looks like a room. They both peered into the impasto darkness, and Augustus, suddenly getting cold feet at the realization of the abyss behind them, hopped down. D'Hachis plumped down beside him. Augustus extended a hand into the darkness in order to reach the *tempio* wall. However no wall met his hand, and the lack of resistance caused him to reel and nearly to stumble as one falls through a door which one is about to push but which is already wide open. So he continued to advance cautiously into the darkness, d'Hachi's heavy breathing blowing down his neck. After they had walked on about ten paces, evidently on a smooth surface, the light came on. Or more exactly the moon slid out from behind the clouds and bathed in its beams was a peculiar object: a cylinder stood in the center of a small platform, a sphere posed on top of the cylinder and on top of the sphere a disc. The platform itself (or small altar) was about three feet high and measured four by four, and was built in the Teotihuacano *talud-tablero* style he had encountered when he first visited the Petén lowlands with the merchant-warriors of Teotihuacan, i.e. inclined walls surmounted by framed panels. On closer inspection the cylinder bore an inscription in glyphs, indecipherable to Augustus and d'Hachis, but one glyph was strikingly eloquent: the profile of an old lord or god, a trifurcated blade circled above one eye and a four-petalled flower clasped the side of the head.

This, said d'Hachis somewhat portentously, looking about now in the brilliant moonlight, is a ball court marker! And they were indeed at the entrance of a vast quadrangular courtyard flanked on the longer sides by broad inclined bleachers of stone, with stucco carvings of yawning-jawed serpents in relief, and down at the further end some sort of edifice or wall with a device set in it, perhaps a ring or a hoop. The floor of the arena itself was covered with hard plaster. Behind them was the low balcony they had just jumped off. Beyond, there loomed in the distance grand pyramidal constructions, which vaguely recalled the summits of one or two of the skyscrapers of Federal Plaza they had observed earlier, but without any of the twinkling lights of the latter.

My goodness, d'Hachis, said Augustus, I believe we are in late-classical Yucatan. About 750 AD. The ball court, the serpent carvings, appear to be in mint condition. And in the year 2002, this ball court marker was, or perhaps is, not here.

Why is it, said d'Hachis sarcastically, you bring to mind a metaphysical Stanley and Ollie? Every time I accept to accompany you in one of your madcap ventures, we end up in an absurd predicament. I have a great deal of research to do for my next book on the underworld—I mean the underground. It is funded by a major institute. I ask myself, what do I now, here! He tossed a stray lock off his forehead irritably. Augustus gazed at his friend quizzically. Clearly Gallic skepticism was in sore discomfort.

We went through the *Öl* portal, the Quadrifoil door. Whether it is a form of mental transference (he said this more to appease his friend than because he entertained the slightest doubt) or a psychophysical rendering, I don't know, but surely it is a fascinating opportunity!

The distinction, said his friend pedantically, is not between forms of transference. It is a question of work on language. It is a question of forms of language.

Augustus gazed at his friend thoughtfully. How very Gallic he was. He would resolve this impossibility through a *lacanism*! No, he said, the figure of the glyph on the cylinder. I know what it is. The trifurcated blade above the eye is the ritual blade used in decapitation. The four-petaled flower is the flower of the blood of sacrifice. It is the prize of the ballgame. That is what the prince offered me. And it is what Princess Butterfly was hinting at with her quips on 'headiness', or 'losing one's head'. A slight breeze swept across the playing field with a dry whispering.

Chut! d'Hachis put a finger before his lips. *Ecoute. Ecoute!* They both held their breath. The whispering appeared to carry across the ball court by some special acoustic property of the stadium. Clouds veiled the moon, and as they scraped along the low edge of the bleachers in the intimacy, which the darkness drew up about them again, the grating screech of a macaw froze them in their steps. The whispering was now quite loud. They stopped in their tracks when they caught sight of the grotesque shape—eight to nine feet tall, it faced away from the ball court and toward an engraved column about five feet high. The monster had the profile of a giant jaguar with a rounded snout and tight ears sitting up on its hind quarters, until they realized there was another profile about a foot beneath the jaguar's—larger than human, with a big, hooked, Roman nose and bulging eyes and a magnificent headdress of plumes of many colors glittering dully in the moonlight, and then just below that profile, still another one became appar-

ent, human and handsome, a very young man to judge by the delicate features carved in the heavy-set mold typical of the Maya. All
these profiles fit together, and they realized that a huge plaster
mask was suspended by means of some hidden device of ropes
and poles set in an outsized backrack strapped to the young man.
The young man's chest and shoulders were covered with jewels of
jade beads and his legs were bare and slung over the throne,
which was the pelt of a jaguar. It was not he who whispered because his head was bent forward attentively toward someone just
out of their angle of sight. The whispering by some echo-effect resounded silvery, cricket-wise, down across the playing court as
they had first heard it. The whisperer remained hidden by the
bulk of the Jaguar-backrack. But the moon shone sharply and
hanging behind these figures cast crisp shadows. Etched in obsidian was a head like that of a large monkey with tufted ears, one
hand stretched out with a brush pen. Clearly it was *ah dzib*, "he of
the writing", and the shadow hand moved now with small em-
phatic nods from the head and the whispering in a stream
soothed.

Come on, said d'Hachis, let's get closer. They moved beyond
the protective shadow of the bleacher-end sculptures and out-
flanked the backrack so now they could see—the "monkey" was
their wise, wiry friend Carl! Somehow transmuted.. Dumbstruck,
they gazed. Squatting close before the backrack, legs folded together in that angular manner of thin and wiry people, hair
springing tuftily from his ears and the great tufted brows, his hair
smoking filmy above his head, the large ears sticking out, indeed
for a moment even outside the shadow, a wise and gentle monkey's eyes radiant with intelligence! Only the domed forehead
swelling up like a light bulb contradicted this *way* self. And they
could see his right hand move with the brush pen in the air before
the eyes of the young crown prince, Smoking Squirrel, for it was
clearly him. His hand moved with irresistible fluency, appearing
to move of its own volition, as if animated by an intelligence all its
own. And his left hand holding another pen moved in synchrony
with the right, sometimes in resistance to it, sometimes in accord,
as if the hands were dancing together in the air, except that
"dance" has too mellifluous a connotation in the ordinary accep-
tance, they were more like combatants in oriental ritual combat
with contrary tensions, sometimes a striking gesture of great ve-
locity, sometimes a fluttering away like a blown leaf, then a spiraling inward of concentrated attention, and it was clear to them
both that the hands were executing a script, a writing of hiero-

glyphs, and these were almost legible through the "mental-phos-phorescent" trail left by the fingers, as when rapid movements are photographed with a slow shutter. And the whisper they had heard before came from his broad lips but was not really a whis-per, rather a staccato flow of gutturals, glottal stops, hisses, wheez-ing, gasps, and now it became clear that this flow of infra-lan-guage was in direct correspondence with whatever he was writing. As he gave voice to the writing with a "boom"—a kind of sono-rous value that appeared to issue from the depth of his belly—his eyes had such intensity that they popped, unblinking, black as ink. Ordinary logic could not pin down what it was they were hearing or seeing, and they began instead to experience physio-psychic movements of contraction, expansion, resistance, progression, conflict, confluence as a form of mimesis, and so became aware now of communication so intense that it penetrated to their in-nermost being, to the impulses before the expression of emotion, and they strove to respond in some bursting utterance, in hissed whispers. It was incantatory, the rhythm of speech before speech, in the throat, in the nerves of tongue and eyeball, throughout the body as if the whole body were an organ of sensation and communication. Yes, this was the shamanic voice. And then it was over. Carl had ceased to "speak/write". He drew back or inward, head cocked, the dark radiance of his eyes welcoming, waiting for the other's response. There was none. Instead, the monstrous jag-uar masque nodded and pawed the air, and the crown prince was off, trotting into the dusk. Augustus and d'Hachis rushed up to their friend who was still squatting on the dusty floor gazing after the backrack with a perplexed air.

Carl, said d'Hachis, what happened, why did this gentleman leave with such impromptu?

Carl stroked his chin pursing his lips with that reflective ges-ture Augustus well knew.

The Maya, you know, on the eve of some great event, do not sleep, but they wait sitting straight up, their hearts and their or-gans gripped by the hope of the red dawning. So I found Smoking-Rabbit when I arrived here before you. We had a good meeting, and talked of the Maya world-tree and the ripples and whorls of the bark of the *Ceiba* tree which are ciphers of coiled energy; and of the pyramids and the landscape in which spiritual energies have been accumulated by ritual—such as your pending ball game. But as I began to speak of psychic travel through the *Öl* portal and the passageway of the Maya to New York, his face darkened with anger and he gave the signal to leave. He did not wait for the dawn. But if he is to be a *ch'ul ahau*, "lord of the life-force", the dawn must rise in his own heart.

Come on, Carl, said Augustus, perhaps we should be getting back. By now the sun was blood-orange red and the pyramids and plazas and palaces behind them awash in its glaze, and even at that distance some of the stucco masks and monsters, such as the *Witz* mountain-monster which adorned a small temple on the top of a raised pyramidal platform, its blood-red maw draped about the front portals were visible. Perhaps, broke in d'Hachis on their meditation, if we made our way to that temple we could get back to Manhattan?

Ye-es, said Augustus tentatively, it does resemble the subway entrance we entered before. Perhaps it is a port of transition. Nothing was as they knew it should be, but somehow they had to deal with what was in front of their eyes.

Eh bien, let us go over on, then, d'Hachis said a little impatiently, it is dawn and perhaps we can get a croissant and a coffee on the way!

Augustus looked at his friend doubtfully. This was not the *quatorzieme*! Admirable, admirable is it not, all in the delicious interlocking play of planes, how they sway in this shimmering ocean of jungle? Carl nodded in agreement, the feathery hairs swimming on the top of his bald forehead. Well, come on then, grunted Augustus, and the threesome pushed off in a beeline for the pyramidal platform. As they trudged along the narrow but well-paved road, even in the dew of the very early dawn, the *yax* of the jungle green had begun to radiate the hot-house tremor that hinted at the enormous energies residing beneath the endless canopy of the Petén lowlands. That breath of humid warmth in the coolness of dawn reminded Augustus of the scent and fullness of a woman's body next to his on awakening. And with that he caught a mental glimpse, longingly, of the little princess's departing back and of the white flash of her calves, and a trace of the smoky perfume of her black hair, and heard her mocking laugh. He mourned at his loss. Carl's deep gaze took it all in, and he said,

I think this shamanic relationship you have is beautiful, my brother; but remember it is no possession. Augustus nodded, touched by his friend's insight. In effect he had not ceased to think of her since that first meeting.

But why, Carl? said Augustus as they trudged on, why a ballgame? Why on earth do you think he proposed a ballgame? And what relevance can it all have for us? What do the 'Maya' have to do with us?

The human psyche, Augustus. The unlocking of psychic energy.

Yes, *Maître*, said d'Hachis. But what of the ball court? Why should we have to do that! It was evident that he was no sports enthusiast.

It's the game of life and death. Having said this, Carl walked ahead of the others, head raised as he concentrated on the small temple on the top of the pyramidal platform looming above them.

I think, said d'Hachis, it's a matter of time.

Yes, said Augustus. The ball court engages time, clearly. But why do the Maya want to engage us? Huge deep-red masks of *Vucub Caquix*, the malevolent bird-deity with its outsized cartoon beak, flanked the broad steps they clambered. Carl flew along the steps with his light and wiry frame.

Malevolence, replied Carl, masks the fear of freedom. Bird-free! Augustus sat on one of the broad steps, still a hundred feet below the temple. The step was wide enough to lie back on. D'Hachis plumped down beside him, his brow bathed in sweat.

He is right, he said. People are afraid to be free. Augustus's hand brushed the dusty step. Perspiration beaded his brow. It can't be more than five or six. They both turned their faces up toward the temple. Carl was already disappearing inside the great maw of the *Witz* mountain-spirit. It must be cool in there, he said. He touched his humid forehead. *Itz*, he said.

It's what? asked d'Hachis.

No, *Itz*, said Augustus. It's what this is. Sweat, tears, blood, se-men. Cycle of life. Isn't it?" The sky had gathered above them into a deep blue half-sphere. The wild cry of the Macaw crashed about them.

Oh *oui*, one day it will anyway, said d'Hachis. And as if becom-ing aware of things now, they both pulled themselves to their feet, and started to crunch back up the steps. Within a couple of mi-nutes they stood in front of the cool shadowy interior of the tem-ple's maw. Time become permeable. What else had Carl said to him? That the bird-figure, the 'head' of the bird appeared out of the eye. The point of departure was in the word *chajjim*, a Hebrew word for the living, the living Shamans of the past. These lived still in the unconscious regions of the mind as Carl in his. They gazed now into the liquid depths of the Temple. In this moment Augustus tasted the sweetness of death. It swam so fleetingly by. He knew it was his brother, Carl: calling him back in time. If they had lived by this code of invisible communication—the radiations of the brain and the heart, regardless of absence, even prolonged absence, even non-communication by the conventional means of letter, fax and telephone—why could it not be sustained in death as well? d'Hachis stepped into the cool inviting shadow of the temple, and Augustus hesitated outside, raising his eyes to the *Witz*-monster face: deep red on the facade of the entrance; furious brows, heavy eyelids, bulging eye orbs, serpent tendrils, the gaping maw and within it, the doorway. But it was the life of the hieroglyphs, which grabbed his attention: an opulent imagery under immense pressure of condensation and formalization. The glyphs appeared as if they would burst their serial frames with explosive scriptural vitality, so that communication might after all be possible with an otherwise unknowable civilization vanished inexplicably more than a thousand years ago. Or was that civilization simply another name for an inner search, which he had not yet put a name to? A few feet farther at the end of this hallway, he came to another   doorway on the right. What, he feared, might await him in this room? In the doorway hung a bead curtain, and in the heavy lintel above the door was sculpted another visionary double-headed serpent with jaws, which yawed about the jamb of the door and painted in a long curved elegant red stroke: the portal of the Underworld. He stirred the beads with some apprehension before stepping through. It was a small gloomy room lit by a narrow side-window: he started when he noticed the two shadowy shapes, one slighter but taller, as if in a supplicant position, the other half-reclining, grossly voluptuous in a dominant posture, huddled by a low table in a murmured conversation with their backs to him. They did not turn, although it seemed to him that the slighter, taller figure nodded imperceptibly, but was that for him? At second look he noticed that what had seemed to be a "coffee table" was really a miniature mock-up of a Maya altar, over which the couple were bowed, and indeed the entire room appeared to be the replica of the *pib na*, home of spirits and ancestors, a sort of fictive plane as he saw it—where "real things happened".

The slighter figure was speaking in a querulous whine: You keep summoning me to these consultations. Your infatuation— sticks to me like amniotic fluid, like a shroud. The other figure, squat, gravitational, unmoving, said:

It's just that I want more of you, more, to suck you inside me, and instead you hold back, you are so dear to me. The sweet hissed tone of the serpentine.

Mother, we haven't innovated on this malady since we started, well, since my puberty! My sharpest and fondest memories..

Darling, she said, to me you'll always be that little boy. You have never really grown up, you know that. After all, I began sucking your pipi when you were still a child!

Please, I am a man now, I have assumed my responsibilities as teacher of the people, a shaman! The fatal weakness of tone of the respondent gave the lie to what he said, and to the irresistible mothering seduction exercised upon him by the other.

A slight cough from the corner of the room to the right of the doorway he had just come in told Augustus that d'Hachis had followed him in and was enclosed parenthetically in the shadows in spite of his embonpoint. Augustus cleared his throat. However if he appeared uncomfortable with the turn of events, d'Hachis was red-faced with shame, fright—d'Hachis, Parisian luminary and sophisticate, was evidently in deep distress. Later he explained to Augustus that his own deeply painful relations with his mother prevented any dispassionate appreciation of the scene. Not for nothing, his patronymic! Neither of the royal pair however paid the slightest attention to them. It was if they did not exist.

Motherhood, she continued, it's not all it's cracked up to be. The two-backed humping beast—and then nine months later the little bastard pops out from between your legs. And it's not even grateful. I gave up everything for you! You have taken my blood, my femaleness..

Smoking Squirrel—for it was he, his younger brother!—removed his cloak and stood revealed in a net-like tunic and pectoral of jade mirrors—a youth of troubling, androgynous beauty. His mother—mention has already been made of her spawning capabilities—leaned forward and placed a clawed hand on his thigh. And she tweaked Smoking-Squirrel's cheek affectionately with the other. She slipped the hood off her own head, and the arrogant hooked nose and the heavy fleshy profile with the faint moustache pivoted left and right in a jerky predatory fashion. The cloak slipped off her shoulders and she was more than visible in her *huipil* which revealed the massive, dark-nippled breasts and the several folds of her belly. The candidate-king stood up brusquely, directly facing the squatting queen, as if he had come to some resolution.

Give me your tongue, he said with quiet hatred. She complied with alacrity, opened her blubber lips and extended a long dark tongue as far as it would go, holding a white napkin below her mouth. Just managing to straddle the huge larded thighs with his bare legs, he grasped the tip of her tongue firmly between thumb and forefinger of his left hand, and raising his right hand above his bent concentrated head with "fish-in-hand" as the glyph phrases it—the razor-sharp tail-bone of the stingray—he sliced down in a trice and pierced the center of the drooling organ. Blood spurted down into the napkin, and he expertly threaded a thin rope knotted with thorns through the hole, and she took the end of it and pulled it slowly through. Now the prince slipped off the net-tunic, remaining only in a brief white underskirt, and pulled out a disproportionately (for his boyish age) long penis. As *Lady Wak-Chanil Ahau* watched with more than maternal possessiveness he pinched the foreskin and drawing it out, slashed down quickly and efficiently, this time with a small obsidian jade knife, through the taut, cupped skin: once, twice, thrice. The blood splashed his white skirt and her *huipil* and he now threaded three little paper napkins, one through each perforation, which quickly turned red. He no longer needed to hold it up to maintain its erect position.. They rose unsteadily and walked hand-in-hand out of the room, twin trails of blood following them, as if exhausted by a profoundly perverse, erotic act. To Augustus (and d'Hachis) who had been bound to every gesture, it was all strangely familiar now, only seen from the different perspective of the adored bastard son. He felt a peculiar sympathy for the youth.

Quel couple classique, murmured the stunned d'Hachis! A murmur sounded distantly, a growing rumor, and they both darted to the window and looked out. What had been a deserted plaza half an hour ago was dotted with hundreds of people, and more could be seen streaming from all the directions, which the limited outlook afforded them. A bass rumble rolled across the plaza, the *tunkul* drums calling the population.

Oh god, murmured Augustus ruefully, I'm not going through that again!

But where shall we go? lamented d'Hachis, but look there! And they both looked at a long crack just behind the *pib na* set-up, and d'Hachis fell to his knees and pawed at the crack and the "altar" pushed aside and they could see that it was a narrow opening in the floor, which had been covered up. They slid the mock-up all the way off and a rectangular opening was revealed with high steps leading downward. After you, *mon cher*, said d'Hachis, with a mocking smile which did not conceal his shaky apprehension. Augustus reached a tentative foot down into the dark pit backwards and it met a narrow stone step, then the next foot. The steps were steep and he felt stirrings of panic when his head dropped below the level of d'Hachis' feet and the opening of the stairwell, and he was engulfed in darkness. There were no railings to hold onto, just the close cylindrical stone and rubble walls of the tunnel

itself which provided some support for both outstretched hands as
he descended the corkscrew staircase backwards and took careful
steps, worried that it might have collapsed at some point below
him. Above he heard only the shuffling descent of d'Hachis who,
with his huge size twenty-something shoes, must be having a hard
time finding toe-room on the steps. They continued on down in
this manner without exchanging a word: just the shuffling of toes
and the crumbling of stone dust underfoot and their breathing
heavier, spasmodic with suppressed panic. When a shaft of light
spilled across the steps in front of him, he shouted to d'Hachis to
stop. A small barred window was set in the wall and sunlight
gushed in. d'Hachis crouched just above him, peering down
through the window. The angle wasn't good, but they could make
out the crowds below still milling in the streets and the occasional
blare of horns.

Well, murmured the historian to Augustus, his face now visible
a couple of feet from the latter as he gazed out the window, we
should be able to just mingle with the crowd. And after a few
more minutes they came to a landing with a little door, which
opened onto the long narrow corridor stacked with boxes of files.
They realized they were back in the Municipal Building on the
36th floor and the elevator bank. They took the brass-gated 1930's
elevator back down and were out of the building, bleary-eyed and
exhausted, as the maintenance people came filing in. They had
been "away" for twelve hours. What this meant was not yet clear,
but, as Augustus remarked to d'Hachis, once the portal to the
Otherworld has been opened, the membrane between "their"
space and "ours" evidently grows thinner with each new use.
When they issued out onto the busy street and its blaring traffic,
d'Hachis wondered aloud if this might be the Underworld the
Maya dreamed when awake.

Do you mean, Augustus said, that Carl has a role here like the
Ah Dzib?

It has occurred to me, smirked d'Hachis, and left the subject
there for the time being and Augustus considerably intrigued. A
monster traffic jam stretched up the avenue ahead of them. Spat
curses and throat-wrenching screams of rage and drivers leaning
hard on their horns and choruses of supporting honkers grew into
a crescendo of fury and frustration on the threshold of the painfully ecstatic. D'Hachis and Augustus walked along at a tranquil
pace gazing at the gesticulating and frenzied mob. When the two
finally reached the head of the traffic jam, it became clear: a very
long canoe, perhaps twenty-five feet long, with several bizarre

passengers, glided slowly at the forefront of the procession of automobiles. The drivers of the front row or two of automobiles were not so much physically unable to bypass the slim canoe as they were mentally indisposed, staring pop-eyed, hands gripping their steering wheels. The canoe did not appear to be on wheels, or if so these would have to be cunningly hidden, because it rode directly on the surface of the street, even swaying slightly from side to side and prow and stern dipping now and then with the powerful strokes of the two Paddlers. He could even swear that he heard the churn and splash of water as the canoe moved forward. More than the sight of a canoe floating up Broadway, it was the spectacle of the paddlers and passengers, which dumbfounded the onlookers. These personages could not have been more bizarre in their brilliantly colored costumes and masks. From the elaborate headdress of the paddler in the rear—closest to Augustus and d'Hachis—floated brilliant blue and green feathers. His hoary head jutted forward along with his entire thorax, and both hands gripped a large paddle, the flat blade of which was half-buried in the surface of the asphalt. Most striking was the stingray spine, which protruded through the septum of his Roman nose. With a gasp d'Hachis grasped Augustus's shoulder and pointed at the personage sitting bent slightly forward at the center of the vessel. One hand was folded about the molded edge of the side of the canoe, the other hand raised slightly: wearing the highest and most elaborate headdress, with what appeared to be a Manikin Scepter standing straight up on his head and two or three horizontal ornaments, a small stingray, a jade stiletto, sticking through his thick luxuriant pony-tail, was the transfigured adolescent, the would-be King, Smoking-Squirrel, in the guise of the Maize God, whom they had left an hour or so ago on top of the Municipal Building—or of the Temple of Inscriptions, depending on whether you were coming or going. All the other bizarre figures in the canoe were imitating the crown prince's gestures in the state of hyperactivity of cartoon animation. Seated directly behind the crown-prince was a large monkey, left paw raised in the air seemingly waving at the gaping drivers, right paw grasping the side of the canoe. Behind the monkey was a figure in a spiny-fish or crocodile costume with long jaws raised and agape, also mimicking the gestures of the crown prince. And in front of the crown prince was a giant parrot-figure with magnificent head feathers of yellow and green and a large malevolent eye, which swiveled balefully backwards and toward them as only a parrot's can, and ahead of it a large jaguar-figure with jaws stretched apart and a long tongue pointed out, both also gesturing like the crown prince. Now looking more closely however, he realized that while all these clownish beasts were waving or flapping paws and hands, the crown-prince's hand was bent at the wrist in an elegant manner and his wrist rested on his temple, fingers and thumb clasped flatly together and pointing forward.

Ye-es, murmured d'Hachis, you are quite right, *cher ami*—the membrane has grown so thin by now that we and they pass through effortlessly, even unintentionally now.

But why? mused Augustus. They are reconnoitering perhaps; their world falling apart, our world falling apart, and the boundaries which defined them blurred. At that moment the canoe tipped to the right as the Paddlers dug in on the same side, and the long vessel slowly swerved to the left, westward that is, all the head-feathers fluttering crazily, and headed up First Street. The traffic roared by with a vengeance, and d'Hachis and Augustus peered after the strange crew. When it was a couple of hundred feet down the street, they saw the stern lift up from the street dripping—yes, distinctly!—and the Stingray God's paddle flailing about in the air three or four feet above the street surface, and all the passengers drawn forward intently in hieratic iteration, and the stern began to slide downward on an angle into the pavement, and next the bow was disappearing below the street's surface, and within seconds the entire canoe with its crew was swallowed up by the choppy waters which flowed from the Municipal Plaza, the primordial waters of Creation.

You know what, Augustus? asked d'Hachis with rare earnestness, with events like these, the vital energy (*ch'ul* I believe?) is going to be sucked out of Manhattan! For the art historian who was a *passioné* of the City, this was a statement to be taken seriously. It seemed unlikely to Augustus though—with Manhattan's history of bloodshed and its huge battery pack of energy.

d'Hachis, I've got to go and see what happened. There must be a trace, something that can tell us. They strode down the side street where the canoe had disappeared, Augustus with a sense of futility, d'Hachis with intense poetic curiosity, another line from Rimbaud having come to him from *Le bateau ivre*. About two hundred feet on they came to the spot. Augustus squatted and touched the pavement gingerly. It was perfectly dry.

Nothing, he grunted. The boy-detective should be here!

d'Hachis a few feet farther on let out a whoop—Look, here, he cried. Augustus hurried over. His friend was pointing at a crack in the street: a bedraggled and soaked yellow feather lay trapped in it. There is our boy, he intoned with mock solemnity. Augustus squatted, leaning on his hands, inspecting, and said, "parrot feather". A dog barked and they both turned with a jump. Milou was sniffing and yapping with his little black bulb of a nose pointed straight at the feather—and a few feet behind him stood Tintin in his brown tweed bicycle pants, bicycle leaning against the nearest wall, his hair sticking up in a curlicue as brightly yellow as the alleged "parrot" feather.

Bonjour mes amis, he said jovially. I see you have come to the same conclusion as myself! I have been pedaling (not paddling!) all over lower Manhattan awaiting this sinking, or better this dive of the Paddler Gods' canoe. Clearly we were right in our premonitions—our two worlds are becoming increasingly permeable, their edges corrupted. This event was clearly predictable because our galaxy is turning and the stars of Orion are being brought to the zenith at dawn![28] The Paddlers, also known as the "Sky Artists", are transporting our friend "Smoking Squirrel" in the guise of "Maize God" to these hearthstones—Orion—where he can be reborn and make things happen. d'Hachis and Augustus looked at Tintin carry on with some bafflement. They shouldn't have however, because they both knew that Tintin and Hergé did their homework thoroughly—the former out of professionalism as a journalist, the latter out of verisimilitude, and the result of their collaboration was always impressive.

Tintin, said Augustus after a couple of seconds of silence, you have done a remarkable job.

Well, said Tintin with his usual becoming modesty, it's not really my doing. Thanks to the Professor we were able to track these events down. And he pointed as if to the wings behind a stage-setting, and from behind the building corner where his bicycle was propped, peeked the dazed-looking, fuzzy-haired, domed forehead and then the diminutive figure of le *Professeur* Tournesol whom Tintin and indeed Augustus had first met in an astronomical setting[29].

He had the fierce scowl of a crossed cat but as soon as he saw Augustus and d'Hachis the expression broke into a child's smile of pure joy—But it is not the Maya at all, my dear Tintin! Why do you mislead me so! It is our old friend Augustus! So saying he flung himself literally upon Augustus and hugged him about the neck, so small and wiry that it was a child's clasp, then he approached d'Hachis and looked him up and down, twice his own size, grasped his hand and shook it vigorously, pumping it a dozen

28   Linda Schele's cosmological discovery in Maya Cosmos
29   Tintin et l'Etoile Mysterieuse

times, Ah! Very content to make your acquaintance sir! Very content!

d'Hachis looked at the Professor and then at Augustus. Dubious, Augustus, he said, dubious. Don't you think this is taking things a bit far? It was not said snobbishly but with that sense of professional seriousness and integrity, which was one of his traits. The Professor had stopped pumping his hand and was looking up at him with puzzled gaze.

d'Hachis, replied Augustus, I do not choose my references or my sources. They simply appear of themselves. Tintin the meanwhile looked on with embarrassed mien.

He said: We prefer not to use this sort of language, it may be dismaying to some of our friends, and he glanced apprehensively at the Professor. The Professor glanced from Tintin to d'Hachis and to Augustus with a look of indignant astonishment.

Mais non, Tintin! Do you think I am a fool! These are not the Maya at all! They went down in the canoe! His eyebrows bristled dangerously.

Non, non, *Professeur*! DISMAYING, I said, said the other.

Mais non, Tintin!! Not "these Maya"! But not at all, my poor friend, you are completely, but completely trumped! The brainy little astro-physicist patted his friend compassionately on the back and smiled apologetically at the others.

Tintin smiled as well and shrugged: Without his hearing-trumpet, you know..

Yes, but—insisted the Dada historian in a not very good temper himself by now, we may not be Maya, but they—you—he said pointedly at Tintin, are BD's[30], and him too, and he nodded at Professor Tournesol, who smiled at him amiably, and I would like to know what they are doing here. This is, after all, an essentially literary domain!

Tintin looked at Augustus in mute appeal, but no assistance was forthcoming, so he said: Well maybe, Mr. d'Hachis, we come to introduce a note of realism here! Your friend Augustus over there is mooning over some erotic romance with a remote Maya Princess while you both drift off on an absurd and wholly implausible trip which, may I say, has more of the fantastic than I would ever consent to!

Augustus considered his friend with solicitude. No, no, my dear Tintin, I'm sure you know I've never treated you with flippancy, nor do I think have I given this impression to the public.

But Tintin, whose ire was rarely aroused, continued undeterred:

---

30   Bandes dessinées or comic strips

Non, non, mon cher Auguste, I am afraid you have not quite got at it! I want to say that although, yes, I am the "boy-hero" and represent a certain role model for Belgian youth (and for you as well not that long-ago!) and perhaps far beyond our narrow borders, a role that I play with professional fortitude, I cannot be reduced to that milieu. On the contrary, behind this montage, and precisely because we occupy it as such, in the *coulisses*, in the wings that is, and back stage, we know life. You with these inarticulate, romantic-erotic yearnings (which so far have come to nothing), can you know what it is like to be tortured for the love? Do you truly believe I am asexual? Augustus had rarely seen his friend so excited and so angrily indignant. And le *Professeur* Tournesol, who was following this harangue (for it could be called that, however uncharacteristic) closely, appeared to bristle sympathetically like a porcupine, the curly black hair seeming to frizzle and to stand out from under the green hunting cap with flaps that he usually wore, little suited to the steamy climate of the rain-forest. So you speculate that Tintin would not know what a bordello was even if he chanced upon one? continued Tintin. Well let me tell you that after a particularly tedious adventure, I have been to the bordello for some other sorts of adventure! Yes! Underneath this boyish garb is a member no less responsive than your own! In a notorious "house" down an alley-way off Eighth Street in Greenwich Village, I was strapped to a special "dungeon" table, cross-dressed in stockings and garters and no more, manacled by the wrists and ankles, and subjected to exquisite "punishment" by young ladies in identical garb! Do you think that I have traveled through the narrow teeming streets of the cities of the Indian sub-continent[31], the sinister port towns of the South American Pacific coast[32], the Arab souks[33] with their variegated illicit offerings, or indeed the sordid *Gare de Midi* back streets of my own capital, Brussels where the ladies wait in the garish, red neon-lit windows with whips and boots and the indispensable garter-belt and little else— without ever, even after hours, after my professional duties, experiencing the seedier side of life?? Yes, even Tintin may have desires which le *brave Capitaine* may not be aware of! Tintin's yellow forelock which had shaken throughout this impassioned delivery, now abruptly came to a stop, and his features recomposed themselves in his customary amiable and alert countenance. He patted down his as always immaculate *coiffure*, and glanced about at his friends who were gaping at him with open mouths. *Le*

31   The Blue Lotus
32   The Broken Ear
33   The Crab with the Golden Claws

Capitaine Haddock appeared most chagrined, tears prickling his eyes. As for Augustus, he had had a revelation: he and Tintin were like two sides of a coin; and even this better self might be contaminated by the flesh!

Now where was I? Oh yes. What I and my friends, le *Capitaine* Haddock, *le Professeur* Tournesol, perhaps even les *Agents de la Sureté Officers* Dupont and Dupond bring you is a taste, a reminder of real life out there, behind us all! Today, for example, following the Professor's studies, we were convinced the Paddlers' Canoe would sink somewhere in Lower Manhattan.

Yes, broke in the *Professeur*, circumflex eyebrows high-raised above excited pin-point eyes, in the Maya Long Count calendar, 9.14.11.17.3 at midnight the Milky Way was stretched across the sky from east to west in the form of the Cosmic Monster[34]. During the four hours after midnight the Cosmic Monster "sinks" as the Milky Way turns and brings the three stars of Orion to the zenith just before dawn! Now in confabulation with Ignatius, my friend and *Profesor de Filosofia de la Universidad de Complutense*, I was able to determine that in extrapolation from this mythical Maya date the sinking should coincide with tnoday's date in 1999, i.e. November 20th! Now it was Augustus's turn to look astounded—

Are you referring to my old friend from Madrid, the author i.a. of the three-tomed work of awesome scholarship of the *Circulo de la Sabiduria*?[35] Yes, yes, of course, who else, muttered Tournesol a little put-off by this interruption. Don't you know that Ignatius has much studied the Mithraic zodiacal constellations, discovering (in parallel with Schele on the Maya) that the iconic elements figure as constellations in the myths? He has shown how the Mithraic *taurocthony* maintains a close link with the celestial equator and the ecliptic, and in particular the equinoxes of spring and autumn marked by the intersection of the equator and the ecliptic. Well, in agreement with Doctor Ignatius I have worked out that the Canoe as Milky Way would be sinking at precisely today's date in the Northern hemisphere. Augustus seemed hardly to listen, however, and stared at Tournesol and d'Hachis and Tintin with an expression of what could only be called beatitude.

But if Ignatius is here, then he is my seventh ball player! With

---

34   Following the original discovery and with the assistance of Professor Linda Schele

35   El Circulo de la Sabiduria (or "the circle of wisdom") published 1998, Siruela, Spain. Among several books of philosophy, Gomez de Liano has also published a founding work of practical philosophy, Iluminaciones Filosoficas, 2001, which was to become the guideline for Augustus' life.

the Philosopher our team is complete! Augustus' tone was triumphant.

Complete? How is that? asked d'Hachis in surprise.

Yes! exclaimed Augustus, exhilarated. Seven is the number of players I have surmised from the wall paintings of Yaxchilan and Bonampak, and besides it is a mystical number. Ignatius is doubtless most erudite in regard to magical-astronomical patterns of language, mnemonic-meditative figures, he should make an excellent forward. Tintin nodded approvingly.

Actually, said d'Hachis, I haven't entirely got at the point of this ballgame.

Oh d'Hachis, chuckled Tintin, the *éternel féminin, mon cher*! Don't you know your man? Augustus here has some odd addiction to *la petite* black-haired pussy-in-boots, the sister of young Smoking Squirrel *ch'ul ahau*, the blood-lord, and the ballgame is the only game in town he knows which might lead to her heart—or panties. Only it may be his head instead which is involved, and if he gets her he may find her to be Smoking Black Cat. But such is the romance, such is the true love. And Tintin rolled the black dots, which passed for eyes and grinned broadly.

Well, quite the man of the world, aren't you! said Augustus with the self-conscious smirk of the moonstruck. *Non*, d'Hachis, well, these paths may intersect, but I was brought here first when I joined the *Pochteca* or Armed Merchants from Teotihuacan at the Butterfly Palace. It's true I went there because "Butterfly" is her *way*, named after that Teotihuacano goddess. In any case the ballgame is about rearranging time and space, about recovering mythic time—in the shadow of the approaching Armageddon which the Maya are preparing for—or exactly 13 cycles, 0 *katuns*, 0 *tuns*, 0 *uinals* and 0 *kins* since the beginning of the Great Cycle. As the wise men throughout the Yucatan say, the world will end in 2000 *y un pico*--"and a little more"—2009, 2011.. As we approach the Day of 4 *Ahau* 3 *Kankin* presided over by the Ninth Lord of the Night, they are coming now to investigate us. Our turn, they believe. Or more accurately, the edges of their world and ours are meshing with impending doom. The ballgame, my dear d'Hachis, with you and my other life companions, is a small attempt to adjust, to shift the time-space. If the Butterfly Princess is to be my prize in the undertaking, well so be it! How else can I reach the soul of the Maya? Carl has identified us as a shamanic couple—whatever that means! And you are aware that since the beginning of these sightings, I rented an apartment in southern Manahatta in order to survey any further arrivals.

Ah, that is why you insisted so extravagantly on the view of all the waters flowing about the tip of the island, exclaimed d'Hachis. And that you had to see the East River edging about to the left where you could spy it just above the roof of the old Customs House, and the Hudson to the right, and the whole Hudson Bay splash in front of you. All water, only water in front of your windows.

Yes, yes, I remember, nodded Tintin solemnly, your observatory for the infiltration of the Maya. In preparation of their arrival en masse one day. No doubt by the great canoes.

I am bringing her to the apartment, said Augustus. It is through our inflammatory combustion that these things will be clarified. Through her I can turn the key!

But don't you think you should bring this up with your mother? You are staying with her presently, are you not, asked Tintin, always the moralist.

Rudely brought back to earth by the question, Augustus turned to him, My BD friend! he exclaimed, not without a drop of sarcasm, Thanks again for reality! Yes, of course, I have already decided that is necessary. And she is not my mother. Oh by the way, *Professeur*, he called over his shoulder as he strode off more purposefully than he felt, where was it you held those conversations with Ignatius?

Yesterday, said the other. He was guest lecturer on his philosophical *summum* at the Spanish Institute, on Park Avenue.

Yes, yes, I know where it is. Well I must go now, thank you. And he headed for the subway and the Upper West Side. It had been a sudden and crude reminder of the realities of his life. How could Tintin have such an intuition? What interiority did he draw on? Apparently not that cartoon two-dimensionality that he had sometimes slightingly referred to. Although he, Augustus, had quickly assumed ethical "paternity" regarding his responsibility vis-à-vis Milena—it was far from easy or self-evident to him. The manly and fair thing was to tell Milena, but now that he had moved from the speculative to the declarative moment of so doing, he was utterly deprived of emotional resources. How on earth could he actually bring himself to do so! He had never told her the truth! It would be so wounding for her (read: wounding to himself). He would just say so in a perfectly natural way, he decided. Through the turnstiles and uptown, across the threshold of her building and an amiable nod at the doorman dressed like the Grenadier Guards. In that proprietary manner of New York doormen who identified with the familial and even intimate interests of their tenants, they looked at him askance, somehow aware through their daily observations of the irregularity of his relationship with Milena, and were even subtly suspicious of him—if always formally correct. Was he seen in the derisory role of the wayward husband? He let himself in quietly at the front door and let the latch slip back softly. This was the home he had grown up in. Or it could be. He tiptoed through the living rainforest to her bedroom, and found her there as usual, stretched out in bed, motionless. Ghostlike, he listened to her quiet breathing in the doubtless deep-sleep stage of the pre-dawn hour. He had always enjoyed this peaceful moment of her sleep when he had awakened before her, inapprehensive of her torments. He was sorrowfully aware that she suffered torments on his account: jealousy, hatred, resentment, bitterness, frustration. Somehow he had been the root cause of it all, and this was the source of his unending guilt. The right question now, however, was, had he escaped the notion of his fate at her hands? Fata Milena. There were moments when he felt so saturated with these emotional bonds, that utter superficiality was most attractive to him. With the gentle sea-surface rise and fall of her breathing, he glided noiselessly into her enormous room. He did not want to wake her! He dreaded waking her. The fluctuations from pity to—yes, terror! —were baffling to him. Far better not to embark once again upon those tormented waters. He just wanted to sniff the atmosphere, to remember: it was close, the smell not unpleasant—sweet, slightly cloying, as of accumulated fine clothes, lingerie, put away in drawers for years. Lavender, rose water. It cradled him—and suffocated him. At the far end of the room, its pillows and sheets fracturing the dusk like frothy whitecaps, the blurred bulk of the double bed with the barely perceptible outline of the slight figure borne upon it: dread, adoration. He caught a movement at one side of the bed, the flicker of a stocky figure.

He hissed—who's there? He heard an echoing hiss. And now only feet away he made out a shadowy yet utterly familiar form. At first it appeared to be one of the Maya, but there was something ineffably tender and at the same time pitiful about the figure that suggested someone much closer to him.

Then the sibilant whisper, *hé mon petit Auguste, elle est souffrante tu sais,* above all do not awaken her! It was his father. His father who had surrounded his mother all his life with a wall of anxiety, worship and alarm. Which doubtless had undermined his health and brought about his untimely death, a quarter century before his wife's. That wall was Augustus' only inheritance, since in the end his father had disinherited him to satisfy his wife's seething resentments. It became in turn the wall with which he surrounded Milena. Mother or spouse, what difference did it make? Saint Sposa. The identification had become hallucinatory; he could no longer clearly differentiate. Yes, his father had been a minor player in his life, but an entirely sympathetic if ineffectual one. While Augustus' ties with his mother had been overwhelming, his kindest memories—tinged with disdain or was it his horror and rejection of resemblance?—remained for his father. His father's tight lower lip betrayed his obsessive concern, a panic-stricken clutching he tried to inculcate in his son—

"Your lower lip is too sensual, he used to tell Augustus, you should bite it in." In this he failed patently, but involuntarily and with no effort he absorbed his father's self-sacrificial, self-flagellatory nature, otherwise he would never have stayed married to Milena for twenty years in a bond of constant punishment. When he occasionally—rarely, but occasionally—caught sight in a mirror of his father's kindly, apprehensive watchfulness in his own eyes, he recoiled. His repudiation, mild and affectionate if determined, was nothing in comparison with his younger brother's unconcealed hatred. He and his father had stopped speaking to each other for years. Had their mother somehow passed on to her illegitimate son her own emotions of frustration and rejection of her husband?

Allez, allez, sors- "get out", the sibilant whisper continued, and he slipped out quickly, gratefully. The bell rang; he went to the front door and opened. Tintin stood there looking larger than life with a broad pink smile and wearing brown jodhpurs[36].

Where're the others? asked Augustus.

Well, d'Hachis said he had to get back to the next chapter of his scholarly biography, and *le Professeur* is designing a new, secret device. Augustus sighed knowingly, d'Hachis was always busy with a book, but he knew this was going to be a *grand livre* and forgave his friend readily, and of course *le Professeur* was always designing something new. That was their being, as no doubt this was Augustus'.

Well, said Tintin amiable as always, what a pleasant apartment you have here.

Well, it's my mother's, said Augustus, or rather my wife's, excuse me, it's a stupid slip I make, I gave it to her. Come on to the living room, it's the most pleasant part, and he led his friend up the staircase to the penthouse "rain forest". Yes, and unsaid was

36   He had first worn them on a trip to Rajasthan, India (The Cigars of Pharaoh) and grown attached to them.

how, with guilt and remorse, he had signed over ever-increasing chunks of the remainder of his personal estate to Milena until it was all gone, which she continuously encouraged for reasons of "safe-keeping"—in case one of your whores tries to get her hands on it, she once said. And she did keep it safely as he would never see it again! Every time he traveled she insisted on seeing his last will and testament, duly dated, to make sure everything was going to her. Tintin bowed his head to pass beneath a huge frond that hung over the staircase. Emerging at the top into the heavy foliage and hanging vines, into the color the Maya call *yax* which is the green of the rain forest, not the green known in the northern hemisphere, but a green with a dimension of depth, green with a tactile quality, green with a fleshy quality unknown in the impoverished plants of the North, a green with an inner animation bordering on the animalistic. Tintin was, for once, speechless, eyes even rounder than Hergé's drawing, perhaps on the edge of ecstasy. Finally he said, as he and Augustus pushed through the undergrowth:

You didn't tell me. Augustus, you must understand that I have been to the Tropics more than once, but it has always been in the context of my *aventures*, and even though it was a very colorful and picturesque world done with lavish detail, it never had this—life! Tintin spread his hands out, palms up in an attitude of rapture. Augustus was astonished by the contrast of Tintin's coloring, one could only say its flimsiness, its lack of conviction, now seen in the midst of the tropical forest. But how on earth—on this solid earth, he repeated, and stamped on the earthy surface underfoot—did you do it?

Oh it wasn't me, said Augustus, it's her. She has a green thumb. He led the way for his guest toward a couple of sofa chairs which to the newcomer would be all but invisible under their covers of crawling creepers and couch grass, and they sat down. However let me tell you something, he said, as his friend adjusted himself among the fronds. Every time I come here this living room-jungle appears richer and denser. I believe that it is one of the manifestations of the edges of the Maya world pushing into ours. In this parallelism of our worlds, we have the advantage of our own unshakeable but how brittle sense of exclusive reality, our cultural hypertrophy. But I doubt that our tinny, colorless, mechanical society can long resist the power of their *ch'ul* which pervades the universe; the soul-stuff which is seeping through our watertight rationalism and technicism.

Tintin gazed at his host with astonishment, finding him every bit as vulnerable in this potent *yax* as his host had found him. But Augustus, he said, were not the Maya a bloody, bloody nation?

Augustus looked at his friend with commiseration, having dealt with the question before.

Tintin, he began patiently, can you not see that the ritual cruelty practiced by the Maya is no worse than our sentimentally cloaked social abstractions?

Non, non, I understand that, continued Tintin, but don't they thrive on it? We mask our cruelties from ourselves, but they rejoice in theirs!

Is a benevolent mask any improvement over a monstrous one? And remember, their cruelty is not an end per se, but an instrument of ecstasy, demurred Augustus.

Ah, yes, your poetic soul must relish that, intoned Tintin with unusual irony, his was a non-duplicitous soul, but with his fact-finding bent, Augustus's vague genius was sometimes just too wooly for him. And does the Dragon-Mother's gross mask conceal a thirst for love, or an ecstasy of self-love? Augustus realized his friend was far too sensitive to speak *ad hominem*. Ahh, yes, I see what you mean. Was there beneath her endless probing at this old wound, behind her lashing at him, her bloody scratches, her maniacal beatings, her homicidal humors, a dark ecstasy of love! He had never really looked behind this curtain. He feared that if he did he would only discover a seething devouring she-monster. Oh spare me your love, mother! He pulled himself together with a jerk.

Yes, yes, of course, my dear Tintin, I understand your wariness, you need the friction of fact and everyday reality just to survive, whereas my only hope is in—in what, really, he wondered? In a fiction: kindness--or deception? Is not avoidance a mild form of deception. No doubt his father's as well; and self-deception? Yes, his father had always been thought of as a kind man; like his father. Not for him the excesses of the whip and humiliation which his spouse might have thrived on. Augustus wondered if this combination of inherited traits on his part did not mask an inability to face the other. No matter how deep his anger might be over the latest insult—and Milena knew intimately how to twist the knife in the wound, whereas he withheld any words, which, he feared, might offend her, irrevocably—he was always quickly moved to pity and guilt. He took a deep breath in response to the puzzled expectancy of his cartoon friend and attempted to pick up the broken thread of his exposition. The slow spread of the Maya throughout the city. If what they believe—that the final phase of the 52nd *katun* of the Maya calendar is culminating, that the wave of our civilization is sputtering to a conclusion on this shore of the 21st century and will turn back, then you and I face a challenge as serious as any you have met with in your career[37]. It is evident to me that one of the most significant portals at this phase of the endtime will be the ball court on which we play against this Classic Boy-King, because they, the shamans, Smoking-Squirrel himself, the *Ah Dzib*, indeed the Queen Mother Lady *Wak-Chanil* herself, have chosen us for this ritual game, for ritual channels dangerous and potent psychic energies.

Eh bien, now you are making more sense, *mon ami,* said Tintin leaning forward. And are these psychic energies what threaten to destroy us then? But first—while the Spaniards no doubt annihilated what remained of the Maya, the cataclysm had arrived six centuries earlier, had it not? Their sudden disappearance in the ninth century throughout the peninsula is still a mystery. The slaughter of the royal families, the auto-da-fe, the burning of libraries, the defacing of monuments by an enraged populace? Do you know what I believe, Augustus? I believe the people were driven to it by the extravagant, esthetically cultivated cruelty of the *Ahau ahauob*. And if that is the case, should we not suspect the true motivation of their visits now?

Yes, said Augustus, but I cannot do any more until I find the Butterfly Princess. Can you help me to get back? Although this living room seems to provide a permeable border with the Petén, the timing is off.

I can tell you one thing, said Tintin, his brows arching and his eyes narrowing as they slid to a backward glance over his shoulder, Police Detectives Dupont and Dupond have informed me that they have personally witnessed Her Royalty Lady *Wak-Chanil* to slip in downstairs before dawn, still wearing her skimpy nightgown and an altered expression. I would be very careful in what I reveal to your Mummy, if I were you. Augustus leaned back at this moment and extended one ear, as did Tintin. A low rhythmic growl could be heard, very softly, through the heavy vegetation. He realized that once again he had adopted the cowardly excuse of "a lack of opportunity" to speak frankly with Milena.

Don't worry, said Augustus, it's not a jaguar. That's just Mummy snoring.

You do realize, Augustus, said Tintin gently, that the reason your apartment "edges" on Maya territory but does not allow you to pass over properly is because of your spouse's lunacy? On this side, she is the shadow double of *Lady Wak-Chanil* on the other

37   Such as "The Shooting Star" which threatened the end of the world..

side of the Black Transformer. This is at the heart of the duality you experience. That is why you have crossed over to the dark realm of the Maya, while you are still bound to the present.

Oh god, what "present"! exclaimed Augustus. Don't you see I am wracked by presentiments and bad dreams? What man does not disappoint his mother! It was only when my "spouse" became a dreaded and censorious "mother" that I began to deceive her! For years I had practiced mental and bodily fidelity! This dam of pent-up frustration and desire broke only after she began to per-secute me for—nothing! It was her hounding that drove me to other women and exotic practices. Well, you may be right about that, but it doesn't help me now, he added quickly, attempting to suppress his momentary hysteria. I need to get back to Tikal--to the seventh century. I've been twice up and down the Municipal Building, I've worn out my welcome there. I can't think of any other floating pyramid or temple in the neighborhood. Tintin, can't you help me?

Do you want my help or do you just want a prop? You do know the Sherry-Netherland Hotel at the Southeast corner of the Park?

Yes of course, thank you for standing in there anyway, Tintin, said Augustus with exaggerated courtesy. He was slightly offended by his friend's truth-telling penchant. And so they left Augustus' childhood home, and walked to Central Park (from the balcony you could see the Park next door). The weather was balmy, the Park swarmed with strollers, there must have been thousands on that sunny and unseasonably warm December afternoon, the dogs straining at leashes, death-defying roller skaters and skate-board-ers, doting young couples and perambulators, and a long single file of horse-drawn carriages proceeding sedately with their cargos of out-of-towners gaping at the running commentary from their drivers. The pop tunes of squealing Lolitas drifted over from the ice rink as these flipped their tiny skirts at aged men's lusting madness, and the City that afternoon appeared to be nothing more than an immense cacophonous carnival. Above the trees they could see the narrow spires of the Sherry-Netherland. When they emerged from the Park at fifty-eighth and Fifth Avenue the Hotel was directly in front of them, with the Pierre Hotel on the left, an austere Megalo-Renaissance palace where Augustus' moth-er had dragged him and his much younger, "baby" sister to dance with the awkward and shrinking children of other good families in their white gloves and formal dress when he was thirteen years old. The rather gloomy building peaked in classic twenties fashion in a Gothic castle-tower with oddly Romanic arched windows, and the saurian snouts of copper-green gargoyles jutted out around its base. Narrow turrets guarded the base of the central spire, which rose to a small platform girding a tiny watchtower, which could not hold more than one or two persons at the most.

There, said Augustus emphatically, is where we shall find a gateway. In the small jewel-box of the hotel foyer there were a couple of astonished glances at Tintin's anachronistic dress and ultra clean-cut appearance (Tintin was so clean-cut because his graphic character was such that all the little irregularities and blurring at the edges of a natural person were just missing. This is what gives him his special "edge", his para-normal quasi-angelic look. And it no doubt explains Augustus' "angel" complex). They asked the elevator man to take them to the top of the building but he informed them with the anonymous amiability of the true professional that it was impossible because the top floors of the building had been converted to a condo, i.e. were privately owned, and he went on to a capsule history of the building, while Augustus and Tintin admired the late 18th century Italian *boiseries* of the elevator and thus passed the time of day until destination. Once they had gotten out at their landing however, they saw the dilemma. A brief corridor came to a dead stop at an apartment door without a number and without a nameplate.

It's odd, remarked Augustus to Tintin, because it would imply that the apartment has the whole top of the building, spires and all, since there's no other way up Tintin frowned and walked up and down the corridor, staring at the door.

I can see you are in your detective mode.

Tintin shrugged: what height do you suppose we're at, here? He took out his journalist's yellow pad and scribbled. Ah, he said answering his own question, I'd say at about the base of the "castle" complex—where the gargoyles poke out.

Well let's see if we can persuade them to let us have a look, said Augustus and he pressed the bell. Immediately the door opened, and a short brown man bulging in a butler's uniform answered. The lateral extension of the shoulders was approximately equivalent to his height. Such was the rounded, ropey thickness of neck and shoulders and plumped out pectorals that it looked as if the butler would not be able to walk without rotating the whole frontal axis of chest and shoulders from side to side. A broad aquiline nose was collapsed on his face and the small dark eyes were entirely impassive.

Yes—Sir, came the voice again, more insistent.

Ah yes, he mumbled, we would like to meet the owner... As he spoke the butler shifted his weight to his right leg, and in the gap between his block-body and the left door-jamb what Augustus saw left him speechless: a row of large, grinning skulls at floor level—and poised above them at an angle the back of a delicate ankle and a slender, graceful calf which flickered and was gone. He could see no more because the swelling torso of the butler in the foreground concealed the rest. Upon closer perusal he realized the skulls were sculpted in deep relief along the edge of a low platform.

Hisss, came the hiss of Tintin just behind his elbow, not a moment to lose! And in an authoritative tone, honed no doubt by years of practice with Captain Haddock's butler, Nestor[1], he said, Thank you my brave man, we shall await your master's arrival inside, and brushing in front of the hesitant Augustus he swept past the impassive butler in the doorway and stopped before—a deep entrance passageway! Augustus nimbly followed. It was indeed a vast interior entrance, through which no doubt the owner of the pretty leg had disappeared, which they found themselves facing the coils of Cosmic Monster, an oversized reptile, rose up and across the top of the entrance forming a writhing lintel in deep relief over fifty feet long, and among its squamous loops sported the oddest little fellows (priests? warriors?) with striated wrist and ankle cuffs and the cocky posturing and face-making of the Marx Brothers. The Butler meanwhile had closed the front door behind them, and now stood with his back against the wall, unmindful of them. Aloof. Tintin and Augustus glanced at one another, and as one man dove through the large interior passageway within the coils of the Vision Serpent. It was a noteworthy experience. I refer to the passageway through the coils.

What do you mean, said Augustus. Ah yes, he garbled, you refer to the existential etc., I always find this so charming, the amateur anthropologist's modest if slightly incredulous subordination of critical faculties to indigenous hocus-pocus.

No, no, insisted the yellow-shock-haired cartoon character, for however prosaic and well-documented he might be, he did not deny his otherworldly origins, I am talking about this, a psychosomatic experience, and Augustus literally felt, as they pressed through that tunnel, the tightening of the leathery coils about his ribcage, the squash of a squamous-clammy surface about his skin, the turbine-pumping tubular enveloping of his entire body, and ahead he could dimly see the larger-than-life, graphically crisp silhouette of Tintin similarly engaged in this psycho-existential squeeze, and he caught a hold of his friend's back-stretched hand

and for once was thankful for his extra animated energy which enabled him to yank them both through and free of this sticky transition. *Eh bien!* said Tintin, brushing his hands vigorously across his bright blue shirt and khaki pants, and Augustus, stunned by the last few seconds of whatever it was, followed suit. He realized as the long filaments pulled off his costume that the salivary glands of the very large ophidian had been only too real.

A disgusting experience!

Eh bien! repeated Tintin in a larger voice, that's a rather bizarre remark from you, with your vast experience! Now you know what it really feels like... Augustus raised his eyes from his gummy clothing and glanced without a glimmer of understanding at the other. Tintin nudged him with one of those spasmodic movements, which seemed to be characteristic of persons of his medium: a high-speed conceptual movement, where the gesture coincided with the thought.

Augustus responded somewhat irritably with a What! Tintin simply nudged him again eye-brows fluttering upwards, thusly ^ ^ in his moon face, and Augustus followed the direction they were pointing—at a giant stucco macaw with a great crumpled beak and feathery cheeks, outstretched hierarchical wings and fat, mitt-like incoiled claws above a portal in the far wall—and saw disappearing through the latter in a twinkle of alluring bare thighs and a long black braid the girl he had been following earlier.

Cherchez la femme! said Tintin roguishly and most irreverently.

That is indeed her, replied Augustus stiffly, and he studied his friend's untoward expression, hoping his unblemished original nature had not been spoiled by exposure to the crude atmosphere of New York, the deceptive camaraderie of its strip-bars and flesh-pots—or indeed his own corrupt character! He took the spherical face in his two hands and gazed inquiringly at the face within. Had this old companion since childhood, he wondered, could it be—

Mon cher petit Auguste, said his erstwhile companion of boy-hood years, she's getting away, isn't this why we--?!

Omigod! exclaimed Augustus, where did she go! He glanced about wildly. Instinct told him where the little princess had fled: to her mother[38], the Dragon Lady, no question about it. He had been there before, so he knew how to go. The palatial compound fanned out before them in an elegant sweep of raised platforms and plaster-floor ball courts and plazas and the occasional step-

38   Princess Smoking-Fox was the sister of the precocious king, Smoking-Squirrel, and his ambiguous relationship with the Old Lady will be remembered.

pyramid. Minutes later Tintin and Augustus stood for a moment at the foot of the steps of the palace he had entered just days ago, and they sped up with a lightness of foot that only a comic book hero and his narrational companion could manage. An occasional warrior *in vivo* nodded them on and then lapsed into the same indistinguishable rigidity of his identical, incised-in-stone comrades, and in the same breath they arrived at the dragon-festooned portal of the Queen Mother and rattled the beads loudly. No hissed response. Tintin stared at Augustus and Augustus stared at Tintin. The silence hissed with added silence.

They're not here, said Tintin superfluously, and Augustus wondered glumly if Tintin really was his doppelganger. A peal of girlish laughter rippled down the corridor.

There she is, whispered Augustus, equally superfluously. Why did they whisper in these palatial hallways? Was it the blood, the *ch'ul*, an atmosphere of fear and trembling? They turned a corner at the end of the hallway and saw an entrance a few feet down. Female voices were clearly audible and the sound of water flowing, splashing. Augustus sidled up to the doorway and peeked in. His attention was drawn immediately, relegating the richly variegated scene to the periphery of his vision, to the entirely naked, girlish form of the Butterfly Princess standing in a steaming pool which reached to her thighs, the sweet, almost childish face alive with laughter, the long black hair wreathed about taut breasts which curved up at the nipples, generous for her girlish figure, the black pubic triangle bringing a quick hard beat to his heart and a thrill to his other parts. An erotic child! He thought. Tintin's round face hovering just behind his shoulder appeared to be rounding further, eyes widened about their usual dot-centers, eyebrows semi-circles arched above them, and all this roundness suffused with such ruddiness that it appeared to be a rising sun. Augustus, aware of this radiance at his shoulder, considered that it was possibly the first time his companion had ever seen a nude woman in spite of his indignant claims to the contrary. Then a racket broke loose in the room as the little princess's eyes as well as the eyes of everybody else in the room were drawn back along the same vector toward the gaze of the two intruders. The girl let out a piercing scream of indignation one hand immediately cupping her sex, the other clasping her over-spilling breasts quite inadequately, as handmaidens jumped up, *huipils* flapping, from the stone benches set against three of the walls and ran to shield and cover her, and a dwarf with yellow and blue plumes bouncing on his head and wearing a net-skirt bounded forward, his features looming as large and scowling as any warrior's, and glared up into Augustus' face. The latter ignored his aggressive stance, and eluding the long-nailed fingers of Tintin clutching at his back, rushed into the room and threw himself at the feet of the Butterfly-Princess who had stepped out of the bath and was dripping on the floor, two of the maidens covering her shoulders with a brightly colored veil.

Sweet Princess, he cried, forgive this intrusion! It was not meant that these eyes.. And he extended one hand and his fingers curled about the slender ankle, and glancing up somewhat slyly he caught a quick glimpse of the delicate creamy thighs and above, where they melted buttery together into the delectable herbaceous mound, veiled in the next instant from his immodest gaze by the dropping down of a long white garment which rustled over her ankles covering his hand. He withdrew it aware of some impropriety. He realized with a slight shock of embarrassment that he found himself in an odd, if not frankly grotesque, posture. He buried his face for a moment in the dusty plastered floor to cover his confusion and perhaps also his untoward and involuntary physiological reaction, and after a moment or two felt her foot nudge his hand. Timidly now he reached out blindly until his fingers-tips encountered the edge of the foot, and then climbed onto the top of the foot in a tentative caress. To his surprise the skin felt rough and horny, as if encrusted and the foot overly large. Twisting his head to one side he peeped up again with one eye, and found himself staring up along a mottled, heavy thigh beneath a net dress into a hairy bush—and recognized it as the Queen Mother's. He twisted his head out from under, and looked up into her glowering face: beneath the hauteur of an eagle-hooked nose bristled a sneering lip and a soft triple chin cascaded toward the powerful dugs hanging to the quadrifold belly.

My darling young man, she said, but her teeth were set and he could see they had been filed to sharp points, now have your pervert leanings taken you to spying on my daughter's exposed quin? Haven't you ever looked into a real woman's gaping crack or are you too much of a pouf to fulfill the needs of a Queen!?

No, no! Mum—I mean Queen, he stuttered, looking about wildly for some—he saw Tintin squinting or signaling to him from across the room, his bright animated form reclining against a wall. Augustus drew himself up joint by joint from the prostrate position at the Queen-Mother's feet, avoiding to graze the massive breasts as he stood up, well above the scowling old Bat (and she did resemble a bat-face with its cruel voracious features stretching into his face) and ardently sought out the princess. She stood combing out her wet, jet-black hair vigorously, wearing the *huipil* beloved of Maya lords for what it cunningly both concealed and revealed of the curvature beneath, and a short net skirt, which concealed hardly anything of the bewitchingly damp groin. He walked toward her and the whole room of servants and dwarves and Queen Mother reoriented itself like a magnetic field about these two. She turned an inquiring look to him, and he blushed dopily, he was so enchanted by the sweetness of her features, the pouting lower lip and huge green eyes, and the provocation of her unselfconscious exhibition of her body, that he could hardly answer. He turned back to the Queen Mother who was standing dangerously nearby, and whose plug ugly form while undoubtedly squatter than he remembered in spite of the platform shoes, had only acquired greater density. As he gazed upon her, dismayed by this potential mother-in-law (yea his thoughts leapt ahead of any such designs), he realized something valuable: the "density" or mental-shamanic nature of such beings was strictly related to the implosive energy of the hieroglyphs:

Almost from the first day I saw you, he added inconsequently to the Princess, I knew you had psychic force. Indeed, in spite of the general bloody-mindedness of her Maya culture he could see her white-flower soul. Well, he said, perhaps we just might have some common ground there after all. A gurgle came from behind, and he did not have to turn to know it was the Mother japing him. The Butterfly Princess meanwhile was studying him with cool, detached gaze. Then and there he guessed that he was no match for her, a deeper truth than he realized then, but he tried anyway. Listen, he said, I don't know my way around here, would you be my guide, my "*Malinche*"[39]? This was said in a bantering tone, since of course the historical *Malinche* was not to appear until some nine hundred years later in the twilight of the Maya.

Malinche, hmm, that sounds cool, why not? she said with an arch and infectious grin. And she grabbed him by the hand and walked out ahead of him with a jaunty step, keeping him firmly in hand, her brief skirt bouncing about her thighs with an insouciance which set His heart aflutter. He glanced back just as they ex-

39   *Malinche* was the name of the Maya maiden who was "given" to Cortes by a local *ahau*, unless it was the maiden who asked the *ahau* to introduce her. In any case she fell in love with the bearded and tall godlike stranger and provided him with invaluable information about her people and their ways, and as well served as his interpreter of the Maya-speaking Indians, and then of Nahuatl, as well as epigrapher of glyphs.It was said that she enabled him finally to defeat the Aztecs in the north, and many in modern Mexico considered her to be a traitor of her own people.

ited the doorway, and saw the Queen-Mother's gaze which, if it could have, would have castrated him on the spot.

Once they were outside in the hallway, she said, Now run as fast as you can. And dropping his hand, she took to her heels, her cute skirt jumping provocatively high, and just the view he had of her upper thighs twinkling in the semi-obscurity of the passageways was enough to make him run after her as if his life depended on it: up to the end of a passage and around the corner just in time to see the back of a white thigh disappear around the next corner. This is the way it has always been, the sweet heart just out of reach, nimble. He never forgot that race together, her hand trusting in his, his girl, his child-woman, and for years he couldn't evoke the image without pain. Finally they poured out of the front entrance of the palace into the blinding light, and all of Tikal lay at their feet. The girl collapsed against the red-stone wall of the pyramidal structure gasping for breath between bursts of laughter. Her breathless giggles were so infectious that he began to laugh himself without knowing why, and he put an arm about her to help her from sliding down the wall, and his fingers encountered the melting softness where her breast arose at the rib cage, and he murmured excuse me, but did not withdraw his hand, and when she did not repel him he curved his hand a little farther around until it cupped her breast, and then he felt her small hand on top of his and instead of pushing him away she clasped his hand tighter to her breast, and he reached up with his other hand and putting it about her cheek that was turned away from him, suddenly silent, he drew her toward him and kissed the upturned lips tenderly. And at the same moment, through and in the softness of her lips, her breasts, he felt himself embedded in the grain of the wall and through this material coextensive with the city of Tikal as it radiated out about them in the broad avenues and graceful plazas and ball courts upon which appeared to float palaces and the truncated pyramids of the Maya.

Is this what it means to be your *Malinche* she asked smiling up at him through lowered eyelashes, half-shy half-sly. His heart was now folded inside the hollow of her hand, and in answer he folded all of her, slight as she was, in his arms, one arm about her right shoulder and down her back to her bottom, and the other arm about her folded legs and her bottom, and so enfolded all of her in one embrace, and this was what he wanted—she was his love-child! His little girl..

Yes, he said, come, show me the city! She untangled herself, whipping her long hair out of the crook of his arm where it had become entangled and muttered tartly that she wouldn't be able to show him much of the city in that fetal position, and he realized then and there that he would never be able to nestle her in the crook of his arm. Just as she straightened out, she gave a sharp shriek at least an octave higher than any other he had heard (has it been mentioned that her normal speaking voice was already an octave higher than the normal? He had felt from the first that she had the vocal cords of a bird.), bent down again, picking up an object and said, look, Augustus (wasn't that the first time she used his name? It enchanted his sentimental ear—most of his organs were just as sentimental, after all!), a spondylus shell! He peered closely at the incarnate spiny shell in the palm of her hand. It's rosy tones and sharp ridges suggested a film of blood which contrasted with a dash of blue. He was quite sure there was not a spot of blood on the childlike white hand (with its very female fingernails) or on the shell.

Why, what's it for? asked Augustus.

It's used in our special rites, she said, it's highly prized by the h-men, a good omen. He took it gingerly out of her hand and let out a little yelp when it scratched a finger and a drop of his blood oozed onto the tip of a spike.

What are h-men, he asked.

H-men say the prayers, she said. He remembered the subway priests.

Ah, he said, and as he turned the shell idly his eye was caught by some hair-fine lines, which had been highlighted by the gloss of blood still on his fingertip on the concave side of the shell. Looking closer he saw the head of a prince, of some *ahau* delicately incised, the head reddish, wrapped in a sort of floppy turban painted a brilliantly contrasting blue with a warm tropical hue to it, an indigo blue—into which were stuck several little sticks, some of which appeared to blossom at the tips, and a curious curved blade-like stick. Look at this, Princess, he said, what is it? She reached out and took the shell fragment and looked at it attentively, then turned it around, and he, following her gaze, saw that some hieroglyphs had been incised in a smooth part of the shell.

Its'at she spelled out slowly. Then her face lengthened, drew out into meditative seriousness. It's the sign of an *Ah k'u hun*, she said in a hushed tone. She turned the shell again and pointed at the blue spot, you see, she said, that is the blue headdress of this exalted scribe, "He of the Holy Books". The blossoming little stick bundles in his hair are brush pens. He must have lost it when he came out this way.

Yes but what was he doing here? he asked. The Butterfly Princess glanced at him knowingly but said nothing.

Let's see if we can find him, she said, and give it back to him. He nodded and they hurried on stage. For the entire city of Tikal appeared replete with stage-settings: this theatre of the urban setting suggested an irresistible ordering hand at the summit, which placed one piece in relation to the other harmoniously, a cascade of planes with the dense tropical blue of the atmosphere flowing from one to the other. The architecture appeared to have been conceived for spectacles (above) and huge audiences (below). He and the princess talked without pause, he poured his wounded heart out, as they strolled through the dusty empty avenues and plazas and courtyards: like a theatre-house before the audience has arrived: a suspended atmosphere of unvoiced characters and imminent disaster. How could a city of such harmony and grace be articulated about a vision of blood sacrifice and decapitation? Because evidently Tikal was organized for the sake of these bloody spectacles! For example, as the little Princess skipped a step or two ahead of him with that heart-stopping flounce of her tunic, he was nonetheless startled repeatedly by some immense stucco Macaw's beak poking through a wall, or a frantic dancing skeleton god, or a crocodile spirit, its snout yawing through the masonry. The amount of stucco crocodile snouts or Macaw's beaks lavished on buildings and ball courts was staggering: a city of monster props waiting for a captive audience to bugaboo. The stillness of the city was stifling; the fakery of the stucco spirits fed on the deafening silence with clownish horror. Was that all there was to it? he wondered. It was in the midst of this silence that a cry came echoing down one of the dusty white streets, Ohéé! And cut out in vivid color against the long street there approached his old friend and companion, Tintin, with a bright smile on his open face and a waving hand! That clarity and clean line of Tintin's face was one of his most distinctive features.

Eh bien, mon ami! he exclaimed as he approached, you two gave me the slip! The little princess looked at him with curiosity. She had never seen anybody with this cut-out presence, this *plus-que-parfait* look. Why was Tintin so admirable? Augustus asked himself as the indeed much-admired boy-journalist approached him and his beloved. It might be the matter-of-factness with which Tintin faced every situation. Nothing was too fantastic or too perilous to be taken account of in the realistic frame in which Tintin dealt with such events. For example *Les Sept Boules de Crystal*, "The Seven Crystal Balls", which whizzed about their victims leaving them in a cataleptic and tormented sleep. What was remarkable was that Tintin was able to absorb such an event into the everyday world, study it, track it down, and find a perfectly sensible explanation for it. It was an eminently reassuring aptitude. No doubt it made his fans, Augustus included, feel that his two-dimensional world was more real than the real world itself and that its problems also could be resolved. The earnest young man wore a broad smile and held out both hands. That and his total lack of guile, thought Augustus, taking the proffered hands in both of his and shaking them vigorously. If only he could be more like his Belgian role model!

Well, he began, Please, *mon cher ami,* he said smiling as well, can you make any sense of this?! And he gestured about with his free arm, encompassing much of the landscape, low hills, the "green sea", the palaces and pyramids.

Exactly so, *mon capitaine,* said Tintin, with a slip of the tongue, *euh, mon brave Auguste!* It seems entirely credible, quite conform to the real world, and the young reporter gazed at Augustus just as guilelessly. Or did he? wondered the latter suddenly. Of course his very profession as reporter was a sort of guarantee of verisimilitude: if there is one fundamental criterion of a journalist's world, it must be precisely his conviction of its conformity with the everyday world. He dropped the other's hands and introduced the Butterfly Princess. Tintin initiated an impeccable *baise-main,* but the princess wrested her hand from his puckered lips with alarm, such courtesy being unknown among her people. She stood her ground, eyes flashing, hand clasped to her breasts, arched under the *huipil* with the same fire!

No, no! hastened Augustus, please darling—I mean Princess he corrected quickly (my god, his and Tintin's tongues were tripping over each other!), Monsieur Tintin only meant a sign of deep respect.

Tintin who was always ethnically sensitive blushed in embarrassment at his faux pas, that is the simple moonlike oval of his face was suffused with a deep flush, and he murmured, *Naturellement,* Princess Butterfly. Her frown vanished and she smiled with a sweetness he knew only in her and the faintest trace of mockery as she answered, I know your heart is in the right place, Mr. Tintin, that is rooted in our Maya ways.

In the dead heat which was causing the sweat to pearl down their necks, a little cold breath seemed to blow with these words, and Augustus quickly, in order to cover up the momentary embarrassment, said, But in effect, Tintin, where is the rest of your family? Tournesol, the *Capitaine*? He purposely used the term "family" because there was never any hint of Tintin's immediate family[40], it was as if he had appeared out of a cabbage, or better, being Belgian, out of a Brussels sprout (*choux de Bruxelles*, Brussels "cabbages"). Was not this lack of familial context, of history, every boy's envy?

We don't always travel together, you know, replied the journalist, he is in all ways in Moulinsart, and the Professor also, working on one of his pet projects—teletransportation.

But Milou! surely Milou! said Augustus.

Oh, Milou, said Tintin looking about in mild alarm, he's off chasing some rabbit around the pyramid. Milou! Milou! he shouted, looking about with annoyance, come here immediately! They had stood there for minutes in the broiling sun in the midst of a *sacbe*, one of those sacred roads which goes nowhere, and the Butterfly Princess had been looking from one to the other in astonishment, understanding nothing of the strange little drama that always seemed to play itself out between Augustus and Tintin, as if the latter were the negative of former and the former the positive of the latter. Then it was as if a window had opened in the top part of the image and one could look down on the graceful if powerfully hinged city and zoom down on the three of them standing in the midst of palatial complexes and temple-topped pyramids, dripping in the sun. Gradually, in slow motion, into this frame trots Milou, white tail up stiffly, wagging fast, and consequent baby talk on all sides which he endures perforce. But wait! Milou is tugging at the pant leg of Tintin who, with his usual respect for his dog's intelligence, yields and follows the little dog while gesturing to his companions with insistence that they follow along. As they plodded through the dusty streets, Augustus marveled at the lack of vegetation in the city proper—the green sea of the *yax* forest lay far beyond—and the Butterfly Princess said yes, all the trees had been cut down, the embryonic cord was stretched thin.. A clump of reeds sprouted near the edge of the pyramid and as they started up the steps, his fingers stroked the feathery dry skin of the plants as he always did. Plant beings speak with the Shaman, he remembered his friend Carl say, and there was something sad and premonitory about this intimate communication with the tiny face or limb of a reed nestled in his palm. The Butterfly Princess, who, though tall for a Maya woman, came up only to his chest, glanced at him with a knowing glance also, as

40   The Boy-reporter's lack of progenitors says much of his involvement with Augustus's—and indeed the young candidate-king's—preoccupation with an overwhelming mother and a dispensable father.

she had seen and understood his communication with the plant beings. They clambered up the steep steps, he breathing hard although the princess did not seem winded—she seemed almost to flutter from step to step! And Tintin bounded with annoying vigor, which seemed to belong more to his Comic Book medium than to the real world. They could hear Milou, now out of sight, barking wildly from somewhere on top of the pyramid. They stopped for a moment at the penultimate landing, staring up at the temple with its roof comb another hundred feet above them, and below at the fluid layout of avenues and ball courts and pyramidal platforms. Then a last effort and they were at the top in front of the doorway of the temple. Milou was nowhere to be seen, but a couple of hollow barks betrayed his presence inside the temple. Across the threshold of skulls and through the usual gaping maws of the portal, they disappeared inside. Although the temple routine was quite familiar to them by now—the dank walls, the warriors in relief, the hieroglyphs, the Sapodilla-wood lintels with engravings of the gods—they stopped short in front of a great wall painting next to the door of the usual *pib na*: delicate crooked fingers holding a brush pen issue from the split-open jaws of a grotesque reptile, the "Bearded Dragon". The little princess pressed against Augustus, taken by a fit of trembling; he welcomed the soft curves pressed into his flank; he even raised his arm and put it around her to accommodate the gentle pressure of her breast against his ribs. The rondure of her breast yielded satisfyingly.

Are you afraid? he asked.

I'm not afraid of anything! she said, eyes flashing. But he is the *Ah k'u hun*. He witnesses the unfolding of the drama that he has set in motion! Tintin looked at her with arched eyebrows, then at Augustus. The latter shook his head, nonplussed. They walked through the open doorway as one man (or woman). A flurry of movement at the lower left corner as Milou scurried up to them whimpering, cowed. Tintin shook a finger at him, and Augustus and the princess bent to caress the quicksilver figure. The little white dog crowded up behind Tintin's legs. Then all three (or four) had eyes only for the reddish-brown figure squatting on the ground in the middle of the *pib na* in a sort of lotus position. He was naked except for a brief wrap-around sarong, and wide jade bracelets. He also wore an indigo blue head cloth binding his short shaggy hair and a bundle of pens stuck in the front of his hair; in the back was stuck the stalk of a graceful water lily. His head was turned sharply in their direction, the whites of his eyes clearly visible against the reddish skin, and he was peering with obvious interest at the Butterfly Princess. His graceful brown body was neither thin nor fat, and the fingers of his left hand were extended in that elegant shamanic gesture Augustus had noticed before, the little finger and the ring finger folded back, the forefinger and the thumb extended out towards them, the index folded into the palm. Unselfconsciousness marked each gesture yet paradoxically he was enrobed with such consciousness that not one of them dared to breathe for several seconds: and now words bubbled up in front of (or in the middle of) his forehead in the most buoyant of hieroglyphs: wakeful eyelight! It was clear he was speaking to the Butterfly Princess, and as Tintin with dot-eyes and Augustus with myopic eyes followed the radiant gaze of the *Ah k'u hun*, traveling as it were along their beams, they also looked into the limpid depths of her eyes which appeared enormous now, a smatter of gray above blue-green as if they were an ocean view when the waters are rocky, and it seemed as if they were all eyes suspended above these eyes..

You are a shamanic couple, he said without turning to Augustus, as if he were looking at him with an eye situated outside of the immediate context, I am happy for you. The latter was deeply touched that the *Ah k'u hun* had understood their being together, although he was not sure what he meant by a "shamanic" couple. Were his eyes watering, then? Why did he feel this happiness to be so ephemeral?

Yes, Lord, *Ahau*, said Tintin with acumen, have we not met before? And the curious, ever-inquiring gaze of the boy-reporter focused in a very unmystical way upon the extraordinary scribe, those elementary eyebrows flickering in complimentary acute and grave accents, so ` ´ .

My point exactly, put in Augustus, for he also had noticed the startling coincidence of the eyes—bottomless, warm, utterly familiar and unutterably intense—of the *Ah k'u hun* with those of his oldest friend, Carl, as substantiated by the footnote[41].

What footnote, said Tintin immediately, glancing downward. Oh, very well, he said, focusing again upon the prince of scribes. Augustus watched the quick reprise of his companion admiringly. He was not unhappy that Tintin had accompanied him on this visitation. His reflexes in these situations were so acute.

Sir, he said, leaning forward in an extension of the upper body and a stretching forward of a lowered head in a mark of respect, and also in order to get a closer look at the eye of the *Ah k'u hun*,

41   There is no footnote—Augsutus was simply testing his old friend.

the eye that is that was turned toward them and which appeared to be suspended almost independently in the atmosphere of that hill-top, as the Maya thought of their pyramidal "mound" constructions, this, sir, is Princess Butterfly, but it was then that he at last recognized his oldest and dearest friend, Carl! *Ah k'ul!* he blurted in confusion, while the girl-princess touched the Scribe Prince's hand.

Uncle, she whispered, eyes cast down, and the little white dog, somewhat older and fatter than Augustus remembered, raised up on its hind legs and pawed at the *Ah k'u hun's* leg panting, tongue out, with the huge grin only dogs can manage. The Scribe rubbed its head and neck affectionately. Augustus watched his companions bunched up about the Scribe with mounting astonishment.

I will never cease to be surprised by the volatility of the human heart, he murmured to Milou, we penetrate deep inside the Petén peninsula in order to reconnoiter and what do we discover? That they are also us! Now the Scribe extended one hand and it was as if they had been peeled out of the present.

Carl! said Augustus again, and the Scribe Prince reached out a hand and enclosed Augustus' hand in his own, and the long, delicate fingers were of such warmth and emotion that it was as if he were held in a deep embrace.

Zwischenwelt, murmured Carl-Ah k'u, remember, my dear brother, that we are neither all here nor all there. And it was as if Carl sat in the midst of a transparent block of jade, and so was limited to minimal gestures, but the warm current which eddied through his eyes and embraced them all with its spiritual electricity made up for any gestures, and he said: I think that we should cut to the chase. Don't forget, we Maya do not have much time left. What you must know is that the "living" Shamans out of the past are still alive in the unconscious regions of the mind. And this ecstatic awakening brings about the release of psychic energies. My dearest friends! And you, Flower of the Air, and the Scribe's smile was tender as he spoke to the little princess, what brings you here?

The long black hair shook about her face in a coiling jumble, him, she said, with a sideways flash of her eyes toward Augustus, I wanted him to see very far, backward and forward, very clearly, like the ancestors, Jaguar Kitzle and Jaguar Night, Not Right Now and Dark Jaguar[42]!

And do you, my brother? asked the Prince of Scribes.

---

42   In the Popul Vuh, the holy book of the Maya, the forefathers, Jaguar Kitzle etc. could see as far as the gods. Hence the gods were careful to cloud the sight of their descendants.

I don't know, said Augustus, for I always seem to make mortal mistakes. Nonetheless his knowledge had become more intense, and he thought he did perceive the transparency of the world, and had begun to see through the stone and plaster, through to the *Yax*-green sea.. His hand still clasped in Carl-*Ah k'u hun's* hand, he turned to the princess and said, Flower of the Air! Come back with me to Manahatta! I have taken an apartment in the southernmost tip of the city as a lookout post, it looks out on the entire Upper New York Bay. Anything suspicious approaching the island would be immediately perceived.

She looked at him with huge mournful eyes, How can I, Augustus? I cannot leave my mother, my brother, my people!

Ah, *mon cher Auguste*! intervened Tintin now, who could never resist putting in his two-cents worth, and who had a strong sense of hierarchy however irreverently he was capable of acting, you must realize she is of the dynasty and has certain obligations. He looked down seriously at Augustus, blinking several times. With his dot eyes this already subtle gesture became almost imperceptible. There were times when Tintin's solar plexus seemed positively to glow with self-righteousness. Augustus glanced back at the Scribe-Prince whose eye gleamed mischievously.

Self-experimentation, Augustus my brother, it is all a matter of self-experimentation in the psycho-physical organism! These words of his oldest and closest friend resonated in his ears. He looked about at his companions. He had been fixated on the inexplicable and ambiguous figure of the Scribe (it fluctuated in and out of focus, from "Carl" to "*Ah k'u hun*"), so now he turned to his old friend of humanist creed (in its definition, physicality, ideal humanity).

You are comforting, he said to Tintin—it's that first presentation which hooked me. Tintin gazed at him non-plussed. Tintin was already in process of self-experimentation himself, he realized. You know, Tintin, he said impulsively, your presence has always been so convincing. It is a matter of not being duplicitous, he added. Tintin beamed at him with his sunny countenance.

It's all part of the *métier, Auguste*. That's my character.

The princess who had been listening intently to this conversation, nodded. Like me, Augustus, she said in her bird-pitch voice. The character *Malinche*. It's written for me. It's mine.

Little Wild Flower, said the *Ah k'u hun*, this is for you. And he drew from behind his ear a tiny ear-shaped flower known as the "ear-flower", the Cymbalopetalum penduliflorum, which was used for chocolate flavoring. Now it is well known that the Maya used chocolate drink for many ceremonial occasions, and in particular for marriage negotiations; so that Princess "Wild Flower" knew exactly why the Scribe was proffering it to her, and so did Augustus. In fact "marriage negotiator" was one of the roles of the *Ah k'u hun.*

Tintin said, with that quick modesty that always became him, Forgive me Auguste, I did not realize that the negotiations had reached this point.

They haven't! I mean I didn't know either, said a flustered Augustus. Wild Flower (her nicknames were interchangeable) pouted, staring boldly at Augustus. She obviously had doubts. Then she blew air through her lips abruptly making them vibrate and shook her head of black curly hair, and said, I'd rather have a cup of chocolate drink, nuncle! And she burst out laughing. Augustus laughed in delight at her whimsy, but secretly he was troubled as well as moved. Milou jumped up and down barking, infected by the general good humor. Tintin caught his doggie by its front paws and sang tra-la-la-la-la, dancing about the small sacred room with him. Princess Wildflower jumped up and down squealing with delight. The others smiled broadly at the odd sight of the comic book character picked out with such graphic brilliance against the backdrop of the grave *pib na* and the Mayan princess, both hopping about and making a racket.

Well, said Carl *k'u hun* to Augustus, as the Song goes, Love is as strong as Death; Death is the next to last; the last is Love. And with that he arose from his squatting position and disappeared. But just before he did, when he had turned away from them, Augustus saw that what had looked like a large quill behind his ear was in reality a deer's ear and just before he disappeared, the last thing they all saw was the two large tufted deer ears fluttering at them!

Well, said Tintin, turning to the others, ever the demystifier, it's not that he's actually disappeared, I've seen this in Tibet[43]. The Shaman is capable of a sort of extreme acceleration as well as a radical slow down, which could be compared to the body movements of Kara-te. Research has been done on the "Bioplasma" which arises out of the movement of electrons between atomic nuclei. Through autogenic training or shamanistic exercises apparently it is possible to potentiate and control this substance. Ultra-weak radiation which was first observed by A. Popp in the sixties arises among gifted and shamanistically educated persons.[44] It seems that our friend *Ah k'u hun* has realized this

43   *Tintin au Tibet*

44   Cf notes on the subject in Zwischen dem Einst und dem Einst,

potentiality. Tintin's round face practically glowed with heuristic satisfaction. Augustus, while nodding his head, could not refrain from looking around at the stone and plaster walls for some crack, some trace of an opening, and Milou, who was perhaps even more logical and down-to-earth than his master, sniffed frantically about the small space of the room. Tintin squatted down and Milou swarmed about his ankles and hands snuffling loudly, as if he were after all much indicated for the job. Nothing there, I'm afraid, *mes amis*, nothing at all, said Tintin straightening up.

But there must be, said Augustus frowning, and stared down at the seamless floor. Tintin began to pace up and down the cell, hands behind his back, a look of deep concentration creasing his brow.

It's the second time he's done that. If only the Dupont(d)s were here! he muttered.

Augustus remained plunged in a brown study. But what was he referring to when he said "We Maya do not have much time left"?

That's obvious, dumbo, said the princess, ruffling his ears, the scribes' writing is beginning to flocculate. Tintin suddenly stopped pacing, eyes widening.

Yes, haven't you noticed, he said, that Long Count inscriptions show us to be almost in the tenth *baktun*? Augustus shook his head, he was embarrassed to admit but he had always had trouble with the famous Long Count, what with the *Tzolkin* meshing with the *tun* in those permutations which added up to millions of years.

And what does that mean? he asked testily.

It means things are beginning to fall apart. It always starts with the writing. The great masters like *Ah k'u hun* Carl, Smoking Monkey, still manage to fuse the elements of hand and eye, brush and pen—but lesser scribes find that their script begins to floccu-late and then to disaggregate.

How do you know this, Tintin? asked Augustus somewhat querulously.

I have spent time in the Petén, you know that,[45] said Tintin. And I can see there is a great deal of anxiety in the air among the Maya.

Yes, said Princess Butterfly, you have put it quite correctly. It is because our world has been breaking at the edges and become

---

Carlfriedrich Claus, Janus Press, 1993, from which Tintin derived this information.

45   This is unverifiable. When Tintin visited the Picaros in L'Oreille Cassée, The Broken Ear, it is conceivable that in his free time he may have visited the Chambers of Inscription..

permeable that our warriors sometimes fall through the cracks to your Manahatta—or you yourselves stumble through into our ball courts and our private steam-rooms, and she glanced provocatively at Augustus, and then burst into the silvery laughter that tickled him pink.

Well then, said Tintin, a light bulb going on above his head like a glyph—then he must have just permeated through! The interconnectedness of reality as a dynamic conversation—that is what he called it! Augustus looked from one to the other. Milou as well: first left, then right.

Well, he said also, after a long pause. Will you come with me to Manhattan then? And without looking back at his *Malinche*, he got up and walked out. The Butterfly Princess followed close behind, and behind her Tintin, and behind Tintin, Milou. Just outside the door they found themselves piled up in extremely tight quarters in the pitch dark, in fact the little princess's breasts were scrunched sweetly into his lower back, and Tintin was excusing himself profusely to the princess because of the embarrassing squeeze and Milou was uttering little shrieks under Tintin's feet. Augustus had stopped short because he had come up against a railing in the darkness, and simultaneously with the delicious softness of her body practically molded into his back, her groin yielding against his upper thigh—what memories this sweet press evoked! In front he sensed a vast cool openness and now that his eyes had adapted to the dark light he saw they were perched on a pinnacle: it was the tiny watch-tower surmounting the central spire, which was surrounded below by narrow turrets and below these by the abysmal drop of the Gothic castle walls with their Mayan gargoyles of crocodile snouts on the south-west wall of the Sherry-Netherland Hotel on the corner of Central Park. Well, they clung together with fright for a moment hanging as it were over an abyss, but soon recovered, this was not the first time was it? Tintin gazed outward, pointing with outstretched hand toward another tower, which stood equally high on the other side of the street in the chasm below. His face appeared to glow even in that gloomy lighting (or was it simply the brighter coloring of his figure compared to theirs?):

Allôôô, he cried out, leaning a little too far over the balcony, so that Augustus in a reflex jutted out a protective elbow to hold him back. The Butterfly Princess glanced up into Augustus' face twinkling with merriment. He shrugged and then froze:

Allôôôôôô, came in answer and with extraordinary proximity, as if rebounding from a vaulted enclosure.

You hear? said Tintin, easing down behind the railing again, and with a broad smile on his pencil-line lips, reverberations still shuddering about them, these edifices have the most remarkable acoustics, especially this Temple of the Masks, it seems that the priests, the shamans, in the old days could communicate with one another from the tops of the buildings, while the masses below were shrieking and drumming.

But—but—but—stuttered Augustus, staring down the drop-away gorge of their building and taking in an immense creeper that ran along the flank of the building many stories below. Then swiveling slowly about, he scanned the faintly violet lurid sky which might have been a harbinger of dawn but only reflected the nighttime city, and as he turned the close-up grain of the tower on which they stood drifted stubbly by his eyes, then receded into the distance while another pyramidal tower, then the *yax*-green of a wide vista of trees, fanned open. But Tintin, he finally said, this can't be the right file, be realistic!

Tintin, who really could take almost anything in stride, glanced at him a little huffily: I think, *mon cher*, you will recognize these glyphs, and he nodded his head backward over his shoulder, his yellow cowlick nodding crossly. Augustus looked behind himself at the doorway through which they had just come, and there along the right side of the door, cut in relief in the cement surface, was a vertical row of distinctly Maya glyphs. How could he have missed it? Butterfly Princess squeezed past them and touched the stone carving sensuously.

You see this middle glyph, she said, with the face, the arched nose and down-turned mouth? That is the King—and this one at the bottom, and she bent down and touched the contours of the carving, and Augustus was annoyed that Tintin should also witness the contours of the soft swell at the top of her thighs, although he was quite sure the latter's virginal nature would no doubt avert etc. He nevertheless glanced sharply at his cartoonish friend who was gazing with (perhaps too) obvious decorum at the glyphs in question. This one, said the little princess, is the noun *ts'ib*, "writing.

Aahhh, said Tintin and Augustus together, it was as if they had exhaled together with surprise. Augustus stepped forward and placed one hand on the stone carving, feeling the inch-deep troughs.

Now do you see? asked Tintin.

Writing, eh? A glib glyph, he chuckled..

It is our profession, the other said seriously. We are all scribes of a sort. I am only a "boy-journalist", but—

Och bih, said the Butterfly Princess with penetration—Carl has entered upon the road. Augustus gazed into the eyes of the princess and their utterly clear depths fluctuated between grey and green and blue: something of the graininess of a pyramid, something of an indigo sky, something of the *yax* green sea. He knew he was lost in it.

The *Ah K'u Hun,* you mean, he said, looking hard at her. She nodded. Carl, he said, bowing his head. Tintin put an arm about his shoulders, and he merged, flesh and blood with the flat-dimensioned, cartoon-color boy-hero at that moment. He shed salt tears and Tintin graphic ones, for Tintin was a good fellow with warm feelings and had shed a bitter tear more than once for fellow-beings[46].

This is the White Road down which all Shamans, lords and princes fall at their death, said the little princess with a transfigured air, they fall along the *Xibal Be,* the Road of Awe. They fall into the Portal called the *Ek-Way,* the "Black Transformer" or the "Black Dreamplace". The Princess spoke as if in trance, and Augustus gaped at her, mouth open. His heart had caught in his throat at her words.

I see it, he said, I begin to understand what is happening here. It's about dying, isn't it? Only by accepting death can the Shaman's form be changed. She nodded with strange authority. And that explains about us, how we can be together in spite of the incongruence... The black dreamplace.

Yes, said Tintin, and the Maya are taking this route to reach us.

No, said Augustus, it is because they always have taken this route that they reach us.

But do you mean, and Tintin nodded toward the narrow tower behind them, that this is a sort of axis mundi?

Yes, she said. And for us the *Ek-Way* is the Portal through which things emerge from that Other World. They know that is how you came to Tikal.

Eh bien, mon cher Auguste, said Tintin with a wry smile (in spite of the paucity of his facial traits, indeed their near-abstraction, Tintin was capable of expressing even the subtler shades of emotion), perhaps we'd better start down that *Wakah Chan* ourselves if we want to keep our feet on the ground and clear up this suspicious affair. Augustus smiled, for Tintin, in his understandable anxiety to render a prosaic and rational universe, sounded a

---

46   In The Blue Lotus, for the young Chinese, Wang; and more than once for a putatively lost or drowned or devoured Milou.

wee bit like his notorious detective friends, Dupont and Dupond. And they headed for the portal and found their way down the internal space-time corkscrew staircase, one person—or dog—at a time, and again predictably back to the dragon-festooned and stuccoed grand entrance past the cubic doorman and out to the elevator hallway. Fifty stories below, Manahatta was much as they had left it—some slight alterations not immediately apparent. Only later did they notice the small signs. But for a few blessed moments, they stood outside the Sherry-Netherland in the fresh air blowing from the Park at the opposite corner. Their attention was drawn by the garbled murmur of a small crowd, which was craning its collective neck upwards to the side of the building they had just come out of. Augustus could feel the air crackle with their anxiety. The princess tugged him by the flap of his jacket and tilted her nose upward. He followed it: what had started the buzz was the giant creeper he had spied from the top of the building just half an hour ago. The creeper was the characteristic *yax* green, you could tell in spite of the late hour because lights had twinkled on up and down the facade of the hotel. It had emerged about half way up the building and then "crawled" seven or eight floors higher. Was it already too late, wondered Augustus?

Come on, he said to the Butterfly Princess, let's go. He held his hand in the small of her back just so he could feel her lithe body pivot about her hips as her legs flew out to the slight oscillations of her back, all these lines of her energy rippling through his fingers. She had not looked at him when he spoke, but just seemed to trust him implicitly. Yes, he said, it is the southernmost building on the island. I got it for its exposure to the Upper New York Bay. I thought it would be useful to have a lookout point, as your people will no doubt arrive from that cardinal direction one day. It's not far from where Peter Minuit once lived. The second Governor of the Island. And of my people—our people, he corrected hastily, catching Tintin's reproachful glance. For he and Tintin did have a common origin in the Walloon people who first settled Manahatta. They had come to the metro now, and so would part.

Why Peter Midnight? said Tintin.

Why indeed, said Augustus. Fit for a rival BD series! The last hour. Ominous. Perhaps the end of a Maya cycle.

Well, said Tintin. I must go. Get some shut-eye.

Yes, said Augustus, although shut-eye was what he least of all had in mind. Tintin and Milou sauntered down the street in the direction of their hotel, while Augustus and his little princess descended into the City Hall subway stop to get the number 5 to Bowling

Green, the last stop on the island before disappearing under the East River to Brooklyn, a foreign country. She took his arm with a sweetly possessive gesture. When they arrived a level down underground, he noticed an immense scaly root, which protruded partly from the tunnel wall.

Yes, said Princess Flower, the root of the *ceiba* tree. The ceiba tree, he knew, was venerated by the Maya and was the greatest tree of the virgin forest. *Wakah-Chan*, she added below her breath.

Curious that it should grow here, he said. Some remnant, I suppose. Still, I didn't think the *ceiba* was a likely candidate for Manhattan flora. A skip in time on the express train to Bowling Green and they were home. Waves slopped up just feet away among the fluorescent-lit piles of the artificial pier, and a dark blue wind murmured still in this early April evening. He kissed the little princess among the wisps of hair at the nape of her neck, and she cried out with the glee of a child at the vista of ocean and sky when they stepped inside the front entrance of the little apartment. After the door closed behind them there was no more witness to their intimacy. Only a mythical language could serve and that would border on kitsch. A jaguar caught in the coils of a boa constrictor, flashed in his mind's eye afterwards.

tu Waybil Ox-Bolon-Chak, she whispered as his body was liquefied in hers, enter into your dreaming-place.. Now as they lay exhausted and trembling on the shore of passion, they rested from the sorcerous combat. It was like giving birth, he thought.

Sweet Butterfly, have you lived all your life in Tikal?

No, I was born in *Altun Ha'* (she pronounced the name with the emphasis on the Ha like an explosive laugh. Near the sea, the Maya traded for our jade and obsidian and conch shell. The color of the water there is Maya Indigo—a metaphysical turquoise, the color of the not-yet-existent. He gazed at the changing tones of the sea off the shores of Altun Ha visible in the blues and greens of Butterfly's eyes. And the coral sea in the girlish pink of her vagina. Above their resting heads now the clouds were scrolls: *tzak* is to "conjure", to conjure clouds, the medium from which the vision comes. He knew that with the Butterfly Princess as his *Malinche* he had entered into virgin territory. It was when they left the apartment that they first noticed the change. As they emerged, flushed as it were, into the garden park behind their building, they were met with a rich gabble of birds—as if spring had just turned the corner. The trees were a more pregnant green and the sea behind them a more fertile blue than they remembered, or was it their heightened senses? It's true that after amorous hijinx and the spilling of seed he would luxuriate in half-dream in the most sensuous colors, bathed in the after-glow of orgasm. But this was no dream, it was quite exactly Wagner Park and beyond the waterfront promenade, the re-imagined sea piles of a concept and sound artist. They walked hand in hand and gazed at West New York across the Hudson and out in the Upper New York Bay at Governor Island etc., and when from some nearby grove a calliope-burst of wild turkey burst on their ears, the phenomenal enhancement was undeniable. And as they walked south on Green Street, he noticed an Escher-like dynamic of stairs climbing up and down at right angles against the side of a building.

I just think I'll take a look, he said.. They went up to the edge of the wall, and he started up the steps. It was an odd climb since he walked up with his left side parallel to the wall, leaning slightly against it for security since the steps extended only twelve inches out from the wall, and when he came to the second flight of steps which started back in the opposite direction, he had to make a 180 degree turn and walk up with his right side now rubbing along the wall, and it felt unbalanced and risky. When the stairs (and he) reached the top edge of the wall, he had to step around and over the edge onto another set of stairs which were situated in a different (frontal) dimension across the front of the building, which now appeared by some architectural sleight of hand to be pyramidal and on a slant—the parallel world his *Malinche* had led him to.. Just before he stepped around he glanced down at the upturned white splash of her face and her breasts that were pulled in a taut upwards tilt by her stretched posture. He swung about the edge of the building and started up this new, frontal set of steps toward an ornate triple doorway at the top. The stair was much wider since it spread right across the steep façade of the pyramid, and the steps were very much higher, so that he had to clamber rather than step up, pulling himself up on hands and knees. He glanced down over his shoulder and looked almost vertically far below onto a great fancy headdress and beneath it a broad rump in a flowery dress, and farther down, onto a pith helmet with skinny shoulders and childlike arms which flailed about the giant building-block steps. American tourists climbing beneath him? he wondered—and then shrugged dismissively and continued on up quickly. A couple of black dots flashed overhead, and it wasn't until he got to the top that he realized they were swallows swooping in and out of the arched entrances. Bending over, he hurried in beneath the awkward corbelled arches of the Maya: dank and perspiring stone and plaster corridors and meditation (?) rooms with their peaked ceilings, vast stone benches far too high and broad for the short Maya to sit on, then he realized that these were the platforms the *ahauob* reclined on, with their pillows and jaguar skins, their enemas and young female attendants. Every once in a while a swallow swept along the low ceilings almost brushing his head. He came to a ventilation slot in the thick wall on the other side of the temple, and found himself peeping down onto a ball court. Dense groves of palm and eucalyptus beyond advanced upon the intrinsic fragilities of this civilization, its structural faults—which one day would be infiltrated by fronds and creepers, and ultimately submerged—the *"yaxing"*[47] of Manhattan. He remained plunged in thought for moments, until he was brusquely awakened from his reverie by the shuffle of feet in the corridor outside. My fellow tourists! he remembered the two remote figures below him on the stairway outside. And to his startled gaze were revealed, wearing the pith helmet, the tiny *Professeur* Tournesol with poodle-cut large moustache and goatee and equally startled gaze and wrinkled brow, and towering above him in flowery and beribboned headdress, the Italian diva, Bianca de Castafiore, with doughy jowls and bright blonde hair, beaked nose and deep red lips..

Wha—what are you doing here! he exclaimed. La Castafiore shook her dyed yellow perm with a tinkling laugh,

Ah, *mon cherrr ami, this galant'uomo,* this Casanova, I'm afraid!! has been insisting I accompany him up this historical monument, I do hope! with no ill intentions towards me!! A cascade of pianoforte laughter.

And the diminutive savant and inventor, pigeon chest puffed out, wispy goatee trembling, declared:

But of course absolutely! But this poor child! It is out of question! Harrumph! Augustus looked at him dubiously. Was he mistaken, he wondered, or did the absent-minded professor have his right hand somewhere beneath the diva's considerable rump? He dismissed the thought as soon as it arose, ashamed of himself. As if the childlike and lovable Man of Science..! La Castafiore appeared to be squirming oddly. But no matter.

Professor, he asked, are Tintin and the *Capitaine* anywhere below there?

The Professor glared at Augustus, his eyebrows practically crackling with indignation, But absolutely not! But why should they "be lovers there"?! Just because they live together in the Chateau! They are but the best of friends! Augustus held up his

---

47   "Yax" it will be remembered is the dark, near-tactile Maya green of the rain-forest.

hands, palms outward in disbelief,

Very well, very well! I just was asking! And he did a sort of semi-circle side step about the couple while still facing them, and as he came around he saw that the little professor did indeed have his right hand tucked in between the sofa cheeks of the La Scala Soprano's operatic posterior. I shall leave you your privacy, he said. He beat a hasty retreat back to the entry of the temple-structure. He had no desire to witness the debacle. He hurried down the steep stairs to the grassy plaza below. A *pibnut* scurried across his path, long monkey-tale a raised banner, long doggy-nose snuffling for possible tidbits. A *motmot* screeched overhead. He gazed across the vacant plaza, not a tourist in sight. At the far left corner of the vast court yard a barman is serving drinks, and in this moment is pouring out some yellow beverage for a personage hidden from our view behind the corner of a one-story ornate building. He hurries over, his own footsteps thudded in his ears, an inexplicable shift has taken place in the urban landscape, foreboding fills him. When he has come within fifteen feet of the scene and can clearly see the white-jacketed back of the waiter, there is a sudden flurry of movement, the arms of the waiter and the tray and bottle and glass he had no doubt been serving flew up in the air, and as he teetered around Augustus recognized the very proper butler, Nestor, unflappable as always—and about him galloped the disheveled figure of Captain Haddock in flapping pajamas, his black hair and beard unruly, eyes popping, who raced into the front portal of the small and noble mansion. Augustus naturally sped after him, while Nestor was bent over picking up shattered glass, a strong smell of whisky[48] hanging in the hot and humid air. Unlike the archaic and time-worn temple he had just come down from, the interior of this aristocratic home was comfortable and pleasing, the floor of polished marble with a Persian rug, wall-length drapes at the windows on the opposite side of the large salon and a Louis XV escritoire to one side. The Captain who had come to a halt just in front of Augustus now was staring toward the rear wall—and Augustus stared as well—at Tintin who was standing on his head, arms clasped behind his neck in a yoga-type position, legs straight up, blue pajamas drifting down the well-shaped pink legs and the famous blond forelock resting on the floor. He appeared to be in excellent shape and was in a certain state, no doubt induced by the invigoration of the exercise. The good Captain walked right up to the upside down Tintin and looked

48   Loch Lomond, the Captain's favorite brand. It is usually represented as having a faint yellowish tint. Augustus who was not a whisky drinker could not really judge.

straight down. Alan could hear the Captain say, *C'est renversant, non?* which literally means doesn't it knock you over, or upside down? No doubt by way of a witticism, but the Captain's gestures were hidden from his sight and Tintin was altogether concealed except for his feet shaking in the air.[49] Again Augustus beat a hasty retreat, although he did not believe in anything other than the platonic nature of this deep friendship. Outside Nestor had gathered up the mess and was carrying it off to dispose of it somewhere, and *Professeur* Tournesol had just arrived although there was no sign of la Castafiore, the poor woman was probably resting from her exertions. As Augustus turned back to the pyramid-temple, the Captain emerged from the entrance of the mansion with a flushed face, and went up immediately to Tournesol, with whom he was soon plunged in consultation. Augustus headed back somewhat disconsolate regarding the lost innocence of childhood, and started to climb the steep steps of the pyramid-temple again aimlessly. Then it occurred to him—why should he not return the same way he had come? Straddling the corner, he lowered himself carefully and dropped down again onto the sideways-climbing stairs along the vertical side of the building. The view was the usual bleak one of the back streets—not a shred of green in sight. To check his intuition, he ran up a few steps to the top and pulled himself about the edge of the vertical building wall, then leaned across the edge of the pyramid to where the stairs slanted steeply down to the green plaza. Off beyond the palatial home on the other side of the plaza was the towering rain forest and of course *yax, yax, yax.* Just when he was gazing, a swish of silk swirled above his ears, and barely a foot from his outstretched neck and head passed the elaborate Diva on her way down, entirely oblivious of him, taking big, awkward steps down the high stairs, knees widespread, hiking her flowery skirts up, proudly revealing that she had discarded her voluminous knickers for the Professor's depredations. He pushed back hurriedly around the wall and dropped down again onto the lateral stairs with their barely two-foot width abutting onto the vertical wall, and took in the street again. The juxtaposition of the radically different views was startling; the angle at which the vertical wall of the building and the inclined wall of the pyramid met was baffling. Below, the Butterfly Princess had disappeared. He hurried down the steps at a risky pace. When he got down to street level his heart was pounding. He ran out into the street—the pyramid was no longer there, of course, its frontal, steeply inclined facade with the broad steps no longer "hinged" to

49   Literally, from Page 4 of *Tintin et les Picaros*, middle top "window" of the lower half of the page.

the side of the building. Now it was your standard flight of six or seven steps leading up to a double wooden door, ugly but sturdy, like so many of the older urban buildings in the city. The door opened and out came the princess, strangely altered. She was wearing a different dress for one thing, dark blue and flowing to her ankles it was adorned with bright starbursts or blooming flowers, brilliant yellow. She also wore a sort of turban with a bundle of sticks or pencils protruding from it in the front, and her hair bound in a sheaf at the back. Finally a large white shell-pendant hung on her ear. But it was more than just the costume that was different. Her already foxy long profile seemed even longer, perhaps because of the way in which her hair was pulled up and her forehead elongated as a consequence. Or perhaps it was simply the well-known Maya custom of binding the forehead. The gaze she directed towards him under her long lashes, a dreamy yet intent look, floated his way. And as she came down the steps he was startled to see that she was holding out in her hand a mask: the hooked nose, pronounced thin chin and fine forehead of an old god.

My god! he cried out to this apparition, and she jumped, arms akimbo (but still holding the mask), stared down at him, eyes flashing, bosom delicate and pointed, heaving. Her eyes resumed that dazed, stunned look and she raised the mask (he saw now that it was very human, perhaps a flayed human face) to her face level. The nose had a strong aquiline hook, the hair was white and short, the lips were drawn back exhibiting sharpened white teeth and the jaw was unusually long, jutting out. Taken as a whole, the traits conjoined to some sense of fine irony, sophisticated cruelty. She flipped the mask about and fitted it to his face. It adhered effortlessly, he put his fingers quickly to his throat where the mask began, the fine edge curved and flowed so seamlessly into the skin that he could hardly pry up the edge, and he quickly desisted. The mask was obviously made of some very flexible material, perhaps rubber from the *Castilloa Elastica* trees, the same used to manufacture their *Pok-a-Tok* balls, and he could see out of the eyes perfectly and even move the thin lips and maxilla. He saw in a different light through these eyes—a brightening it might be said, and what became patently clear was that the princess was an *Ah k'u hun* in her own right. In his heart he now knew he could not simply cast himself into the abysm of her flesh. She could never be his. She was already beyond the flesh. This is what he saw with the mask, for it was no mere concealment or disguise but a projection of what had been hidden of himself. Then he turned to take another glance at the building with the staircases behind him and realized that they were a representation in architecture of the underlying metaphysics of this doubled city which he on the one hand and the Maya on the other had been exploring. The impossibly hinged walls and angled staircases were the way in which these civilizations communicated. It was clear to him that it was high time to get in touch with the last and seventh member of the team whose vast philosophical undertaking had been the diagnosis and tracking of just such architectures and diagrams. Ignatius had traced the diagrams and palatial architectures of a fundamental figure known as the Circle of Wisdom[50] from the astral religions and the Mithraic mysteries to the Gnostic groups. Similar numeric-geometrical and cosmogonic images had evolved during exactly the same period across Maya Civilization, and its roots plunged with the *Wakah-Chan's* into the Zodiac—above, that is, in the celestial sphere, and below, in diagrams and architectures. He pivoted on his heel and stared into the Butterfly Princess's eyes, transfixed. This was the insight, which the mask had given him! She had become illumination in the flesh for him. He snatched the mask off his face, and handed it back to the princess.

You have opened my eyes. You know what is in my mind before I conceive of it. That is what this "old god's" mask is about, isn't it? He stared at the sweet face she lifted toward him, her great Isis-eyes rolling comically at him.

Of course I do, Augustus, she said. I always know what you are thinking before you think it. That's why you had better be careful what you think! He glanced at her sharply, thinking he must remember never to play poker with her.

You see what I am thinking, then, that not only this building with its odd stairs, but all the buildings we have been 'transiting' through are interiorized (by the shamans) numerical-geometrical orders which can be reflected in diagrams or architectonics. This peculiar building makes it particularly clear in its wrap-around duality, but basically it's the case of those inexplicable passages between all those buildings in Manhattan and the Maya pyramids: their numbers are at work. It is in their mind.

Yes, she said, and her eyes always lit up at talk of numbers and geometries, and what are the numbers? She was pulling off the beautiful, ritual gown because the ritual was done and it was hot—it seemed as if a breeze from the Petén had slipped into the street from around the putative pyramid. Now stripped, she wore only the short white tunic she had on before; when she bent over

50   Ignacio Gomez de Liaño, El Circulo de la Sabiduria, Siruela, 1998, two volumes

to fold the gown the hem of the tunic rose to meet the twin curves of her bottom.

The numbers—the numbers—he murmured distracted by her spherical geometry. He remembered that Ignatius had spoken of that most beautiful of the platonic Pythagorean triangles, with its sides in proportions of 3, 4 & 5: the vertical (3), Osiris; the horizontal or base (4) Isis; and the hypotenuse (5), their fruit Horus.. Threes, fours and fives, he said as he reached out his hand for the fruit, his fingers between her thighs—

What do you mean, threes, fours and fives! she exclaimed, slapping down his hand before it could nestle there. The slap and her tone stung, but her smile was sweet.

Alright, he said, Ignatius quotes Tertulian's comments in the third century on the Valentinian (Gnostic) system, that their heavens have many floors, like apartment buildings—i.e. like our Manhattan "sky-buildings"! These are the buildings whose portals we have been crossing. But what of the numbers? she said.

Those are the numbers of Mithraism and the Barbelognostics! whereby the universe is organized in fours of which Barbelo constitutes the fifth. *Dixit* Ignatius.

On the Tablet of the Cross[51], enjoined the princess, our scribes wrote '*hoy wakah chanal waxacna-tzuk u ch'ul k'aba yotot xaman*, that is, 'it was made proper, the Raised-up Sky Place, the Eight-House-Partition, its holy name, the house of the north.'"

Yes, yes, said Augustus excitedly, that is the important point: these architectural diagrams are reflected in the cosmos, the stars.

Yes! exclaimed Flower, whose mind flared up when she was intellectually excited, as the Raised-Up-Sky House is centered on the axis of the World Tree! The crown of the World Tree, or the Foliated Cross as we call it, lies in the celestial north at the polar star and its roots in the celestial south in the constellation of Scorpion. But what does it all mean?

I don't know, said Augustus, but Tintin recalled that the Paddlers' canoe had sunk into the constellation of Orion, and Professor Tournesol, that with the zodiacal drift the Canoe dipped and sank vertically into the Milky Way at a given time, becoming the *Wakah Chan*! It comes together in the constellations![52] But only Ignatius can tell us, we must talk to him. Right now. Where did Professor Tournesol tell me he had seen him?

---

51   This inscription is one of the most important of the Classic-Maya texts to reach us.
52   *Maya Cosmos* is the title of the most inspired book by the Maya scholars Linda Schele, David Freidel and Joy Parker, in which Schele describes the discovery of the astronomical patterns of Maya cosmogony.

I don't know, I wasn't there, was I! sniffed Butterfly.

At the Spanish Cultural Institute on Park Avenue, where else, he murmured ruminatively. In fact I was on my way there when I was distracted and ended up finding you instead in your birthday suit at the Sweat Baths. He was giving a lecture on his new book, *El Circulo de la Sabiduria*. Maybe he's still lecturing. I don't know how time has gone by.. Perhaps it is yesterday. Either time gets lost or we move at different speeds on the two sides.

Well, the simplest thing would be to go and see, she said with characteristic matter of factness. They took the Lexington express line and within a quarter of an hour were at the 72nd street station. He didn't like the way two business suits had been sneaking glances at his girl's slender honeyed thighs, and got her off in a hurry. He worried about people's reactions at the Institute, but supposed the scandalously short tunic would pass as the latest Versace chic. In another ten minutes they were in front of the Institute on Park, the doors flung open, and people in formal evening wear already bursting into the splash of light the Institute cast onto the dark sidewalk. A couple of hundred people were milling about on the ground floor with glasses of champagne in their hands, happily with hardly a glance for Princess Butterfly's revealing hemline, bunched as they both were in the midst of the crowd, and they made for the narrow crowded staircase. He turned left at the first landing, and realized just as he pushed the door open that the reception was on the third floor. He jerked the half-open door back again but not before he and Butterfly caught sight of the naked, broad, plump, brown back of a man in a wrap-around white tunic of the kind pulled up between the legs like a diaper and an immense beribboned and bundled turban on his head in the small book-lined room. He was leaning backward and his right arm was sharply bent, his right hand pointed backwards over his left shoulder in their direction. In his left hand they could see a vertical strip of a codex with glyphs running down one column, and Augustus immediately surmised that he must be a Maya scribe. Just before the door closed, it became apparent as a face leaned outward to the left of the bent right arm that another man had been blocked out by the first man's back and high turban and was squatting in front of him. He saw half a visage and one eye with a cruel slanted wink, a pronounced muzzle and a flattened nose instead of the ruddy aquiline Maya features he expected, and saw this was a humanoid Monkey, as was no doubt the squat-necked scribe who had his back to him. Right after the door closed he realized the obvious but unthinkable: the latter had been pointing back at them before he had opened the door.

Hun Batz and *Hun Chouen*, murmured Flower. We must be careful. They are malevolent and cunning[53] He looked at her in dismay. But what are they doing here! It's senseless. In the heart of Manhattan! The Spanish Institute of New York! And then his flesh crawled. Of course, Spain! The return. I think the situation is becoming dicey, he murmured to her as they hurried up the steps, hearts pounding, elbowing their way through the crowd. The Scribal Shamans had chosen the Spanish Institute! As if any of the snobbish beau monde of Hispanophile Manhattan cared. The Princesa de Braganza, Honorary President of the Institute, with her wide sexy mouth and socialist sympathies, was honey to the socialite buzz of these Manhattanites. She was standing in a flurry of black chiffon in the center of the formal reception salon, unmistakable even in that seething swell of cocktail dresses and male strut, the frenzied feeding on *tapitas*[54] and champagne refills (the Institute's receptions were particularly well attended), bright laughter like crystal tinkling, a posh occasion in a word. As Augustus and the Butterfly Princess stood at the edges of the solipsist crowd, only one other figure rose above the flood: not because he was particularly tall, but Ignatius occupied space with a kind of quiet authority. It was as if he held court, but in the most disarmingly unassuming manner. The *Princesa* evidently had just asked him a question, and a retinue of young women were hanging on his lips with rapt attention while a dark-eyed, dark-browed, young latino with a blaze of died yellow hair looked on with knitted brows and lips sneering with disdain and—possessiveness.. Augustus pressed at the crowd's breaking edges resolutely with Princess Butterfly in tow on his arm. This interview, this warning! could no longer be put off.

Ignatius! he cried out. *Amigo mio! Filosofo de mi vida*! And the crowd broke and surged, pulling them under and in. Ignatius' grandee profile swerved about and his lips curved in a delicate smile and his eyebrows rose like seagulls above the waves,

Querido amigo mio! he said, well, it's time we met again!

Princesa, said Augustus, Ignatius, may I introduce you to Princess Butterfly de Tikal! The tall elegant red-headed Princess de Braganza, all rustling black organdy and gracious smile atop swan-neck, and the little princess, lithe and tan-limbed in the

---

53   The half-brothers of the Hero Twins of the Popul Vuh. Scribes par excellence.

54   Those exquisite tiny edibles of infinite variety which only a people delighting in late-night snacking and drinking of vino tinto in packed bars like the Spaniards could invent.

revealing white tunic, with a smile as frank and belligerent as a warrior's and black hair swarming about her shoulders, rendered a most poetic chiasmus.

Ah yes, said the former, the indigenous royalty..

Ah yes, said the latter, the royalty of the arrivistes.

Ah yes, said Ignatius, lifting a highly articulate eyebrow, something about pyramids--I seem to remember—

Excuse me for interrupting, interjected Augustus, I urgently require enlightenment on an obscure point. Urgent because, as no doubt is known to some, and here he dipped his head imperceptibly in the direction of the Spanish princess, aware of the faint ridicule his apocalyptic tone might evoke, there is an alien presence about the city and indeed in this very house. As he did so, he asked himself why on earth a Spanish princess would harbor two Maya *Ah K'u Huns* in her Institute when her ancestors.. His thought drifted off into the suspension points of a revelation—perhaps precisely because her ancestors..!

Now then, Augustus, said the philosophical skeptic with a teasing smile, what is this obscurity which requires the logos of illumination?

The *Wakah Chan*, Ignatius, the World Tree of Maya Cosmogony, also called the Foliated Cross, is a fourfold structure. Now the Maya Zodiac shows the constellation of Scorpio is the Milky Way. And the two-headed Vision Serpent, which is draped around and through its branches in Maya depictions, had to be the ecliptic, which actually crosses directly overhead and occupies the zenith position of the sky.[55] Do you believe that this core figure, this celestial north of the Maya, could have a universal correspondence in the civilizations you have studied in your opus magnus. Ignatius had frowned slightly during his tangled description of the great central Mayan mythogram. The outside edges of his brows appeared to widen or stretch apart and then the entire brow to rise like wings taking off, and this produced a sort of extra depth and breadth in the already large eyes, as if to swallow additional light.

It is notorious in the gnosis, he said in one expiring and resigned breath, that Draco, the Celestial Dragon or the Great Serpent, wrapped itself about the Cosmic Tree or the Luminous Cross formed by the equinoctial and solsticial meridians which intersect at right angles at the pole of the ecliptic. In Mithraism, the Cross was the instrument through which the Selfborn acts upon the structures of the Universe.

---

55   Maya Cosmos, Linda Schele, pp. 78 foll.

But then! cried out the Princess de Tikal, that is who it was! The Double-Headed Serpent lying across the arms of the World Tree or the Foliated Cross in the teaching of the *Ah K'u Huns*! The Vision Serpent fed by the blood of my ancestors! The ecliptic lying in its East-West position across the Milky Way!

Excuse me, said Augustus, rubbing his eyes, dazzled and confounded by all this stellar esotericism, but how could the Self-Born possibly be the Great Serpent?

Ah! said Ignatius, You have not quite got it! Let me put it in another way for you, my dear Augustus. Knowing murmurs and nods accompanied the philosopher's ensuing q.e.d: "And then in the Heavens will appear the sign of the Son of Man.." wrote Matthew, and that sign is precisely the Cross upon which is wound Draco in the Mithraic cosmogram. [56] Dead Silence fell upon the crowd. Gone was the clink of glass and the suck and crunch of tooth and tongue and the vocal humdrum. The Princess of Bourbon and the Butterfly Princess appeared to be isolated in the ornate drawing room, Ignatius standing to one side with the faint smile of a Jesuit Counsel. The rest of us including Augustus receded into the shadowy background of supporting cast. An overpowering feral whiff floated over the scene. Augustus guessed that the two Monkey *Ahauob* had in fact joined the fiesta. There was some jumble of motion in the crowd, some scatter and reassembling, which suggested a sudden repulsive smell.

Well, said Princess Butterfly, loftily ignoring what appeared to be a colossal fart, it seems that when your ancestors arrived carrying their Cross, they benefited from a sort of instant translation into our constructions, however erroneously, which allowed them to finish up my people.

I had heard, the Princess de Bourbon finally spoke up throatily, that a certain *Malinche* provided a better—and certainly more seductive—translation. A transparent allusion to the passionate attachment of the Maya princess to the foreign intruder. She rustled a step putting her best silk-clad foot forward.

There is a translation for building up and another for pulling down, said the latter-day *Malinche*. Today you have forgotten your Cross and we have returned with ours. The Princess de B. appeared to be at a loss for words.

It was Ignatius, the Spanish philosopher, who supplied them: Barbelo could have been carrying it, he said, for the Maya. There

---

56   This is an extremely summary conclusion of the lengthy evolution traced from Mithraism via the cruciform division effected by Barbelo in the Ogdoada of the Pleroma to the Johannine Mystical Gospel by Ignacio Gomez de Liano in his great Circulo de la Sabiduria.

was a murmur of relief and an adulatory smattering of applause from the lip-hanging crowd, who obviously hadn't understood a fuck of what had been said. Q.e.d., reflected Augustus, the Maya Universe and the Gnostic Universe are structurally equivalent, and Manhattan and Tikal are *vases communicantes.* But no one had really listened to his philosophical friend's conclusion anyway, delighted and comforted as they were by his rhetorical flourish with Barbelo, and they were crowding in on the momentary celebrity in their midst, the gnashing and the chop-licking taking up again, as if they wished they could gobble him. And the Princess from the old Country had taken him possessively by the elbow again, exuding quite another appetite. Augustus was able to catch his friend's eye for an instant before the crowd surged away with him, and to nod quick confirmation of the football game tomorrow. Ignatius was borne off and he and his Flower princess were left standing there.

PART II

THE GAME

Next to them stood the blonde youth with the twisted mouth and the gimlet eyes. The point is, said Augustus to the thin air, that the dualistic West is heir to the ghost on the cross.

But my dear chap, said the thin air with a honeyed snarl, do you really believe all that academic phooey about the 'foliated cross' and the Barbelognostic cross and the Draco hanging from it, and so forth? I mean our Ignatius has an adorable profile but hasn't he become a little mad with his great learning? The youth giggled at his witticism.

He may not have been struck down on the way to Damascus, said Augustus, but he has shown that a fundamental figure moved underground from West to East in the first centuries of our era which represented the gnosis, the dark knowing. After the orthodox Cross ran its course, this disembodied daemon, the Barbelognostic Set, rose again out of the dualistic split of mind and body, subject and object, matter and spirit in Western rationalism.

Ah, indeed! cried the youth, then give credit where credit is due, to the Sodomites, for as you know, he continued with a patronizing wink, Damascus was the original Sodom and Sodom of course was the city where the Universal Savior, Set, appeared, verbatim from Ignatius' opus[57].

The Butterfly Princess appeared contemptuous of the entire proceedings. She slapped Augustus on the cheek,

Stop it! Enough! Stop talking right now! He looked down at the little princess: her eyes flashed, her white breasts billowed in the loose tunic like a choppy sea. He realized she meant business.

Well, well, all right, my dear fellow, go join *le maitre*, we're off. He offered his arm to the Tikal princess, she took it, and they made their way across the room and down the—before they actually got to the stairs a dark rush or a shadow passed before them trailed by a delayed sound effect, a grunt, or throaty cough. The feral stink that accompanied the grunt was all enveloping and brought up phlegm to the throat, and they both realized the furry coats of the Monkey Scribes had brushed past them, and Augustus drew back with an instinct of horrified avoidance. The Butterfly Princess on the other hand was unperturbed, as befitted

57   Circulo de la Sabiduria, Vol. I, pp.

a female *Ah K'u Hun*,

This is their way, you know, tricky beasts! The moon bathed the avenue, as well it might after such an evening, and they breathed the summer-fresh air with relief. Augustus pointed out to the princess the monumental sculptures splashed milky-white in the moonlight, which had been set up at regular intervals on the traffic islands, as was the custom on Park Avenue for special artistic occasions. But those are *te-tun*, "tree-stones", she exclaimed, what are they doing in Manhattan? He was rather taken aback as well, but he explained the above custom. Yes, but, she replied, have you heard of any exhibition of Maya artifacts?

I don't think so! he concurred, and suggested they go and take a look, so they crossed to the middle of the Avenue to check out the next stela. It was all of seven feet high, solid stone, maybe six or seven feet in girth, a half-effaced relief carved into it. The princess touched it with a knowing hand, but could make out no familiar features—he took that literally as "family". They were obviously the real thing, more than a thousand years old, and it seemed quite implausible that the Avenue should have been lined with a score of them. What a kkkkkkicker of a show, he murmured.

Augustus! she exclaimed, that's no show! There's a major rearrangement of psychic powers and energy zones going on here! These are from Tikal, my people have been to this place, it is they who have brought the *te tuns*. They are trying to—I don't know what—to set up some sort of field of magnetic influences. a portal.

A bit fantastic, Butterfly, a bit far-fetched, don't you think? scoffed, I am afraid, Augustus. The princess just shook her head with an air of "hopeless innocent". A couple of tourists from Des Moines, Idaho, had crossed over during a lull in the traffic, and were admiring the stela with little nods and overhearing the conversation of these "New York literati" as they imagined, with fascination.

You see, Harold, the wife exclaimed during a lull, these are the Stonehenge dolmens!

How did you know they're from Des Moines, asked the princess.

They always are, said Augustus. They strolled on in the pleasant moonlit evening, wondering how a score of two-ton stone monuments could have been transported and deposited along the avenue by the princess's countrymen.

Our warriors are very strong, proffered the princess. Unlike your steroid-stuffed hypertrophic Americans, they are built like blocks close to the ground, they are so compact that no light escapes them, that is why they can handle the *te tuns*. Augustus feared that this did not bode well for the ball game. He said as much to his companion. You cannot use strength against their strength, she said, you'll have to be—I don't know—original? He looked perplexed. They had strolled across town and southward to get to the IRT subway and had now arrived at the corner of 52nd and Sixth opposite a Citibank branch. His mouth dropped open: as high as his chest, the finny roots of a *ceiba* tree plunged into the concrete in front of them, great cracks splitting open to make way, and the astonishingly smooth-skinned, almost feminine trunk rose up from the splintered pavement and towered vertically into the dusk hundreds of feet above their heads.

Whew! he blew the exclamation out of his mouth. The magisterially savage presence of this tropical growth in arguably the most sophisticated urban setting on earth was a shockingly effective artifice, he reflected. Again, the princess looked on quite composed.

Ch'ul, she said, and pointed upwards. He stared up and could make out little white blossoms on the horizontal furry branches of the tree.

Why? he asked.

Soul residue, she said. My people have been around here, they have been very active, they are preparing for a great event, these are traces of their stagecraft.

Well, you know, said he, this really goes beyond the pale. The *te tun* could be explained as a public relations display event, these things are not unusual, but they could hardly have planted this tree over night, whatever their arts budget.

Trees, said the princess, pointing. He followed her outstretched finger and saw ten blocks down the demotic avenue the unmistakable phallic erection of another *ceiba* tree, and many blocks beyond that a feathery wisp which the 20/20 vision of his companion no doubt could make out as yet another *ceiba* tree. A distinct chill traveled down his back. I do not like the fantastic when it is manifested in everyday life, he said at last, it irritates our sense of our being, it smells unhealthy. There must be a rational explanation for this incident.

There is, *mon ami*, there always is, said a friendly voice behind them. They both swiveled around It was Tintin, his shock of yellow hair as implausible and cartoonish as always, with the fuzzy bundle of Milou leaping and straining at his leash, pawing the air between himself and these old friends of his master.

What an incredible coincidence! said Augustus, obviously not much surprised, so that the little princess shot him a meaningful glance, and he hastily sought to correct the impression: My dearest Tintin, he gushed, I am always so glad to see you, but how did you come here?

Oh, *mon cher Auguste*, it is not such a coincidence, you are in our territory here, we are staying at the New York Hilton just up the street, and I always take out my little Milou for his evening walk. Milou looked at his master with a skeptical tilt of his black nose, as if to say, Hmm, not half enough though, but he's a good sort. The timing of the encounter was not ideal in light of Augustus' discomfiture regarding the phenomena occurring about him.

Look, Tintin, you have always been a sound fellow, and I appreciate that, but just look at that thing! Tintin gazed thoughtfully at the giant piece of vegetation.

Have you read about the murders in the Post, asked the latter abruptly. Augustus stared at his friend in shock; again the shock of reality! What? Yes, he had glanced at some screaming headlines on the front page of the New York Post about some particularly gruesome murders. I have inside information because Dupond and Dupont are cooperating with the NYPD on this one, continued Tintin. The papers speak only of 'mutilated bodies' in Queens and the Lower East Side, but I have been told that in all three cases the hearts were removed from under the rib cage on the left side. He turned and shot a brief meaningful look at his "realistic" friend.

The *Popul Vuh*[58], murmured Augustus as if mesmerized, the 'gentle death' of heart removal..

Now you know as well as I know, continued the boy-journalist with impressive, incisive, reportorial concision, because you were there with me at Pier 43 at one such arrival, that waves of illegal Maya immigration are taking place in this city. I am convinced that the Maya are preparing for some major event—perhaps the fifty-second *katun*, the beginning of the great cycle of their Return. I don't know. In any case they are gathering, trust the intelligence of the Dupon(d)t's for this. Augustus gazed at the grim-faced boy-journalist, musing.

And you believe that for an event of this magnitude, no effort—including the installation of these trees—would be too great? Tintin nodded slowly, his forelock bobbing, his little o of a

---

58   The Maya "bible", founding myths of the Maya peoplest, a tardy document which exists only in the Spanish translation of the original.

mouth pursed seriously. This was, suddenly realized Augustus, much in the manner of Tintin's *Aventures*. Well, that makes sense, he said. The little princess, who had been playing with the irrepressible Milou and was just now shaking his paw, looked up. What has always impressed me about you, Tintin, he continued, is your seriousness. Your innate ethical instinct. I know I can place my trust in you, and I think this is what others feel about you. I really doubt this is true about any other figure of your status (he was always delicate when he touched on this aspect of his friend's nature. He understood his natural susceptibility.). Why you? He looked at Tintin as if he were looking through him to some significant background. I think it's because of your uncompromising commitment to reality. People watch you, and they see how you act, and they feel reassured. About life. About their difficult, tenuous, messy lives. Tintin glanced at him nonplussed. It was not often he heard anyone speak to him with such intimacy regarding his nature.

Well I'm glad you do not reject my idea as preposterous. I have studied the reports of the Dupont(d)s, which I have in this briefcase. For the first time Augustus noticed Tintin was carrying a briefcase. In fact if he wasn't mistaken, when he had run to his help at the dock he had it then as well. Here, you may have a look if you wish. Tintin held out the brown *calepin*, more school bag than briefcase, the kind they used to carry in Brussels as boys, taking the tram to school in the cool drizzle of the early morning. On the other hand, perhaps Tintin had never been a boy, and then again perhaps he still was—but a sort of old boy. Tintin might be in his fifties or even sixties, but he still had that utterly boyish look.

But why would they be murdering people in Manhattan—did you say in Manhattan or Queens?—because they are planning some major event? It's absurd!

Manhattan and Queens, replied Tintin. These things almost always start in Queens. That's where the Maya community has forged its ethnic enclave.

It's cracking, it's splintering, went on Augustus, I can feel it in the air. You remember that *te-tun* you stroked on Park Avenue? Was the writing legible?

It was, barely, said Butterfly, but worse, it was clumsy, so wooden, which is a terrible thing to say about *yuxul*, or stone carving. The tree stone was dated 827 AD. My people were clearly disintegrating. The princess, whose grandfather had been one of the great *Ah k'u hun's* of stone-carving, was obviously pained.

Listen Tintin, said Augustus in the next breath, then what will the great event the Maya are waiting for consist of, in your opinion? What is this 'return'?

All I can think, said the other pensively, is that it is connected with your ballgame, and as such is otherworldly, since we know the ball court is the major portal. However we do need to apply our minds to it. All three looked pensively at the *ceiba* tree.

It is, said Augustus, pensively still, as if we were subject to the thought of the Maya. In the presence of the *ceiba*, that is. The great trees of the Mayan forest stretched down the Avenue of the Americas as far as the eye could see. Now he could make out tufts of deep-green vegetation sprouting here and there at the intersections of the street. It was getting very late. Or very early, perhaps, with the first light not yet breaking but some dissolution at the edges of the night sky. The tentative cries of the birds in the trees punctuated the nocturnal urban dread. But from what trees? Not the occasional moribund anemic plastic trees planted by the New York Park System. Exotically melodious cries and whoops, the metallic music of creaks and the wooden rattlings, snickers and snackings came from the altitudinous *ceiba* trees, and they looked up in wonder into the still gloaming and could just make out the giant, horizontally spiraling monkey-arms of the tree above them, but still not the birds. And then, as this first awakening of the birds subsided, beyond just this tree a vast and gorgeously orchestral swell mounted of a multitude of birds of an entire forest.

Look, look, cried the Butterfly Princess, and they followed her finger. In the first striations of the paling sky the three friends saw a flutter of the atmosphere above the *ceiba* trees, two and then three and four blocks south of them, and then looking up, became aware of a rustling rush of air in the branches and saw the swirling flocks of parrots and ravens, and pelicans in formation, soaring giant harpy eagles and hawks, the fluttering of tiny neon blue *dacnis* and hovering hummingbirds, the quibbling *tucan* and the resplendent iridescent green-tailed *quetzal* and *pirre* warblers and in the ecstasy of their song and flight, the three friends, however disparate, the princess from the Classic era of the Maya, Tintin from his comic book milieu, and Augustus, of Belgo-New York literary origins, were of one mind in that moment.

Finally the latter said, Maybe they are just in time.. Each of them understood his words with a shade of difference, but none of them was thinking of the birds.

Well, said Tintin, bending down and fluffing up Milou's scruffy neck, I think it's time we got back to our beds. Tomorrow will be another day. Milou jumped up and down yapping loudly, almost bumping into Tintin's nose, and they all took better cognizance of one another as flesh and blood. Or to put it differently, they recognized one other.

Goodnight, they said, goodnight, and took leave, and as they drifted apart in the *entre chien et loup* of the dusk, they appeared like specks in the street beneath the *ceiba* trees to the great, blue, banner-tailed *macaw* gliding overhead who let out a warning scream—for what? When Augustus and Butterfly got back to the apartment, he went first to the window as usual to check if anything was amiss on the Upper New York Bay, but saw only the customary tugboat nosing along a black oil barge. Again that night he drew the intricate puzzle of her body open with delicate manipulations, she gazed up at him with astonishment, mouth rounded in an O as her womb flooded, and his heart broke with the orgasm. Her trust and dependency had something of the child, a daughter, and this emotion wounded his heart exquisitely. In the sexual act the flesh is electrified, he thought, it becomes metaflesh. In the extreme instance of its unselfconscious joy the flesh, as something outside of ourselves, disappears. As he watched his princess's pale buttocks, and the tuft between them when she walked, in its vulnerability and crudeness, he loved her the more. Butterfly came up and hugged him from behind, her breasts jelling up against his bare back. He reached back and stroked her left thigh and buttock. She told him she was going to bed. He said alright, I'll come later. He turned around and pulled her into his arms so that he could feel the softness of her whole body against his, her lips velvety as raspberries in her sleepiness. Usually he loved nothing better after love-making than to melt into a diffuse body with her in sleep, to feel her hip pressed against his or her fine warm hair on the pillow laced in his fingers, but tonight he needed to look at the dark bay for a while. She left and he stared out the window again. The water a couple of hundred feet from his window was muddy in tone, nondescript, opaque, barely reflecting the lamp lights along the shore of the mouth of the Hudson where it opened out onto the bay. And beyond, the bay was a lead sheet under the heavily clouded sky. No moon, no lights, no ships were visible. A foghorn wailed thinly and a minute or so afterward a church bell's metal ring reverberated flatly in the night. He continued to peer out, a deep disquiet pervaded his soul. After all, what did the "shamanic" mean, he wondered; ec-stasy, to stand momentarily outside the flesh? Carl of course.. But Carl, the artist-scribe, was already on the other side. Since childhood Carl had cultivated experimental living with karate-like detachment—life as self-experimentation. He carried it to its most extreme consequences, until that day when the blood streamed from his eyes and nose. The poet's shamanic nature arose from an apprehension of the delicate exchanges between the psychic and physical organism—even in the terrifying state of decay. It was well known among many friends that Carl deliberately explored his own state of dying. Thanks to shamanistic training, with his papillary-fine tracing he was able to direct the floating ions between the atoms of his body in what is known as the "very weak force". This was what Carl believed to be acting in the darkness of the "in between" zone. Augustus, to the contrary, was aware that for his part he had been born with a kind of spontaneous and primitive shamanic sense, and that having neglected any discipline, aside from moments of unsolicited grace, had not sharpened that sense. His undirected abilities, he felt, were in large part due to his unresisting attraction to the "weaker" sex. At this point of his reflection, he glanced toward the bundled shape in the bed clothes; with her bottom thrust up unconsciously and her black hair spilling out over her flushed cheek and white shoulder, she was a picture of vulnerable and wanton abandonment, which only confirmed his point. He was so tired by now and the ocean swept up such long calming waves over his spirit that he could no longer withstand the fatigue, and almost crawling to the bed and to the mortal form of his longing, slipped down beside her and into sleep. The one barely articulated thought that accompanied him in this nocturnal drift as his hand snuggled down between her cheeks, is that Carl's supreme shamanic testing may have been the "love experiment", as he called it: the directing of sexual stimuli and energies toward the heart, i.e. the solar plexus region, beyond any sexual act. He recognized the higher nature of his older brother's life-project, but felt quite incapable of it. Could that be what he meant by a "shamanic marriage"? Non-possession, non-fleshliness? He had fallen far short of it. Still, just before he fell into deep sleep his lips formed the shape of a kiss for his child-lover, and he slept with a smile on his face.

Aq'ab'al – 1
(The Last Night)

Night

The next morning, the next year, the next tun.. So turned the intermeshed wheels of Maya time and it seemed normal by now to Augustus—and of course to his consort, Princess Butterfly—to live by them. First the cycle of the magical *tzolkin*, in which the numbers one through thirteen mesh with the twenty name-days, *Kan, Akbal, Ik, Imix, Ahau, Cauac* etc. to make a 260-day period. All the peoples of Mesoamerica shared the sacred cycle. This wheel meshed next with the "Vague Year" of 365 days with its eighteen named months, *Pop, Uo, Zip, Zotz, Tzec* etc., so that any day in the 260-day count had a position in the Vague Year as well—and one of these positions could only be repeated by one full turn of the meshed wheels which took 52 years. Finally, there is the Long Count which really jumps us forward—and backward, calculated in *baktuns* (144,000 days), *katuns* (7,200 days), *tuns* (360 days), *uinals* (20 days) and *kins* (days) and so on. Now when Augustus and Butterfly woke up, each one of those cycles had clicked forward by one notch, a rare event, and the date is the one seen above. The Upper New York Bay this morning had the metallic, no-nonsense ding-dong of the bell that rang out the hours from the church across Wagner Park and which seemed to accord with those notches. When he scanned the horizon as he always did in the morning, it looked as normal as ever: the usual tug scudded across the top of his window while at the lower right portion of the same a long flat black strip of a tanker eel-slipped past the frame once again. He asked himself, what on earth (or on sea) am I looking for anyway? He had acquired the apartment at an unreasonable rent just in order to be able to keep watch with

Princess Butterfly over this watery approach to Manhattan. He gathered up his Butterfly's long black hair from behind and thrust his face into it like the fragrant summer grass, which made her giggle with glee at what she called his exaggerations. Embracing her from behind, he said,

I feel I can divine coming events from the smell of your hair, *Malinche*, like the botonomancy of the ancients.

Bottomancy, you mean? She inquired, laughing.

Plant beings he continued seriously, remembering the words of his brother, Carl. They speak to the Shaman.

Suddenly becoming serious as well, she said, Listen to me, my love—you must be very attentive today. You are so careless! My brother is not merciful. And he has a risky sense of humor. He would love to have your head. The question is, is your head attached firmly to your shoulders? He could not give her any assurances. Women had always asked him that. He trusted in his flair. That was perhaps a mistake, but what else did he have to trust in?

The day was crispy clean. It was a day for the *ah ts'ib*: the hand that writes the glyph draws the figure. When they walked out the front door of the building, the doorman as usual greeted them jovially. Augustus glanced at him in surprise—for the first time, he realized that this black-haired, swarthy, heavy-set man was probably Mexican or Guatemalan. As they left the building, he felt the man's eyes boring into his shoulder-blades. This Manhattan bay in late autumn lay in an almost tropical air. How could that be? Tones, moods drifted across the water in a moment's turning—yesterday melancholic, choppy, harsh, today quasi-indigo! Signs, subtle but distinct, could be made out in the air. Perhaps already touches of the *ah ts'ib's* hand? For example: *Ceiba* trees were now growing in Wagner Park and along Broadway, on the way to the Municipal Building where they were going to take the subway. These avenues appeared to have a channeling force, like the *Sakbe*[59]. And there were more meandering cracks in the sidewalks and the roads, through which exotic grasses and other undergrowth appeared to be pushing. People in the usual morning rush appeared incurious, oblivious, transparent New York figures. Only occasionally a short dark-complexioned (opaque?) girl would nod at the strange, rubbery-legged trees to draw her girl friends' attention, and they would break into inexplicable hilarity. As he and the princess turned up Park Row from Broadway, the building at number fifteen with the bulbous towers and the copper-green cupolas thirty floors above J&R's exhibited some unusual activity. In the vertical slots in the towers, which served as windows, they could see tiny dark figures waving their arms above the street.

Look, said the princess, look over there! He looked toward the Municipal Building where she was pointing, and saw a procession of small brown people pouring out of the great eagle-winged building into the street, which was strange to start with because on an early weekday one would expect people to be pouring into the building. And above, on the colonnaded *tempio* just below the Golden Female Warrior in the billowing gown, they saw those balconies were occupied by many small dark people; on the top of another building just north of the Municipal Building, golden pyramidal roof (late-Romantic French chateau) topped with a needle spire, heads and hands were poking out of the slot-windows in the roof. And suddenly he understood—

It's the shamans and the princes, Butterfly, they are communicating from summit to summit as they once did in the Petén from the tops of the pyramids in the steaming mornings.

Of course, said Butterfly, looking up at him faintly surprised that he hadn't realized this sooner. It's a sky-building event, isn't it? Her eyebrows were faintly raised, no doubt with quiet hilarity at him. How is it she seemed to know these things without a word being said? Well *Malinche*, of course, had an inside track! They made for the subway next to the Municipal Building, joining the scores of shuffling, small brown people with the large quadrangular faces and features set in stone. It was time to go. It was the day and the hour to cross over. Holding hands, he and his princess passed with the solemn crowd through the maw of the Underworld, into the rococo, bearded and skeletal jaws no doubt freshly stuccoed last night, and plunged downwards on the escalator. Masks painted deep-red of *Caquix Vucub Caquix*, the malevolent bird-deity, flanked the tunnel as they cascaded along with a horde of Maya among whom they had so suddenly found themselves. This squat people who were almost invisible in the city, whom nobody noticed, who were not even Dominican or Puerto Rican "Latinos" with their pretty faces and sexy exposed bodies, this underground Maya-Indian population which was the humblest of the humble, overridden and trampled by the "West", had taken possession of the Underground now. Few whites appeared to be using the subway system; he had doubts concerning his own whiteness. Wasn't he a mixture of amber yellow and rose? He knew this odd journey to the Kingdom of *Xibalba*[60], the *Ox-Bolon-Chak* or dream-place, was really the test of truth of this people. Each time the number 4 express train stopped it took on a few more non-Maya including a smattering of so-called Whites, and slowly the initial solemn mood was cracked, the crowd was stirred and excited by the prospect of the game, especially the young males who mostly wore Yankee Stadium caps and uttered sharp yelps and hoots to provoke their consorts, white girls in blue jean jackets and very short jean skirts and a curlicue of a tattoo on an arm or a thigh and adorned with silvery nose-rings or lip-rings, and black and brown girls bursting with sexuality, bottoms and breasts packed more rotundly and firmly than their white sisters and stuffed into even tighter and shorter skirts. Black and white and brown, they responded to their mates with bird-shrieks, and thus a diffuse, light-hearted eroticism steamed into the air. Human sardines in the subway car, their color distinctions faded as body was added to body and buttock to belly and breast to back, and they melded in their common humanity to a single jouncing sexual polyglyph. He braced his arms about the princess to preserve her bodily attributes for himself, and the thrust of her breasts against his midriff and his right thigh wedged in the engulfing warmth of her pelvis was eloquently demonstrative of his success, and not without noticeable effect upon his own physi-ology for which he turned apologetic eyes upon her scandalized (?) glance. It was as if the entire crowd in the subway car held its breath in order not to interpenetrate and mutually fit and become interlocked in one another. An old puzzle he was familiar with and once quite adept at: the fitting, the wedging, the imbrication, but now with the Butterfly Princess in his arms he was no longer interested in the anonymous welter. There was no question, he reflected, that the subway car was far from just an efficient means of conveyance. It was an erotic parlor, a brown study, a *chapelle ardente* (especially: the relation of the underground train to the Dead was less evident but profound. Momentarily separated from those Living-Above, denizens of the subway system experienced a detachment from the normal daytime world and traveled, psychi-cally, in the vicinity of—or toward— the Realm of the Dead). The excitement of the crowd on its way to the ball game bordered on erotic hysteria, both a flight from—and an intimacy with—death. Finally as if the trip had passed in a dream they were coming in

---

60   The Maya kingdom of the Dead where the ultimate ball game was played out by the Hero Twins, Xbalanque and Hunahpu.

now at—Augustus and Butterfly recognized the Yankee Stadium stop when they saw the mask of *Itzam-Yeh*, the giant long-beaked bird of *Popul Vuh* fame, its finger-like claws curled around the top of the big metal name-sign of the elevated station which had to be many decades old, and it seemed to glare down balefully at the jocular crowd. The jocular crowd paid it little heed, it was hardly in the mood for archaeology. Only the Maya glanced up with respect as they passed beneath, the way Catholics do at the image of Mary. He glanced down at Butterfly's face when they passed beneath, but her expression did not alter. She was not, as she occasionally pointed out, a churchgoer. They joined in the clangor of the crowd as they trotted down the metal steps--in a fundamental transition from the utilitarian-consumer world to the world of *Itz*, of dream. As to the Butterfly Princess, well, he watched her breasts flounce as she stepped down the narrow stairs in her high heels, and with each step down a fresh wave rolled within each breast. Ah, it was delectable, strolling out by the seashore with one's girl! That is what he was thinking, and it was quite often what he was thinking. They spilled from the staircase out into the street, and found themselves on the edges of a crowd milling about, washing one way, then the other. The usual festive crowd description: sports caps, souvenirs, small kids hopping beside their dads, clouds scudding, the perfect day, the girls raucous, sexually aggressive with their guys, the vendors, the hubbub, conversations shouted, noise-makers, whistles, the pervasive acidic stink of hot dogs, cartoon-blue sky, the All-American carnival atmosphere, the guys clutching their girls possessively, cardboard trays piled high with goodies, the shrieks of children chasing each other, the occasional fat cigar (stogies) jammed between teeth, the plump and blooming families from New Jersey, the occasional bright red Corvette, plenty of family SUVs, and ticket vendors crying out the last few remaining seats.

Look! There, there! The Bat! cried the Butterfly Princess jabbing a finger into his ribs and he stared to where her finger pointed still throbbing in the air, but instead of the monumental pop-sculpture of the raised Baseball Bat, favorite rendezvous of sports fans and their agreed place of meeting too at the Stadium, hanging by its tightly curled toes was *Camasotz*, the huge Bat of the Maya, also called Snake Tooth, with its cruel little eyes and beaked nose. Its leathery sail-like wings attached to its feet flapped idly open and displayed one great globular decorative symbol on each wing. Its huge dangling obscene genitalia were equally impressive. The sports fans literally shrank from it—naturally enough when they were keyed up expecting to see their *baseball* bat! Augustus and the princess recognized the standard of the "Maya Nation" carried before their king into battle. Underneath the "Bat" standard waited a delegation of Maya warriors and shamans; people they knew well and who knew them well. And hereinafter we have: foremost the very young candidate-king, or Prince Smoking-Squirrel: helmet headdress with the usual and wonderfully elegant blue quetzal plumes tossed back archly spilling about his shoulders, a mask with the snout and pig eyes, the image of the Jester-God with its Pinocchio-nose, bracelets of bright red feathers, extra large ear-flares, and of course that gorgeous green jade pendant which we have had occasion to admire (in his chambers), on which was incised his own royal figure on one side and on the other a text not yet entirely deciphered, de rigueur in such a situation! He cradled in his arms an oversized Double-Headed Serpent Bar. It looked as if some envious *ahau* had put the largest royal scepter he could find in the fourteen-year-old boy's arms in order to emphasize his immaturity. And of course the ritual, if real, shrunken human head slung at his broad belt. After all, thought Augustus, from his most tender age he had always affected the grandiloquent poses! A dozen courtiers pressed about him now, in frankly fawning attitudes, as if they were posing for the official court photographer. Those who were engaged with the Prince adopted clearly subordinate attitudes, the posture of the head bent slightly forward beyond the sternum, chin out, ingratiating smile. Some sat cross-legged, others knelt, leaning back on their heels, they were brown and red and half-naked, none as elaborately dressed as the Prince, most of them with gracefully wrapped tunics and plumed *ah ts'ib* (brushes and quills) headdresses, and they appeared to be arguing incessantly. As for the Prince himself, the beautiful, one might say girlish, face was raised toward us an instant, eyebrow cocked and a seductive gleam darted out at his half-sister, Butterfly, who blushed.

Yes, he said sotto voce to an adviser, yes, yes, we'll take care of them in a moment. His adviser of course was none other than the wryly elegant (more is less) *Ah k'u hun* they had met beyond the temple compound confines the other day—the one the boy-prince referred to as "Uncle", and whose name, Princess Butterfly reminded Augustus in a hiss, was Lord Smoking-Rabbit. And the *Ahau* they knew was the Lord of Motul de San Jose, plump androgynous with the fashionable, dangling, white-plumed cap and the drooping paps, and his attendant dwarf in brilliant carmine hose. The former wore his immutable faint sneer. In fact, apart from the servile smiles with which they invariably addressed the Prince, most if not all of the noble personages wore sneers or fierce scowls, which appeared to be the right "form" among the courtiers. The sole female attendant wore a sweet expression and stood a few feet behind the group, bare-breasted and with a slight loin-cloth which fell between her thighs, holding in one hand a leather syringe-bag fitted with a bone tube. It was said the Crown Prince never traveled without such an assistant. All the movements, the exchanges, were very slow. However aside from the flashed glance of the prince, the *Ah k'u hun*, the other *ahauob* and the attendants appeared oblivious of the princess and Augustus who, in their elevated position (up a flight of stairs on a balcony), were not very visible for that matter. The sports fans milling about were filing through the entrances and up the stairs of the stadium and did not stare much at the Maya dignitaries, perhaps believing them to be a coming attraction during the game intermissions, an *entre'acte*. The occasional pubescent girl gawked with consuming passion at the too-pretty prince who might as well have been a teen rock star with his band of hardened older instrumentalists. And in fact there were some instruments among the Maya delegation: the red-cloaked and pantaloon'd dwarf held a rattle, and from somewhere in the backdrop behind the royal delegation the dull obsessive thud of the *tunkul* was audible, so that the would-be groupies might have thought the "band" was warming up.

Have you noticed, whispered the princess who noticed everything, that people are behaving differently? And indeed, of the great swarm of people who streamed past the delegation toward the multiple portals, which gave access to the arena, it was clear that more and more were bowing respectfully in the direction of the princely party, which they skirted. Looking closely, said Augustus, more and more of the ticket-holders appear to be Maya! And indeed why shouldn't more Maya inhabit their *barrio* than live in Tikal? And why, in light of the monuments and land-art projects which had modified the face of Manhattan over the last few days in preparation for this transcendental event, and with their *Ahauob* and Shamans and the noble warriors pouring down from the skyscraper summits of Gothic New York, wouldn't every able-bodied one of them be attending? It became equally apparent that the royal party was not simply standing in that area by chance, but was situated on a dais of some sort, which both separated them from the crowd and allowed them to be seen.

Listen, darling, he said, I think I have to speak up now, don't you? She nodded gravely, her black hair shaking about her shoulders.

Respect, she said, but no sign of fear. And remember to keep scowling. Her winged lips appeared to bring him the message of the gods, and so he began.

He leaned up over the balcony, and cried out- Lord! He had not cried out in a "stentorian" blare as he had no wish to over-play his part, but firm, yes, and at the last moment he put on the snobbish frown as well. No point in eating humble pie, after all the other was his long-lost brother!

Ah! replied the Prince, a curlicue issuing from his mouth and the glyphic logographs lining up in two neat columns by his head for this historic occasion, their elegant calligraphy already providing a clue as to his intentions, carefully parsed by *Malinche* who was extremely sensitive to such expressive quality, mellifluous at one moment and slicing, razor-sharp, the next. And their phonetic cues completed a reading of the Prince's tonality, *le mot juste* and so on. Thus: Ah ha, *mon ami* (the Prince could be most charming when he wished. This was when you had to tread most carefully, Butterfly had warned him)! I dared to count entirely on your honor and your great-heartedness! A fine heart it must be! My sweet little sister no doubt has aided and abetted you! I, as you see, have spared no pomp. *Malinche* smiled with wry amusement at the allusion to her role. This maligning of her role eventually would become a Mexican pastime. Still, there was time enough for that. With the prince's words a sea of brown faces tipped up toward him and the Queen shifted beside him: squat, impassive, unsmiling. He strained to look the prince in the eyes.

Well, he said finally, glad to say, your panache has not been disappointing! This city—and he spread his hands in a gesture of unfeigned admiration. Indeed, his younger brother had always been a bit of the charlatan with a taste for the grandiloquent pose. The Prince looked pleased. Well, he said, I do what I can. But this isn't really all me, you know, there's Smoking-Rabbit here who is a master of such legerdemain.

Legerdemind, amended the *Ah k'u hun* with a wink for Augustus and his bride to be. The fine nose and high delicate cheek bones of the latter were family heirlooms. Hadn't you noticed? he asked in his high musical tone, and Augustus glanced up in the direction of the scribe's gaze, and on the wall of the great

concrete arena which they had walked around to get to their rendezvous he saw the PPS This was a large horizontal band of huge
glyphs encircling the arena just below its rim as if it were an enormous bowl—followed by the word for "blood", which Butterfly
pointed out to him. What is of particular interest to us here,
she said, is that the name of the artist/calligrapher appears here,
trembling lightly and high on the three-story stone walls, after
the glyph reading *u ts'ib* ("his writing or painting"): the name, in
papillary-fine strokes, of Smoking-Rabbit, the brilliant *Ah k'u hun*
before them.[61] It was much like the difference between the owner
of a work of art or the patron and the author of that work of art.
The former is negligible except insofar as he is incorporated in the
work. Augustus also realized that the issue of authorship was critical here. It was a matter of responsibility. When he and the princess finally lowered their eyes from the great wall "scroll" which
shuddered with the huge energy with which the glyphs were
packed, they became aware of a startling quiet. Several hundred
pairs of dark eyes and absorbed brown faces made it eloquently
clear that the crowd of Indians had been following the *Malinche's*
translation. Evidently they were not able to read the magic symbols either. She made a short but respectful bow to the *Ah k'u hun*.
The prince seemed a mite put out by these remarks,

Ah, dear *Malinche*, you seem to be providing an education
not only for your new companions but for my people as well. The
princess smiled less tolerantly, she was growing tired of her royal
brother's glib references to her persona as well as of his derisive
posture of utter superiority.. . He had always had a taste for the
histrionic gesture, exotic dress and the pose of spiritual teacher! In
any case the shaman's powers serve the King's game, he continued,
and this, by the way, is the future King's team, and with a flourish
he embraced with a wide-flung arm the six warriors surrounding
him. All very high-ranking nobles and some even members of the
young crown prince's family. You could almost feel shock-waves
from the compressed meat of these men—jostling one another,
packed like the glyphs, rounded muscles bulging out of the sleeve-
less jackets of cotton armor and the calf-length leather-skirts over
the loin-cloths (for wider lap-span to receive the ball). Their hel-

---

61   Thse indications regarding the PPS are cited from The Art of the
Maya Scribe by Michael D. Coe and Justin Kerr. They along with the other
distinguished epigraphers responsible for these discoveries appear to be
assistant-scribes following in the footsteps or better the glyph-strokes of
the great Shamanic Scribes more than a thousand years later.

mets festooned with golden feathers and apple green jade pieces
nodded with approval at their crown prince's words. The sheer
jangle and dazzle of ornament, chest-platelets, nose-pieces, pendants, pink spondyl shell and blue wrist and ankle feather-brace-
lets—but none with the world-tree loin cloth which hung between
the thighs of the Prince alone—were packed with the bustling
overspill of the hieroglyphic texts. Of course the Prince alone
bore the green jade pectoral with its fateful dates. Several carried,
in addition to axes and obsidian-bladed clubs, spear-throwers,
curved like a hockey stick but shorter, which gave tremendous
leverage to the hurled spear, odd accessory for a ball-player! And
then the human face-skin shields, always so disconcerting.

Just the psyching-up of the ball game, he whispered to his
princess, who whispered back,

I wouldn't bet on it. This mix of ballgame gear and military
trappings is quite usual. For good reason.

And your team, cried the Prince complacently, don't they feel
quite up to it? Are they going to forfeit the game? Chickened out?

Oh yes, my dear chap, of course, well it's to protect our privacy, you know, their names...

So have they mistaken the date? Fled the coop? Augustus
looked about the crowd with a touch of panic.

See here, oh crown prince! cried out a pure, Galahad-type
voice, a voice which could have trumpeted out of a Benjamin
Britten Serenade. All heads turned including Augustus' and
Butterfly's and the crown prince's and the *Ah k'u hun's*, and they
saw stretched up in all his rather slight build the golden-locked
Tintin. This latter had obviously sensed a theatrically apt moment
which could affect the Maya, much as when he cried out to the
Incas[62] that the sun would darken.

Ha! cried out the Prince with an infectious boyish grin, I see
your team's golden spearhead is here! Oh thank you *Itzam-Yeh*
for comic-strip relief! A rumble of laughter bellied out from the
soldier-team, and the crown prince smirked complacently.

Well, cried Tintin again, shaking the forelock to good effect in
the radiant sunlight, with Professor Tournesol I have been studying your Paddlers, whom we consider comic-strip colleagues
(and it was true that the awesome Paddler Gods who canoed

---

62   In *Le Temple du Soleil*. Here Tintin had been able to calculate
the exact time and day of the sun's eclipse, and consequently used this
information to amaze the Inca. He did not appear to have any such instru-
mental knowledge this time however.

through the Milky Way could have come out of a contemporary comic book!). And we would like to ask you, what is the date? Augustus gaped at his old friend. What on earth was he thinking? No eclipses were going to come to their rescue now![63] Not even Walter Aleph..

The crown prince glanced at Tintin as if slightly taken aback, and then conferred for a moment with his Scribe. Well, my young cartoonish friend, he then said with contemptuous bonhomie, my *Ah k'u hun* tells me that in our calendar it would be 13.0.0.0.0 4 *Ahau* and soon will come the 3 *Kankin* with the Ninth Lord of the Night ruling. The Long Count cycles have returned to the symmetry of their beginning. The thirteenth *baktun* has been completed. The return of the Maya has begun. Is that helpful to you? I'm afraid it may not be. It doesn't appear to be highly propitious for your people. The Prince burst into a harsh barking laugh and his team roared, gurgled, wheezed and gasped with him, their vibratory density shaking the surrounding air. Augustus began hurriedly counting on his fingers and toes (the basic counting unit of the Maya is twenty, counted with the whole person which includes fingers and toes, and the smallest calendric cycle is the *uinal* or "week" of twenty days—and all further calculations done in multiples of twenty to eternity) but he couldn't figure it out. He looked at his *Malinche* in dismay but she merely grinned. The Maya enjoy a good calendar joke when they hear one.

It is today, she said.

West, added the Prince for good measure, and in the black quadrant. "Armageddon", I think you'd call it. Subtle smile.

I'm afraid you've misunderstood, replied Tintin with astonishing although not unusual smugness for a Belgian. I really was asking you about back home. I refer to that other time. The Paddler Gods would be sinking along the Milky Way above Tikal, the Professor tells me. The Prince's face grew black, if such a fair and beautiful face could be said to blacken. He was so admired (and desired) that he had been compared more than once to the Maize God, and he turned angrily to the *Ah k'u hun* now. Again they conferred in hurried, angry whispers.

He says, the early eleventh *baktun*- began the Prince tersely, say 10.4.0.0.0..

---

63   This could be a reference either to Walter A.'s "Eclipse Fever" or (more likely) to "Tintin chez les Incas", in which the Boy Hero saves himself and his companions from incineration by the Inca thanks to his knowledge of the pending occurrence of an eclipse .

Tintin broke in, And in our calendar, your Lordship, Tryphon[64] tells me about 909 A.D. I believe. And Tintin, who was not more than a couple of hundred feet away, shot a meaningful glance at Augustus.

We'd call it, "Apocalypse", he said. Shocked silence, palpably. The teammates looked at each other, and at their Lord. Even the *Ah k'u hun*, normally unflappable, looked uncomfortable. This number was revolving in Augustus' head slowly, like the interlocking circles of the *Tzolkin*. Then it came to him. The last Long Count recorded anywhere in the Maya world, he said. It was incised on a jade pectoral. The end of Maya civilization. Tintin pointed one long unwavering finger at the Prince's chest. The Maya in the audience began to disperse, albeit with ugly looks for Tintin and his interlocutors. The warrior-team stirred uneasily about the stage as if the show were over but they were not sure where to go next, and Smoking-Squirrel and his uncle the *Ah k'u hun* conferred intensely and quietly, glancing down toward Tintin and up toward Augustus and his *Malinche* now and then, for the latter an unmistakably malevolent look.. All the glyphs which had hung in the air above their heads drained away. Nonetheless Augustus got a good look at the glowing pectoral of the Prince, and could certainly make out the fateful date, and remembered the image of the beautiful Maize God on the other side (the Prince's reflection that is, facing his heart). What puzzled him was why the Prince would wear such a dread inscription as if it were a *nota bene*. Now the Prince rose again, in his hand a Manikin Scepter now, obviously passed to him by the wily *Ah k'u hun*.

The grasping and raising of the serpent-footed *K'awil* with the long blade protruding from its mouth (thus forming an axe) is a common ritual, whispered Butterfly hurriedly in Augustus' ear, in the Royal iconography. His full birth name is *Tzuk Yax Ch'at K'awinal Winik*, or "Partition First Dwarf, K'awil-born Person[65]. It means that as a novice shaman my older brother has set his foot upon the path to the Kingdom of the Dead. The axe is the instrument of the sacrifice of decapitation practiced upon the losing captain of the ball game. Why else do you think is the ball court considered to be a Portal into the Otherworld? You must be prepared, Augustus, if you really go into this ballgame. And indeed this detail gave him pause, food for thought. It was not for noth-

---

64   Professor Tournesol's first name. Used only in moments of great stress or great relief.

65   From Maya Cosmos, Linda Schele

ing that he had always been averse to team sports! Why would his—more than putative--brother want his head, even if they were on this side of the mythic divider? Sibling rivalry? The cruelty and madness of the ball court had been evident to him, ever since his school days. He had fled their ball games for solitary walks in the woods, and for the otherworldly voices of recorded opera from the tower where he used to sequester himself from the games. How he had trembled at those silvery-voiced, agonizingly sweet temptresses.

It is the *ch'ulel*, the princess whispered into his ear, the blood, the holy spirit, which animates the game. The shaman speaks through the blood, he understood, the *ch'ulel* inhabits the blood.

And where are your warriors, *Ahau* Coyote (improvising this title of nobility with patent irony), where are your knights, except for this puppet! said the Prince and snorted with unseemly crudeness. The Prince's men looked up from their crestfallen postures, and visibly began to preen and strut again, and then the most unexpected chiming voice arose, like one of those operatic temptresses of his boyhood, and swelled progressively into a very big sound, a huge, glass-shattering, one might say, bloodcurdling, soprano voice:

Ah je rrris de me voir-r-r si belle dans ce mirroir! It was of course la Castafiore, the Milan "nightingale" as the popular press called her, Tintin's friend and Captain Haddock's bane or succubus—or girlfriend?—in her favorite role, Gounod's "Faust", "*le fameux air des Bijoux*" as she called it. Augustus was profoundly— well, shocked, because at this solemn moment of confrontation and intimidation, of the male feints and lunges which always precede a combat, nothing could have seemed more out of place and, well, ludicrous, than this shrill, tremendous, female voice.

Ah! rang out the sarcastic voice of the Prince, This is your team, my poor friend! This is what comes, you know, from employing BD characters, I'm afraid they bring a lot of baggage along with them.

In the meantime it is necessary to correct a possible impression: whereas transcribed as it is here, it may appear that what was being said was graphically clear-cut, in fact the voice of the *rossignol* de Milan had reached gale force, and now the capitaine Haddock could be seen in the wind-swept crowd holding on tight to his dark blue captain's cap with a look akin to panic in his eyes, for he was half-naked in what had been momentarily transformed into an opera house, and appeared to be wearing a shoulderless dress with a plunging décolleté which disclosed the swelling of breasts. He blushed beet-red and the audience stared at him indignantly.[66] He was about to gallop away in the opposite direction, but just then he noticed Augustus,

Allooo, marin d'eau douce, he cried, and they all stared at him, and the Prince turned to Augustus and said,

It's very odd that "Castafiore" is "Chaste Flower" in Italian, isn't it. What meaning is there here, some sexual dysfunction? Are you and my little sister…? Well at least it all stays in the family, he concluded with a wink.

At first Augustus felt a hot flush of rage, then astounded at this—acknowledgement, he decided it was wiser not to respond to the prurient intimation. He noticed that the *Ah k'u Hun* was watching him sharply. The Prince betrayed his adolescence with such crudeness. Unless..

Ah, brother," said the princess bending in his direction, what a relief for you with your budding *machismo*! She spoke the word in Spanish, in the language of their conquerors that is, with the intention to prick him.

You took a fool to guide you! continued the Prince. She may talk Mayan and she may be good in bed, but just take a look at la Castafiore.

Why should I take a look at la Castafiore, asked Augustus with petulance. What's she got to do with it! The Diva as if to signal this reference to herself punctuated their conversation with an ear-splitting trill that she was particularly notorious for, and in spite of himself, Augustus (and Tintin) took a closer look at the billowing-bosomed (fake) blonde as she sang: her bucal contortions were obscene. Exactly how she projected that quality was difficult to say. Her lips wrapped around the notes with caricatural pouting and wrinkling and slobbering; the sharp thin nose bespoke a lascivious turn. He had never really noticed before, not having wished to look beneath—beneath what? What was he thinking? Perhaps her skirts hid some contraption? Her make-up must be ladled on. He dreaded to think what she must look like the morning after.. Why was she eyeing him in that sly way as she sang? No doubt she had reduced the poor *Capitaine* to such a state. He turned away with a tiny shudder from this unexpectedly perverse

---

66   This very ambivalent and intriguing image does indeed appear in a small oniric window in Herge's *"Les Bijoux de la Castafiore"*. Some might be tempted to read into it a reference to Augustus' boyhood escapism.

companion. Then he realized that two or three of the Mayan warriors were tittering behind their hands, and that the whole group, like a tableau, was watching him, the Prince with particular keenness. He glanced at her—the little princess—she was looking at him in surprise and dismay. Tintin alone appeared oblivious of anything out of the ordinary. Was it his inherent purity of nature? Then he realized, from a quick sideways glance from the Prince's uncle, the highly inventive *Ah k'u hun*, that psychological, if not psychic, tactics were afoot, and that the latter was no stranger to such.

Ah! he said, and nodded to the Uncle instead of to the Prince, our team is quite feisty and on the *qui vive*, he said with a confidence he did not feel. And as if to confirm him, a voice rose from the outskirts of the crowd of Maya—

K-k-keekk, or something like "kick", and then it came clearer, Kick off! *Monsieurs les Maya, shootez les premiers!* Thus challenging the Maya team by inviting them to take the advantage by kicking off (or whatever one did in *Pok-a-Tok*) as in soccer and to get the game going. The massive, improbably buoyant form of d'Hachis loomed above the crowd of short Maya to the left by the Temple (or Stadium) Portal. He smiled mischievously at his sly historical reference and waved gaily at Augustus, whose heart was warmed by the timely arrival of his faithful friend.

You see, Prince, he said, turning again to the royal party, the Manhattan team is quite feisty! The Prince's warriors, his team, stirred about and jangled their ornaments, pendants, ear-flares, jade mirrors, short stabbing spears and whatnot, even the dull thud or klunk of one or two of the shrunken heads hanging from their ceremonial belts was distinctly heard. It was an intimidating sound. Then a very New York voice rang out from the other side of the crowd, slightly curved by the warmth and the cockiness of a Brooklyn origin,

Rattle those knuckle-heads, boys! cried out Phil, and the jaunty white pony-tale flipped up as he waved both arms at Butterfly and Augustus, a radiant grin on his handsome face. A warm current of trust in his friends run along his spine. He turned toward the Prince and his muttering team, apparently they were having second thoughts, or were frustrated, or simply aching for our blood, when a slight mocking "ahem" sounded almost at his elbow, and he turned to see the sparkling wide gaze and then stretched back a hand to clasp Ignatius' hand, and the little princess jumped up and hugged his old friend impetuously, who looked slightly taken aback—he was of so mental a composition that he often shied from bodily contact—and smiled and said—

If your spirit folds back upon the contents of your mind, through deep concentration you can explore those interior spaces and cast the hook of an image to fish up what you will need, and he winked affectionately at the couple. Well now only Walter Aleph was left and no sooner had Augustus and Butterfly turned back to the crowd below than a restrained laugh burst out, and the teasing voice of the novelist issued from directly below.

Oh come on, now, came the coaxing, highly modulated, hypersensitive, classic, New York-Jewish intellectual's tone, Surely you can't be serious about this utterly lethal game, I mean, they actually decapitate the loser! This last word produced in a quasi-falsetto and an incredulous high-pitched laughter peeled out, and they peered down into the crowd until they caught sight of the black eye-patch on the up-turned, obviously vastly amused, face of Walter Aleph. I mean, he repeated as he gazed up at the couple, these are obviously people who take their ball game very, very seriously! Augusto as a castrato! That will be the day! and another whinny of merriment. A muttering assent ran through the crowd of Maya, and the opposing team smiled without humor or benevolence and obligingly rattled their hanging skulls, which sounded more numerous than the first time, and sent out a pleasingly clanking noise which reminded Augustus of cow-bells in high mountain meadows.

I have given some thought to this problem, answered Augustus, and turning to the Crown Prince, he said, Smoking-Squirrel *Ahau Ahauob*, which was a highly flattering form of address and somewhat premature as the young man had not yet actually become King, Couldn't we waive this messy piece of the business? he asked coaxingly, After all, we are all sportsmen here, and the game's the thing! A murmur rustled through the crowd again, grunting, belligerent, and it was picked up and amplified by the chorus of warriors on stage.

That's the tradition, Smoking-Coyote, replied the Prince contemptuously, you see how the people feel, what would be the point without decapitation, that's what gives the game its pimento and drives the players beyond the plane of mere mortals. That's why the *wayob* come down to dance with us! And indeed in this small peroration the Prince's face appeared transformed, or deformed rather, darkened. Augustus could tell that he was not at all kindly disposed toward himself! Sibling dread might be more appropriate?

Animal-sprits, whispered the princess, the 'companions'. It is they who charge the space of the ball court.

Yes, broke in the Prince, my sister has that right but it won't save you! They draw it out elastically into an extension of *Xibalba*, the kingdom of the dead. Coming and going in the darkness, thought Augustus, and looked again at his beloved *Malinche*, hoping that perhaps she would help him here, but she looked distractedly into the empty air as if she were searching for a word. Whispering and rustling of the public. Now another voice boomed out from the courtyard, not so much a matter of volume as resonance, a wave harmonic, as if it bodied out in the air, an embodiment of the mind..

Birdfree, Brother and Sister, called out Carl, for it could only be he, don't forget that in the bird-spirit we know the rise and the fall, we know the dying already, there is no fear! What was it was about Carl's voice, Augustus wondered, that it takes on the shape of his body? Carl had the rare capability of projecting his soul, of making manifest his aura. Even without his body he was within his voice. For that matter his voice would keep on vibrating forever as a wave harmonic. Augustus looked proudly, even though his eyes were clouded by some wetness, at the Prince and his Family Portrait standing around him.

These, he said, are my brothers and our team is complete. The Prince glared back with what he doubtless intended to be withering contempt.

You do understand, old chap, he said with preppy aloofness, that regardless of the old school tie and the level playing field rah rah rah, that the penalty for the captain of the losing team—for losing his head and challenging the King of Tikal is—to lose his head. His manner may have been jocular but his voice was cold. Augustus blanched a moment, he tried to conceal it and Butterfly squeezed his hand hard, but then again the luminous, full-bodied voice (like a wine which has reached perfect balance) of Carl rang out again:

Do not forget, Augustus, that I was elected captain of this team long before you conceived of the match, please do me this kindness. It is a question of the experiment which converts the sex-drive into endurance and combat-readiness, into the *karate* empty mind. I think this is not yet your undertaking, dear Augustus! At this, sympathetic chuckles were audible among the otherwise gaping and rapt audience. The little princess glanced archly at Augustus, and shook her head with mock resignation (a

word cloud floating above their heads, flashing with the pulsa
tion of writing, words emerging occasionally in brilliant bursts),
but the Prince's "uncle", the *Ah k'u hun*, had crouched down with
his hand in front of his face, as if measuring or estimating Carl's
cipher, and he suddenly cried out, *Xbalanke*?! A tremor rippled
through the serried ranks of Maya warriors at the sacred name.

Yes, nuncle, and is this not my brother, *Huhnapu*[67]? So saying, Carl (or, at least momentarily, *Xbalanke*), his heavy black
eye-brows bristling, stretched out his hand toward Augustus who
gaped—like a fish out of water. A surge of another being flooded
up his spinal cord and vibrated it (a chord). He knew that these
two personages were the hero-twins of the Maya "bible", the *Popul
Vuh*. And she, said Carl/*Xbalanke* and stretched his other hand
toward the little princess, a descendant by way of an illegitimate
love-child of Black Butterfly of the ninth generation of the Lords
of Quiché, as listed in the Generations of the Lords. And these
two are joined in shamanic union!

Not if I have anything to say about it! A voice with a cracked
ring, harsh and imperious, called out from the rear of the warriors, and from behind the curtains which hung on the wall behind their muscled mass on the dais, stepped the formidable figure of the Lady *Wac-Chanil-Ahau*, Dragon-Lady. I will not permit
it! she said again in a rasping voice, striding forward in full warrior regalia. A purple-blue quetzal plume swept behind her and
large bone ear-flaps caused her lengthened lobes to bulge, a couple of shrunken skulls hung by her side. At the center of her embroidered skirt, something like a kilt, hung a huge, what looked to
Augustus like a *Witz* monster face buckle, with sharply glittering
jaws at about the height of her crotch. *Vagina dentata*, he mused.
The portrait was completed by her warrior's calves and massive
horny feet with large ornate purple feathered shoes which fanned
above the top of the feet with pompoms in a row and were bound
about the bottom of the feet with twisted thongs. The words issued in front of her face in heavy, rubbery, squat hieroglyphs:
sexual and murderous. The young Crown Prince glanced up at her
from his squatting position with peevish astonishment at having
been upstaged. Undeterred and unperturbed, the Dragon-Mother
swept down to the front of the dais and glared up at the girl who

---

67   The Hero-Twins of the Holy Book of the Maya, the *Popul Vuh*.
Xbalanké fascinated (and finally destroyed) the Lords of Death by self-
decapitating, then reviving himself. In the process he saved his brother,
Hunahpu.

had dared to supplant her.

I have something to say about this cheat, she said. There are thousands of little trollops like her hunting for a meal ticket. Just lying down and spreading their legs, she sneered. Little Missy Cunt! I'm just sorry for you, my dear, and for what awaits you— she smiled at the girl showing sharpened yellow teeth—like all his floozies.

The little princess glared back, and shrilled out—you old sow, how could those larded shanks have ever gripped a man's dipping and plunging tool! Her cry echoed the age-old hatred of the younger woman for the murderous jealous mother. The Queen-Mother merely grinned with spiteful gratification and went on:

But him! I was told a long time ago by a girlfriend who had been married to one never to trust a Belgian! *Faux chien!* she spat at him. Hypocrite! He reddened, aware of the curious glances from the Maya crowd as well as friends. He has sucked my blood dry! she cried, I gave him my youth, my beauty, I sacrificed everything for him, my career! I was a tender girl too, once! In my innocence I dreamed under the moon and awaited my young prince.. I put him on a pedestal. I gave him my all. But I wasn't good enough for him, was I? Silly old bugger needed fresh blood! A girl so young she might well be his daughter! As if she could possibly care for him! I would slice off his fat member myself! She drooled at the thought, and wiped the spittle off her jowls with the back of a bristly hand. I was a famous beauty. I could have had any man I wanted. I refused far better offers! He has stolen my life! The blubbery lips trembled. Her chins wobbled. She scratched her groin. Was there not something touching about this barbarous Walkyrie and the delicate sentiments which she uttered? Yes, thought August, and I was young enough to be your son.. These clichés had been run past him hundreds of times. I am living in a nightmare. Something vital has disappeared, the ground of my life has crashed under my feet, the temporal lags have slipped. What has happened? Whose mother, whose son, whose spouse? It was difficult for him to remember how passionately he had loved her once. She whom he had known as the Tropical Island "Princess"— yes, old enough to be his mother, but he had been very young at the time and she irresistibly seductive. For decades he had been haunted by unplumbed depths of guilt toward her, which she assiduously cultivated.

The Diva, la Castafiore, whose opera presence had been trumped also by this grande dame, examined the latter with professional jealousy, while she plumped up her heavily dyed blonde locks with dainty taps to the back of the head with bent fingers. As to the little princess, if looks could kill she would have died then and there at the feet of the Diva who sympathized generationally with the Lady *Ahau*, in spite of her wounded vanity. Meanwhile the Dragon-Lady swept off the dais preceding the Prince and his warrior-team with superb disregard for any effect her interruption might have had. The Maya audience who had followed the exchange with stupefaction from the outset flowed out in the wake of the royal retinue.

What do you think of this, appealed Augustus to Ignatius, is there much risk to us? The friends indulged in light-hearted banter, but they all felt the tickling behind the armpit under the ribs.

Bon bon, said Tintin brusquely, waving aside tension and preoccupation with a hand. He really had no particular interest in the sport. They all surged across the entrance. Alas ye friends all, he whispered almost inaudibly, we need better entrances and exits. Lady Butterfly mulled this over as she fled across with the others, she didn't quite get it although she knew his theatrical bent. And as they came through the tunnel up the narrow stairs they all heard a great murmur, he well remembered the dank touch and musty smell of that long passage-way, the feet of his companions thudding in his ear, and when they emerged into the light of the great arena—it fell about their ears like a waterfall, the hiss and racket and jumble of chatter, shriek and guffaw of the immersing crowd. *Bain de foule* the French politicos call it. d'Hachis stood there arms akimbo with a look of hilarity behind his spectacles. Walter Aleph frowned, more troubled than amused, amused nonetheless but still troubled, for he was fundamentally distrustful of very large gatherings of the human beastie, and much given to complex rumination. The mass of fans was seated in the decks and the upper decks on the shady side of the arena in this brilliantly sunny day. The sort of day really made for a ball game.

K'at – 2
(Day One)

fire

The friendly hand of Phil, the shopkeeper-poet, settled on his shoulder,

Have you noticed? There are so many more of them than of us! His eyes gleamed with amazement, and while we're on the subject of death and life, he continued imperturbably. Augustus did now take his first good look around the arena and realized there were about 40,000 Maya to judge from the mahogany-red hue of the huge crowd. Whites and blacks stood out like blank spaces and punctuation in the monotone redline text. And then he looked down: they must have been very high up in the stadium seating arrangements. The arena dipped away like a giant bowl at their feet. He teetered—a careening drop from the cusp where they stood—and gazed down the steep narrow corridor of the aisle below them past the rows of thousands of seats to a remote and tiny black stone platform at the edge of the playing field. And in the confusion of the vertigo, of the rhythmic clapping and the guttural cries of the crowd, and the *tunkul, tunkul,* the Maya drums with their sullen thud, and the swallows and pigeons soaring and wheeling above the crowd and diving in low as if intoxicated by its excitement, he became aware of a soft but equally firm hand wedged at his back under his belt, and the chemical reaction that his skin always had with hers told him it was the princess's fingers in the small of his back even before he heard her voice.

Augustus! You are at the *Wak-Ebnal,* the Six-Stair-Place, quick don't look down, and she practically jerked him back into her arms, where he rested a moment luxuriating in the soft twin pressure points.

The Six Stair Place, he murmured as if he were speaking of heaven.

The place where the *Te Tun Ahau* is thrown and bounces down like a ball! she exclaimed with exasperation. I don't know why I put up with you! Augustus craned his head backwards and gazed, besotted, into her eyes. She released him and he stood up a little shakily. Cloudlike shadows of the wheeling fowl drifted upon the crowd and the field. At the back of the stadium he saw the huge white block of the Brooklyn Courthouse. Opposite the little group on the other side of the stadium sat the "bleacher creatures" in the dazzling sun: the cheapest seats and the most fanatic fans. He heard his name boom above the arena through the P.A. system, and shuddered with that fright that comes over us when we are suddenly exposed, vulnerable, to the crowd, and the jeers and imprecations of the "bleacher creatures" only reinforced the shock, and then Carl, and then d'Hachis, and the others, their names rolled over the air amid raucous laughter. And as they gazed down, the companions realized that their names were being flashed on the huge electronic scoreboard. Yet nobody in the stadium glanced their way or realized that the small huddled group was the challenging team. And now the names of the opposing team, first Prince Smoking Squirrel and the crowd roared its approval throughout the stadium and the *tunkul* banged out again and again, and the fans in the bleachers jumped out of their seats and imitated playing movements of their sports hero, such as the short jabbing movements of the spear arm, or the flip of the hip with the yoke to catch the ball, and the names were blared out, *Lord Bird-Jaguar*, then *Lord Great Jaguar-Paw*, and Augustus found himself doing a little dance step with Princess Butterfly to the rhythm of the crowd's scansion of the names and the roar of drums, and *Six-Hell-Lord* and *Lord Storm-Sky*, and other warriors fell into a similar step, and down below they could see the mass in the bleacher seats jerk backward and forward with the same rhythm. The electronic score board spelled out the word "clap!". And dutifully the crowd began to clap. It was deafening. And the mass of brown bodies skipped to one side, then skipped back again, and jumped forward a step, then jumped back again, and the slap of the thousands of feet in rhythm added to the racket. And Augustus and his crew would skip forward two or three steps, then a step back as in a conga line, and gradually they made their way down the aisle between row after row of crowded seats, and they had to be careful not to be bounced over when the people in the rows skipped sideways together. The clapping stopped sporadically as the teleprompter stopped prompting, and

Augustus and his team mates came to a stumbling stop also. And then they saw the Shamans and the Princes and the *Ahauob* and the *Ah k'u hun*, the scribes, dancing at the far end of the ball court (which was the length of a football field) on a much larger blood-red platform no doubt red stone, or perhaps it was stucco stained red with some dye. Our team had come down almost to the level of the field itself and could look straight across to where the Lords were dancing. It was the *ak'ot* glyph, the raised heel which inaugu-rates the dance. It was stately, only a sort of strident flute could be heard. And what was wonderful was that intuition, as if the glyph were spelled out, that someone had stepped on the base of the mountain and this of course meant the dancing!

Look, you see there, and Princess Butterfly points with excite-ment mixed with awe at an animal-headed and elegant dancer, that is the Lord of *Tzum* who was prancing on the name-glyph of the *Wuk Ek'-K'anal* or the "Seven Yellow Black Place"—that is to say he was in suspension in a place not visible to the onlookers because it was situated outside this ritual space somewhere else where his dance-steps had carried him to. They could see it was precisely below the glyph of the White Bone Snake's gullet which signified a portal to the other world. And now came the dancers in full body-suits of otherworldly creatures: these dancers were plumped out in furry, spotty, jaguar suits which would have been comical if they had not been vaguely sinister. The long muzzles with streaming whiskers swiveled toward each other, their big eyes bugged out and they flung their upper paws about with abandon as they strutted fantastically about the stage. The plumes nodded even behind these swollen jaguar heads. It was tangible as the various animalistic feet scampered and scraped the pavement delicately that some current was charging them up and the crowd around them, who watched with respect and rapt attention.

It is the dead, hissed the princess, they are charging the space here, preparing the ground for the ancestors and the bloodletting.

The what! exclaimed Augustus with dismay if not surprise, isn't that rather unsportsmanlike..

Carl at his elbow flashed him a reassuring glance—You must remember, he said, the ball court is the place of life and death, of victory and defeat, of rebirth and triumph. And that comes through sacrifice here, indeed decapitation is the crowning event (no pun intended) in the career of the hero. What's reassuring about that, wondered Augustus. As they came to the wall, the tingle of green energy that zapped at their ankles told them they

had reached the charged arena. They looked back up at tier upon
tier stretching around and above them, and he realized that when
they played they would have to keep their heads down, because
the effect of those thousands upon thousands of reddish bodies
hovering above them could be daunting.

Quite so, murmured the aristocratic Ignatius, who tested the
spongy ground with the toe of his Church shoe. It's hard underneath this Astroturf, feels like…, his voice trailed off, feels like that
essential material of their dramatic décor, a plaster stage!

d'Hachis dropped lightly to his knees in spite of his imposing
girth, and scraped at the turf until he scratched the stucco surface.
But of course, he beamed up at Ignatius with relief, this is theatre
after all!

Ah, yes, the others looked around and nodded, that's what it
was of course.

Ouf! cried Tintin, half-crouching, hands on knees, bent forward, as if he could not believe what he was seeing, Augustus and
all the others now stared in the same direction as the ancient
king, Pakal, danced across the watery surface of the ball court in
the net skirt of *Hun-Nal-Ye*. What did this mean, their eyes asked
as they all looked toward Princess Butterfly,

Well, she answered, it was clear enough from the unmistakable long-nosed profile and noble features that it was the old King
Pakal, original and infatuated husband of the *Dragon-Mother*,
whom, rumor has it, she sacrificed on a propitious occasion.
When he had died from a lingering painful death that eventually
rendered him speechless (cancer of the throat), it had seemed
to Augustus to be a bitter accomplishment and metaphor of that
condition of non-communication that had characterized the
manner of his relationship first with his beloved queen and then
with the younger son. He had little enough concern for himself
for he was overwhelmed with (inexplicable) pity and sorrow for
his spouse, and by means of a long pole he would poke out mes-
sages on scraps of paper into the hallway separating their rooms
assuring her of his undying love. Had his last (and probably only)
extra-marital romance—which only briefly preceded his mortal
illness—contributed to the pathetic nature of his demise? In any
case his ineffectual and kindly character ensured his non-survival
of his spouse. As to the "watery surface", this strange ripple and
brilliance as of splattering rain on the court surface, the ball court
notoriously was on top of the watery underworld of the Xibalba,
much as if one rode in a glass-bottomed boat over the depths of a

lagoon. And a "boat" was a good analogy here because the experience of the underworld hads that connotation of "travel" in it.

Yes, mused Ignatius, but this dance, that is what is determining..

Self-loss and concentration, said Carl finally, this is the meaning. *Dis-tanz* in German, to dance away from oneself. And Augustus and d'Hachis remembered that fateful evening on top of the Federal Building. When you observe yourself, you notice that through concentration on a point something pulls together, and that an interspace comes between what otherwise would be stuck together—because normally different spheres of consciousness stick together. But with concentration these interstitial spaces—or the distances that you gain with respect to yourself –are realized to the extent that you manage to press forward to the psycho-nuclear core.. That is what the King's Dance means here.

Well, we all supported him as our Captain, but we also wondered what the hell he was talking about! Not everyone is capable—but just as these thoughts coursed through their heads, this time the little princess let out a cry and pointed: it was the Prince, Smoking-Squirrel himself, who was dancing toward his mother, so that the other dancers had left a swath of space around them. Yes, the dread Mother had returned to the scene dressed outrageously, barbarously, even if it was par for the course for the Maya Queen, but in the heavy net skirt, the Jaguar-Lady (that was another of her names, she was often portrayed sitting on the double-headed jaguar-throne), or the Lady *Wak Chanil Ahau* as we know her by now, and nods went around our entire team as these names were bandied about, with the jaguar belt or large pendant hanging at her crotch and the shrunken skulls clustering about it, her meaty shoulders bare, and her huge sagging breasts barely covered by the assorted mirrors and shell ornaments and jade plaques, and the huge bone ear-flares protruding through her lobes. She was heavy-lidded and it seemed as if she might be drugged from the fumes of copal resin that wafted even to where we stood and the *balche* liquor that accompanied the sacrifices before the ballgame. In any case she entirely overwhelmed the smaller boy-king in spite of the enormous palanquin he was rigged out with, a complex backrack consisting of a great Draco-Serpent with its plumed crocodile head, holding in its arms the two-headed royal scepter, at one end of which peered a goggle-eyed mustachioed gentleman that recalled a sinister Groucho, the whole prosthetic body so littered with ornaments and knots and braids and pendants, bracelets and belt pendant and flayed skin shield that the plethoric figure was roiling with graphic energy. The boy-prince was ensconced within this clumsy theatrical machinery, his slight, nude form quite visible within, and he appeared pathetically vulnerable next to the formidable beldame. Now he was dancing towards the Mother as was originally pointed out, and she tendered him the *K'awil Manikin* scepter, the Manikin with the fish-foot and the curled snout, foolscap on its head and an axe through its forehead where a mirror glittered fitfully, its meaning the taking of blood and decapitation in particular of course, and the youthful would-be king was overtly anxious to take possession of the scepter, but each time he reached out to gather it graciously into his embrace, the Queen-mother twirled ponderously away again with a blare of conch shells and he had to prance off as yet ungraced with it and clearly put out, a rueful and rigid smile affixed. For that matter, their gestures appeared to be lingering in the air as in slow motion, and looking closely Augustus noticed a thread of blood running down the Prince's inner thigh from the groin, and he realized why they both appeared to be groggy. Her blubber-lips did appear ruddier and more swollen than usual.

Oh yes, whispered the princess to the members of the team around her, all this dancing and folderol is a preparatory mechanics, cranking up the stage machinery. It transforms the playing field into a battle field. Fat drops of sweat mixed with blood pearled down the jowls of the dowager mother, and the young candidate-king also gleamed with a fine film of perspiration all over his near-naked body within the giant "puppet" for which his entire body was the hand. It was perfectly clear to Augustus and his companions that the royal couple were engaged in their central role—as performers for the populace. The tiers closest to the field of the sports arena had fallen silent, and they gestured at those behind them to be silent, and the silence swept slowly wave upon wave up the crowded tiers until the whole stadium was studiously quiet. The previously rowdy spectators stared now with worshipful attention as their kings and nobles enacted other beings, another space, a time outside of their time and perhaps within this very time.

I have only begun to realize, he whispered back to the princess, that this archaeology of manners has been resurrected just for us! Whose would those roles be otherwise? Why else would we be here? What would be the point? She nodded in assent. Yes, he thought, our lovers, our mothers and fathers, our failures, our fates--what else could it be about?

The clap of feet of these living dance-glyphs across the arena was dry and percussive in that dead silence. "Uh!" and "Oh!" ran through the public in a hum like a plucked string, providing a sinister background beat for increasing numbers of dancers who spread about the horizon of the playing field now and even approached Augustus & Co.. Hearing a tap-tap very close by, his and the princess's eyes dropped to the floor at their feet and to their astonishment they saw that Carl's left heel had risen in the *ak'hot* position and his right foot now tapped again at a catchy rhythm and in the next moment he was moving out in a partly gliding, partly swiveling dance-step, very smooth, very ball-room competition style, and as his team-mates gaped after him, the strangest *way*[68] or soul-companion they had ever seen hip-hopped up to him. This was White-Three-Dog, literally three dogs, one quite large, plump, hairy dog and two others, smaller and hairless, but with equally unpleasant snarls, locked together as if copulating or articulated in a glyph-like formation as a single (vertical) being (but in triplicate), in which the dog forms were graphically functional as well as phonetic symbols for a glyph, which no doubt spelled its name (White-Three-Dog), but on second sight (not a second look) it became apparent that "they" were a human being dressed in dog-fur and a dog-mask with a dog-tail curled up fluffily behind his posterior dancing on his hind legs, but as he danced opposite Carl, he could not maintain this stance for long and would drop down to the ground into the actual three white dogs again, a hallucinatory spectacle and one hard to understand either rationally or optically. Carl, all bristling black brows and piercing dark eyes, danced away from himself, obviously deliriously happy and not one misstep. And this was increasingly the model of the ball court having been converted by these couples and the supporting drums and cymbals, trumpets and a kind of castanets, into an ancient dance-hall (like the grand old ballrooms in Manhattan and Brooklyn), just the outsized macaw heads grinning down incongruously on the throng, the pairing that is of noble and unmasked figures like Carl and grotesque, monster figures like his partner. The entire team was frozen by another, still more bizarre sight, and the crowd seemed to have been hushed just now

---

68   The *wayob* are the demons or divinities which descended upon, danced with or emanated from the shamans in trance-dance, much like the *Orishas* and the *Vodoun* in Candomble dances of Brazil and West Africa.

by this same spectacle:

Nupul-Balam, the *way* of the *ch'ul ahaw* of Tikal, the princess hastily whispered in her fright to Augustus, its face raised ecstatically toward the sky and in its paws (yes, because instead of hands it had the spotted muscular paws of a jaguar) a large pot of sorts, was literally floating (perhaps in some Nijinsky-like dance-leap?) above the *Ch'akba-God A*, while the latter sat on the ground, oblivious of the rich scene about him, studiously, fastidiously, cutting off his own head!

Clearly beyond the pale of dance! Tintin whispered sharply to his companions. The companions glanced at each other in a state of alarm. It was evident that this spectacle was in the airy stages of hallucination. The squeal of pipes, the steady deep drone of the great horns and the incessant calling of the antler-beat on drums. The whole team now followed their captain's lead, Phil tripped out in a kind of jig, Ignatius in a most sophisticated and at the same time mocking tango, d'Hachis spilled onto the dance floor with a fat birdman, a heavy boa constrictor hanging about its neck, and they both danced what looked like a greatly slowed-down version of rock'n roll. Well, well, well, said Augustus to himself, it looks like it's time to go! And he jerked elbows and shoulders and high-stepped it in some reminiscence of New Orleans street pomp, and sidling up to him was a *way* with razor-sharp flints on its knees and elbows, naked, testicles repellent and dragging, clearly a death-god. He was just watching out of the corner of his eye as Walter Aleph sallied out in the smoothest World War II style fox trot, in that moment he could swear the big bands were playing their song, in fact the strangeness of the costumes, the mixture of familiar faces and aristocratic warrior-lords, and especially of the exuberant and sinister *wayob* who were anybody's guess –or nightmare— were such that neither Augustus nor his more level-headed female companion of bed and board, the *Malinche*, could be faulted for some little confusion regarding dance-tune eras. Oh the hell, he thought, where are we all going, it was as they had been siphoned out onto the plane of the playing field-cum-dance club. And at some moment they clicked—they all clicked. It was as if everybody (and every thing for such dancers as could not be clearly identified as human personalities) fell into a dance lockstep, they jelled—it was jolly and at the same time vaguely threatening, and a kind of interior illumination came on as if ir-radiated from the inner beings of us all, and it was then that we realized clearly just what the charging and/or the purification of the time-space meant. Augustus noticed the *Ah k'u hun*, the supreme artist-scribe and "uncle" of the pretender to the throne, as he hip-hopped syncopatedly by in a still fluid and graceful manner that only a *Ah k'u hun* could manage. He caught his eye as he by-passed, and it was humorous and full of titillation and sundry charm and deft wisdom which Augustus could not quite get the ken of. The *maître* (as in the formal address to the artist) called out as he whirled past with his way companion *Nab Ix*, the Waterlily Jaguar who danced on his hind legs as if he were a graceful human being but who roared like a jaguar, "Welcome home!", only he pronounced it *Hom*, and *Malinche* whispered into Augustus's taut ear—

Hom in ancient *K'iche* from the holy book means "ball court", but in today's *K'iche* it means "grave", so you must take it as you see fit.

Thank you, he cried back after the master's dwindling form, always happy to drop in—momentarily! He reflected upon this latter reference: *Och bin*, already Carl had "entered upon" this road, and what if the whole purpose were to meditate upon one's eventual death (no, my eventual death, he corrected)? He stopped dancing with this glyph hanging above him, and the murderously obscene *way* who had been doing a pas-de-deux opposite him left. He went up to Butterfly who had been waiting for him on the shore. Yes, because the playing field was also like a lake according to the Maya mythology—beneath their feet, pairs of supernatural players in this watery upside down world…and on the shores, egrets, crane and other water fowl stood and peered through the glaucous surface, or pecked and skipped along.

So, Lady Butterfly, he queried, is it not this sense of danger that inspires us, these monsters, these self-projections, and well, the possibility of our own demise?

Phil, who had been lolling about behind Augustus at this point, cried, Just the ticket! And thus have I identified myself always! My self with my self passing.. With a slightly impatient shake of her head and her long black-fiery hair, the princess said,

No, it is the *ch'ulel*, the sacred which lies hidden, in caches beneath the floor of the ball court.

The 'sacred'? repeated Augustus, shaking his head incredulously, or with some glimmering of an illumination infringing heretofore barriers—

No, she said, no, you don't understand what this is about, *ch'ulel* is power! Most of the team were gathered around them now, and people had stopped dancing, the *wayob*, those sinister projections, appeared to have left.. Tintin was staring aghast at Princess Butterfly, spots of perspiration flying out from his face graphically. A bloodcurdling yell interrupted this conciliabule with its religious overtones, and other screams punctured the atmosphere--at the highest, almost vertical reach of the stadium's upper rim, a flurry became visible, the form of motion resolved itself into a tumbling ball-like object; it appeared to become more shapeless and sodden as it continued on its downward course, until it came to the last, very long and vertical, set of stairs, and then with one last shove from the audience it rushed down leaping up into the air once when it hit an obstacle, and then plunged on downward until it collapsed in the flat altar carved as the spread gullet of the Vision Serpent at that end of the ball court. A red stain spread about the sad sack. A deathly silence spilled over the crowd again. The front of the bundle appeared to stir, then stopped.

Well, we've seen that one before, he said grimly. Celebration of the game! Now we know what we are playing for. He looked up gravely from his bowed position at the team players behind him. Milou tugged at his rear right pant cuff; without him Tintin was not really Tintin. They were so attached that Milou could be said to be a part of his persona. Indeed, it could be argued that he was Tintin's very soul. The spell of the human ball, whoever the poor sod was, was broken. We were all half bent over behind him observing the prone figure, and we must have looked like a football team just before the scrimmage. Yes, death was the vehicle of the game, and they would play accordingly. The first to arise from this bowed condition before the corpse was Captain Carl: he had been bent over in sorrow with his belly bowed to the earth, for the shaman poet knew better than any of us the bloodiness and the lies of the power-brokers and the priests at the altars on high on the peaks of the pyramids and the office towers. It was as if Carl had been buried with the dead, such was his dream-bond. And now, as in the triple burial of Til Eulenspiegel, the visionary folk hero of the thirteenth century dear to his heart, his living skeleton was slung by colliding and converging energies of hope and rage into a vertical posture buried in the earth under his stone, on which the two figures of the Eul or "owl"and the spiegel or "mirror" were engraved, the owl holding the mirror in its claws in which the writing could be glimpsed. Captain Carl rose straight up now as if out of the ground from the dead and assumed his captaincy of our clattering and hitherto disconnected troupe, with an infectious smile. And a cloud of hilarity surrounded the band of friends. Tintin who was clutching his ribs quite helpless with laughter tried to draw their attention by a violent nodding of his yellow cowlick in the direction of the other end of the field, and when they finally managed to look that way, they caught sight of the team of the Kingdom of the Dead which had been trotting out onto the field with the hulking swagger, the rolling hips and shoulders, of an American football squad, and at the sight of this classic American super-machismo their cackling and wheezing and hee-hawing peeled out hysterically. The latter stopped dead in their tracks: stripped of their finery, their plumes, their gleaming pendants and skull, they wore deerskin trousers or loincloths with calf-length leather skirts over them and, surprisingly, they wore gloves. Cotton padding was attached about waist and pelvis, and cloth padding about one forearm and a single kneepad as well. What was incomprehensible was the stone yoke many of the men wore about their waists. The weight was so unthinkable that Augustus felt he must be looking at a comic strip. He had always imagined the yokes were wood, and that the stone ones which turned up in the "digs" were only the remains of statuary. Evidently he was wrong! They were the real thing—and as our boys' laughter drifted off in long plumes it appeared to hang in suspense in the humid and otherwise hushed air of the arena, for the huge crowd, which had been plumping for its favored heroes, had fallen into an awkward silence, as if disconcerted by this raucous and untoward behavior, without a clue as to how to respond. Pulling themselves together and still gasping for breath, Captain Carl's team began to trot in formation along the edge of the playing field with Milou closely attached. A bizarre object swung into their line of sight, and as they came up, they saw, ten feet tall and twenty long, a solid wooden rack neatly crammed not with hats and umbrellas but skulls of players of the past who had lost their match. Row after row of grinning skulls appeared to hail them as they loped about the rack and out onto the field in a sinisterly humorous twist of the cliché-ridden "*morituri te salutant*". It looked like a visual joke by Magritte. So Captain Carl's team trotted out onto the field, well aware that they were not dressed appropriately, and each of them sort of thinking over what had brought them to this impasse, much of it owing to Augustus's persuasive skills, although that was not the case for their shamanic captain who alone could show them the way inside this interior realm, the mirror

realm, for he had knowledge whereas the others not a clue. And
the young Prince's team resumed their trot as well, and the ru-
morous rumble of the crowd picked up again as if it had suffered
no interruption--then came a high-pitched scream of glee like
that of the *Muwan* bird, which resounded beneath all this scree of
mountainous rumble, and we all looked up to where it came from,
the precise location of the voice, everybody looked, from the
bleachers, from both the teams, from the few odd *way* still left on
the field and then we saw them, two voluptuous women with
swans in their arms stood looking down on the field from on
high, from a dais where other high nobles and dignitaries with
bowls of flowers had flocked—no not swans but what they had at
first taken for swans with their long white twisting necks were
white serpents which they held in their arms above their bare
breasts, their white *huipil* dresses billowing about, getting entangled with the serpents tails, the serpents writhing, their tongues
flickering among the pink nipples, and a third girl, and it was obvious that it was she had screamed, for her red lips were still open
as she leaned forward with her arms bent by her sides as if she had
just—and everybody else, to judge by the collective sigh, and every eye followed the slow descent of the huge pok-a-tok ball with
glyph 113-Nab which started the game, while she was wordless
and the swans screamed, or no, the serpents, or was it the long
white-necked damsels with said snakes who stripping off their finery quickly with the serpents twisting about their nude limbs, accompanied the large ball slowly tumbling through the air with
streams of pink and white blossoms, its glyph perfectly legible
throughout the great breathless stadium, and then when it landed
with a huge *Castilloa Elastica* bounce and exactly on the rebound
the crowd let out a clammering vast roar of excitement mmm-
mm—the game was on! There was the cry, "*pitzen!*" or "play ball!"
in Mayan (Cholan), and at that moment he spied the Tikal ball-
court marker in the midst of the court: a thin cylinder surmounted by a sphere and a disk that he had seen before on top of the
Federal Building. An ear-clapping bellow of the crowd jerked him
back to the game, and turning with the others to the enemy team,
he saw one of the largest, in sheer girth, of the Maya, Lord *Six-
Tun-Bird-Jaguar*, so broad-hipped that his hips constituted the
dominant axis of his body as it moved or swung, now bent and
swiveled along this axis and the huge stone-grained yoke which
lay about it toward the sun and the descending ball. The ball, it
may be remembered, was on its rebound and since the sun lay be-

hind it and the ball passed slowly in front of the sun it was hard to keep an eye on it, even now the only clear perception was of its 113-NAB glyph rotating over and over as it dropped, and there was that huge interval before it actually would fall when it seemed that almost anything was possible, and he looked back at his teammates whose cantering roll of shoulders and hips and bowing up and down of necks betrayed the intense effort and seriousness with which they ran even though this moment, this interval, provided no such luxury of reflection and tactical thinking. Think of their "running"—not moving across the playing field but running in place—not like the inability to move away as in a nightmare, but in the mind, no, in ecstatic movement. Learning to see; to see. And not to see. It was at this moment that the large ball (bigger than a basket ball but smaller than a medicine ball) landed on the tendered yoke. Lord *Six-Tun-Bird-Jaguar* extended his left leg and knelt back on his bent right leg in a classic position and absorbed the huge blow unflinching, as if he were sculpted out of stone, and the elastic ball rebounded again. The ball is thrown out: the ladies with the serpents—sexual connotation—what is the original time if not childhood and its ecstasy? The rush backwards. Out of anguish, out of death. The perfection, the grace of the game, transcends time and death and disease and aging, the curses the Maya wished to conjure away (*Xbalanque*'s killing of the *Xibalba*[69] Lords of death & disease). Childhood and grace: every blow and bounce of the ball reverberates in that world/time. The ball had passed the apex of its arc and was dropping down now again. Augustus could only see the faces of the Maya players, all seven of them, the broad reddish-brown faces, noble, symmetrical, and glowing—with what? With murder-lust, with the desire for suckling under the rib? Or simply with the competitive spirit, what they called the jock mentality in prep school? Was there a difference, he wondered idly?

And his eye followed the lazy arc of the ball and he remembered as if it were yesterday playing baseball with the Buckley School team on Staten Island, or not exactly playing but lying

---

69   The Maya Kingdom of the Dead in the *Popul Vuh,* the holy book of the Maya, visited by the hero-twins, who vanquish its Lords thereby overcoming death, disease etc..

in the grass in far outfield hearing the cries of the boys and the dry crack of the ball on the bat and the remote lofty drone of a tinny plane in the still heat which would never again float out of that blueness and the drugging rich smell of the cut grass he was drowning in and he knew ecstasy for ever. The ball dropped with ominous speed and enormous, and he stretched to meet it, his hands out, agonized he knew he would never be able to reach it, the massive glyph beating down on him with such unanswerable violence. And moments before it would have got him, crushed him, a figure seemed to spring out of the ground. It was the wiry energy of his brother Carl who jumped like a released spring, like the irrepressible Til Eulenspiegel himself. The broad grin flew by,

Not with the hands, he shouted at Augustus, the eye of the hand—the hand that sees! And with these words he leapt to meet the ball, and he knew that the slight frame could never stand up to such a battering, and he saw Carl's body torque in the air, shoulders and head and arms twisting out of the path of the ball and rearwards while the hips and the legs faced forward, which gave the impression of tautly wound-up energy, and there must have been a collision although Augustus failed to witness it because the ball reversed direction and sped toward the great iron ring sunk high in the wall and the faces of the other team were no longer red but ashen, and our team screamed like monkeys with fists beating at the air, and there sounded a whoosh with the universal sucking-in of air by the thousands of onlookers. It seemed like such an expanse of space and observation, but it must have been only moments, no one—not a member of our team, not a member of theirs, not a single onlooker—seemed to breathe or to stir even, such was the peacefulness, the leisureliness of this gesture. The large ball dropped through the iron loop softly and sweetly. The Maya team screamed with rage and horror and the crowd, well.. Down here in the pit it's the maw of hell, the noise of the crowd drops like a cataract, incomprehensible. It was flattening! Our team felt like quitting even though they were winning.

Look, murmured Tintin, the golden boy, flipping the forelock out of his eyes, look who's therehrhrhrhrhr! He practically neighed as he pointed toward a tier of seats, which was close to the field and had some special kind of protection against the sun's glare. We looked.. Then, then.. Watching her, just watching her—it was the Queen Mother. Her broad face seethed with hatred. It was clear she considered the goal to be lèse-majesté. The body-armor clanged on her thighs, the pendants of jade mirror on her large breasts and of silver on her groin clattered, the shrunken heads dangling from her belt jerked and spun. In the midst of all these unmistakable manifestations of annoyance, Augustus caught a cunning ophidian glance—a kind of mother's greed, a look of tender and devouring prurience. Do you know those mothers who would eat their child, such is the desire to possess this beloved flesh? Such was the regard lavished by the granddame. And how well he sympathized! Whatever horror and repudiation as a virile and up-standing member of—well—self-respecting male society, he wanted to be ingurgitated by that female psyche, oh god how he desired that maternal appetite, and he knew how to whet it! By god he did! Such were his fugacious and barely self-avowed musings as he witnessed the above. For that matter, the entire stadium of forty to fifty thousand ticket-holders sitting above the players' heads, thighs akimbo, thick and hairy or slender and gently curved, mottled and freckled or silky, stuffed into cut-away jeans and shorts, and breasts bursting with pulchritude out of tight halters and pectorals with sculpted nipples in clinging T-shirts, in an irrepressible outpouring of vital sexuality—a *trôp-plein*, a potency displayed for us in the field below, at our disposal, communicating vases through all their proffered apertures, this fleshly offering pumped the players' hormones. *Bird-Jaguar*, slighter than *Six-Tun* but tough and wiry, muscles rippling up along the shoulders to the neck, was being applauded at the moment because he had flipped up the ball on its bounce with one foot and knocked it off his shoulder toward a team mate, *Six-Hell Lord*, who with his fierce beetling brows and machete-sharp nose, filled the bill. And then, then, a quite extraordinary revelation as d'Hachis as well, remember d'Hachis also, was in hot pursuit, halali! Without more ado, then, it consisted in this: when the ball dropped from, after, that is, the ball had dropped from the hoop, it was the sensation of the ball dropping through the iron hoop all the way down to and through the floor, yes, passing through the delicate membrane of the floor and into the depths leaving a trail of bubbles. In a moment our team, that is Tintin and d'Hachis and Walter Aleph and the others, had all crowded about this "wat'ry grave" as the ball plummeted downwards (in slow motion to be sure, what with the density of sea water), Princess Butterfly with them, and as they peered downwards in relief (was this the end of the ballgame?), she said—

It is the portal of *Öl*, a doorway that happened to open into the watery world of the Maya Kingdom of the Dead. Nobody really took it in, but they were all fascinated by this peep into the underworld, a glaucous, still world, and by the other players who moved beneath them, their counterparts, the *way*, the spirit-companions of each player, who in some way predicted or anticipated their every move, upside down under their feet, always a little ahead of the players' moves, not merely their moves on the field above but in life. Tintin threw himself down now next to the hole, which was like a rippling circle which grew no larger, fluid but never overflowing its borders, and looking up at the others, said,

I am going to exercise my cartoonish prerogative in a situation which I think lends itself to such invention—because otherwise this game is kaput! And reaching down a curved arm which under water took on a distorted angle and elongation, and as they all craned their necks they could see the long arm and hand curve downward and feel about until he could just scoop up the big, buoyant (in the salt water) ball and fish it up to the surface, pulling it all dripping and soaked back through the hole with both hands, and as soon as he had done so the fluid aperture drew itself together again with an organic squelch, any excess drops sucked up by the parched soil, and the ball perfectly dry!

Well, said Walter Aleph, looking down his nose fastidiously at such tricks, what do you think this means? As if it were a word puzzle. The intricate novelist had a way of asking seemingly simple questions, which required complex answers. Augustus could well imagine him as one of those sensitive and introverted friends of his childhood, who were also the most disquieting. When on one of those damp, still-dark, early mornings he would travel by tram to school, the rich smell of rotting leaves beneath the trees along the great boulevard where his family home with its manic turrets stood amidst embassies and other mansions, and the penetrating, sickening but intoxicating, smell of the electricity geneconflationated along those tram tracks with him even now, which would set his teeth on edge, you could almost taste it. In his schoolbag he had the latest Tintin album, which he was keeping for perusal a little farther on in this long morning ride. He liked the dawn darkness outside the large windows of the tram as it sped with the gnashing of steel on steel, he enjoyed the sense of the unknown and its dangers out there, and here inside the coziness and warm light. Several stops farther on and the pale rays of the sun reaching tentatively along the facades of the buildings rushing by, he now fully engrossed in his album, *Tintin et le Retour de la Mère des Maya*, forgetful of the outside world as it gradually became prosaic, one of his schoolmates climbed up the tram steps and joined him. He was pleased to see his friend but also annoyed that he would be distracted from his hero's adventures. It was Walter Aleph. The sensitive and clever boy peered over his shoulder at the pictures as he feared he would.

Ah, said Walter Aleph, looking down his nose fastidiously, what do you think this means? For this distinguished wordsmith life was a word-puzzle. He had a way of asking these very simple questions which had not even occurred to Augustus and which doubtless demanded difficult answers. And he pointed a long and inky finger at the cartoon frame in which Tintin had just fished up the *pok-a-tok* ball to the surface of the underworld, pulling it all dripping and soaked back through the hole with both hands, and the next frame, as soon as he had done so, where the fluid aperture drew itself together again seamlessly, with any excess drops sucked up by the parched soil and the ball perfectly dry! Walter Aleph had a way of pressing on the surface of things, or of the words, which represented them rather, as if he suspected sinister forces of lurking behind them. In fact while retaining an air of detachment and incredulous amusement at the world about him, he also appeared to move cautiously through an atmosphere thick with dread. These Maya of yours, he said, they're colorful and personable, and one would like to engage them in a conversation. But have you ever tried to do so? Without waiting for an answer, he pursued his line of thought. One fears, doesn't one, that they may draw one into their undoubtedly dangerous world and, and, here he glanced mischievously at Augustus, perhaps cut out one's heart?

Actually, said the latter, according to this footnote (Hergé also loved to insert lengthy erudite footnotes which gave his cartoons a kind of legitimization and worldly context),[70] the Maya were more given to decapitation than to removal of the heart, although the latter was the sacred essence, as described in the *Popul Vuh.*

Walter Aleph continued to look at him curiously, his head cocked slightly to one side,

Yes, but what does it mean? he asked again. Augustus stared at the faint, tremulous impression the aperture had left on the floor of the ball court,

I don't know, he said finally. Perhaps something sexual? The

---

70   Decapitation was typified by the sporting event, but the removal of the heart, far more subtle and loaded with symbolism, was of course the sacred act *par excellence.*

"vulvular hush"?

Yes, I think so, said Walter Aleph, especially with Death lurking within the vulva. And he neighed with laughter. Oh my goodness, Augustus, you're too much! Well, neither of them had had any experience with the other sex yet anyway, although probably neither had le petit Marcel in spite of Augustus' quotation[71]. The tram lurched on. It will surprise nobody to hear that at the next stop, not far from the final, school stop and with the dusk being vacuumed upwards out of the morning, another one of his little friends got on board with a briskness and an authority that could only be Tintin's. And it was indeed the boy reporter, more youthful than ever, who strode purposefully over to where he and Walter Aleph were perusing the album.

My friends, he declared, smiling and looking each one of them in the eye, that was Tintin's approach, self-confident, open, a manner that inspired admiration and emulation on the part of his fans, but fear and murderous loathing on the part of evil-doers who etc., there really is no time for this sort of thing now. We have urgent business to attend to out there, and he pointed out the tram window. It was not the school stop they had come to but the tram stop at the sports arena. Tintin who had never actually been a real boy like them, nor would ever become a real adult, was an aged adolescent who thwarted adult machinations, and having said this, he gestured, and they followed him back down the steps. They were greeted by the roar of the crowd as the tram pulled away steamily in the suddenly tropical atmosphere, and by the drumlike rattle of galloping feet as the team of *Xibalba* bore down on them. More than by this "fatality" of the other team (and much of life seems to be summed up by such an impending sense of "doom" brought by others, and how futile that is!), they were caught and lifted on the roaring crest of the crowd, and it was quite evident that the other team possessed no energy proper but was inflated and propelled balloon-like by the massed breath of forty or fifty thousand lungs. His companions seemed to have been scattered like chaff, he glimpsed only the erect white tail of Milou disappearing in a remote puff of dust. No, no, he said to himself, just step aside and breathe quietly by yourself, and he listened to this calm voice. Throughout his life in moments of disquiet and dread, he had appeared to himself in the second person, and this person was able to counsel and to calm him in a

---

71   From *A la Recherche du Temps Perdu*, Marcel Proust, Gallimard.

manner and with an authority that reflection in the first person was impotent to. What after all, he said to himself, is this charade of the ball court, the warring teams, the thread of life itself, which suspends us—and our lives always hang in the balance of these great games of life even if we don't believe it—about? This side of death? Neuroses? Sexual dysfunction? God, just when he thought about his immediate family, his sexually repressive (and jealous!) father who had fought him—and his own urges!—for years, until in the last year or so, just before dying of cancer, he had found a sweet blond who treated him like a king; like a man! When Augustus, as a boy, found her photograph as he fiddled about idly in the drawers of his father's desk one day (yes, these were always a source of fascination to him), which was situated in his father's large dark bedroom on the other side of the family mansion and at the farthest remove from his mother's and younger brother's (!) rooms for these were side by side, he stared at it fascinated and put it aside carefully, becoming an accomplice in his father's deception of his mother! His father's last (and only) fling shortly before contracting throat cancer and being condemned to as rapid as it was painful (no doubt guilty!) a death—in the photograph she is shaking the blond wave of hair out of her eyes, laughing with happiness. God, in this moment he loved his father! And he remembered the day his father had once turned to him, suddenly, surprisingly, and told him he was the child who had loved him the most (not, interestingly, whom he loved the most)! And he remembered his mother's desperate telephone call late at night crying out with the revelation and the very peculiar and tardy recognition that he, Augustus, had been right in his choice of life since his father had found ecstatic self-fulfillment in another woman as well!! And what about his mother, her perverse character, exhibitionistic and *sado-maso* as the French put it so quaintly! If he had worn her dainty provocative panties and garter straps in his boyhood, how thoroughly would he explore all her darker sexual yearnings through his adulthood! And above all, what of his spouse? Her mothering possessiveness, her decades-long jealous persecution of him, her insatiable narcissism! But after all it was his own hallucinatory conflation of mother and spouse, which was at the bottom of it all—sex with his mother and filial tenderness for his spouse! No wonder the latter had wanted to murder him in the last years of their marriage!

Then he remembered the Butterfly Princess—sassy and sharp-tongued, but with the sweetest arms around his neck that he had

ever known. His tender feelings for her were tinged by more than
a touch of the paternal! If the beginnings of their romance had
been marked by amorous excitement, indeed she had appeared
to lust after him, recently her attitude had become querulous or
mocking, and she was growing physically distant, yet at the same
time emotionally dependent, as if she were marking off a filial
boundary. One that still remained incomprehensible to him.. That
is what the game of *pok-a-tok* has to do with our life. The ball
must be kept up in the air at all costs. The ball is death or mortality or the vehicle of these. The crowd conveys our own impending
sense of doom. Now in the stead of the crowd's huffing bray, he
could hear his own breath: small and private, it alone carried him.
An elegant silhouette fell into step with his and a smile so broad
that it englobed him, and as if curtains had been pulled aside
from the deep eyes, these filled with light, and the caressing tones
of his friend Ignatius said:

It is sweet emptiness that allows us to become wise, my friend.
And nothing changes in the world but ourselves, and perhaps we
do not know even ourselves. And his friend put an arm about his
shoulders, and the thunder of the herd gathered behind them.
And first they saw *Lord Smoke-Shell* balancing the huge medicine-
ball on his winged elbow, that is to say that he bore a prosthetic
bat's wing on each elbow and one of these formed a kind of support for the ball. Long lean hard muscles writhed beneath the gaggle of bright feathers and a cruel curve bent the mouth as he
leaned in their direction. Remember, phenomena or magical rep-
resentations are theater, my friend, and so saying Ignatius rose up
in the air in a slow-revolving leap, and since he wore those knee-
length pants one could see his knee as it swiveled toward the
Amerindian and Ignatius leaned behind his knee to give it more
support. What had sounded before like a distant murmur, began
to gather now, and so far this also sounded like a straight-forward
description but now the cries oddly (since they came from the
tiers of fans above) appeared to swirl from about a foot above the
ground and then to mount in a sort of vortex, gathering into a rising mass-whine, laced with panic, spreading out more and more
widely at the top of our screen, and we realized that this cry of
anxiety had started its rotary course at the bottom tier who could
most closely and early observe his knee and then spiraled up
around and to the top of the tiers of seats. The philosopher had
made no perceptible effort in his upward leap, a small smile
played on his lips and his eyes were half-closed as if he did not be-

lieve in the reality of what he was doing. Quite simply, as he half
lay against the dark blue sky (for Augustus it was the sky—for the
vast audience which had fallen dead silent as if asleep in anticipation, the elegant greyhound body was revolving a little above the
red dust of the court), the encounter of Ignatius' knee and the
large ball reverberated with a THWACK which traveled around
the arena like an immensely expanded cartoon balloon, and every
eye was on the ball as it lifted off the shoulder cum batwing of the
Maya player and rolled lazily through the air toward the wall in
which the iron ring was attached. There were a couple of seconds
of silence as if the Maya audience were in a state of suspended belief, and in the next moment their screams and jeers battered the
air with such rage and vigor that he and his team mates felt their
ear drums being bombarded. It appeared that the psychic violence
of the uproar was aimed at deflecting the ball itself from its goal;
as if the massed will might affect its course if only by inches. And
it seemed that their stimulus might have been effective if by other
means, because at this moment *Six-Hell Lord* had caught up with
them, and while *Lord Smoke-Shell* went stumbling off to one side,
his large leathery wings flapping uselessly, *Six-Hell Lord*, pumped
up with the crowd's mania, harsh beak-nose and bristling brows
leading, followed the ball up to the iron ring with a piston-thrust
of the squat red muscle-bulging thighs and calves which positively
glinted in the sun, and the rage of the crowd tipped into rapture as
the fierce Lord's fingers grazed the bottom of the ring in a desperate attempt to deflect the dropping ball, but his effort failed and he
fell back leaden and gravity-bound as the ball slipped neatly and
handily through the ring. Screams, catcalls, groans sundered the
chaotic atmosphere, and Augustus and Tintin hugged and danced
and Phil jumped up and down with the unsurprised philosopher,
and the Maya War Lords stopped in their tracks as if they had
been turned into *Te-tuns*, the massive stone warrior-stelae which
populated their plazas back home, and stared incredulous at the
prospect dawning upon them that the home team might lose the
match—which was unheard of—and face (if one can face one's
face) decapitation. Again a cloud of heavy silence cloaked the
crowd and the teams in tense expectation, and a single voice,
etched out in the steamy air, was heard above the hissing of
massed silence: "penalty for the crown-prince's team". It was the
Ah k'un, uncle of the crown prince, ultimate umpire of the game.
Augustus sought him out, not far away, standing near the Queen
Mother with her barbarous revealing S&M outfit, who, he would

have sworn, grinned mockingly at him, as she sat with her mottled thighs stretched apart revealing her hairy snatch available for
all to savor. Was this obscene exhibitionism the Mother's last pleasure—or threat? But the subtle and delicate Maya priest did not
look in his direction. A smattering of laughter traveled around the
crowd at first, then uncertain applause (w-w-w-what for? they
asked each other), and the electronic billboard lit up and the giant
electronic hands began to clap, and the entire crowd clapped dutifully as one man, as is the usual media and the vibrations stirred
the red dust of the court yard. Carl and Augustus and Walter
Aleph shook their heads in disbelief, and the reanimated *te-tuns*
stirred to life and chatted in low tones, but did not look at Captain
Carl and his visitors' team. It was half-time, and both teams
walked back to their portals of entry slowly, while the crowd
lapsed into cheery optimism, and trailed down into the bowels of
the stadium and the girls in their tight shorts and bulging blouses
and bared belly-buttons and the guys with proprietary satisfaction
and flexing of muscle and male yelps lined up to buy foot-long hot
dogs and guzzle soft drinks and beer, and micturate. Speaking of
micturation, he stole another look at the Queen Mother. She was
plunged in conversation with someone behind her, so she had
half-swiveled on her massive hips without, however, moving her
legs. This produced a spiral effect and about her neck and spine
and hips the folds of fat positively spun, and with the effort drops
scintillated and dripped down her crotch and her thighs. It was
now possible to see whom she addressed—it was La Castafiore
who had become her favorite. A "gasp" or a "gulp" sounded by his
elbow and he turned around and saw that his friend, Tintin, was
white as—well, as white as his beloved Milou, who stood in front
of his feet, tail rigid and unmoving, and a slight "grrrr" emanating
from between bared teeth. The *faux blonde* grande dame of light
opera (remember Gounod's Faust! and why was it that Bizet's
Gypsy song always rang in his head like a loony tune?) was squat
and her girlish short skirts revealed shanks too thin for the bulk
they had to carry but of which she was inordinately vain. She
spoke in a self-consciously loud and grating British accent and
shook her fake curls, and glanced with complicity across her
hooked nose at Tintin. The latter went from white to beet-red because, it must be said, he had to his ever-lasting regret lost his vir-
ginity (certainly not she hers) in a brief and ungratifying S&M encounter with her, which he sorely regretted. Tintin who had obviously been so effectively neutered by sexual guilt (thanks to Hergé

of course, aside from the absolutely platonic relationship with le *Capitaine* Haddock) that he had written off sex altogether in his adventures (there was that excessive avuncular fondness for the young Chinese boy), presumably determined one day that he should be punished—sexually punished—and had resorted to the Diva for this service. There was no lack of opportunity since she was notoriously in pursuit of the Captain and often visited the Chateau de Moulinsart, the latter's ancestral home. One morning when Tintin was exercising in his blue polka dot boxer shorts he had "inadvertently" left the door ajar—she tiptoed in and molested him from behind--"goosed him" was the schoolboy term he used. It was on that occasion that he proposed that she punish him in a perverse manner. He confided afterwards in Augustus, and out of discretion suffice it to say that it involved ropes and an implement in which Tintin adopted the passive role and it was quite unpleasant. So her complicitous manner was not altogether unjustified, although ever since that first fiasco, Tintin had tried to discourage her attentions. Although the intervention was crudely fleshly, so he put it to his schoolboy pal, Augustus, he had never felt more like a character in a cartoon (although certainly not one of his!). The whistle blew, and half time was over. The two teams trotted out to their respective positions, and Tintin tried to keep his rear view (the view of his rear) out of the Diva's line of sight by keeping between Augustus in front and the large d'Hachis behind. He was determined to make up for his inadequacies in bed on the playing field like all other sports fans. He had a strong sense of duty. He reminded Augustus of his own father—his father as a boy of course. Or as Augustus imagined him. Thoroughly repressed, romantic and ashamed of his sensual yearnings. Somewhat as he himself, Augustus, had been? Immutably guilty.

Listen, Tintin said, catching up with Augustus, please tell the Captain that I may be late for the line-up—but that I will be back soon. There is something I must do, he said. Augustus nodded. He knew. Tintin was the ghost in the back of his own mind—however animated and colorful such a ghost might be! Like his own soul. Tintin turned back where the 104 bus had dropped them earlier. The 104 appeared soon enough, and he vaulted up the steps with his usual light-footedness, and slumped into a seat. Wistfully, he watched his team mates trot on out into the field. The bus was empty except for an obvious Mayan (squat red body, large pentagonal face, scowling brow) dressed in a yellow nylon running suit with red lightning on the chest.

I am seriously conflicted by this course, ran the thoughts in his mind. I am acutely aware that the game is about to resume. And my sense of timing, of realism, of consistency, of moral fiber.. I wonder if I am *pneumatikos*, that is to say, blown up like a flotation device by some god? It was very obvious indeed that Tintin was being borne away from the game by some force more powerful than himself in a move as uncharacteristic as this one. Uncharacteristic that is for someone who played by the rules, who was highly responsible in his own actions and toward others, and above all rigorously logical, *cartésien* in his way. Hergé would not have been *d'accord*. It was a swerving out of the path of ordinary awareness. For that matter, who else, besides Augustus, could exhibit any such conscious transparency?

Meanwhile the others had arrived at their various positions on the field. Captain Carl raised his hand and glanced back at his team with a huge, embracing smile—they were tense, excited, determined: d'Hachis pretended to *piaffer*, that is to make like a horse, and pawed at the ground, with a mischievous wink at Augustus. The latter was buried in thoughts of the mystifying exchange with Tintin: Tintin as father-figure, but when he was a child! The engendering of the father by the son.. Is that who Tintin was, then!? The son he should have been? The son will address the father as *'nuk jo'* my son, according to Maya mythology. The Resurrection of the Father by the Son, the central mystery: the father engenders the son but depends on the son's courage in dancing across the abyss to dig him out from under the ball court floor to renewed life!

Yes, but who is my father, wondered Tintin. Hergé? I don't think so. The problem is not authorial, not textual. It is the story of life and death. He reflected on the ballgame—its distorted powers had something to do with his anxiety, the uncertainty he had been struggling with for five decades. Now I can come to grips with the father story, he said. That's why I am here. There were cries of the crowd as they surged forward. Short vigorous unsealings, were the last thoughts he could remember. As in "the last days". The pentagonal red face of the Indian stretched toward him from the rear seat,

"Or the first days," the face whispered. This was the tragedy of Tintin's life, that he did not know his father or his mother. Or they had disavowed him, they did not know him. They did not wish to know him. The bus lurched to a stop. Tintin got up and out. He stared up at the mostly black façade of the building. She was up there, waiting. And now we shall leave him in this "window", standing in a pool of yellow lamplight, bent backwards in a crooked stance, gazing up at another window several floors above, an uncharacteristic posture for him—in order to return to the game. Tintin's career had brought him back to his home in la Wallonie[72] to the portal between the Maya world and ours. That is, it had brought him to confront the essence of his being.

The crowd's swelling and ebbing roar: it grumbled like the dull roll of thunder before the storm. Augustus started as if he had heard a voice behind him, then crouched again in defensive formation with the rest of the team. He saw Phil, who seemed quite oblivious of the game, meditating no doubt upon grammatical slips and *double entendres* which might serve for his next move in the game. And Ignatius appeared to be looking both through the ball court and at it as representation.

All it needs, said the latter in an aside, is for a little black curtain to be raised at its next act. Arch tone as he shot a glance at Augustus who was known to have a weakness for black lace curtains and other intimate veils. The latter was obviously caught up in some such dream: when the frothy, curlicued fringe of that curtain lifts on the female mystery, when it is drawn up the creamy thighs.., and he looked most dreamily toward where the princess sat at the edge of the field, leaning back lazily on the bleacher, her knee drawn up in her folded hands. It was of course known in the profession that he was a sucker for lingerie, especially Perla, the Italian brand name, which she wore for him, with its cunning allusion to the pearl enclosed within the violaceous lips of the oyster, just awaiting the scoop of the lascivious tongue.. In other words, continued Ignatius imperturbably, the phenomenon (which is what appears as representation) is the basis of life, and in the thought of the skeptic Sextus Empiricus everything is reduced to pure representation. In fact, continued Ignatius warming up, and several of the team mates were pricking up their ears as he spoke, seemingly oblivious to the pending onslaught of the Maya team, the world presents itself with the traits of magic reality, as the work of a magician. Ignatius looked around at all of us then,

---

72   Or southern Belgium, the gently undulating hills and valleys (the "vallons" of la Wallonie) of which were indeed the home of his honorable parent.. Moulinsart, a vieille famille, a family with claims to several centuries of nobility. This had always seemed irrelevant to him in his adventures and peregrinations, but after all, these ancestors were in his blood. If he could truly be said to have blood and not just ink in his veins, as she would say.

and we all nodded. That is its fascination, its peculiar adherence to our deepest pulsations, and also why only consciousness can begin to free us from it

Phil to Walter Aleph and Augustus: That is how I see it. As nothing at all.

Augustus, dubiously: Hmm.

But if that is so," said d'Hachis, with a flush of excitement, following up on Ignatius' exposition, we should be able to intervene in this ball game very effectively. This opens up an entire field of new consciousness: one may see life as a sequence in which cut-ups could be introduced, planes unfolded, moves made instantaneously to something else.

Let's simply say that Ignatius made us aware of a more creative approach to the game. Already the floor of the arena rumbled with a herdlike beat and it wasn't beef on the hoof although when the Maya team swept in—squat red faces and dense bodies bolted to the ground except when they were in hot pursuit, as they were now—they could have been wild buffalo with the speed and ferocity they displayed. *Lord-Storm-Sky*, his black hair streaming in tangled strings, his jaws—but enough, suffice it to say that his appearance was horrible, and *Six-Hell-Lord* with his tusks and *Lord-Six-Tun-Bird-Jaguar* with the extra-large ear flares and pierced nostrils, and the wiry monkeylike howling of *Lord Bird-Jaguar* and *Lord Jaguar-Paw* with his jaguar-like bristling brows and sharpened teeth were all quite repellent as they rushed down the field wielding their short spears (god knows why, this was a sporting event; presumably the Prince's idea of "psyching them out"), and yet there was something stereotypical about them.. Naturally enough our team was intimidated by the precipitate *Ahauob*, baleful they could be described, and as they came crashing down, the Captain turned and yelled at his mates in stentorian tones,

It is the *Kalachakra*[73], boys! Psycho-experimentation is the only way to take them on!

It has to be so amazing, remarked Phil to nobody in particular, when did this happen to anybody else recently? The air continued to be shaken by tremors. Nobody was quite sure where they came from—arrgh! shrieked Augustus, almost dropping the glass of Prosecco he had been toasting with, as a horseman

---

73   In Circulo de la Sabiduria Ignacio traces the evolution of the Greek skepsis and the mnemonic figures to the most radical form of Tantra in the Tibetan Kalachakra

brushed by too closely, and he spun into a *Nei Kung*[74] stance with the three interlocking circles: lower spine and pelvis inscribed in one concave curvature, in-turned toes and outbent knees in another, and rounded embracing arms and concave chest in a third: this conferred upon him quiet stability and sureness of success and the horseman's coup failed. He observed the Captain dead ahead to hang as loose and flowing as a rag and nothing in the rush pell-mell even flustered or fluttered him. But then Carl was not the Captain for *nada*.

This is the subject floating before us on the horizon of time, cried out the latter in a loud voice so as to be heard above the dry thunder-thud of hoofs, the puzzling In-Between-Reality of communication--in the broadest sense! All the mates seemed greatly animated by this, to Augustus, rather opaque and, yes, puzzling apothegm. However it was not to remain so for long, Carl was not one for empty rhetoric, and this time *Lord Smoke-Shell* himself appeared out of the storm of dust that had been raised by the preceding onslaught of the savage cohort. He was mounted on a dainty purebred fleet as the wind on those sharp little hooves, although *Lord Smoke-Shell* overspilled his mount with his large and blocky form and his wide and scalloped bat-wings appeared to hang over them both as he bore down on our team. And yes they hung over the tiny group of survivors now, and primarily the Captain who undertook self-experimentation as if on a transparent sheet of paper upon which the traces of feet on the ground were indicated as a sequence of sign-impulses. This is to be understood in accordance with the In-Between Reality. And you must understand that as he followed this abstruse "map", the Bat-Lord was bearing down rapidly on him! The difficulty consists in making conscious the reversal of movement in imaginary life, hence in the folding and unfolding of this moment as if it were a transparent sheet of paper.

If I want to grasp the inversion simultaneously, thinks Carl, I would have to split myself or be doubled. And so perform a perfect move. Or move out sideways from myself by a one-half turn so that I would be standing in front of myself. Or, corresponding more closely to the foot, the moving and the path, I could let myself fall forward (or backward), thus describing a half-circle on a transparent material of the imaginary. So that my second consciousness would be standing on its head under my feet. In

74   Ancient Chinese *kara te* martial exercise assiduously practiced by Augustus

this self-experiment I introduce an imaginary diaphanous ball or a transparent circular cylinder. In whatever regions the simultaneous grasp of folding should lead therefore, or, going-beyond that, the Shamanic dance is active on two or four or six pages (= folds, or dimensions). Through imaginative energy this is what I self-probe with.[75] The Maya warrior ball-player who had borne down on him by now was wholly disoriented and disjointed and quite incapable of following his counterpart in the quick-silver dance mode he had adopted, and hence always felt himself to be on the outside or going off on the wrong angle, but of course things can always get worse, so that if the appropriate angle and slope and trajectory are chosen—but the flying minotaur was far from this capability and *Smoke-Shell* simply gave up in a state of confusion not understanding how the Captain could stand like that and move one way but then not be over there but at the obverse. *Smoke-Shell Ahau* was like a dog chasing its tail for the wily *Ah K'u Hun* (the Captain) had him running around in circles without moving. Needless to say the *Ahau's* large ball, which had been tensed on his shoulder ready for the killer shot at Captain Carl, plopped onto the arena floor in a limp fiasco when it was over. Instead of provoking a huge uproar of revenge from his teammates an uneasy silence ensued. While Augustus's mates sat around watching their Captain in the perfection of his play, the other team, the royal cousins and brothers of the Prince, dismounted and looked on as *Smoke-Shell Ahau* staggered in confusion, his great cloth bat-wings drooping, and Captain Carl stood there—and here—attentively. And slowly they began to applaud. Carl, with his unselfconscious smile, waved them to silence. *Bird Jaguar Ahau* approached, his fine traits knit together in puzzlement.

Its'ab, he began, it's been amazing to watch you. I don't think we in Xibalba have ever had occasion to witness such Brownian movement, how can one do this? He stepped back, now each man's face was wreathed in smiles.

Simply, said Carl, the fact that our acts are realized with instant precision at a point of intersection of space-time is only the outcome whereby the observer is observed truly by a hundred eyes, changing darkness into brightness and light into black rays.

Wha-a-what? exclaimed the other, wrinkling brow.

It was evident the Maya warriors were both awed and envious of his ability.

75   Carlfriedrich Claus, Zwischen dem Einst und dem Einst, pp 83-84

Can you show us how to do this? they almost pleaded: the tusked *Lord-Six-Hell* and *Lord-Tun-Bird-Jaguar* with his pierced nostrils, and the wiry *Lord Bird-Jaguar* and *Lord Jaguar-Paw* with his jaguar teeth.

You already are, answered the Captain, and was gone. This is only what Augustus and his mates expected of him!

Meanwhile, at about eighty blocks from the ball field, Tintin unbent from the crooked pose he had held during these several minutes below the window, the small of his back aching, and proceeded to the glass portal of the place, quite aware that his fate awaited him several stories up above. He got a funny wink and a nod from the porter who appeared to have some inside information about him, and who sent him up after a quick jocular call on the intercom. And why "fate", one might ask oneself, as he sped upwards in the elevator. Well it's quite simple, isn't it? Tintin was "born" without parents (who has ever seen even a reference to the parents of Tintin in all his many albums?), and here he was hell bent on the search for the Mother! The door was on the latch as he expected, and he walked on in. The demonic roar of howler monkeys greeted him punctually as he closed it behind him. The lush fleshy green or *yax* of the vegetation had covered the door by now and one or two tendrils had even slithered across the threshold.

Mother!" he called out then, or some say it was: Mummy! It's me, it's— (and here in an odd and unfathomable lapsus, he said) Augustus! I mean it's me, he quickly corrected, Tintin! Well, the lapsus was understandable, it was after all his place, who else do you think Tintin really was? And this matter of mothers—remember, *Prince Smoking-Squirrel* himself had obsessively made a point of posing with his mother for all those stelae, and his father never once portrayed. Not once! While Tintin was notorious for his parthenogenesis. And Augustus's own ambiguous relations have been amply portrayed—I refer to his hallucinatory conflation of mother and spouse. So there is obviously a significant convergence here. In the former you could see, as it were in a negative, what was hidden in the latter. He smelled her before he saw her—she approached with a rustle of foliage and was standing behind him, her fetid breath on his neck. Tintin turned, a tentative smile trembling on his lips—he had become so human in the end! He glimpsed—the henna hair—the sharp teeth. And a large balloon-shape floated above his head, a phylacter which contained nothing, no glyphs, signifying a silent scream. They had no doubt always both harbored this terror of woman.

Tintin, said the queenly and very buxom female, you are always so histrionic. Do calm down, darling. When she laid the hambone of her crooked elbow about his neck, he flinched. When she pressed a mountainous breast against his arm, he shrank. He was apprehensive that his worst-case scenario would be consummated as she walked him firmly down the well-trodden path through the undergrowth to the paternal bedroom. The tree canopy overhead so darkened the apartment that he felt it was evening and hence bedtime. He trembled and wanted to pee, something he had never done in the comic books.

Mummy, he started, but he couldn't remember what or who it was, something about the *Kawil*? About his inheritance? About who his father was? No more could be heard other than a mumble with the discreet fade-out, and now we return to the football game.

The psychic game, which had just played itself out between the two teams in the persona of Captain Carl, was over. The huge crowd was a-gog, they had understood nothing. They had seen their favorite, *Lord Smoke-Shell*, bear down on Captain Carl, and then some fancy leg-work by the latter, but what actually happened didn't register on their collective consciousness. By the normal rules of everyday mechanics and realities, what they had just seen could not happen. Therefore they did not see it. What was the score? Augustus looked about in disquiet. The crowd had lapsed into inchoate and intermittent calls of "play ball" and cat-calls and laughter, but it was all scattered, unfocussed. The Prince, plumes bobbing, had led his team off and they were stalking out to their positions on the field. Augustus was struck by the slightness of Smoking-Squirrel's back in the midst of the solid muscularity of his warriors. Scuffles broke out not far above our team's heads in the bleachers, girlish screams, vague hysteria. Among the two or three hundred people closest to them, Augustus could see erratic movements and gestures, a kind of frantic collective shifting in the postures and attention of the people like a herd of wildebeest, which has scented the approach of a predator. He was disquieted by the momentary absence of Carl who was conferring. What was it then, this instability in the atmosphere--a "spectral" event!? The Great Cycle coming around; the grinding wheel of the thirteenth *Baktun*. The plash of ghostly oars—Augustus and his team mates glanced up at the clouds and saw a dark vanishing shape. Jasmine in the air. In any case the question none of us had posed—why would a people who has never been here before be returning? The question seemed to be a mind-trap. And this was just a game, right? The answer to such an ordinary American question, it seemed, could only be lethal. That is the point of the game, isn't it? This latter question was addressed to the back of the Prince, and the latter half turned with a warped smile. Carl had returned, and with a couple of murmured instructions, he sent us scurrying. Flutter of many voices in the stands. The game would be played according to rule. They had after all a grand model: the *Popul Vuh*[76].

The second half was about to begin: the drums tunkulled, the pipes shrilled—tusked and hairy-nostrilled, *Six-Hell-Lord* planted himself face to face with Ignatius, who wrinkled his nose. *Lord Bird-Jaguar* who was the wiriest sort, like a howler monkey, perhaps in fact a reincarnation (or re-presentation) of One Monkey, the malicious uncle of the Hero-Twins, landed jabbering in front of Captain Carl, paws raised with caurled claws and much the monkey—Carl sort of yawned. *Six-Hell-Lord* with his tusks and *Lord-Tun-Bird-Jaguar* with the extra-large ear flares and pierced nostrils, and the wiry monkeylike howling of *Lord Bird-Jaguar* and *Lord Jaguar-Paw* with his jaguar-like bristling brows and sharpened teeth set the ambiance of our encounter. Not gemutlich.

Well, let's play ball, boys, someone said. And Augustus and Carl were asked by *One-and-Seven-Death*,[77] and the words were enrolled in the curl of smoke which usually depicts the speech of the Maya heroes. The question being if the time had indeed come to say these things.

Where might you have come from, boys? Please name it. Now it is true that *One and Seven Death* had not manifested themselves to this moment, but the Maya had so charged the playing field with mythic dimension, with *ch'ul* or soul-force (what else could sustain that energy but living blood?), that these gods of death who wore the masks of the Maya Warrior-Players (or vice versa) were recognizable. Anyone who has played football will know what I'm talking about. ●

Well, wherever did we come from? We don't know, was all the answer Carl gave them, with a sly wink at Augustus. And the lat-

76   The Bible of the Maya, and the main frame of reference for all the events which appear herein. Indeed, without it the Maya would barely exist for us.

77   the aura of inevitability which hangs over these words is doubtless owed to their authenticity, as the various players are quoted from Tedlock's translation of the *Popul Vuh*.

ter well understood that they were not to name Manhattan, as the reference might rip open the present occasion and betray their identities. In fact he did not altogether understand the nature of the threat, which hung over them, just that he should not so designate it.

Very well, we'll just go play ball, boys, the Maya gods told them in the most unforced manner.

Good, they said. Let's do. What else could they say? There are things one does or says in a given situation which we know may be self-destructive, but we cannot turn away.

Very well, said Augustus, and the team crouched in readiness. And now Captain Carl and *Lord Six-Tun-Bird-Jaguar* I think it was, with a determined shake of his ear-flaps and bristling brows, knelt each on a knee, the large organic "ball" supported on their arm guards and about them the murmur of many hieroglyphs as this was a momentous occasion, the glyphs fat and squat and animated as if they spoke in lieu of the Maya themselves, of the entire Maya civilization and its *raison d'être*, in fact the buzz of the glyphs appeared to pose the question of the very existence of the Maya people. Then the Maya warrior bumped the ball off his sturdy hip-yoke and Augustus watched the out-sized skull-ball plummet down upon him and flipping himself hipwards, batted ball with yoke, and contemplated the following: has anyone calculated the richness of this scene? Just look at *Lord Six-Tun-Bird-Jaguar!*—all tensed muscle in daintily scalloped sleeves of red feather, a grand swish of quetzal plumage blue and yellow from his back, studded pectoral collar of green jade fanning across his chest, grinning Joker-God scepter in hand, red-feathered shoes and pencil-like nose-plug etc.. But more than the individual players it was the scene itself which saturated the senses--crowded with snakes, decapitated heads, spraying blood, grinning skulls, birds' beaks, claw-feet, and camouflaged in this sinuous and compact lattice-work, the ball players! It was, a *trop-plein* of vitality, a self-devouring world.

The only object of this undertaking, he murmured and he felt the pressure of the eyes, or better the eye of his friend, the pressure of the one good eye of his friend Walter Aleph on him, or was it rather the pressure of his non-eye, of the blind eye behind the black patch which after all was no doubt the far-seeing eye of a master of fiction?

What! What is it, Walter? He asked with a slightly hysterical edge to his voice, the stakes were after all his own head, he had played his life on this roll of the dice, the ball game was no picnic. Walter Aleph looked at him with sympathetic understanding: after all the truly "devouring" imagination was his, Walter Aleph's, gentle and suffering, probably the closest to the pain-obsessed Maya of all his companions—weren't his novels a game of pain and cruelty?

The Codex, my benighted friend, he hissed, with a friendly hand on Augustus' elbow, the Codex is where it all is. Indeed Augustus, whose head still echoed with hoofs and the curdling screams of the warrior-players, had suspected from the beginning that it was all in the Codex. After all was this not the very first sign he had received of the Maya—from the hands of his spirit-brother Carl himself? In the form of a facsimile of the Dresden Codex? A present when he was in his twenties? And that moment had taken four decades to come to fruition just now! What had simply appeared to be an exotic document had turned out to be the cipher of his life now!

Walter Aleph's's blind eye pressed further upon his own sightless membrane. Packed in bubble wrap! He cried, in bubble wrap!! [78] Augustus had retained this part—the bubble-wrap—as concrete reference. Walter Aleph had reminded him at this precise moment, when he had been in the midst of a meditation on the self-devouring, frenzied Maya culture, that it was all there, in the Codex! No elsewhere! In the meantime the pounding of hooves, the sweeping regalia of the Prince's ball team, his own mates clattering about, were a reminder of the intoxication of the game.

Shall we have a look at it? Augustus asked.

I don't give a hoot what you do with it. In any case at this moment the wraps came off and the codex was unfolded before their amazed gaze, all of them, including Walter Aleph and Carl who had sent the original facsimile to Augustus, and it was all in there, the beat of the half-human feet of the Maya warrior-players pounded their way back into the consciousness of the present, and now, not Augustus, not Captain Carl, but Walter Aleph himself arched his literary and soft body in an impossible twist and roll and slugged that damn skull-ball right down the middle of the stone hoop jutting out from the playing field walls. It plopped through the hoop and the crowd went bananas, Walter Aleph himself was jumping up and down whooping, and the team-

---

78   Page 269 of Walter Abish's novel, Elipse Fever—when the purloined treasure of Maya history is finally within the grasp of the American multi-millionaire, Preston..

mates screamed dizzily and sweeping him onto their shoulders ran around the field. The glum faces of the Maya royal cousins and the Prince's crestfallen, quetzalcoatl plumes were a more than eloquent witness of the incomprehensible literary defeat just inflicted. For *Xibalba* was again defeated by the boys.

Well, don't go boys, cried out the captain of the *Xibalba* team, we can still play ball, but we'll put your ball into play.[79] This they said as an incitement, because otherwise they would have lost the match.

Just one important point, boys, said Captain Carl to his assembled and glad-hearted team: please note that this has been accomplished under an unseeing eye.

Very well, they said (in answer to the *Xibalba* team's proposal), and this was the time for their (authentic) rubber ball, so the ball was dropped in. The crowd was ecstatic. And how curious that it was precisely the intervention of his distinguished friend, Walter Aleph, which had brought this "epiphany" to the fore—i.e., could cruelty be practiced for the sake of beauty? For were not the floating plazas, the quetzalcoatl plumes, the obsidian knives—beautiful? Furthermore it was at this moment that the prize was agreed. The *Xibalbans* asked,

What should our prize be?

It's yours for the asking, was all the boys said.

We'll just win four bowls of flowers, said the *Xibalbans*, a most unassuming request, and above all reassuring as to the Maya attachment to beauty.

Very well, said the boys, heartened, what kinds of flowers?

One bowl of red petals, one bowl of white petals, one bowl of yellow petals, and one bowl of whole ones, said the *Xibalbans*. And they looked around at the audience for applause. There was a smattering, uncertain. Princess Butterfly looked somber, her black hair flat against her back, her hue sallow, her gaze dark. Augustus could never get used to these black moods, but he had come to recognize that her instincts were right. And that she was not pleased with him.

Very well, said the boys, and *Hunahpu* (Augustus in mythic drag now) and a member of the other team crouched, facing each other, the gross ball balanced on their arm guards once again. Augustus peered into the face of his vis-à-vis, *Bird-Jaguar*—glistening with sweat, the heavy rubbery features fixed, the gaze veiled, opaque. How could he possibly grasp who this other re-

79   page 121 of Dennis Tedlock's translation of the *Popul Vuh*.

ally was? He had always believed he could touch the other's soul, know the other through the skin. Now he knew he was wrong. Was that also at the root of the Maya's cutting, piercing, slicing through the skin? The pain of self-knowledge? What was that the Captain had said about the above events? Not-seeing? Was that what Walter Aleph and Captain Carl had in common? The (un) seeing eye? Everywhere in his soul-guide's translucent sphere were eyes, innumerable eyes. Eyes upon which were threaded the innumerable scenes, characters and outcomes of our lives. Carl saw it all without seeing. So with the Captain at his left, ready, and with young Prince Smoking-Rabbit on the cleft side of his man— proud, haughty, splendid, hermaphroditic, beautiful boy, whose gaze glanced swordlike into the soul, hence "cleft". Then their ball was dropped into the game. Beautiful art! cried the prince as the game went on. And the boys played with very good thoughts[80], and made many surprising plays. The audience already had some acquaintance with their thinking. Interstitial spaces, which had not been observed to this moment, which one had overlooked because they ran close to the edge of the moment—were discovered. Often Carl had spoken of the Eulenspiegel Reflex—

The nose, said Carl, the young Eulenspiegel is lacking a nose. And the explanation of this came to me like a stroke of lightning one night, in my study of Hebrew. "Nose" is *aph* in Hebrew, and *aph* is also, by synecdoche, the face or visage. Furthermore, aph signifies anger, or yearning. Now it is very likely that in the speech act, in the taking of words as words, a tear or break of the verbal veil occurred—the "Light of the Breakdown". And the source of the nose lies in this sentence, or rather the lightning that evokes it. Then there were Walter Aleph's narrative paths through the labyrinth of the psyche; and Phil's word-slippage, word-coinage, adverbs, adjectives, nouns and verbs slipping into and out of each other and out of everyday existence; and Tintin's perfectly sensible non-events—well it's not necessary to sum up everybody's thinking in a popithy phrase, but the idea is simple: that they were all thinking good thoughts. This was their playing. And this, the *Xibalba* lords and ball-players—found disorienting. Indeed, they were recorded earlier as saying to each other,

What's happening? Where did they come from? Who gegot them and bore them? Our hearts are really hurting. Because what they're doing to us is no good. They are different in looks and different in their very being.

80   literally, from the Popul Vuh

Balivernes! muttered *le Capitaine* Haddock, his teeth chomping down on his cigar which he had lit for the occasion, to watch his little companion play, and Tintin himself stepped up to the rubber ball, his yellow forelock nodding with his vigorous step. He looked around at the others with beady eyes, and they knew he was ready to play. Actually, the way Tintin's eyes were drawn, at least when you look carefully at the earlier drawings, they appeared to be sightless as well!

Mes amis, he said, getting right down to the nitty gritty, dispelling the merely mythical, I believe there is something very suspicious here. After all, he said, staring Augustus right in the face with his unseeing eyes--I mean, there is a reason for this ball game thing, is there not? The *Captaine's* hair was disheveled and his perfect borsalino slightly cocked, and he was trying to fix a monocle in his left eye but it kept popping out, and Nestor, his butler and valet with the impassive quasi-canine features who had accompanied them onto the playing-field with a hamper of cool prosecco and fine English cucumber sandwiches, would dive and retrieve it for his master. Tintin had on a bright yellow sweater and those bicycle pants caught up above the ankles. While all his little household seemed quite persuaded by Tintin's suspicions, his team mates and indeed the Maya ballplayers as well sort of shuffled about on the field, bewildered by this idle talk.

Goal! cried out the umpire, and the Maya looked up, bewilderment written even larger on their faces at their success. In the following sequence, however, the boys gave themselves up in defeat, and the Xibalbans were glad when they were defeated—note the expression "gave themselves up"—it was a tactic they had plotted in advance.

We've done well. We've beaten them on the first try, said the *Xibalbans*. Where will they go to get the flowers? they said in their hearts. Truly, before the night is over, you must hand over our flowers and our prize, the boys, *Hunahpu* (Augustus) and *Xbalanque* (Carl), were told by the *Xibalba*.[81] It is also true that throughout this essentially "scripted" (Holy Maya Script) episode of the ball game, the boys (signifying in particular Augustus and Carl) were supercharged with their mythical characters, *Hunahpu* and *Xbalanque*. This was due to their authenticity. And all of this curiously elliptical, poetic dialogue is verbatim.

Very well. So we're also playing ball at night, they said. This

---

81   Again as quoted directly from Tedlock's poetic translation of the *Popul Vuh*.

was a cunning allusion to the fact that the ensuing episode of the ball game from the *Popul Vuh*, which underlies this ball game in which the two teams confronted each other, was only a psychic aspect of the game. In this "mortal trial" (which after all is what the ball game is) the Heroic Twins are put inside the "Bat House", which was filled with snatch bats, monstrous beasts with snouts like knives, long curled toes and fingers between which stretched their black wings, and on each wing the distinctive marking of a gouged-out eye. A long penis and large balls hung grotesquely between their arched thighs. In the *Popul Vuh* account, [82] the twins slept inside their blowguns in order not to be bitten by the bats. But then they gave one of themselves up as follows, because "it was actually what they were asking for, what they had in mind"! And it went this: all night long the bats were going,

Eek-eek! Eek-eek! and they say it all night. Then, the canon continues, the bats were no longer moving about so much, and one of the boys crawled to the end of the blowgun, and *Xbalanque* asked *Hunahpu* if he could see how long it was until dawn.

Well, perhaps I should look to see how long it is, he replied. So he kept on trying to look out the muzzle of the blowgun, he tried to see the dawn. And then a snatch bat dropped down and snick-snacked off his head, leaving his body still stuffed inside. And *Xbalanque* still inside his own blowgun could get no answer from his brother, and realized what had happened, and despaired. And the head in the meanwhile went bouncing into the *Xibalbans'* court, much to their joy. Such is the mythical account.

It is of course an allusion to the decapitation which awaits the defeated captain of a Maya *pok-a-tok* game. Augustus' sacrificial bent destined him to this end, although he had expected it would be Carl now because Carl was the Captain—not only the Captain but the only one capable of living on this side and that. We have not yet reached that moment in the account of the ball game however—but at some point it must take place. Augustus knew this. His heart was pure, although he had been corrupt in his life. He loved all his friends and the princess, even though he saw in her shadow now the Cipher of Death. Why? Did she need to destroy him in order to fulfill her destiny? What were the Maya after all if not the consciousness of such? The Maya were the Ecstatic Consciousness of Death. Such was the finality of this game of ball, after all. Although many of the fans in Yankee Stadium may not have been that aware of it, such also was the finality and the end

82   Dennis Tedlock, op. cit.

of any ball game, baseball, football, basket ball, all games they inherited from the Maya thanks to their *Castilloa Elastica* rubber tree. Don't forget that the ball court was considered to be a grave! Our baseball fields and football fields are mortal battlefields! And why was Augustus there, why was d'Hachis there, if not to fish up their fathers from the grave? And did he stand in for Princess Butterfly's father? And Tintin—do you remember that he has been left back there, in the apartment on the upper West Side, the shadow at the window, Tintin's ascension (by elevator), the mother's seduction—but he had heard something else.. Memory can be the lucid suppression of what you wish had not been there—the whisper, the hoarse recall of life. The fiasco of the father! That had been the father's ghostly presence. That nightmarish squall—only the father could have stayed it. Wasn't it the lack of the father that allowed it to happen in the first place? In fact, the denial of the father! Augustus may have never envisaged this, but Tintin! Tintin whose ethereal existence did not carry so much cumbersome luggage.. Now something was breaking through their mutual and often frivolous unconsciousness.

The ball game was nearing its end, goals were marked left and right, we no longer knew who was actually marking them, no one cared anymore as we were coming to the climax. In the rush back and forth across the field feathers and fur flew, the fans cheered, their throats bursting, they didn't know why, sports as usual, but in fact it was the mystical them, was it not, Augustus, Tintin, Carl, who were dancing across the transparent watery surface of the playing field, of the world of the dead, in the net-skirt of *Hun-Nal* to disinter the fathers? Life through rebirth, son will address father as *nu'k'jo*, my son! The father engenders the son but depends on the son's courage in dancing across the abyss to dig him out from under the ball court floor to renewed life. At this point, Augustus sensed rather than heard the heavy breathing, and saw right across from him *Six-Tun-Bird-Jaguar Ahau*, face darkened, creased and streaming with sweat, feathers shaking on his head; and next to him, *Jaguar-Paw*, serrated teeth and big-cat bristle a-whorl in the red-savage face; and next to him, the Prince, with his startlingly delicate features, his hermaphroditic beauty:

My poor Augustus, said the latter, with the faint smile of the spiritually supreme, what on earth has happened to your head?

Have you ever turned to look at yourself and seen no head? Have you never noticed that this is, in fact, how we see ourselves—I do not mean in a mirror which is an ancient deception—but if we stop during our everyday activities and look about at our surroundings and at ourselves we are visually aware of our body/world but not of our head? It is just a kind of airy nothingness floating on top of the body. (This is the contrary of that more quotidian and obsessive gesture which is the quick look into the mirror to assure ourselves not so much of properly combed hair or accurately applied lipstick as of that mirror-fiction that we are still there and especially our head). And of course we are convinced that it is this null that allows us to perceive the world and our body-self, that contains the organs of sense that enable us to perceive them, but as Ignatius points out, we cannot perceive it perceiving. In reality, has not Augustus always been featureless? Who can describe him? In all these encounters and queries and misadventures, who could even recognize him? Who in fact is he? It's as if we'd been taking him for granted all along, and nobody had even noticed that "he" wasn't there. In any case he was struck dumb with anguish by this clear "perception" of the null and void at the top of his shoulders, and now that he noticed the ring of faces of his team mates beyond the gloating Maya players, he saw Tintin with his own rather insubstantial bloop of a head, 0 0 eyes popping with horror, and d'Hachis, eyes dark with sorrow in the leonine noble head, and Phil, tears welling up in his blue eyes—and beyond, at the edge of the field, his little princess, his darling, the sheer disbelief in her dark sky-eyes matching his horror vacui—and in effect, when the ball was dropped in the game again, it was the head of Augustus that rolled over the court! Just as in the *Popul Vuh* episode, in a cartoonish version!

Well, this is the one we should put in play, here's our rubber ball, said the Maya ball captains, picking up the large ball-like skull—but obviously no rubber ball. Carl and Ignacio and Phil and Walter Aleph and Tintin exchanged doubtful looks.

No thanks, they said hurriedly, this is the one to put in. Here's ours. And Carl and Augustus again proffered their standard rubber—from the *Castilloa Elastica* tree—ball, a unique Maya export to the rest of the world along with the Cigar. But of course all along they had planned for their refusal. The decapitated head of Augustus-Hunahpu was planned.

No it's not. This is the one we should put in, the death-gods repeated, with gross, mocking winks at one another.

Very well, said Carl, imperturbably.

After all, said the gods, as if to justify their awkward and inelegant insistence, it's just a decorated one.

Oh no it's not, said Carl. Oh no it's not at all, said Augustus.

It's just a skull, said Carl.

It's just a skull, said Augustus.

This, said d'Hachis, who had been looking on with narrowed eyes beneath the brim of his brown fedora and a slight smile curled with amusement, is what we say in return, that it is only a skull.

No it's not, said the death-gods, firm and immutable, and that was that. It should be noted that the boys had practiced long and hard for this exchange, and felt they had got it down pat.

We've won! You're done! Give up! You lost! chanted the Maya team in anticipation. But even at that moment, Augustus was shouting,

Punt the head as a ball!

It was no doubt at this point—his detachment from his head or his head's from him—that allowed Augustus to become this not-self. In offering it up to the game—ah, what game? The game of whose memory and death?—that he could so become. For what did he shout from in that moment? What streamers of voice, throat, neck and inner body? The no-show of the body, let alone of the head! Such was the essence of his decapitation, such the aim of uncle *Ah tzib*, remember? When in the original flight from *Xibalba*, he and Haddock and Phil and the others had fled the on-coming horde, and they had met the *Ah dzib* who had pointed out to them the constitution of the city, there was already an *aperçu* of what has now become apparent—*sehen-zucht* (the lust to see) floated through his mind—to see himself feeling, thinking, see-ing.. This, after all, was the point of *pok-a-tok* and of the Maya Nation. And so he recalled how the Teacher of the Nation, the Prince of Scribes on that occasion, had shown him the gossamer pyramids, the smoking mountains, and had made clear that real-ity wasn't separate from the writing and that the hand was not what wrote, the hand which does not see what has been writing itself.

And the *Xibalba* lords sent off the ball, and the crowd screamed itself hoarse, and Carl received it, put a stop to the rush of the pounding sphere of Augustus' head[83] with his yoke, hit it with a sharp crack which ricocheted about the stadium—he hard-ly appeared to move, it was all grace, soft summery swirl, more

---

83   This moment has been preserved in an Early Classic Maya ball-court marker from La Esperanza, Chiapas, as noted in Dennis Tedlock's "Popul Vuh, pp. 129.

dance step than sports hit, and his eyes appeared to be closed and a faint smile playing on his lips, and the ball took off and passed straight out of the court, bouncing just once, just twice, and seemed to stop among the ball bags, but then bounced up again with unexpected vigor and the whole *Xibalban* team headed by the shrieking Queenie Prince took off, and the crowd went wild, practically foaming at the mouth, practically choking on their threats and insults, because once the Prince got the Head!! it would be over..The crowd reveled already in the smell of blood. Only it was a lure—a deception, a decoy! Walter Aleph, himself master-novelist of deception and false trails, had noticed it: just after the ball-head stopped among the ball bags, what bounced up again was no head but a rabbit. The *Xibalban* pack had gone after this red herring, baying like hounds, and the crowd with them. Carl and Augustus had discussed this move earlier, after the latter's accident:

You don't play in this one, had said Carl to his friend. Just a lot of shouting and screaming insults, in the Maya manner. I'll take care of the rest with the rabbit. Walter Aleph did not have much use for folklore, but he understood that only the most skillful player could make the play—only Captain Carl, that is. This interlude, with the Maya players out of sight momentarily in the cloud of dust they had raised in hot pursuit, permitted Carl and the others to recover Augustus' head. And after that, the boys called out to the baffled Maya players,

Come back! Here's the ball! We've found it!" However they had dropped in a squash in the place of Augustus' head, which had been made up to resemble it closely. And the game resumed with more verve and ardor than ever. And the players made equal plays on both sides, and the electronic sign board flashed out goals and names of performing players, and the crowd, as was its wont, went wild, more hotdogs were eaten and beers and soda pops guzzled than ever, and the girls were being felt up and the boys feeling their oats in the crowded rows and queues, you only need remember the typical ball game to get the picture, and just add a little more blood lust than usual to it and it will be picture perfect. And after that the moment came, and Captain Carl kkkkkkkkkkicked or punted the ball, and it was the moment they had all awaited, it was again his practice of the kara-te, the concentration on a single point in self-observation, which drew things together, so that where normally spheres of consciousness are "glued" together here an interstitial space swells up between them, a new, naked distance is there where one may act, a time-space where no one else has time or space. And after the squash was punted by Captain Carl in such an in-between-space, it burst open with its bright seeds, and the team of *Xibalba* was agape:

How did you get a-hold of that, they asked. Where did it come from? And from this moment, after the fiasco of the "decapitation" they had thought to have obtained, the Maya team lost heart, the crowd was struck dumb, and indeed the rest of the mythical encounter ends with the actual removal of the hearts of the Lords of the Dead, that exquisite trick or treat which the *Popul Vuh* calls "suckled on their sides and under their arms", even dearer to them than decapitation. And so the Masters of *Xibalba* were defeated in the end by *Hunahpu* and *Xbalanque*, the mystical stand-ins for Carl and Augustus, even though the game had seemed to be won. The crowds subsided through the stadium like water draining from a basin or a toilet, accompanied by a trickle of applause and some catcalls and a final gurgle as the last of the crowd disappeared.

PART III –
THE RETURN
Of
THE MOTHER OF THE MAYA

KAN – 3
(End Day)

THE PLUMED SERPENT

Very well, my dear, said Walter Aleph, with a quizzical smile, does all this mythology add up for you? He aimed this rhetorical device at Augustus but it quickly became, in his star lecturer's manner, a little talk for the two ball teams assembled in the Swan Bar & Grill in the Wall Street area to drink to each other's health. Isn't it so—he groped for the right word—outlandish? What do the public care about all this Maya astrology anyway? The last time that approach worked was Valhalla, the Master Race, and you know where it all ended, with an arch wink of his good eye—Nuremberg. Come on, Augustus, if there's to be any survival of myths and mannerisms it'll be of the new plutocracy, they're the ones who buy art, for god's sake! Walter Aleph obviously was feeling at ease with the world, Maya or otherwise, having just this morning received a very substantial check as a retainer from *Señor* Salas, Director of the new Mexican Museum of Maya Artifacts [84] for the bubble-wrapped Codex. The extended article, no doubt the lead article, that he had undertaken to write for their new publication, would be an amusement for him, a bagatelle, he could do it with one hand tied behind his back, throw in a couple of mystifications and that labyrinthine story-line that he was famous for..

    Mais Messieurs, said d'Hachis, shaking a finger of remon-

---

84   A character from his novel, Eclipse Fever.

strance at the assembled Maya team, what one doesn't understand here, and his eyes lit up with mischief, is where the mythical game took over from the real one?

Perhaps, said Phil, who had been rather quiet, myth is the only game left in town.

I think, said Tintin slowly enunciating, spreading his hands palms downward, gentlemen, you need to keep your eyes fixed on the ball, no pun intended! There have been many unexpected turns, such as this unstoppable spread of the vegetation—and so saying, he brushed aside a bright green tendril, which had curled up over the edge of the bar, with his little finger. I firmly believe there are sinister intents—unresolved family relationships—behind all this. I shall have to travel back to Yucatan.. *Capitaine*, I'm going to call Nestor right away to pack my bags.

Ah non! Tintin, I beg of you! *Nom d'une pipe* [85], we have only just begun to relax! Captain Haddock sat hunched over the bar with an oversized mug of Trappiste ale in front of him and looked chagrined. He raised the glass and quaffed it at one go. He shook his shaggy head and beard and said, I'm going to put my foot down on this one. I won't be dragged off in every hare-brained scheme you come up with. Ah no, for me the Chateau Moulinsart, my slippers and a good pipe, and *le brave* Nestor bringing me a glass of Glynwidden. The Captain gestured to the waiter to pour him another glass and looked as if he were going to cry. The Crown Prince looked over at Haddock from across the bar.

Haddock, he said, Must you whine? It was a very nice game, and your young friend played well. Too bad he lost his head, he said archly, and the whole bar, at least on the Maya side, broke out in guffaws. The Prince turned the jade pectoral slowly over in his hands before he spoke again, and a darker tone crept into his usually sardonic drawl.

Wasn't it to do with the fathers after all? Whose father is which and all that? Some unspoken regret appeared to loom through this declaration. The heavy-jawed, quadrangled faces of the Maya players around the bar all sort of champed equine-wise and assented to his words, and Carl and Augustus and their pals gelled into self-recollection.

Yes but--I think I can safely assert, said Augustus, that there is not one of us who does not relate overwhelmingly to—his

---

85   = "name of a pipe". The Captain, despite his rude exterior, liked to play these word games which were not a recall of his compatriot Magritte by pure chance!

mother! To the instant response of raised and acidulous eyebrows he added—I mean who hasn't been overwhelmed, suppressed, trussed up, cooked, swallowed, ingurgitated, digested—by the mortuary mother! There arose in every mind in the audience the shadow of that dread figure, the Mother of the Crown Prince—the *Dragon-Lady Wak Chanil Ahau*. The Prince himself, looking extremely juvenile and vulnerable, shivered deeply like a duck throwing off the cold winter air, a strange analogy in light of the pervasive semi-tropical humidity of the barroom!

When I think of the cool untouchability of Mummy—Augustus continued, and her hints of sadistic pleasures, resulting in my self-punishment and penitence, bondage and masochism? Or when Walter Aleph recalls his inaccessible and glamorous mother whose remoteness from her little boy would have the legacy (in his novels) of generations of erotically charged and provocative but cold and elusive women, or when d'Hachis considers his hard and domineering mother who, if she had not succeeded in destroying him, had left his father literally a suicidal *hachis*—and himself enormously vulnerable and suspicious of woman's embrace and motives! And what of Tintin, one can only surmise his mother's smothering embrace, her hypertrophic Belgian breasts, which had left him in an airless universe, stripped of female sign or presence, in an arid lifetime pairing with a father-like figure, sympathetic but hopelessly outdone at every turn by his dynamic hero-son. Which brings us back to our forgotten fathers, added Augustus in the startled, silent café, which had hung on the words he had first pronounced. Our absent fathers. After all, what boy has not played ball with his well-meaning if slightly ridiculous father? Sorrow rises through my chest and chokes me when I remember how my father struggled in vain to communicate with me, and I rejected him, evading him again and again! I can barely remember the last look in his eyes, his too-hasty surrender to his own son's complacent superiority! Despairing, I think. This relationship also was swallowed up by the Mother. How could I ever recover the father, when I can hardly remember him, whose heart nonetheless burns in me! While my mother occupies my viscera and my genitalia and my imagination..

A fresh, birdlike voice piped up from the rear of the barroom—and don't you think a woman is annulled by her mother? Reduced by the Mother to a replica of herself? It was of course the Butterfly Princess, the only woman in this male territory, and who knew what we were talking about. Butterfly, so small among the hulking ballplayers, stood her ground, luminous eyes flashing, long black hair shaken out in a sheet of storm wind, mocking. The whole room revolved as one man to look at her. I'll tell you who your fathers are, she said. They are you, yesterday, defeated by life. That is why you have not disinterred them! There was bitterness in those flashing eyes, and Augustus knew that she had loved her father beyond all else; who was he himself after all, if not her ersatz father? It had taken him years to understand that. And in reality he had loved her as if she were his own daughter—she had sought in him the father she had lost to cancer as a child. Because she had needed him so desperately as father, not lover, she had slowly withdrawn away from him, gradually their relationship had become disembodied, much to his pain, humiliation and confusion. A stunned beery silence was tangible in the taproom. Then Tintin turned impulsively to the *Capitaine* who was gazing morosely down into his beer—or rather his empty glass—

Nu'k'jo, my son, he said, and embraced the old salt, who stared at him in alcoholic stupor and wide-eyed disbelief. And for the first time Tintin appeared to be an adult and was hardly recognizable as Tintin, an inconceivably paternal Tintin! The entire team mourned for him through this ersatz reconciliation between son and father which each of them longed for! The Captain, whose gruff exterior sheltered a very sentimental soul, was sobbing uncontrollably in Tintin's arms, although whether he had actually understood the greeting or was just caught up in some intoxicated confusion was not evident. Similar male, embarrassed and half-choked, greetings could be heard now in the crowded and semi-obscure atmosphere of the pub—

nu'k'jo, my son—

Amid muffled noises of sorrow and relief and happiness in the mingling crowd, for athletes and soldiers are far more vulnerable to the male emotions than the ordinary man, he could not make out just whom the members of the two teams were greeting, until he saw a young man, a boy almost, excessively plump and fair and painfully shy-looking, who had his arms about Carl, and he remembered Carl's young protégé, Klaus who had never been able to affirm his male identity against this kindest of men and spirit-father who had no need of self-affirmation. In a desperate attempt to find this self, Klaus had begun his personal pursuit of women, perhaps inspired by the carnal self-assurance of Augustus who would deeply regret it—until finally, inevitably, he became entrapped in a sexual imbroglio and would kill himself. Augustus recognized then that it was us, his own team, who were being greeted with "*nu'k'jo*, my son" by these young men. It was then that he exchanged a shocked glance of recognition with his mates d'Hachis and Ignatius and the others, that it was they who were the fathers, the grey-heads, wrinkled, they were the fathers whom they had dreamed when they were boys, when all this started, when they had set out to explore the Maya country of *Xibalba*, the people of the Dead. They had traveled through another time, decades had passed unawares while they thought to be away a few days, and now they had caught up with themselves as fathers in the land of the dead. How could they be this, here, he wondered, and he looked about at his once youthful companions, companions of his life-journey: Ignatius, who had been a beautiful youth, head wrapped in the wisdom and beauty of an Apollo, now still handsome, distinguished, but an older and portly man; and Phil, the iconoclastic, startlingly handsome rock-singer and jack of all arts of the sixties, now white-maned and morally exhausted; and d'Hachis, his noble rhinoceros-head with the handsome, plunging slant of forehead and nose, his devastatingly precise wit not dulled, but his once light touch gone, now leaning on a stick with one arm and on a beautiful young woman's arm (not his daughter) with the other.. Augustus remembered the promise he had made as a boy fifty years ago to his future self (how could it be? How could all these years have come so suddenly between them? And yet here it was, he could summon up decade after decade of his own history, yet all meaningless, as if compressed like an accordion, squeezing empty air), the promise not to fall into the mold of the older man whom he would join fifty years in the future, and while it was the boy, Augustus, who had breathed that promise forward fifty years ago to the man he would become, and whom he now was, it was the old man who spoke it back to the boy, now fifty years in the past. What difference was there between this "Once" and that "Once", as his Captain said? Yes, they were the Fathers whom they, as Sons, had "rescued" from the grave of the ball court half a century later. You are already there as well, do you know that? There is no break between the "Once" and the "Once". Which is emptiness, *epoche*, as Ignatius would say.

No break, added Ignatius, whatever changes must change in an instant but cannot change in time past nor time future since these times do not exist, nor in time present since neither does the present moment exist, or if it does it must be indivisible. This is what the journey of our life means, this is why we entered the land of the Maya.

In the midst of the sentimental brouhaha, the door of the tavern opened, and in the doorway stood "he of the holy books", the *Ah K'u Hun* whom they had met when they first entered his world—Smoking-Rabbit. He wore the bundle of sticks on his forehead, which denominated his ultimate function as Prince of Scribes. The whole room had left off its murmurings of reconciliation and was staring at him. He lifts up the huge fright-mask of the monkey-man god, who was in effect the father of *Hunahpu* (whom Augustus had played or who had played Augustus), god of scribes—and now, opposite him, on the other side of the door, stands a female *Ah K'u Hun*, fierce, decided, it is Princess Butterfly wearing the mask of an ancient wizened god, alien to him. They stand on either side of this doorway opening onto the elaborate ceremonial stage of the tavern, witnessing the unfolding of the drama, which they had minutely planned. Her delicate hand holding a brush pen, through some "speaking gesture", such as one sees in paintings of the Maya nobles with their long refined fingers, issuing from the jaw of a grotesque reptile, an avatar of *Itzamna*[86], the Father of all the gods of the Maya. The other slender arm of the young woman is stretched out, pointing to the doorway—she seemed a girl to his wounded heart, with her light form and her black hair curling like a storm-cloud about her face—why had she become so distant, Augustus asked himself, and why threatening?

They're coming, she cried in that unnaturally high pitch which seemed to be closer to the birds than the human race, and she cried out again, now from behind the mask of the ancient god, which no doubt muffled and distorted her voice, for it came out hoarse and shrill, they're coming! she cried again, but it wasn't clear if the words were "they're" or "we're", although the latter made no sense since "we" were already there.. Was it terror that made her voice so strident?

In such thoughts he peered through the door from behind the billowing pants of the *Ah K'u Hun* and saw green: thick foliage, creepers, vines, boughs weighted with exotic blossoms, and all this in a narrow street somewhere off Broadway in lower Manhattan, i.e. nowhere near Central Park!

Remember, said Carl, the dark light twinkling always in his fathomless eyes, plant beings talk to the shaman. Augustus looked

---

86   This formidable image of transforming creativity is incised on a bone from Hasaw Ch'an K'awil's tomb.

at his spirit-brother, with prickly awareness of the green growth
outside and remembered with sadness the tiny white feather
which had clung to the hat of Carl's long-deceased mother, and
which had appeared to wave a goodbye when stirred by the air,
a micro-sign from the other side. Yes, there are other mothers,
he thought. And with a gaggle of heads peering out behind him,
through the gloaming of the bar entrance, who should come tack-
tacking on his high leather heels out of the preternaturally deep
tones of this rain forest greenery but le *Professeur* Tournesol! His
nose was buried in a tome, the once tight black curls ringing his
ears now in a white cloud, and the wispy ghost of a goatee was
threatening as a poodle's. Evidently he also had made the generation leap. He finally looked up as he came in to the open door of
the bar.

Yoo-hoo, he called, Tintin! He stood there, resting both hands
on a polished black cane with a gold knob, obviously a present
from Haddock, and swayed back and forth anciently, nodding like
those wooden balancing birds.

Yoo hoo, called the others near the entrance turning back
inside and mocking him, yoo hoo Tintin! When Tintin reached
the door and the light of day, Augustus and d'Hachis especially,
the two in the crowd also of Walloon background—were startled
by the vapid grayness of their boyhood friend. Tintin, who has
been painted in the most vivid colors for generations, with his
bright pink cheeks and yellow shock of hair, now was quite sallow and with more than a hint of a sagging double chin. He was
still the intrepid boy-reporter he had been for decades, but like all
those who have appeared to skip a generation and preserved their
youthful features, and suddenly show their age, he appeared oddly
older than those companions who had aged normally—a wizened
boy. He poked his head through the door—

Alors? What is it, Tryphon[87]?

Mais non! *Pas du tout triomphant! C'est les Maya!* answered
the astronomer-inventor-botanist-ethnologist-epigrapher,
Tournesol, irritably. They have arrived right on time. Here, he
said, pointing at the relevant column in the facsimile Codex[88],
the volume that he had been perusing. Walter Aleph, who had

---

87   Tintin only called the Professor by his first name in moments of
tender solicitude; and in cases of extreme urgency.
88   Or was it a facsimile? It suspiciously resembled the Codex which
Walter and his benefactor Mr. Preston had sought—some say stolen—in
the Yucatan.

squeezed out the front door beside Augustus craned his neck,
his good eye peeping over the Professor's shoulder. Or precisely,
continued the Professor with a more solemn tone than was his
wont, 13.0.0.0.0 4 *Ahau Kan* 3, with the Ninth Lord of the Night
entering upon his round. In a word, it is almost the end of the
13th *Baktun* which signals the Return of the Maya. Most eminent
epigraphers concur with this date. He beamed with pride, leaning nonchalantly against the pale trunk of a *ceiba* tree. From the
dusky recesses of the Barroom emerged hysterical turkey gobble.
Our Maya mates were obviously excited by the news. And from
somewhere beyond this immediate tangle of the Wall Street
neighborhood an atmospheric murmur, an immense brouhaha
of voices, a rumble as of thousands of feet in the distance, could
be heard. There was nobody to the left toward Platt Street, just
the new growths of vegetation shuffling through these streets and
a tramp steamer docked at the far end of John Street in the East
River, M A Y A Q U E E N in Broadway Marquee yellow letter-
ing across its stern, and it wasn't moving or making any noise—
and there was nothing to the right up to Maiden Street. Princess
Butterfly appeared in the doorway and walked out into the street.
While the senile mask still concealed her features, the slender
raised arm and arched breasts belied the disguise and the contradiction of these traits seemed to echo Tintin's:

L....oo....oo....oo....oo....oo....oo....k!!!, she cried with the
great looping cry of that water-fowl, the loon, beloved of the shamans, and the Swan Bar & Grill regurgitated its contents, and the
dozens of team mates and family and fiancés spilled out onto the
sidewalk, and all eyes were pinned to the dotted line which flew
hypothetically from her finger almost vertically upwards—and
in fact the buildings were so densely packed in the narrow streets
that at first the soaring height of the AIG building farther up on
Pearl Street was not even visible, each terrace rimmed with silver-
embossed shields or lunettes which carried up the modernist
silvery flower motifs in relief which were linked in a glittering belt
at the first floor level above the entrance doors, and the onlookers
had to bend over backwards in the classic New York *Adoremus* attitude to see to the soaring needle spire toward which the princess
was pointing.

Look, there—a voice came near Augustus's ear, it was Phil,
whose shaggy white mane appeared tinted with the silvery reflections, and he pointed to the base of the spire, and at this moment
of focus the brouhaha seemed to have abated, and Augustus saw

something, and there were two or three cries among the crowd staring up, I see him! And then he also saw a tiny insectoid figure climbing the spire, and there were gasps of astonishment and someone cried out, no, no, he's coming down! And yes, it was obvious that the figure was sliding down, and then another figure after him, and then another, but one could not tell where they were coming from. As the group from the bar shifted about in the street and murmured in oddly muted voices they began to notice other dots milling about the turrets beneath the spire, and realized crowds of people were swirling down from the turrets from out of the empty air and disappearing inside the building. It was as if a film were being run backwards. As the group pushed across the street, they spied an enormous green cupola with turret and spire which loomed beyond the AIG building, visible above the roofs of the smaller buildings on the Pearl Street side housing the Swan Bar & Grill among other establishments, and this also swarmed with tiny figures descending in concentric circles from the top. They could not make out what building this was, and several of them, essentially the ball team, Tintin sprinting in the lead having apparently recovered his youthful speed, Ignatius and Phil and Augustus and Carl and d'Hachis close behind, and trailing them, Walter Aleph and the little princess, headed up Pearl and made a right on Maiden Lane in an attempt to get a closer look at the domed building. They left the bar crowd behind them, and their footsteps resounded now in the tight twisting street, and next dashed through the Louise Nevelson square, it's thirty and forty-foot black metal sculptures raising their angular profiles and limbs around the sides of the square in mute anguish against the urban sky. They plunged back into the canyon of Maiden Lane between the immense (40 foot circumference) pillars of 2 Federal Plaza on the south side and the massive late Renaissance building blocks of the squat and impregnable Federal Reserve Building with its heavily barred windows on the north.. As if borne by an arroyo through this canyon between dark overhanging buildings they rushed, but the uncustomary undergrowth that clogged the street and reached to their knees slowed their progress. When they popped out like corks on a stream into Broadway, dazzled by the open space and light, they glanced instinctively north to the Woolworth Building five hundred feet farther on. Broadway looked unlike its workaday thoroughfare self, lined as it now was with white elephant-footed ceiba trees, and it seemed more like an avenida out of, well, a city of the Yucatan. Streams of people headed up the street, far more than the usual gawkers and shoppers and thru-traffic, and they gathered in a growing flood. Craning their necks to the east they still could not find the green dome behind the mass of buildings. The crowd was animated, no doubt over-excited but not hysterical, and Carl remarked to Augustus that they appeared to be gesturing toward the Woolworth. The team hurried past Trinity Church and across the cemetery; behind the church a mock portcullis arched high above a street passing at a lower level and led to the front gate of a many-turreted and grandly columned building. People were pouring out of this building over the normally unused bridge. Now everybody came to a halt beneath the Woolworth: a cathedral in the flat-faced and rectangular manner, it was the essence of New York *Spaet-Gothisch* and soared like nobody's business, its four vertical columns leaping from the foundation to four step-tiers of terraces with embattlements and ornate balconies which one expected to flutter with banners—and yes, here again tiny figures clamber down the central turret while others scurry along the parapets, and the vast crowd at the foot of this immense and remote stage of spires and turrets being reconnoitered "from the top down ", surged and stirred fitfully. For those who have not grown up with the little Woolworths of America, the 5 & 10's, the soda fountains, the ritual healing of the inner life of those churches of mini-consumption, it is difficult if not impossible to understand the emotional shock of this violation of the Cathedral-like solemnity of the great Woolworth Building of Manahatta. Augustus and d'Hachis and Tintin and the others felt uncomfortably hemmed in at the heart of the crowd, and began to press their way north across Federal Plaza, a proposition no longer so simple, overgrown as it now was by a veritable maze of vegetation.

This borders on the comic book realm, remarked Tintin to Carl, the crowd murmuring around us, and a sense of impending doom. Tintin's remark was well taken, and Augustus for one agreed that it didn't quite seem to be happening, and indeed what was it? The others shook their heads, and they all decided to skirt the BD[89] "forest" of Federal Plaza and to head up Park Place toward the Municipal Building. A woman screamed next

89   The "Bande Dessinee' or comics which Tintin consummated for the non-American world in the 30's and 40's and into the 50's; remember the Forest of the Chateau de Moulinsart, a moderate and sparse wooded domain compared to the sub-tropical density of the Maya lowlands or even this Federal Plaza overgrowth, nonetheless one which concealed mysteries and perils behind the bucolic poetry every Walloon affects.

to Augustus's ear, and turning his head along with his team mates
to see who it was among hundreds of others at the foot of the
Woolworth Cathedral—Princess Butterfly just behind him with
her outstretched hand was de-scribing by some visual language
of the fingers a warding-off of the Municipal Building, the building of the Golden Walkyrie. And as they looked farther, at the
top, about the little scalloped tower above the colonnaded *tempio*
where he and d'Hachis had visited Carl—an unmistakable reference to the Lantern of Lisicrates, remarked Ignatius—animated
stick-figures crawled about the man-sized stone pawns which surrounded it.

It's the Valentinian architectural figure of wisdom, whispered
Ignatius, they are seeking their way, they are thinking their steps,
they have arrived at the conclusion of their mystical journey.
And of course this grotesque palace of air, with its Baroque and
Renaissance hodge podge, was now covered as well with scram-
bling figures, and so it was with Augustus, his sense of harmoni-
ous life now to be sacrificed! Why did he think this? What sacrifice was demanded of him? He glanced down at his little princess,
once his companion, his guide, sick at heart—he felt he could
touch it, its painful throb. His shamanic marriage.. Was it to be
"suckled", then? He knew the Maya ritual well enough. The tumult
had left them in a kind of deafened isolation. He heard screams in
the distance, the crowds grew ever denser with the dark-red, squat
people. Someone else was walking in step with him just behind,
he could hear the crunch of the vegetation underfoot. In spite of
the press of the crowds heading toward Federal Plaza, it was as if
a small clearing of space and time had been created about them-
-a friendly pressure on his shoulder and Tintin's unmistakable
falsetto broke in on his brooding. He glanced back into the gui-
less visage of his old schoolhood friend: Tintin's hairless eyebrows
were quirked over the dotted eyes.

Augustus, he said, have courage, it's just a matter of having the
courage! Augustus looked into the incorrupt face of his old friend
with anxiety.

Yes, but the courage of what? he asked.

Mais le courage d'aller jusqu'au bout de ton voyage avec elle
("going to the bitter end of your voyage with her")! replied the
other, from the tic to the tac, as the French put it. Before their
eyes, from one classic skyscraper to the next—beginning with
the Italian Baroque *tempii* on top of the Municipal Building and
the Gothic turrets of the Woolworth on the southern corner of

Federal Plaza came the Maya captains and shamans as if on landing stations. Captain Haddock, who was quick-stroke johnny to
his friends, pulled a small maritime telescope out of his vest pocket and handed it to Augustus who clapped it to his right eye and
peered at the Woolworth looming directly behind and above. A
shape flickered briefly at the base of the mock ramparts about the
tower, and then a blue-green flame of quetzalcoatl flashed and was
gone. And this continued throughout the city, at the US Realty
Building at no. 15 Broadway with its triple-story gothic windows,
slipping down the golden-roofed French Chateau which sat atop
the staid United States Court House, and shimmying down the
copper-green steeples and gargoyles of the Sherry-Netherland at
the corner of 5th and 60th. Nobody could discern just how they
were able to get there, although it will be remembered that the
Maya Portals of *Öl* made it possible to enter one of four "quadrifoil" doorways and exit out of another simultaneously like an
electron in the famous Heisenberg experiment and find oneself in
a different space-time. As Tintin spied out the many-hued feather-
dresses and the short-spear-launchers of the Maya visitors,

This is, he remarked, an eloquent reminder of our family relations.

Dear God! exclaimed Augustus, the hands, the hair, the presence of his princess were slipping from his fingers. How can this
be? He turned mutely to his friend and erstwhile mentor, Ignatius,
for now the entire "team" was bunched up in a hiatus of the rushing crowd. He tried to fix his friend's eyes in his own, why is it so
painful, he mouthed.

Ignatius responded: I think, he said, it is your whole world
slipping from its time and–yes, you stripped of your fleshly heart!

What do you mean? he begged.

Who else can you think? said the other, what is wrong with
this picture, do you think? Well, Augustus knew there was something very wrong but did not know yet just what.

Well, said d'Hachis, who leaned on Augustus's left side, beef-
like, I'm not sure we all understand what you are after when you
speak of the "slipping away" of the Butterfly Princess's organic
parts. What has this to do with—love? Meanwhile the rumble of
the crowds is growing louder, there is a movement and danger
afoot and aloft.

Listen lads, said Augustus desperately, the Captain knows
about this. All turned to look at Captain Haddock, who with
downcast eyes demurred, heavy black facial hair (moustache and

beard united), his eyes shut, his hands joined and at the fingertips, nodded downwards as if to say,

I'm afraid I'm entirely too modest to..

But no! exclaimed Augustus, not Haddock, ours! And Carl's dark eyes and bushy brows swam into their purview:

The possible negation of the sexual drive, he says. The child-life: the yearning for a life freed from the sexual drive. New consciousness. His eyes shadowed. Do you remember, brother, the first dream? Augustus wanted to grasp these filaments that drifted out of the palm of his brain. What did it all mean? Tintin nodded, his eyes bright and all his colors.

A long loop is in the mind's palm, muttered Tintin.

d'Hachis leaned over solicitously: you really have understood nothing at all, *mon cher.* You are not in control of anything here.

Listen, says Tintin, I sense disintegration under way. Now it was coming to Augustus however: the cloud-body of the Maya angel floating balloon-like above their heads! That was it. He moved forward with the crowd, oblivious of the body press about him—the imprint of a thigh, the nudge of a knee, the soft brush of a tender breast against his forearm, once even, fleetingly, the nuzzling clutch of a female groin pitched for an instant against his thigh in the thick of the flurry. It was the meaty generality of the female kind. Quite oblivious to it all, he used to tell Milena. Milena. He had never understood that she wanted to kill him for it. And the fruity, fluted vowels of Quechua came across with the body part impress. Evidently they were in a crush of Maya, his Captain on the right hand and Ignatius on the left hand and Tintin close behind, d'Hachis not far behind. With such an entourage he was capable of advancing "blindly" as it were, for he could be guided by the bony-fingered, prehensile, left hand of Carl on his right side, an extended skinny hand with dark hairs on the back and at the wrists, the fingers spread open, palm upwards, the medullar and the little finger bent forward slightly ahead of the straightened and flattened forefinger and ring finger and uplifted thumb, and in this posture they appeared clearly as the "brain-fingers" Carl had spoken of—the consciousness of the hand. Why "conscious", because the fingers of his hand moved in a dance in assuming this ancient figure, imprinted upon Augustus's somatic cortex. If you think of the emotional and psychic pulsations which accumulate in the tips of the fingers—Carl's fingers stirred lightly as if they were producing the papillary-fine lines of a drawing or writing—one could speak of the "dark light" of the hand? And beyond—for the hand is also the exposed component of the sexual nexi of the body, the erotic and amorous relations expressed by the hand-finger movements, pressures. And on Augustus's left side, the right hand of Ignatius, the smooth, hairless hand of the hidalgo, only his nails were hard and well-shaped, also "spoke gesturally" to him, as Ignatius' smooth feminine fingers closed in a tight balled fist that signified "cataleptic apprehension"[90]. Why? He wondered. Theatrical representation he could understand, from Carl—but why "cataleptic"! Could it be that the mind closes onto a—what is this, asked Augustus, looking askance at a jumble of letters! And the brush underfoot was ever thicker, and a tropical early-summer evening glow suffused the air, and in the thickness of the vegetation that dragged on our feet was the glow of the flesh:"hot" and "pink". You will ask, why did he not simply look about him if he still did not understand? He raised his eyes and all the wrong words fall into place, and the little princess with a told-you-so look, for she had always known her price would have to be paid, her long black hair leonine bristling about her fierce little features; the Maya everywhere, dark clay-red, squat, powerful bodies, tight to the ground. There was a tug at his jacket and looking back between the fronds and creepers he saw the extra-vivid pink face of Tintin with the bright yellow forelock.

Augustus, hissed the latter, look about you, don't you see that the landscape has taken on a mortal hue? Augustus straightened—yes, the hue had changed, like Tintin's face one of the Maya pyramids rose brighter and bigger than life. People were hurrying up its huge central staircase with its too high steps, and were hacking at the great stucco masks which hung oppressively above them, projecting from the side of the building, huge chips and splinters raining down. In the paved courtyard before the pyramid, small groups clustered about the stone stelae and stared up at them, apparently seeking some solace for the loss of their city-state, a record of lost glory, and were frustrated by the absence of any inscriptions at all, for the late Maya had lost the art of writing and could no longer integrate writing within relief sculpture or painted murals, so, enraged, they defaced the features of the latter. A single-minded fury inhabited these small powerful men and

---

90   It is remarkable that both these great friends, who had such a central influence on Augustus Psyche's mental growth, had each arrived, while following entirely different itineraries, at the *mudra* or speaking gesture. Carlfriedrich Claus, *Zwischen dem Einst und dem Einst*, p. 66; Ignacio Gomez de Liaño, *El Circulo de la Sabiduria*, Vol. II, p.277.

women, and a crashing as of forest trees becomes audible. But the noise is too surd, too one-of-a-piece for the organic, not splintering and tearing, rather a crunch of parts of speech—and it was clear that the city was being torn down glyph by glyph by its own people. Maya temples and palaces reeled and disintegrated some twelve hundred years ago in the Petén, and Maya newcomers were trashing Manhattan in the present! Walter Aleph, blanched, with his hand to his good eye, and uncharacteristically groaned,

My god I never thought it would come to this! d'Hachis waved from behind them,

Il faut les amenager, mon cher, he mouthed (you've got to learn to handle them properly!). Augustus understood him to be referring to women and in particular to his Princess Butterfly—the *Malinche* who had brought them to this pass! Now everybody had always told him how readily he was manipulated by women—but by the little Princess? Why would she? The mob was howling about them like a storm now.

But why are you against her, he hissed back at d'Hachis, frustrated and hurt by the insinuation.

Because, he answered, she is dangerous and will destroy you! Imagine, he said, this entire story is a product of the *Malinche*, from beginning to end! Haven't I always told you that you need to see my Lacanian analyst! Augustus glanced uneasily at his girl who was up ahead and who bore her great coil of curling hair like a black halo. He knew nobody could understand her! Was there something he hadn't understood, that he couldn't see because of his very constitution? That he had taken the place of her deceased father, he had finally accepted. What did this have to do with death? His chest was hollowed out with the quaking.

Carl held a steadying hand on his forearm, remember, Augustus, yours is a shamanic marriage! The edges of the entire scene trembled slightly, the golden-patina, quadrilateral pyramid glinting in the glowing rays of the sinking sun just north of the Municipal Building. Yes, but what is this shamanic marriage? he asked himself fearfully, taken again by uncontrollable trembling. He had given up his soul for her. And little by little she had drawn away from him. Her melancholy visage had told him so. Ever-lengthening periods of sexual abstinence as they plunged deeper into a psychic relationship. But his frivolous nature had not allowed him to understand this at the time: that she was departing from the flesh. The mass of dark-red, powerful men and women and children in the street was intent on dismantling what they could—not the common vandalism of smashed store windows and stolen TV sets—they attacked only the ornate and symbolic art deco, such as silvery wall medallions or barrel-ceiling tiles, the various ornaments and emblems of Empire, much as they were doing next door, on the other side of the portal in another millennium and civilization. In effect it was the *Tzolkin*: the beginning of the 14th *Baktun* here, the end of the 11th *Baktun* there, a full cycle of the *Tzolkin* calendric clock—intersected now. On the United States Courthouse rooftop "pyramid", bunched groups of half-naked people wrested loose glittering tile-sections and sent them spinning down into the street below, causing havoc in the careening traffic, police and firemen were overwhelmed by the Maya horde. However, the mood was not so much ferocity and vandalism in the streets as celebration, a wild and jubilant destructiveness. People were caught up in a moment of extreme fluctuation, butterflies, blossoms, scent scattered in their wake.

I wish I could toast this with a glass of prosecco, murmured d'Hachis.

Perhaps we should do so with the wine-froth of the sea, murmured Augustus to d'Hachis.

The time is rushing by, moaned the latter, I can't get a hold on it. But Augustus could not convince the rest of the group. The Butterfly Princess only eyed him sorrowfully.

I have this grief, he murmured to his friends; shards of language flying about my ears. We are all very—ah—mindful of the delapidation of words. It was much the same situation back in the Petén, when they were up on the "mounds" (the rubble upon which the temples were built): the images could no longer be read there either. Great sections of the city of Tikal lay in ruins, smoking, half-erased.

Ah, put in sly Walter Aleph, who had been rather quiet—uncustomarily quiet—until now, I always knew the Pyramid Project would fail! I'll, I'll speak for myself: things are only destroyed when they are already falling apart, don't you know! But you can't simply stop everything because of calendrics.

Oh, said the *Malinche*, mocking, are you going to put it all on the account of the *Tzolkin* in the end? Finally Carl's burning eyes with the great sprouting eyebrows swam before them all. The Captain was discrete and unemphatic but he had felt their disorientation, and when he spoke they listened.

Abulafia, he said, spoke of *dillug*, which means to jump from one concept to another. Synapse-thinking, it might be called. It is the gap from one thought to the next which is important, and that is why the *dillug* is necessary, there is no smooth continuous transition, no necessary logic. If anything, disassociation must be practiced, which is to say dis-integration, demolition, so that only detachment (from the ground) of the jump can take you to the next step. This jump is only made possible by intensive sharpening of focus and a repelling of attention, coherency. This seems to be pure contradiction, but through the extreme tension it produces a mental break, and as Abulafia says, every jump opens up a new sphere of a formally determined character. It is in this sphere that thought can associate freely. The synaptic jump brings together free and directed association and is achieved in heightened consciousness. Then you can move on. And they all sort of nodded, and Augustus reached out his hand to Carl first: the warm grip of the Captain's hand shot a live current up his arm and about his shoulders and up his neck! It was the embodiment of the *dillug*, it was to skip across the unfathomable gap between two persons. I feel here, continued Carl, as the team strolled on, an organic, borderline landscape, which has been fully integrated into thought and language, and as such speaks to us and of us. Perhaps on the threshold of death one steps into a landscape of such features, of geological faults, of hills and hillocks, and one can sense the glacial streams, the rivers, the vegetation coming out of words and phrases towards one. In the feverish and icy rush of dying perhaps one's last thoughts glide over such in-between worlds, line upon line, and identify with them. And this land surface suddenly becomes the brain cortex, just before we enter fully into it, blurring everything, dissolving into shreds, white sheets, mirror surfaces; blood flows over them, cries. And then the sudden stillness, the endless distance..[91] Carl was speaking of himself, but not only. Augustus was still incapable of understanding, through all this, his pending loss. The team members did as their Captain proposed, overcoming their earlier presentiments and loss of direction. They now rolled resolutely through these Elysian fields of Lower Manhattan, as their friend spoke which rose to meet them through the words and sentences of a devastated landscape.

Ah, said Tintin, a fluorescent pallor in his usually agreeably flat-colored traits, all this talk of death is somewhat off-putting, although I understand after that ballgame. Le Capitaine Haddock grunted and puffed on his pipe, and Walter Aleph looked up anxiously and murmured something about really having to get back

91   The actual words of Carl to Augustus in a letter dated 10.9.67

to a meeting of his coop board, with his delicate and warm appreciation for the very interesting occasion of the ball game, and that he was most pleased with the small artifact etc. and drifted off into the evening, and Phil had to go and pick up his son, and gave Augustus a hug. Ignatius' noble and long-nosed profile bent toward the latter, and he spoke in a low voice and with affectionate urgency:

The experience of the other precedes that of the "I", he said.. My friend, I leave you with this hope—do not lose heart. He gave Augustus an affectionate pat-pat on the shoulder and the warm light of a sad gaze, and left as well. Tintin and Captain Haddock and d'Hachis walked along with Augustus now, and a little ahead of them went Carl with his arm about the lithe slight form of the Butterfly Princess. She appeared to him to be utterly detached from him now, his heart caught in his throat. It was about dying, he now understood.

Hmm, cogitated the Boy Reporter, it is curious how they all have some reluctance to cross this terrain. The *Capitaine* and I are used to these perceptions of the landscapes of the mind—here, for example, this bright green shrubbery, part of the *yaxing* of Manhattan, just as, in the gardens of the *Châââteau* of Moulinsart, the alleyways are decked with the most fragrant bows of dark green leaves, and the gravel kicking up underfoot—

Ah oui, broke in the Capitaine, ah my dear forest! *une source d'inepuisables richesses.* I sniff *la marguerite* and it has the light innocent *parfum,* which the word suggests. Here the *Capitaine* fitted a monocle in his perfectly good right eye, and gazed fixedly upon a brilliant red hibiscus bloom which of course does not grow in Manhattan but rather in the lowlands of Guatemala and Belize. Then the *Capitaine* straightened up again with the ramrod bearing of an old salt who had stood on many a tossing deck, and cupping his pipe with one hand, was about to strike a match when a voice came out of the gloaming under the trees.

Allow me, *mon Capitaine,* and the slightly guttural accent in French was then followed by the emergence from the shadows of a graceful figure, loins swaddled in a white cloth, and carrying in one hand his long zoomorphic pipe and in the other a long lighted match which he now extended toward the bowl of Haddock's pipe. Well, said the newcomer, whom they immediately recognized as their old acquaintance, the *Ah k'u hun,* Smoking Rabbit. The kindly, fine-chiseled features of the old sage turned toward the little group: I see we are speaking of the words! Smelling the perfume of one now, inhaling the sweet dense smoke of *"une pipe"*! The *Capitaine* muttered some incomprehensible appreciative guttural in return. Augustus did not pay much attention because he was gazing out after his Butterfly Princess who was only just perceptible ahead under the deeper shadows of the trees with Carl, compressed energy of wiry with grace of lithe, why this sense of suffocation, of dread? He wanted to call after her but Smoking Rabbit's voice piped on,

What you may well ask yourselves, was this charade of the ball game?

I asked a lithe lady to lay herself down, mused Augustus sadly. He felt despair regarding himself.

Well, continued the *Ah K'u Hun*, it was a necessary condition for the empowering of the *Öl*, the Portal through which our people would return. Augustus felt the anguish begin to drain down his windpipe, his speaking organ, and then to his gut, the locus of his appetites, and he reached out a hand to her dwindling form. Why was his friend, his Captain—why were they.. Tintin looked at him distantly, his round cipher of a face not comforting, and the *Ah K'u Hun* placed a restraining hand on his arm.

Don't be disturbed, friend, he said, the *Malinche* was given to help you translate this vast event. She knew her short life..

d'Hachis, whispered Augustus to his soul-brother, unable to speak aloud, in a desperate gesture for help, why didn't I understand this sooner? Or you, d'Hachis? His companion since boyhood, the closest friend since the death of his brother, Carl, had understood nothing... Is that why then? murmured Augustus, this brooding "suspension" in the atmosphere? Even though they were approaching enchanted Bowling Green, which he had too briefly inhabited with her, and the fresh cool breeze slipped into their lungs off the Bay.. The atmosphere obviously weighed on the two comic book characters. Tintin turned a gaunt face to his old boyhood friend, his face washed of its unambiguous coloring,

Augustus, he said, I have been with you in this through thick and thin, played the Ballgame in the Land of the Maya, but I cannot accompany you farther.. I have exhausted all the recources of my nature. His friend, *le Capitaine*, was already receding rapidly backwards, now smaller than Tintin in accordance with the rules of perspective, scaled down, the colors of his maritime-blue cap and jacket not quite right nor of his bulbous red nose, dilated as it were in comical panic, his finger poking in the opposite direction, no doubt to Moulinsart..

Excuse me, *mon ami*, I think my friend is tired from his exertions in this *Aventure*, it has been good as always, but the hour rings (from *l'heure sonne* in French), and as if to provide proof for his words, at that moment a bell rang out from across the water, and a large literary tear spilled out of one eye. He smiled gracefully and exited, following his companion. Augustus arose as from a deep sleep. He is no longer anxious--he has lost hope. Even though his girl's figure is almost swallowed up by the branches of the graceful little woods of Wagner Park, rendered immeasurably richer and denser through the interlacing of exotic flora and fauna—the screech of a howler monkey—beyond the woods lay only the Upper New York Bay.

The *Ah K'u Hun* was especially animated, dancing as he talked. Yes, he chortled, the *Malinche* has been much more important than her brother, she was able to translate to the white man's truth—to yours, that is—our entire Kingdom of the Maya: that is, to betray it.

I would say for myself, put in d'Hachis who had been following closely, that to write *is* to betray. That is why I would even say, he added with peculiar Gallic sophistry, that when *je m' écris*, I write myself, I betray myself. So my friend, Augustus, you have betrayed yourself.

This, said the Maya Master Scribe, is what I have wished to tell you. What you have explored here is only what has been written. Remember, my people have fallen apart under the sway of the White Man's separation of word and image! All that I have done— is drawn out the thread of this tale.

Well after all, said d'Hachis, it's a matter of keeping this language informed and tight. In a word, a silvery thread!

Most literary! But neither of you have got it right about my little Missy! exclaimed Augustus heatedly. Hard to get these words out, the atmosphere caused this resistance—that the *Malinche*, through her translation (and, well, "guided tour", if you like), had realized the Maya in herself, so this entire *Pok-a-Tok* ball game was just the means for me to get, to possess her.. Neither of you have got that, he insisted a little desperately, it's about la *Malinche*. This is not about the vengeance of the Maya, nor about their Return, it's about her return. What none of you understands is that it has only been about her, the *Pok-a-Tok* game has been a metaphor for—he was visibly under extreme stress, every word seemed to cost him trickles of sweat-

A metaphor for what! d'Hachis shrieked back nervously, put

out (*outré* in French).

A metaphor for, a metaphor for—well, he ended lamely, a metaphor for love.

Listen to the *jonge,* said the *Ah K'u Hun,* lapsing into Manhattan Dutch, *zijn andere als een Vaudeville akt*! ("his other as a Vaudeville stripper"). Augustus stared at him—he was ready for a good time, that liberatory feeling, but instead he—well, remember, the former speaker said to the latter, it's high time we got our minds together on this! It was about then that the small "scouting" party got to the seawall, beyond which lay the vagrant will of the sea..

Princess Butterfly!!! he cried out, where are you! Only the *Ah K'u Hun* and his soul brother, d'Hachis, were left looking after him now. Why isn't she here? he inquired grief-stricken, there's nothing left after the woods, we're at the end of Manhattan! His brother, d'Hachis reached out a fleshy hand and touched him on the right shoulder, the Spirit-Teacher, *Ah Tzib,* touched him with a spiritual hand on his left shoulder—

She is gone. Then their presence became irrelevant as well. Abandoned by d'Hachis, and Carl returned to the other side, he sat down on the wall, his legs dangling over the slap of the waves and gazed seaward.. The Caribbean sea at *Altun Há*: the moon's silver on the waves is of such an intense glow that it approximates a patina beyond life. In the dove coo of the waterism[92], the sinewy rush, a mystical intensity gathers, and he identifies the liquid interiority of the vaginal sea of his princess: remember the translucent life of the coral reef, the selfless motion of its creatures produced as much by the denser medium of the water as by muscle and fin—a seamlessness of inhabitant and habitat. Remember the astonishing depth and brightness of color, the flutter of shadow and being, the dreamdrift in which all creatures are taken, the slow motion of their dance—and the abrupt shocking frenzy of feeding or capture of prey by the predator—over almost as suddenly, peace returned. His grief was at once mystical and sensual: to bathe in the liquid moonbeam—transcendent eroticism. Sea-warm, mothering, all-enfolding, sensually caressing his limbs, and his entire being absorbed in the vulvular embrace.

92   Indeed, the K'iche Masya at this terminal moment of the Maya witnessed a "young maiden" and "white birds ", footless birds, (Doves of Mary) etc. Tekum Uman, eagle-shaman (*way*), who had soared above the warriors to strike the final blow, was blinded by Virgin Mary & Holy Ghost, and hence the turning point of the great battle.

One with nature, as when the princess told him, let's become one. He had wrapped his mind about this sweet-cruel world of the Maya, his arms and legs about his beloved *malinche*. Dusk was coming now quickly and the Verrazano Bridge was shimmering with magenta lights across the bay, and the lonely trumpet call of a foghorn sounded from beyond. Bright specks flashed irregularly out across the open ocean.. Foam spattered about his feet as the sea grew rough, and he rubbed his eyes as the specks multiplied. He sucked in a deep breath of the dark vaporous air. The specks seemed to have vanished in the thickening fog and veiled moon, and the heaving black pelts of animated water had lost any trace of the very sweet touch of *Altun Há*. It was indisputably again the Upper New York Bay. The moon slid out from the unfurling S-shaped cloud-scrolls of the lowering sky, and he remembered with a stab of nostalgia the *tzak* or the conjuring of cloud-writings by the Maya shamans. Out of the metallic polish of the waves, stilled, momentarily suspended as if by a thread, and at only a few hundred feet from where he now stood, surged the narrow black prow of a great canoe. He recognized the Paddlers from the incised bones of the tomb of *Hasaw K'an K'awil*, the King of Tikal. Just behind the looming prow the grimacing features of the Stingray Paddler, the saw-toothed stingray in a flourish above his head, paddle raised high, then the prow smacked down again among the remote surging waves and disappeared, and he couldn't believe that he had just perceived that twisted rubbery mask so vividly, but of course the Paddlers were artists, sky-artists they were called, and perfectly capable of such projections. Other canoes were approaching, yes, splicing the waves, bristling with heavily armed and highly ornamental warriors, the theatre of axe-war underscored by the screech of pipe and the roll of drum, the sullen thud of drums, the animal shrieks of the Paddlers could be heard now at a few hundred feet from the seawall between the promenade and the bay when the command canoe rode the undulating moonbeams back into sight with its colorful collection of cartoon masks, he was crying bitterly, he had carefully numbered them in his head, the Graceful Parrot and the Laughing Iguana, the Howling Monkey and Spotted Barking Dog.

It was no surprise to see the girlishly beautiful Prince in the middle of the canoe, near naked in the Maya manner in his splendid battle-gear, all manner of colored feathers, yellow feathered bracelets, headdress of shimmering blue-green feather of the Quetzal of course, *Quetzalcoatl*! The beloved Prince, brief kilt fluttering above the slender thighs, jade pectoral over the chest and a belt of shrunken skulls, black hair a roiling plume in the wind and brine, when the right arm draws back bearing a small and delicate spear and from behind the left side of the pectoral slips a full and perfect pink-tipped breast—Augustus shakes his head soddenly, lethargic as a dreamer dreaming he is awakening from an equivocal dream, then awake, sees with the lucid sensuous focus of dying moments how the light battle-skirt hugs the vanishing contours of the pubic mound, and how her breast arches up with the out-stretched arm, and sees finally, with horrified understanding, the glee of the Mother in the unseeing, seagreen eyes of Princess Butterfly as the obsidian-bladed spear speeds his way. The bitter sweetness of its penetration just under his left nipple is unspeakable.

ABOUT THE AUTHOR

Alain Arias-Misson's nomadic character has brought him to live and work in the U.S., Belgium, North Africa, Spain, Italy, France and Central America. He currently lives in Paris and Venice. He has published six novels and four art books, and his stories have appeared in many publications such as *Partisan Review, Paris Review, Brooklyn Rail, Fiction International, Evergreen* and *Black Scat Review*. His "literal objects" have been shown in museums and galleries around the world and his "public poems" enacted in the streets of a score of cities. His novel, *Theatre of Incest* (Dalkey Press) is currently being published in France.

Sublime Art & Literature from
Black Scat Books

BlackScatBooks.com